**SEXY, AMBITIOUS AND TOTALLY
RUTHLESS, SHE'S OUT TO WIN
THE RATING GAME . . .**

Monica pushed open the door, stepped over a
single Clive Shilton court shoe, and surveyed
the room with satisfaction. It was her way of
saying – well, my fine world, so much *you*
know! . . .

A quick summary of the day before she
dismissed it altogether. Sales meeting, OK.
Board meeting, OK. Brian Callaghan not OK
at all – have to watch him, he could be
dangerous. Sir Peter had been very
complimentary – have to watch him too. She
afforded herself a little smile as she slowly got
up and strolled over to the dressing room.

DAVE CASH

THE
RATING GAME

A SIGNET BOOK

SIGNET

Published by the Penguin Group
Penguin Books Ltd, 27 Wrights Lane, London W8 5TZ, England
Penguin Books USA Inc., 375 Hudson Street, New York, New York 10014, USA
Penguin Books Australia Ltd, Ringwood, Victoria, Australia
Penguin Books Canada Ltd, 10 Alcorn Avenue, Toronto, Ontario, Canada M4V 3B2
Penguin Books (NZ) Ltd, 182–190 Wairau Road, Auckland 10, New Zealand

Penguin Books Ltd, Registered Offices: Harmondsworth, Middlesex, England

Published in Penguin Books 1992
1 3 5 7 9 10 8 6 4 2

Printed in England by Clays Ltd, St Ives plc

05369988

For
Mottie and Alfred

I would like to thank the following people for their help in making this book possible: Anne Orange-Bromehead, Tim Binding, Fanny Blake, George Alexander Gellhorn, Patricia Martin, A. Sabrina Grimwood, Marie Jeanne Smith and Steve Newman.

Also thanks to the management of Capital Radio for the time off; Gary Pearmain and all at ADM for keeping the Amstrad on line; my family for their patience; Andrew, Jane, Kate, Jennifer, Blurbs, and all the other Penguins.

Most of all, thanks to Debbie Cook for the encouragement, help and understanding at the beginning, when it all seemed far beyond my reach.

PROLOGUE

In 1973 the Independent Broadcasting Authority, under a mandate from the Home Office, licensed independent local radio in Great Britain. Two London stations went on the air in September of that year. London Broadcasting, or LBC, first; Capital a week later.

LBC was also responsible for IRN, independent radio news, which would provide a national and international news service for the network.

After initial financial problems, including the three-day working week of 1974, both stations were successful and remain so today.

No more licences were granted for London stations until the late 1980s.

I always thought that a third station using an adult contemporary format – that is to say, playing album tracks combined with selected oldies and the 'class' end of the pop charts – would have been successful if launched with Capital and LBC in 1973.

This is the story of that third station, in the summer of 1990.

CHAPTER 1

Monica Hammond knew something was going on. It was crackling in the air, like electricity before a thunderstorm, making the hairs on the back of her neck stand on end. No one was saying anything of course, not yet, but every instinct told her something was going on.

Monica trusted her instincts. They were not the trivial feminine intuitions that told her who was on the phone before she answered it, or made her aware of when a member of her family was ill; but the sharp subliminal senses of a jungle animal that killed before being killed and ate before being eaten which had stood her in good stead in the past.

On the first day she met Duncan Hammond, for instance, she had known instinctively that she would marry him. It certainly wasn't love at first sight, but a certain knowledge that the young playwright would make his mark, and that if junior secretaries like herself rarely achieved glory on their own account, they could often achieve it by association.

Two years later she divorced him on instinct.

His success as a television playwright brought him a contract for a novel, which everyone predicted would be the literary event of the decade. But Monica watched her husband sitting night after night struggling with the unfamiliar complexities of English prose, and knew that it was more likely to be the alcoholic event of the century. There would be no more glory following in the wake of Duncan Hammond.

Her original instincts were not entirely misplaced.

She now had a circle of friends who were involved in the media to one degree or another, and when one of them told her she was leaving her job as Harry Connaught's PA to have a baby, Monica knew that was the job for her. At that time, Harry was the equivalent to a lieutenant-general in the ranks of the BBC, but with ambitions to be a field marshal. He had taken her on, realized her potential, trained her, taken her with him when he moved away from the BBC and into the independent sector, pointed her in the right direction and generally nursemaided her career to the point where he felt she could survive on her own and be a credit to him.

And she was. At thirty-five, Monica Hammond was now the managing director of City Radio FM, the most successful independent radio station in the country, and Harry Connaught, now chairman of the IBA, felt justifiably proud of her – as she did of herself.

Monica entered her office just before nine, rang for coffee, and wrote herself a couple of notes on her jotting pad. She had to speak to Nigel B., the breakfast jock, about the minor fiasco that had occurred on the eight o'clock news; it wasn't particularly important, she was sure it wouldn't happen again, but it did the presenters good to realize that Big Sister could – and frequently did – drop in on them at any time. She wrote a memo to her sales manager regarding expense forms, then started doodling in the margin, her face forming into a scowl, the lines of the doodle becoming hard and angular on the page.

What was going on? It had to be something to do with the Cornwall and Dundee situation, but if so, why didn't she know about it already? She kept her ear to the ground, listened to whispers, drank in the gin-and-rumours served up at every cocktail party. Why wasn't anybody saying anything? She looked distantly at her secretary as the coffee was brought in.

Radios Cornwall and Dundee had, for some time, been the lame ducks in the IBA's network of independent local radio stations. Set up a couple of years earlier, Radio Cornwall was failing because, with every good intention possible, it could not pull in enough money from its franchise area to keep afloat and had sold a major shareholding to Radio Dundee in a last-ditch attempt to stay on the air. Radio Dundee, on the other hand, was an ambitious little station which had grown to a position of prosperity and respect through the efforts of two astute and experienced managing directors: the first had retired in the fullness of his sixty-five years, and the second had been *coup de grâced* by his sales director. Unfortunately, this new sales-turned-managing director had proved a congenital idiot and, over the last six months, the stations had been losing both listeners and revenue at an alarming rate.

Each in their own way, Cornwall and Dundee exemplified two of the greatest myths in broadcasting: the first being that good will, high ideals and hard work have any relevance whatsoever to success, and the second being that any second-hand car salesman, given an expensive suit, a computerized playlist, and a ten-day course in man-management, can run a radio station. But if Cornwall and Dundee saw themselves as merely lame ducks, they were guilty of culpable naivety. As far as the wolves in the media forest were concerned, they were already dead, plucked and ready for eating. All that remained to be seen was who got the juicy bits. What Monica didn't understand was why CRFM was not in there howling with the rest of the pack?

She stopped doodling, looked at her watch, and

reached a decision. There was a board meeting at ten, and Sir Peter French, chairman of the board and head of French Enterprises, would be there. She would ask him outright what was going on. He wouldn't be able to fudge, not in front of all the other directors.

Meanwhile, however, there was Nigel B. to be given a bollocking; he would have finished his show by now. Monica pressed the button on her phone that would put her directly through to Studio One.

Nigel Beresford-Clarke, known to millions of breakfast-time listeners as Nigel B., was having an interesting sort of morning. It started with the tall blonde outside the station doors when he arrived at his usual time of five fifteen, and whom, for some inexplicable reason, he could not get out of his mind. He was used to being propositioned by leggy blondes at odd hours of the day or night – as far as Nigel was concerned it was one of the perks of the job. It was that she hadn't made a proposition that worried him. She merely asked for his autograph on a crumpled newspaper cutting about him, and disappeared into the summer morning. None of the usual crude offers or coarse demands for sexual gratification, just a big grin and a shake of the long mane of pale hair as she walked away from him. It was all rather unnerving. But not, however, as unnerving as the sight that greeted him as he entered the studio.

Bernie Bonelli, the all-night jock, was winding down into his last few records. Nigel looked through the sound-proof double glass window and thought he caught a glimpse of large and complicated expanses of female flesh sticking out from under the console. He pushed through the door and had his sighting confirmed. Bernie leant back in his chair, grinning from ear to ear.

'Morning, Nige,' he sniggered, 'I have a surprise for

you. Meet Tina and Jenny.' He nodded down at the two pairs of legs, now a little grubby from the studio floor. 'Of course,' he went on, 'they're mainly into each other, but I should think they'll be ready for breakfast soon.' Bernie's face contorted into a lecherous leer, and Nigel felt the beginnings of a cold sweat break out in all the places that his expensive deodorant had promised it wouldn't.

'For Christ's sake, Bernie, are you mad?'

Tina and Jenny shimmied out into full view, giggled, and looked doe-eyed at Nigel. Nigel's face hardened. 'OK, ladies, time to go.'

Bernie sat bolt upright with surprise. 'What's up, man? Come on, you've got time to join in. Tina's got a throat like the Grand Canyon.'

The girl Tina giggled again. It was a rare compliment.

Nigel leaned across the console and stared hard at the startled disc-jockey. 'Look – asshole – if you don't get these two out of here before the daytime security arrives, Monica will get the glad tidings faster than shit off a hot shovel and you, my son, will be an unemployment statistic.' He paused and allowed his voice to lose its venom. 'By the way,' he went on, 'your record's finished.'

Bernie's reaction was immediate. Glaring malevolently at Nigel, he spoke into the microphone. 'CRFM, twenty-four hours a day. That was Bob Seeger, here's two from Eric.'

He loaded his next commercial break into the digital memory system and was just about to give Nigel his best earful, when the truth of what had been said sank in. He looked regretfully at the two girls. 'OK, girls, Goody Two-shoes says it's time to take a break. Move out.'

Tina and Jenny scrambled to their feet, replaced the various missing pieces of clothing in roughly the right order, gave each other a perfunctory brush-down, and giggled out of the door. Nigel waited until they were well out of sight before he spoke again. 'You're tacky, Bonelli,' he whispered. 'Very tacky.'

After that, it had been more or less plain sailing until the eight o'clock news. He started the commercial break at seven fifty-eight and twenty seconds. There would be a sponsored time check at eight and Nigel noted with satisfaction that he was dead on time. But, as he loaded the last thirty-second advertisement slot, his satisfaction turned to horror: there was no one in the news-booth. He pushed the newsroom talkback switch and yelped into the microphone. 'John! Get your ass in here!'

The commercial ended, with no newsman in sight.

'It's eight o'clock,' said Nigel over the air. 'Good morning from CRFM.'

Still no newsman. Nigel forced a smile into his voice and carried on. 'Just before the news, a quick reminder of the day on your favourite station. At nine, it's Nick "Family Man" Glover, and his special guest today is Jane Fonda, talking to us through the electric megaphone from Los Angeles. At noon, Trevor Jones continues his look at the career of David Bowie, with FM Reports at one o'clock. Kenny Parker at three, and then Mad Maggie Lomax firing on all guns at six this evening. Give her a ring if you can, it might be your turn to cross swords with the first lady of radio. At nine, Frosty Brian Forst plays good soul to take you through to midnight, and then Bernie Bonelli will keep you company till breakfast. Twenty-four hours a day, we never close. CRFM!'

Nigel had run out of things to say and was getting

desperate. He glanced at the news-booth and saw, to his immense relief, that John Thorne, head of news, was finally in place. He punched him up on the matrix.

'Good morning, John!'

'Good morning, Nigel, good morning, London. This is John Thorne with CRFM news. For the latest on the fire in London's Docklands, a report from James Grey.'

John Thorne started the taped report and slumped back into his chair, pulling a maniacal face at Nigel as he did so. Nigel had replied by shooting John through the glass with two fingers, thanking the gods that nothing worse had happened.

Nigel finished his show and was clearing his bits and pieces from the studio, when the ex-directory phone light flashed on his console. He picked up the red handset.

'Eagle laundry. We wash eagles. How can I help you?'

'Very funny, Nigel,' said Monica, her voice exuding all the warmth and intimacy of a SAM 7 ground-to-air heat-seeking missile. 'Why wasn't the eight o'clock on time?'

That's my girl, thought Nigel, never waste a word. He adopted his most reasonable voice. 'I think John was waiting for the fire report. How are you?'

'Astounded, Nigel. You put the news up thirty seconds late and still need to ask how I am? I want to see you and John in my office at half past nine.'

The phone went dead. Nigel replaced the handset, and pondered the consequences of this last statement. Monica in a bad mood was the last thing he needed, and a nine-thirty straffing would mean a lucrative commercial voice-over would go by the board. Some days should start at noon.

★

Monica Hammond's office was noted within the business for the thickness of her pile carpet. It had inspired hundreds of juvenile jokes and the odd piece of self-consciously crude graffito in the gents' loo. The reason for such extravagance was that Monica liked to work barefoot whenever possible, and it served the dual purpose of impressing hell out of anyone who wasn't sure of who was the boss. Apart from the floor covering, the office was furnished with a glass and chrome desk, matching conference table and chairs, and a four-seater sofa which had given rise to at least one good joke concerning all-night DJs. Monica was well aware of both the jokes and the graffiti, and secretly revelled in them. She felt they made her appear more approachable.

Nigel was the first to arrive. He stood outside the door of her office and looked at his watch. Nine-thirty the lady had said, and nine thirty it would be. Counting the seconds, he rapped on the door at nine twenty-nine forty-five, and was sinking into the legendary pile carpet at nine-thirty on the dot. But the look on Monica's face was enough to stop any smart remark that he might have considered making. 'Morning, Monica.'

'Where's Thorne?'

'Still covering the fire, I guess. I haven't seen him since the nine o'clock bulletin.'

Monica pressed the station tannoy button on her desk intercom. 'John Thorne to my office. Now!' She glared at Nigel. 'We'll wait.'

Nigel shrugged his shoulders, sat down on the sofa, picked up a copy of *The Times* and pretended to read it while Monica went back to her paperwork. Two minutes later, John Thorne burst into the room.

'Can't this wait?' he asked. 'I've got the biggest story this year and we're two hours ahead of TV.'

Monica peered at him over the rim of her glasses. 'That, John, is what you have reporters for. Sit down.'

John reluctantly took his place beside Nigel and looked at him for some sort of comfort, but Nigel only folded his paper and remained expressionless. Monica removed her glasses and stared at them both.

'What the fuck happened to the eight o'clock?'

John and Nigel both knew that Monica only used that sort of language when she was on the point of firing someone. They looked at each other, hoping against hope that the other would provide some sort of acceptable explanation. Neither of them did, and Monica continued to stare.

'Well?' she asked eventually. John was the first to answer.

'Umm . . .' he began, 'we had a first report from James, and it took me an extra thirty seconds to cart it. I thought it was worth being a bit late for an exclusive like that. I'm sorry,' he said unrepentantly, 'I should have told Nigel instead of hanging him out to dry.'

Monica spat out her reply. 'Sod Nigel. He's paid to be quick. You and your damned exclusive could cost this station fifty grand.'

John and Nigel looked at her in disbelief.

'You're joking!' said Nigel. 'How?'

'Timeprice, that's how.' Monica stood up and walked barefoot round the desk, coming to a halt in front of the astounded pair. 'Gentlemen. Last night I spent the most boring evening of my life with three execs from Timeprice. Apart from one of them causing me continuous personal embarrassment, and notwithstanding the fact that their copyline is "Timeprice, Always on time, at the right Price", I managed to convince them they should sponsor the seven, eight and nine o'clock news because we were always – I repeat, *always* – on time.

And you two jerks blow it the morning after. Not the week after, not the month after, the bloody *day* after, for Christ's sake! You had better pray they were too hungover to listen, that's all.'

The two men looked at each other and then at Monica. John was the first to speak. 'God, I'm sorry, Monica, I didn't know. It's nothing to do with Nigel, it's my fault.'

Nigel looked at John in surprise and wondered briefly if he'd been to Eton. Monica cracked a slight smile. It wasn't so much that she admired loyalty and honesty, more that she enjoyed seeing other people display their exploitable weaknesses. But whatever, John had just about cleared Nigel of all charges.

'As I said, gentlemen, pray I got them drunk enough to oversleep.'

Nigel sank back into the sofa. 'I've got an idea,' he said. 'Assume they didn't hear. Let's get the log tapes, edit out the thirty seconds and send that to them. Aside from the time, the fire is a great scoop, and the bulletin was sharp as hell.'

Monica walked back behind her desk and eyed Nigel with a grudging respect. 'Sold. I want the tape by ten-thirty today. Thank you, John. Nigel, please stay, I'd like a word.' Nigel's heart sank.

Monica waited until Thorne had closed the door behind him and assumed her 'I want information' pose, leaning back in her black leather chair and showing about three inches of thigh to Nigel through the glass top desk. Nigel wondered whether she did this to attract, or merely to unnerve, him.

'What time did you get in this morning?'

'About five-ten.'

'Did Bernie have any women in the studio with him?'

Nigel decided – rightly – that the thigh business was

designed to unnerve. Monica rarely asked such a direct question, and could hardly have expected a direct answer without first reducing her opponent to a state of mild shock. But after years in broadcasting, it took considerably more than three inches of directorial thigh to faze Nigel B.

'No idea,' he lied. 'I was at my desk and in the newsroom. I didn't go into the studio till five fifty-five.'

Monica didn't know whether to believe him or not.

'Besides,' continued Nigel with the innocence of a new-born, 'against the rules, isn't it.'

Monica now knew he was lying. 'Yes, Nigel, it is,' she said, sitting upright and straightening her skirt. 'I don't care what you lot get up to outside, but I won't have groupies in this station, and that goes for you as well.' She paused. 'That's all. Thank you.'

Nigel felt well and truly dismissed. He backed out of Monica's office resisting the temptation to give her a mocking bow as he reached the door. It wasn't worth it, he thought. She'd probably think he meant it. Only one thing for it, two hours of sunbathing on his balcony. He smiled at the thought and headed for the foyer.

The street was hot, the underground car-park chilly. As he approached his car, he noticed the tall girl from this morning's autograph session standing beside it. He tried to think of a cool witty line to impress her, but something about this girl produced the same effect on him as a partial lobotomy. All he could come up with was, 'What are you doing here?'

She shrugged her shoulders as if it was totally obvious what she was doing there. 'Waiting for you,' she said.

Nigel was flattered. 'You mean you've been here all morning?'

'No, silly, I went home and listened to your show.'

Not so flattering, but the girl was still smiling, so he carried on. 'Where's home?'

'Cricklewood.' She looked slyly at him from under her eyelashes. 'Is it right what you said in the article – about liking stockings?'

'Yes.'

'How do you like these?' She slowly lifted her skirt until the word Dior was visible on the stocking top just before it connected on to the black suspender belt. Nigel thought about suing his deodorant company for negligence.

'You're as subtle as you are beautiful,' said Nigel. Oh God, he thought to himself, is that really the best you can do?

'I don't like wasting time.'

'Do you like sunbathing?'

'Anything you say.'

Nigel turned off the car alarm and unlocked the door. 'Get in.'

The girl grinned and slipped effortlessly into the passenger seat, exposing, as she did so, a length of thigh that was infinitely more attractive – and infinitely more unnerving – than anything Monica was ever liable to come up with.

Sir Peter French, chairman of the board of CRFM, drove his Corniche convertible into the underground car-park at the same time as Nigel B. was driving his 911 out of it. As they passed, they waved to each other, and Sir Peter caught a glimpse of the blonde in the passenger seat. Lucky sod, he thought, as he parked in his reserved place next to the check-out kiosk.

It was board day, and Sir Peter was in his element. He knew he had enemies on the board and, with the finance meeting preceding the full board, his thoughts were focusing on Brian Callaghan, the sales director. Now there is a man full of ambition, he thought, desperate to achieve a position far above his capabilities. I'll have to watch him.

Sir Peter's arrival at the station coincided with that of Maggie Lomax. Mad Maggie was forty in years, bust and hips; twenty in clothes, hair and make-up; sixty-five in the brain but a babe in arms at heart. She was also number one in London between six and nine in the evening by a good twenty-five per cent. The trainee security guard with his crisp new uniform and shiny shoes handed her a stack of messages and three letters. She took them, smiled, and realized she hadn't seen this smart young man before.

'Hello, I'm Maggie,' she said, extending her hand. The young man took her hand and shook it enthusiastically.

'Yes, I know,' he said, 'I'm Robin Trower. I started yesterday. Pleased to meet you.'

'Well, Robin Trower, welcome to the madhouse.' She retracted her hand, and walked over to the studio doors.

The studio complex at CRFM was an ergonomic quirk. The original owners had decided to build the actual studios near the front of the building, reversing the practice of most stations, who prefer to do their broadcasting well away from entrance lobbies, and secure behind locked doors. This meant that to reach the rest of the complex, everyone had to pass by the On-Air studios. At first, this was thought to be a big disadvantage by Monica and Co., but the spacious hallway and ante-room had fast become a meeting place and the On-Air jock could see everyone who came in or out of the station. Coffee, cigarette and soft-drink machines were installed and bingo – instant communication and five hundred Brownie points for Monica with her new board.

Maggie stopped just outside the studio doors, rifled in her handbag, and then scrabbled through all the many pockets of her outfit. Sir Peter French, treating himself to a Diet Pepsi as he watched her, was reminded of nothing so much as a demented squirrel who had forgotten where it had stashed its nuts. Maggie swore under her breath and came over to the cigarette machine to replace the missing Silk Cut.

'Maggie, dear lady, how are you? So nice to see you. Have a Diet Pepsi, it's disgusting.'

Maggie continued feeding money into the machine. 'No thanks, sweetie, I'm trying to give it up.' She collected her cigarettes and turned to face him. 'So who's been calling you chubby-chops, then? Or is this a public show of virtue to cover up a private vice?'

'Maggie, you cut me to the quick,' said Sir Peter cheerfully. 'Actually, it makes me feel good. Besides, after your show last night, I have to stay in shape to fend off physical assaults from disgruntled cabinet ministers.' He smiled benignly. 'You were jolly rude about the Education Secretary, weren't you!'

Maggie feigned a look of surprised innocence. 'So? He's been jolly rude about me. At least I didn't say he was a destructive influence on the moral behaviour of fruit bats, or whatever it was he said in the papers last weekend. Everything I said was true.'

'I'm sure it was,' said Sir Peter smoothly. 'I thoroughly enjoyed it. Smashing stuff. And I'm sure you know what you're doing. I just hope I never upset you.'

'Oh, you couldn't.' Maggie gave him her sweetest smile. 'You haven't got the bottle.'

There was a loud click as the security lock on the complex door was scraped open. James Grey ran through the hallway to the news room.

'Oh, my ears and whiskers!' said Maggie.

'A man in a hurry,' said Sir Peter as he and Maggie watched James disappear in an almost visible cloud of dust.

'It's the fire in Docklands,' said Maggie.

'There'll be a fire in the boardroom if I don't get going.' Sir Peter toasted Maggie with the dregs of his Diet Pepsi, tossed the can in the rubbish bin and followed James through the newsroom door. Maggie exchanged thumbs-up with Nick Glover through the double glass window and headed for her desk. The sun was shining and Jackson Browne was on the radio. That'll do me, thought Maggie. Come on, world, let's be having you. One at a time.

Monica resettled herself more comfortably in her chair at one end of the long boardroom table, and pretended to listen to her sales director's report. Brian Callaghan, his suit new and his watch antique, was being more objectionable than ever. It wasn't what he had to say that was objectionable; sales were up, revenue was up, Mrs Thatcher was in Downing Street and all was well with the world. It was the way he said it that was so irritating – to listen to him, one would think that this happy state of affairs was entirely due to Callaghan's hotline to God. And to make matters worse, Callaghan was playing to the gallery this morning. He raised his left eyebrow and smiled sardonically; he raised his right eyebrow and looked quizzical; he knitted both eyebrows and pretended to be an elder statesman of the economy. It was a masterful performance.

Monica glanced across the table at the primary target of this display, Jemima Stewart, one-time actress, one-time dancer, now trying very hard to be taken seriously as a writer and 'broadcaster'. The fact that Callaghan directed most of his comments at her was enormously gratifying; at last Jemima felt she was being given credit as an intellectual and influential woman. It didn't occur to her that Callaghan merely wanted to go to bed with her.

As Brian Callaghan laboured on, Monica surveyed the rest of the table. Captains of industry: dry, grey, bored and boring to a man. Her eyes rested on Sir Peter French, not so much a captain of industry as a fully-fledged admiral. He wasn't grey or boring; Peter French was the suave and elegant product of fifth-generation education bought by fourth-generation money. During those generations – and more – people had found it all too easy to underestimate the Frenchs, and throughout those generations were scattered the sad and crumbled bones of those who had made that particular mistake.

The family name had not always been French – until the Napoleonic wars, they had been the Comtes de Courcy d'Amiens. But when Comte Jean-Luc de Courcy and his brother Pierre had decided that they would rather give the benefit of their advice to the English crown rather than the French, on the basis that the English were a little more generous with their rewards, it was their nationality that distinguished them rather than their name. King George III had enjoyed his clever little puns enormously. 'Never trust the French,' he had said, 'but always listen to them. And always watch them very, very carefully.' And in 1990, wise people still said that to themselves.

Brian Callaghan drew to the end of his tedious self-congratulatory dissertation, and Peter French rose to his feet, thanked him most graciously, and proceeded to give his chairman's report. Monica listened attentively. Congratulations were given for previous performance, plans were outlined for future improvements, suggestions were made for development. But not a word was said about Cornwall and Dundee. Eventually Peter concluded, smiled benignly at the company and sat down, thereby signalling the start of the informal fat-chewing session that inevitably followed these meetings. Monica Hammond decided that this was the moment to take the bull by the horns.

'Peter,' she said, her voice innocent, and her eyes gazing at the far wall, 'tell me something.'

'Anything, old chap,' beamed Sir Peter, 'fire away.'

'Well, for a start,' said Monica archly, 'why do you always call me old chap?'

The room dissolved in delighted chuckles, partly because Peter's habit of calling everybody 'old chap' had been getting right up everybody's noses for years, and partly because the board members realized that whatever was going to follow was not going to be heavy enough to demand a great deal of their attention.

Monica waited with satisfaction for the titters to subside, and smiled. 'Seriously, Peter, I want to ask you about Cornwall and Dundee.'

There was not a millisecond's hesitation from the chairman. 'Oh yes?' he asked. 'What about them?'

Monica kept her tone light. 'Well, just that, you know – I mean, everybody knows they're going under and as far as I can gather, everybody bar Mr Patel in the corner shop seems to be gearing themselves up to make a take-over bid for them.' She paused and studied Peter's face, which beamed affably back at her, but made no response. 'I would have thought,' she continued, 'that those two particular stations would have been a prime target for us – for CRFM. We've been looking for suitable ways to expand our operation for some time now and, well, I just thought acquiring another couple of small independents would have been the obvious way to do it.'

Sir Peter stretched contentedly in his chair. 'Absolutely, old – sorry, *ma'am*,' he grinned. 'Nothing I'd like better. Suit us down to the ground as you so perceptively say. Just a shame the old piggy bank won't stretch to it. Still,' he said, gathering his papers together and preparing to leave, 'perhaps we might have a little bash at the next one to come up, eh? Morning, gentlemen, ladies.'

There was a general mutter of farewells as the meeting broke up. As he left the room, Monica watched the retreating back of Sir Peter French very, very carefully.

He walked down the corridor, smiling and exchanging pleasantries with the various people he met, and made his way to the men's lavatories. Locking himself in a cubicle, he looked at his watch, decided to give Monica ten minutes to get back to her office, and sat down to wait, unconsciously clenching and unclenching his fist, and grinding his teeth so hard that a small vein stood out on his forehead.

Monica had been back in her office no more than five minutes when the door opened and Sir Peter French bounced in.

'Oh, bother!' he exclaimed cheerfully. Monica looked up in surprise. 'I live in perpetual hope that if I arrive unannounced I'm going to find you *in flagrante delicto* with a filing cabinet or something.'

Monica smiled. 'D'you do that to everyone, or is it just me?'

'Absolutely everyone,' said Sir Peter, 'and no one's ever *in flagrante delicto* with anything. It's jolly annoying.'

Monica suppressed a grin until French turned his back and wandered over to the window, where he stood, hands in pockets, gazing out over the morning skyline, giving it his blessing. Monica waited patiently, knowing from past experience that the degree to which Sir Peter resembled a character from P. G. Wodehouse was in direct proportion to the importance of the information he had to impart. This morning, he was very Bertie Woosterish indeed. Without moving, he spoke over his shoulder. 'You know your trouble, don't you, old thing?' he murmured.

'Tell me,' said Monica.

'You're far too good at taking the wind out of a chap's sails. You never let anybody have any fun.'

At that point Monica knew she had been right, but said nothing.

'Having something of an eating session at Eaton Place tonight. Care to come along and massacre the odd oyster?'

Monica's skin stood to attention. She would have to cancel another appointment, get her hair done and re-arrange an awful lot of things – but had it involved a biblical slaughter of the innocents, she would have done it. Bertie Wooster plus dinner at the Frenchs' town house equalled very important.

'Er . . . yes, I think that might be possible. Let me just check.' She opened her diary to the wrong page so that French would not see the scrawl of engagements, and closed the book quickly. 'Yes, that would be lovely.'

Sir Peter smiled to himself. He knew perfectly well what it would cost her, but that was all part of the game. 'Nothing amazingly vast, you understand, just you, me, the Old Lady, Freddie –' he paused for effect '– and, of course, Harry and Jessica Connaught.'

The Old Lady was Lady Isobel French, Sir Peter's mother; Freddie was his reprobate younger brother who, despite his alcoholism, was a significant shareholder in the French empire; and Harry, Lord Connaught, Monica's original benefactor, was chairman of the IBA. Monica's spirits soared. Oh goody, she thought to herself. All that and oysters too. By now she knew why the dinner had been called, but she couldn't resist asking, all the same. 'I don't suppose this has anything to do with Cornwall and Dundee, by any chance?'

Sir Peter raised his eyebrows in mock innocence. 'Dear girl, it is merely an excuse for old chums to get together on a summer's evening and pig out on assorted goodies.' He started towards the door, but stopped with his hand on the doorknob because he couldn't resist telling. 'Though I daresay the subject might crop up in passing, as it were.' He winked and disappeared through the door, closing it gently behind him, leaving Monica to wiggle her toes happily in the deep-pile carpet.

Maggie spent the rest of the morning preparing her show and herself for a six o'clock start. She shuffled through her pile of letters, selected the most violently abusive, and impaled it with a drawing pin to the noticeboard beside her desk. Not many people got letters like that. It was the tails side of the coin that had stardom as its crowned head, thought Maggie, but even that wasn't strictly true, for Maggie Lomax was a 'character' as opposed to a personality.

She had come into radio from a national newspaper where she had run a merciless gossip column – not scandalous, not merely dirt dishing, but merciless all the same. The trouble was twofold really. On the one hand, the Satirical Sixties were long gone and Maggie was rapidly approaching the inner boundaries of middle age; on the other, she was very good at her job and could pull an audience otherwise unheard-of in that particular time-slot.

When Monica Hammond rescued Maggie from a potential backwater at Radio Two and offered her her present job, she knew it was a gamble. She confided her worries to Peter French, saying that she hoped Maggie would find a comfortable place at CRFM. And Peter French had accurately replied that Maggie Lomax was a brilliant and terrifying absurdity who would never find a comfortable place anywhere.

Now, at one o'clock, Maggie decided she needed a drink. She wished she didn't, but there it was. Resigned to lunching on her own, she was crossing the reception area, when she caught sight of John Thorne standing behind a potted palm, an expression of exasperated fury crumpling his pleasant face. Treading softly, she approached him.

'Boo,' she whispered through the fronds of the palm. Realizing he was discovered, a strangled snarl escaped John's lips.

'Get me out of this loony-bin before I disgrace myself.'

'Come on, I'll buy you a drink.'

They left the building and blinked in the dusty brilliance of the street. Maggie linked her arm through his and led him gently to the nearest pub, waiting patiently for the explanation until he was calm enough to give one. She bought them both pints of bitter and sandwiches and propelled John to a quiet corner table.

'There!' she said, pushing plate and glass in front of him. 'Eat it all up and then tell Maggie who's been horrid to you.'

John took a long drink of his beer. 'Piss off, Mags,' he said. 'The world is full of fools and wankers except thee and me. And even you have your moments.'

Maggie munched on her sandwich. 'Don't tell me, let me guess. Monica.'

'Well, she started the ball rolling, I suppose. That woman has no conception – none at all – of what it's like at the sharp end. No allowances, no reasoning, no empathy, no understanding. I mean, what the hell is she doing here? She's got no talent, no skill – how does she do it? How does someone who has so little to offer get to be Great White Chief of a radio station?'

Maggie considered carefully. 'By staying sober at IBA parties and wearing Gucci shoes. Easy. Everyone knows that,' she said. She could well have added several of her own comments, all of them more or less along the same lines, but her views on Monica Hammond were already widely known, so she restrained herself.

John took a mouthful of his sandwich and stared hopelessly at the ceiling. 'And my new junior ... oh dear sweet God, my new junior. All she had to do, honestly, *all*, was to go along to the Docklands fire with James, park the car out of the way, and smile nicely at policemen who don't like the media. What does she do?'

Maggie opened her mouth, but didn't get the chance to ask.

'I'll tell you what she does,' continued John. 'A sergeant comes up to move her out of the access area – a reasonable enough request, you would think – and she accuses him of being a fascist lackey and a corrupt instrument of an establishment trying to cover up the lack of safety precautions in a helter-skelter development for money-grabbing capitalists.'

Maggie nodded. 'She has a point.'

'I don't care if she has Cleopatra's fucking Needle!' screamed John, to the intense amusement of several innocent bystanders. 'You can't say things like that on tape and then burst into tears and call your boss a sexist pig when he won't let it go out!'

Maggie stroked his hand maternally. 'There there, dear,' she cooed. 'Just give her the sack, and you'll feel a lot better.'

John pushed his plate and glass away with slow deliberation, thus clearing a space directly in front of himself. He rested his head on the table. 'I can't,' he sobbed. 'She's the vice-chairman's niece and Lady Isobel French's goddaughter. I'm trapped.'

The amusement of the innocent bystanders had turned into slightly alarmed fascination at this performance. Maggie stroked John's head reassuringly.

He rested his cheek on the table and looked up at Maggie. 'Oh, you bad bitch,' he muttered. 'Why aren't you head of station instead of her?'

'Me?' chuckled Maggie as she finished her beer. 'I'm far too young to settle down and do a real job.'

She wandered back to the station with John, offering the sort of comfort that only one beleaguered journalist – however ex – can offer another, and spent the next couple of hours answering mail, collecting some oldies from the library and chatting on the phone to a few friendly publicists about their respective clients. Maggie knew that ninety per cent of what she was told was bullshit, but part of her talent was to sift out the ten per cent truth, or at least reasonable credibility, which, in this business, was just as good.

At four o'clock, she decided to take a break before her show, and go for a stroll in Hyde Park. She entered through Speakers Corner and headed towards the Serpentine. The park always made Maggie run through a fair cross-section of her emotions. She always felt sorry for the prostitutes, not because they worked any harder or earned less money than she, but because she at least thought she knew what her job cost her in real terms.

The lovers, sprawled carelessly on the grass, made her envious. She'd had lovers in the past, of course she had. She had lovers now. But she'd never be that innocent again. Or that slim, she thought, remembering the lunch-time beer. And then there were the loners, the disparate collection of individuals who trotted, jogged and shambled round the park, wanting and needing to be with other human beings, but too terrified to make any more contact than a polite good afternoon as they passed. There but for the grace of God, thought Maggie.

She stopped at the Serpentine café for a black coffee. A young student dressed in jeans and a UCLA T-shirt approached her. 'Are you Maggie Lomax?' he asked in a north London accent.

Maggie studied him briefly before answering. His dark hair was carefully tousled, his skin was tanned, and his face wore a self-congratulatory expression that had been practised for hours in front of a mirror. 'Yes I am. What can I do for you?'

'Lots,' said the young man with an air of winning in his voice. 'I always listen to CRFM. I never miss your show. How about dinner?'

'How about coming back in ten years?'

The young man struck a pose that Maggie imagined worked wonders with provincial sixth-formers. 'Oh, come on, Maggie, I like older women.'

That was the wrong thing to say to Mad Maggie Lomax, as over the next three and a half minutes the young man, three joggers, a party of delighted American tourists and a small bull terrier were to find out.

The six o'clock news was exceptionally gory. A plane crash in America claimed 172 lives, starving children continued to starve in Eritrea, and a family of four was wiped out in a car crash on the M4. The bulletin ended with a slightly lighter story about a gun siege in south London. Maggie switched on the microphone and started the weather report.

'After that lot, rain would be an upper! Don't worry, dry and warm tonight, minimum temp. 16 Centigrade, 61 Fahrenheit, tomorrow sunny and hot. Good evening, this is Maggie Lomax on CRFM. Our lines are open on 01-493 1000 if you have something intelligent or interesting to say. If you want to say something stupid, call the BBC and do it to them. Musically this evening, the usual mixed bag, starting with Genesis.'

She closed the microphone as the record started – she never bothered with voice-overs – and sat back in her chair. All six phone lines were flashing.

Monica Hammond arrived home at 6.03 p.m. She automatically switched on the radio in the kitchen, heard Maggie introducing Genesis, and switched it off again. Not tonight, she thought, I have to concentrate. In order to accept the Eaton Square invitation, Monica had had to cancel a dinner date with Frank De Wolf, a promising young lawyer she had met the previous week at her health club. He wasn't in The Business, wasn't married and wasn't after anything, three factors which were something of a disappointment to Monica – she never felt easy going into battle unarmed. But he was tall, good-looking, and his choice of car showed a certain style – a Series Two Bentley rather than a Roller, which Monica had learned to regard as mere ostentation. Any lawyer as young as that who can afford to support a Bentley must be very promising indeed, and you never know when you might need one of those. So, all things duly considered, when De Wolf had asked her out, she said yes without more than a moment's tactical hesitation. The cancellation didn't give her too many regrets, however, for Monica Hammond had very clear priorities.

Her flat was on the top two floors of a converted house in Cadogan Square. She had her own lift, and her own maid who lived in Notting Hill Gate and caught the bus in. Like her office, the flat was always spotless and sported thick-pile carpets in every room except the kitchen. On the first floor, there was an entrance hall by the lift, a kitchen-dining room which connected to the main reception area, and a small study. To the right of the kitchen, there was a guest bedroom and bathroom, complete with double bath and separate shower unit. The main bedroom was decorated in cream and blue with a king-size bed from Harrods and various antique bits and pieces gathered from exclusive dealers. It was also the one room in the flat without a radio – just a Bang and Olufsen hi-fi record player and tape deck. On the wall opposite the window hung a print of a David Hockney painting, the original of which hung in the living room, and more than one ex-lover had suggested that this was significant in terms of where one could expect to get the real thing.

Monica mixed herself a vodka martini, drank it fairly quickly, then mixed another one, this time remembering the ice and lemon. Kicking her shoes off, she walked through the hall. The panel to the left of the lift was a disguised door which led to the stairs and the top floor. She had converted one of the upstairs bedrooms into a dressing room and bathroom *en suite*, and had left the other as a very personal bedroom. Monica sipped her drink, opened the secret door, and climbed the stairs to the one place in all the world where she had privacy.

No visitors came up those stairs, ever. No friends, no lovers, no one. Not that there was anything particularly scandalous to hide. It was just that Monica's whole life functioned around secrets. She flourished on them: the good, the bad and the trivial. She saw this tendency as proof of her business acumen, but the reality was that she did not wish to be the only person in the world whose life contained nasty little messy bits for which there were no excuses.

As the maid was included in the list of people who were not allowed up the stairs, this private bedroom definitely qualified as a nasty messy bit. Although the shelves in the sitting room were crammed with leather-bound volumes of the classics, glossy books by famous photographers and first editions of *Winnie the Pooh*, the books up here were mainly paperbacks, dog-eared with time and neglect, and by the kind of authors who mainly make a living out of tired travelling salesmen in cheap motel rooms.

The furniture was good, but each surface was littered with debris: empty nail varnish bottles, dead stockings, hairbrushes, crumpled balls of Kleenex; and where the debris had not yet collected, the dust had. Clothes waiting to be taken downstairs to the official linen basket lay in tangled heaps, although those yet for public display hung neatly in the dressing room, and over all, the smell of stale, but expensive perfume.

Monica pushed open the door, stepped over a single Clive Shilton court shoe, and surveyed the room with satisfaction. It was her way of saying – well, my fine world, so much *you* know! She walked over to a small Georgian cabinet, chose Handel's *Water Music* from the collection of over a hundred tapes that were stacked there, loaded the cassette player and flopped on to the bed. A quick summary of the day before she dismissed it altogether. Sales meeting, OK. Board meeting, OK. Brian Callaghan not OK at all – have to watch him, he could be dangerous. Sir Peter had been very complimentary – have to watch him too. She afforded herself a little smile as she slowly got up and strolled over to the dressing room.

Standing in front of the full-length mirror, she unzipped her dress and let it fall to the floor. Her slip and several items of underwear that Janet Reger had laboured long and hard over followed the dress, and the whole pile was kicked unceremoniously out of sight of the incriminating mirror. Monica studied her face and body – the narrow shoulders sloping sharply away from the neck, the stomach hanging loosely between the pelvic bones, and the breasts, never full, but now threatening to develop an unfulfilled scragginess. Only in the face did Monica see anything that pleased her. A firm jaw line with no hint of spare flesh under it, and above it, what someone once called her wall-to-wall bone structure. And set in the bones, clear ice-blue eyes that never missed a trick. She looked at her body in the mirror, decided it was all down to a long day, and that Monica Hammond was not the woman to be beaten by any sort of day. She stood up straight and took a deep breath. Miraculously, the sagging flesh firmed, the muscles tightened and Monica Hammond stood an inch taller. It was an art form. 'Not a line anywhere,' she said to herself. Her smile broadened. 'All right, my girl, it's your turn to relax.'

She went to the bathroom and turned both taps full on. Then she returned to the bedroom and pumped Handel's *Water Music* up to full volume to cover the noise.

Robin Trower, the new trainee security man at CRFM, left the Number 37 bus one stop before he needed to, which enabled him to walk the extra two streets to his

Mum's council flat in Hobart Road. He was Admiral R. T. Shipworthy back from the most arduous assignment in the Pacific, and as people who had known him since the time of his paper round waved hello, he graciously acknowledged them, pretending they were the grateful townsfolk of Greenwich, welcoming their hero back from the wars. Robin liked daydreaming. As he approached the Jericoe Estate, reality gradually returned. This was Deptford, not Greenwich, his uniform was that of a security guard, and his sixteen medals were no more than his name tag surrounded by its little plastic CRFM pin-holder.

His mother greeted him in the hallway of their tiny flat. He looked so handsome in his neat blue uniform and he was working with such nice, interesting people that her heart swelled with pride.

'You go and change out of your suit, now, lovey,' she said in the soft voice he had loved all his life. 'Then I can have it brushed and all ready for you tomorrow.' She helped him off with his jacket. 'Your sister's in the kitchen doing her homework. Did you manage to get that Nigel's autograph for her?'

Robin smiled sheepishly. He hadn't plucked up the courage to ask yet. But he would. 'I've only been there two days, Mum, give us a chance.'

'Explain that to your sister,' said his mother as she inspected his jacket for the tiniest specks of dust. Robin walked through to the kitchen and grinned at his sister as she looked up from her algebra, feeling a lot more important than Admiral R. T. Shipworthy.

Monica paid off the taxi outside the house in Eaton Square and took a couple of seconds to savour the mixed perfumes of the cooling night air. Top notes of diesel fought with undertones of warm tarmac, but over, under and through all this came the scent of bay trees standing to attention in their tubs. As she mounted the steps, the front door was opened by the butler who had obviously been watching for her. He took her coat.

'The verandah, madam, as it seems to be a pleasant evening. May I show you through?'

'No, that's all right, thank you, Simmons,' replied Monica, 'I know the way.'

On the verandah, Lady Isobel French was holding forth in her customary fashion. 'You can call it what you like, Harry, quango, quongo, whatever it is, it sounds like stuffing a bloody chicken.' She stopped and sipped her drink viciously. 'But the truth remains that we have a bunch of ill-informed amateurs shaping the legislation – no, I'll rephrase that – imposing the legislation whose effects are going to be more far-reaching than they have the brains to imagine. Tell me I'm right.'

Harry Connaught smiled indulgently but said nothing.

Lady Isobel rounded on her younger son. 'Freddie, Harry thinks you're going to be affected by this new legislation; if you'd had the wit to see this coming – Freddie! Pay attention!'

The Honourable Frederick French glowered from under his eyebrows at his mother, whom he held exclusively responsible for his alcoholism. But, as he had done since the age of six, Peter French stepped in on his brother's behalf. 'Actually, old toad, I think you're utterly wrong. Fred's spent a great deal of effort making sure his areas of interest fall well outside the scope of the Act, haven't you, Fred. Jolly cleverly too, if I might say so.'

Freddie grunted, turned on his heel and walked away, leaving a nasty hole in the little assembly. Harry Connaught cleared his throat uncomfortably, Peter French gazed at the sky and muttered 'Oh, *shit*,' and Jessica Connaught, coming from a family in the diplomatic service, bravely started a conversation about the best way to pot out camellias, at which happy point Monica appeared through the french windows. Peter turned with relief.

'Monica! I'm so glad you're here. We were just about to start disembowelling each other with the family silver.'

Monica glanced round the embarrassed faces and made a pretty accurate guess at what had been going on, but knew better than to comment upon it. Instead, she took Lady Isobel's limply outstretched hand and gave it a small formal squeeze, before turning to the Connaughts and giving them each a brief and formal peck on the cheek.

'Peter,' said Lady Isobel imperiously, 'stop pretending to be an ass and give the woman a drink.' She looked Peter in the eye for a second before continuing, 'And then you can go and find Freddie.'

Peter poured a glass of champagne for Monica and handed it to her, winking as he did so, before going off to do as he was told.

Eight thirty-five p.m., and Maggie had held back the Flash Jack record for the last half-hour of her show, knowing all about saving the juiciest items to keep people listening. So far this evening, she had talked about abortion, premarital sex, the economy, and the odd snippet of music gossip. She had one spiteful caller who accused her of being a lesbian, a matter she dealt with by wishing him a fun time at his parents' wedding. But she knew that that would merely be a prelude to the big one. Flash Jack's new record was cued up and the commercial was ending. She took a deep breath and switched on the microphone.

'CRFM, this is Maggie Lomax. I'm going to play the new Flash Jack single now, so you can all stop asking for it. Why you're all asking for it, I don't know, I think it's a bit sad, myself, considering all the good stuff he's done in the past. It's such a shame that a talented man like Jack should let a little white powder get in the way of making good music. Smarten up, Jack, before your nose drops off.' She started the record and sank back into the battered softness of the studio chair. Six phone lines started to flash simultaneously. You want to argue with me? she thought as she reached forward to take the first call. That's fine by me. I hate dopers, especially when it's my punters that pay the pushers.

Dinner at Eaton Square was something of an awkward affair. As always, and despite the fact that there were only six people, Lady Isobel took the head of the table, with her sons to her right and left like a pair of medieval bodyguards. Jessica was seated next to Freddie and Monica next to Peter, with Harry Connaught taking the far end. Monica surmised – quite rightly – that this seating plan was arranged in order that Jessica and Freddie might have each other to talk to while everyone else got down to business.

There were indeed oysters, followed by various artful confections of fish and vegetables, but Monica was in such a state of tension that she hardly tasted a thing. As course after course was advanced, the conversation bounced from Goodwood and Wimbledon to rose-growing and compost – anything but business. At last, the dish bearing the few remaining tiny, wild strawberries was removed. Simmons placed a salver of coffee things on a side table by Lady Isobel, decanters of port, brandy and liqueurs at intervals down the table, and withdrew.

'Thank you,' said Sir Peter.

Lady Isobel drained her coffee cup, dabbed her lips with her napkin and rested her elbows on the table. 'Monica,' she said, 'we're taking over Cornwall and Dundee.'

The tension slid from Monica like warm jelly through a cracked plate. She turned to face her hostess. 'Oh yes?' She paused, knowing there was more to come, and that it would come from Peter. She turned her attention to him.

'I think it makes sense, don't you?' said Sir Peter. 'A consolidated operation, a union of interests, a marriage, if you like. Three can live as cheaply as one and all that.' He glanced at Freddie, who was muttering quietly into his brandy at the mention of marriage and three-somes.

Monica transferred her attention to Harry Connaught, chairman of the IBA. 'And you're happy with this?' she asked.

Lord Connaught swirled the brandy in his glass and considered carefully before answering. 'Happy is not the word I'd choose, Monica, left to myself. I'm of the old school, you see, and I do find all this a little difficult to swallow. I mean, when we set up the ILR franchises, we really thought they could operate independently – we really wanted them to – that was the whole idea.' He took a sip of his drink. 'But it hasn't worked like that and we all know it. As I see it, we're faced with the choice between two evils. On the one hand we can allow free enterprise to have its head, and smile as the inter-national media giants come in and take over. If we do that we can kiss goodbye to any sort of moral independ-ence. On the other hand, we can allow what we have to gel into workable units, and at least maintain some of the status quo.'

Peter chuckled. 'What he's trying to say, Monica, is that the IBA will see him hung, drawn and quartered before they allow the Australians in.'

Monica nodded, and chose her next words with care. 'So who is actually going to buy the stations, CRFM or French Enterprises?'

Down the table, over their brandy glasses, Harry Connaught and Lady Isobel exchanged glances. Peter started to speak. 'In the final analysis, CRFM. But, as you know, at the moment the old purse is a teeny bit skinny. So dear old Harry will ensure that the IBA will waive the station's secondary levy for a couple of years, which will help, bless his little cotton socks.'

Lady Isobel raised her eyes to heaven and sighed. 'Do grow up, Peter,' she said.

Monica watched the electric flow of more exchanged glances, and decided to go fishing. 'That's all fine, but unless I'm mistaken, there'll be a problem. As soon as CRFM puts in a bid for the shares, the price will go up and it'll be an unholy free for all. Even with our extra money from the levy, Aylford could still bid us into a cocked hat if they wanted to.'

'They can't buy what's not for sale,' said Freddie, smirking as he poured an extravagant measure into his glass. His mother gave him a warning look but Freddie ignored it. 'Oh, for Christ's sake, let's stop beating about the bloody bush. She has to know sooner or later.' He took a mouthful of brandy and looked directly at Monica. 'I'm buying the sodding stations. Me. Old Failure Fred.' He grinned at Monica's startled expression. 'The word you want is thank you,' he said.

Lady Isobel looked distastefully at her son. 'I think it's time you stopped drinking, Freddie,' she said. She turned to Monica. 'Various companies under Freddie's control have been buying shares in Cornwall and Dundee for some time now, as have companies controlled by Peter and myself.'

'I don't think I should be hearing this,' cut in Harry Connaught.

'Oh, rot!' snapped Lady Isobel. 'You know perfectly well what's been going on. Anyway,' she went on, 'we've done nothing underhand.'

Monica wondered why she hadn't heard about these manoeuvres before, and suddenly realized that the Frenchs must have been restricting their share purchases to less than five per cent – the level at which they would have to declare an interest. Therefore, when CRFM and Aylford put in their official bids, there would only be a limited number of shares for sale at all. And even if Aylford bought every share that was available, it would still leave them without a majority shareholding. The IBA would sanction the Cornwall and Dundee franchises going to CRFM, and the various operating companies controlled by the Frenchs would sell their shares to them at a highly competitive price.

Monica loved it. It was a plan after her own heart. Her only small annoyance was that she hadn't thought of it first. She brought her mind back to the conversation.

'It's not insider trading,' Lady Isobel was saying.

'By a whisker off a flea's bum,' replied Harry Connaught sourly.

'Which is quite good enough,' continued the old lady. 'Which brings me to why you're here, Monica.'

Monica winced inwardly. It was typical of the old girl that she made sure Monica was in no doubt that the only reason for her presence was in a business capacity. Outwardly, though, Monica kept a polite and interested face as Lady Isobel went on, 'While remaining managing director of CRFM, you will also become Chief Executive of Radios Cornwall and Dundee.'

I will, I will, thought Monica. But it would have been nice if you'd said please.

'With commensurate stock in the holding company, of course,' said Lady Isobel, concluding her official statement.

Of the people present, only Sir Peter caught the twist of gratification and humiliation on Monica's face. He took her hand and patted it. 'That is, if you don't mind, dear girl. Need to have someone we can trust, you know. And frankly, there's no one who knows the business quite like you. Do say you'll take it on. Please.'

'Of course I will, when and if it happens,' smiled Monica, praying the angelic hosts to shower rose-petals in the path of Sir Peter French, wherever he should walk.

Lady Isobel looked at the still-clasped hands. 'Peter. No canoodling at table, if you please.'

By five past nine Brian Forst had replaced Maggie on the radio in the full and bleak knowledge that ninety per cent of Londoners were watching the James Bond film on ITV. He waved to Maggie through the double glass, emptied her overflowing ash-tray, and set out a four-record segue pattern.

Maggie walked through the foyer and out into the warm evening air, debating how to spend the rest of the night as she stepped into the pre-arranged mini cab waiting at the kerb. She had a choice. She had just acquired a VHS of the Martha Graham dance troupe, New York, circa 1958. She loved the lady, and had a semi-envious longing to lose herself in the fantasy of the dance. On the other hand, there was the snooker hall in

Cricklewood beckoning temptingly to her, and as she settled into the soft imitation leather of the Granada's back seat, she was still undecided.

A strong Irish accent came from the driver in the front seat. 'Where to, Maggie? Home? Or are we on the boogie?'

Maggie wondered whether or not to slice the man to shreds for his impertinence and decided that she had done enough slicing for one night. She crossed her legs, thought of Martha Graham's, heard the sharp roll of the driver's accent as he pattered on about the weather, and made her decision as she dragged on the last of the current Silk Cut.

'Kilburn Pool Hall,' she said, letting out a laugh that made the refugee from Crossmaglen remember better times.

The Granada stopped outside the building in the Edgware Road and the driver shut the car down. 'Shall I wait?'

Maggie thought for a second. 'You play snooker?' she asked.

The driver looked at her in surprise. 'I do,' he replied.

'Come on, then,' said Maggie, gathering her life together in her handbag, 'I'll give you a game.'

The driver looked at her to see if she was serious, decided she was, and followed Maggie into the pool hall.

This part of the day belonged to Maggie. She loved snooker and most of the patrons of the Kilburn Snooker Club were so astonished to see a woman who was actually interested in the game that, on the whole, they tended to forget who she was. The ensuing frames went very well, the cab driver showing Maggie a few tricks she didn't know, until some unenlightened jerk asked

Maggie if what she had said about Flash Jack was true. Her reply made the driver reflect that even if there was quite a bit he could show Maggie about snooker, she could still teach him a hell of a lot more about the English language.

Chapter 2

It was all over bar the shouting. The boards of Radio Dundee and its sad little satellite, Radio Cornwall, had been told by the IBA that their franchises would not be renewed. The financial papers published the pre-tax profits – or lack of them – and the dozen or so disc jockeys employed by the stations started to look at their track-records and liveried company cars with new and questioning eyes. And in the offices of accountants and stockbrokers all over the country could be heard the baying of wolves.

Foremost among the wolves after the carcasses of Cornwall and Dundee was the Aylford Group, a broad-based conglomerate sometimes referred to – more in spite than humour – as the Australian Yuppie Loan Finance or Death Group. Having started life as a company specializing in transport and property, Aylford had rapidly acquired more than trifling interests in the media both in Australia and the States; City rumour whispered that their recent heavy investment in Japanese and Korean electronic research signalled a future involvement with satellite communications.

But, for all that, Aylford had little stake in the UK media. True, it wasn't for lack of trying, and true, they had recently acquired a major shareholding in Air Time Services – a company that supplied national advertising to radio and television – but they were still in the galling and frustrating position of outsiders at the feast. Even more galling was the fact that all Australians tend to look the same to your average Brit, and the mud flung at Packer and Murdoch stuck to them as well. The mud but not the money.

Wallace Pike, chairman of Aylford UK, resented this enormously. He was one of the new breed of Australians – sharp, original, creative and totally uninterested in the continued survival of koala bears. He had been head-hunted into Aylford from the embryonic Australian film industry, where his acute and selective investment had played no small part in making the organizers of film festivals sit up and take new note of what was happening in kanga-land.

In the boardroom of the Aylford offices, high above Millbank and the queues of dutiful Americans waiting to see the Cubist exhibition at the Tate, Wallace Pike swung back dangerously in his chair and fashioned a paper aeroplane from a report submitted by his financial director.

His vice-chairman, Bruce Hamilton, in an adjacent seat, sourly surveyed the carnage of the morning's board meeting. Half-empty glasses of orange juice jostled empty coffee cups, and the remains of desperately smoked cigarettes lay shredded in each ashtray. 'Bloody Americans got a lot to bloody answer for,' he muttered. 'Breakfast meetings! Who the hell can think at breakfast, for Christ's sake?'

Wallace Pike finished his plane, screwed up his face and took aim. The missile flew into the air, circled twice, and somersaulted to land in a glass of orange. 'Me.'

Hamilton looked at him. 'Think they'll go for it?' he asked.

Pike thumped his chair back to land and twisted his face into a fair approximation of Paul Hogan's. 'Don't see's how they got much bleedin' option,' he drawled. 'They may not be as chuffed as a bowl of badger fat, but it's that or nothing. They go for this or they go home. Simple.' He relapsed into his normal cultured tones. 'No,' he said, 'as long as our friend Longshore plays his part, I don't see any problems. Cornwall and Dundee are not the Beeb, but they're a start and a start is all we need. Great oaks and all that.'

'How worried are you about Longshore?' asked Hamilton.

'Not enough to lose sleep over, but enough to watch.'

Sir John Longshore was Aylford's riot-shield against the mudslingers. The lone Englishman on the board of Aylford UK, he also had a place on several Select Committees in relevant areas and was on golfing terms with most of the Home Office. Although his place on the board was little more than spurious snobbery, his would be the job of persuading the powers that Australian involvement in British Radio would not mean the end of civilization as we know it.

Wallace Pike left his chair and wandered over to the tinted window. Whereas on the previous day, Peter French had gazed benignly out over London, wished it good morning and marvelled at the grace of the soaring pigeons, Pike stuck his hands deep in his trouser pockets, and applied all his willpower towards influencing the bloody pigeons to go crap on Soho and not on him.

Freddie French was also watching the pigeons at that particular moment, but with even less enthusiasm. Standing at his bedroom window, his pyjama bottoms slack and rumpled under his incipient pot-belly, he shouldered an imaginary twelve-bore and potted them, one by one, as they flew over Eaton Square to the richer pickings of Trafalgar Square. He dropped his arms and stared down through the open window to the garden below, remembering his stroll with Harry Connaught the previous evening.

They had said nothing for the first few minutes. They had stood, he and Harry Connaught, puffing on their cigars and not looking at each other.

'I wouldn't worry if I were you,' said Freddie at length. 'It'll be all right.'

'Bloody better be,' muttered Harry. 'I could end up selling double glazing.'

'Monkeys,' said Freddie, and in answer to Harry's puzzled face he continued, 'hear nothing, see nothing, do nothing. That's what you want and that's what you're doing.'

'Complicity by default's the phrase they tend to use when they fire you,' said Harry. 'Or even worse, they promote you sideways out of harm's way.'

Freddie aimed carefully and deposited a large wodge of cigar ash on one of his mother's cherished lilies. 'No,' he said, 'everything's all right. Except for that bloody Hammond woman, that is.'

'I warned you about her,' said Harry. 'She's bloody good at what she does. How did she find out in the first place?'

'Peter reckons she just guessed. He certainly didn't tell her and nobody else would have done.'

Harry Connaught stared thoughtfully at the backs of other people's houses for a moment. 'It could be worse,' he said at length. 'She'll run the stations like clockwork for you.'

'Terrific,' snarled Freddie. 'Fifty years of radio and still we have clockwork stations when we need every bit of high tech we can lay our hands on. Now me, Harry, I'd have run the stations like micro-electronics, not clockwork.' He paused before speaking very deliberately and quietly. 'I cannot tell you how much I resent that.'

'I know, I know. Don't worry, Fred, your turn will come. Besides, running the stations was only a bit of a whim to you, wasn't it? Another string to your bow, as it were. No, this time I have to agree with your mother. The best way to keep the whole thing sweet and silent is to give Monica Hammond a vested interest in doing so.' He transferred his gaze from the backs of other people's houses to the polished caps of his own shoes. 'Not, you understand, that I know anything about any of this business. You do realize that I am merely speaking hypothetically.'

Freddie puffed on his cigar and smiled to himself, wishing that he'd had the foresight to secrete a small tape-recorder somewhere about his person. He looked down to the garden where his wodge of cigar ash still lay in its lily, and decided that he would not be so remiss in the future.

Soho is a curious place. In its narrow lanes and broad thoroughfares, big movie businesses stand cheek by jowl with small-time production companies, massive dubbing studios overshadow Chinese pharmacies and seedy sex shows vie with art cinemas for the available custom. Also vying for the available custom are a catholic admix of £50 prostitutes, second-division solicitors and third-division management companies, usually housed three to a room above Italian restaurants in flats no longer deemed suitable for human habitation.

One such room housed Tony Lazer Management. Tony Lazer, né Goldstein, was a West Ham boy made bad. He had been in the rock and roll business for six years, having made the logical graduation from selling dodgy Ford Escorts in the Old Kent Road, and for five of the six had floundered badly. Then had come the magical day when he first heard Flash Jack sing at the Green Man, and had recognized him as a winning ticket. It must be said that this had nothing to do with any artistic insight on Tony's part, but it would take more of a fool than he to stand in a pub full of hysterical pubescent girls and not realize he was watching something exploitable.

Flash Jack had needed little persuasion to sign a five-year exclusive, and at the moment was celebrating his sixth hit record while Tony booked his fourth sell-out tour. Although Tony could now afford offices in Regent Street at the very least, he stayed in Soho, partly because he thought it gave him some street cred and partly because, with only the one earning client, he didn't see why he should spend the money.

There is an odd relationship between those who play music on instruments and those who play music over the air-waves. It is not so much that the musicians feed off the DJs, or even the other way round; it is more as if they are both together in a very light boat on a notoriously unpredictable sea. And while there may be many arguments as to who holds the tiller and who rigs the sails, there is complete agreement about one thing: nobody jumps up and down and rocks the boat – especially if you're not sure which way the wind is blowing.

What Mad Maggie Lomax had done on her show the previous evening definitely counted as rocking the boat; unfortunately, neither Tony Lazer nor Flash Jack had the experience to be particularly good sailors.

Jack arrived at Tony's office at eleven o'clock. He made a quick stop at the second-floor loo to powder his nose before climbing the tatty carpeted stairs to Tony's third-floor, eight-by-twelve room. They had both heard Maggie's programme and neither of them was in the mood to mince words.

Jack immediately went on to the offensive. 'You're

my fucking manager, Tony, why don't you just waste this woman and be done with it?'

'Calm down, Jacko, and stop talking like fucking Kojak. This is business, not bother, we got to sort it out properly. Legally.' He noticed the tell-tale white ring that surrounded the singer's left nostril. 'Anyway, the way you keep hitting that damn nosegay, it's not as if she's saying anything that's not true, is it!'

'I need my boost to cope with all the shit you make me do, and besides, since when has the truth got in the way as far as you're concerned?'

Tony leaned backwards in his Corbusier office chair – bought from the proceeds of the second hit and the only luxury he afforded himself in his otherwise tawdry office – and eyed Jack with cold-haddock eyes. His suppressed Jewish nature came to the fore. 'Listen, my boy, we've done very well in the past two years, thank you very much, and I'm not going to let some DJ screw our chances of another ten. Remember, Cliff Richard can't last for ever, and you, my lad, are in a perfect position to go "family". So, let's stop accusing each other of malfunctions, and fight this thing. First, you stop this nasty habit right now.'

The horror on Jack's face was akin to that of most people the first time they saw the alien coming through John Hurt's stomach. Tony continued before Jack could mutter a protest. 'How much are you carrying?'

Jack reached into his shirt pocket, produced a neatly folded white packet and opened it on Tony's desk. 'About two grammes,' he said, taking a small pinch and inserting it with expert precision up his unpolluted right nostril.

With the calmness which can only be described as very upsetting to a user, Tony seized the open packet and threw it across the room, spilling its entire contents over the stained paisley rug. 'If you want it that bad, snort the shit off the carpet.'

Jack looked at Tony in disbelief. The thought of his life-support system being scattered irreverently across this necessary evil's office stirred hatred in his heart. He was not stupid enough to resort to violence; his looks constituted at least fifty per cent of his talent, and Tony was an East End boy who knew enough about street fighting to do him considerable damage. Anyway, he could always buy more. He sank philosophically into the Habitat deckchair. 'You're right, Tony, I'm sorry, we can make millions. I'll stop. Hell, I survived twenty-two years without it.'

Tony smiled. 'That's more like it,' he said. 'Now, how many people know you do coke?'

'Sheila Graham, Billy the Roadie, the dealer I use and you. And since last night, four fucking million listeners to CRFM!'

'OK. I'll take care of it. I'll call Annie and work out a press release denying these outrageous allegations. I think we'll use John Dillman as the eagle, and let's shit on this camel-driver's hooker from a great height.'

'I'm going to call you Razorbrain from now on. Lazer the Razor.'

Tony smiled in gratification. 'All part of the service.' He chuckled, 'Lazer the Razor. Yeah, I like that.'

The English summer had been very kind so far, abstaining from the kind of spiteful outbursts that came as a godsend to hard-up *Sun* copywriters, and ruined the odds on the July course at Newmarket. Brian Callaghan marched briskly down Park Lane, hoping that people might think he was ex-Coldstream Guards, and it seemed to him that the girls in their summer dresses, the trees in their summer leaves and even the air in its shimmering summer dust had been laid on by God specifically for his benefit. He always felt like this when he was about to do a deal.

Brian Callaghan could sell sand in the Sahara and compasses at the North Pole, and had built a brilliantly successful career on a basis that was only slightly less improbable. Within the station itself, he was known as 'Dirty Harry', which he assumed was a reference partly to his name and partly to his marked resemblance to Clint Eastwood. He assumed wrongly. He bore more of a resemblance to a slightly less animated version of Kermit the Frog, and any secretary at CRFM would snigger and tell you the real reason he was called Dirty Harry: Brian Callaghan screwed anything that moved.

His destination this morning was the BMW showroom a couple of hundred yards further down Park Lane. He looked at his watch, which showed seven and a half minutes off his appointment time, then twisted his wrist towards his companion. 'How's that for timing, eh?'

David Westbury, scuttling along on shorter legs beside his boss, glanced at the flashy watch. 'We're going to be early.'

'No we're not,' said Callaghan. 'Berris's watch will be slow.'

David looked puzzled. 'I'm not with you.'

Brian explained with a patience born of total self-satisfaction. 'We'll be early, Berris will be caught on the hop, we will look at our watches with tolerant amusement, he will think he's in the wrong and be apologetic. Good start.'

David considered this for a second. 'OK, I'm with you,' he said, grinning.

Unlike Brian Callaghan, David Westbury was a quiet fellow, not really the type one would expect to be a hard-case media salesman. But he did have the knack of luring his clients into a sense of false security just before lowering the boom, and also had the remarkable record of closing over forty per cent of his contacts at the first visit, which is why Callaghan had taken him on as his sales manager. The man they were talking about was Stanley Berris, media manager of BMW, and prospective client.

Callaghan, a past master at finding out all there was to know about prospective clients, had a Dun & Bradstreet operation performed on Berris, and knew him to be a small, balding man with an obsession about punctuality and a genetic dislike of Arabs, which was rather unfortunate as they made up over sixty per cent of his trade. He also knew that Berris had a great and abiding love of tennis, which is why Callaghan had two tickets in his black crocodile briefcase to the following day's men's semi-finals.

As they approached the showroom, Callaghan and Westbury slowed their pace a fraction in order to confirm the final battle plan.

'OK,' said Callaghan. 'What we want out of this are at least four cars in lieu of cash, and we're not willing to go above twenty per cent below book. Right?'

'Right,' replied Westbury. 'What if he won't play ball?'

'Then you will make your excuses, more in sorrow than in anger, and go back to the office. I shall tell him he has an hour to deal, or we take the package to Volvo.'

Westbury looked doubtful. 'He won't wear that.'

'He will if he thinks you're lying about the office, if he thinks you're actually on your way over to Volvo to close.'

It was not quite the way that Westbury liked to do

business, but he was not about to argue with the Master. As they drew level with the showroom window, he nodded his head at one of the cars and grinned at Callaghan. 'That's the one I want,' he said, 'pearl grey with black interior.'

The air inside the showroom was cool in contrast to the heat of the day outside. Glistening BMWs lurked like great shiny insects amid the obligatory jungle of potted palms and *Fatsia japonica*. From behind a large desk, a well-polished receptionist looked up at Westbury and Callaghan as if they were the most physically fascinating and intellectually stimulating creatures she had ever met. Callaghan gave her his most knicker-wetting smile.

'Callaghan and Westbury for Mr Berris,' he said, before raising his left eyebrow a millimetre. 'CRFM.'

'Of course,' said the girl, pressing a button on the console before her. 'One moment, I'll tell him you're here. Do take a seat.'

Stanley Berris was having a totally, absolutely and completely rotten day. He had left his house this morning with his wife howling about the washing machine. He had been stuck in the most horrific traffic jam all the way from Blackheath. His secretary had told him that she was pregnant and it was his. As if that were not enough, he had spilt coffee all over the proofs of the company's new catalogue and his own new trousers, and was in the process of mopping up the mess when those bastards from CRFM were announced. He had made himself respectable – just – when Callaghan and Westbury were ushered through his door by Miss Fertility herself.

'Hi, hello,' he stuttered. 'Come in, yes, hello, have a seat, sit down, hello.' He stuck a podgy hand out. 'Stanley Berris. Sit down.'

'I'm so sorry,' purred Callaghan, taking the sweaty paw and shaking it, 'it's obviously our fault. I thought we'd said ten-thirty.'

Berris looked quickly at his watch and Westbury looked gratefully at his shoelaces.

'Yes. Quite right,' said Berris. 'We did. Ten-thirty. Right. Absolutely. No problem.' He looked at the two men with eyes that were panic-stricken and already defeated. 'Coffee?'

Twenty-eight minutes later, Callaghan and Westbury descended the wide spiral staircase that led from Berris's office to the showroom below. They had done a deal: Berris would pay for a very average package of advertising with an impressive package of above-average cars. David Westbury had his pearl grey with black interior and Berris had his centre-court tickets. What Callaghan was after – apart from his car – had yet to be achieved, but he was quietly confident. As they reached the foot of the staircase Callaghan whispered to Westbury to go on ahead.

He pretended to examine one of the glossy cars to allow Westbury time to clear the doors, then approached the reception desk where the girl was adding to her polish with the help of a small nail-file.

'Listen,' he smoothed, 'I know this is outrageously forward of me, but I was thinking of taking in *Salome* at the open-air in Regent's Park tonight, and I really do hate going alone.' He put on his little-boy-lost face. 'I don't suppose you'd care to keep me company, would you? And perhaps join me in a little supper-ette afterwards?' His tone was winsome and innocent.

The girl smiled and batted heavy fringes of eyelashes at him, before answering in tones that came from Roedean by way of Balls Pond Road. 'Bugger off,' she said sweetly.

Oh well, thought Cállaghan as he bounded after David Westbury, one out of two's not bad. Can't win 'em all.

Maggie Lomax wheezed up the stairs to the top floor of the CRFM building. She could have taken the lift, of course, but every now and again, Maggie liked to kid herself that forty cigarettes a day weren't killing her. She was not quite sure why she had been summoned to the divine presence, but she had a pretty fair idea. Well, to be accurate, she had several fair ideas. The Education Minister might have turned nastier than he already was; or perhaps the God Squad had taken exception to her remarks about the Pope last week. Then again it could have been a richly deserved pay rise – but she doubted it. Outside Monica's office, Maggie stopped and brushed a fragment of ash from her jumper. She was just about to knock on the door when a small fit of coughing took her.

'Come straight in, Maggie,' came Monica's voice from inside the office.

Monica leaned back in her office chair and glared at the sheet of paper she held in her hand. Then she looked up at Maggie, slouched defiantly in the chair on the other side of the desk. 'What *am* I going to do with you?'

'Leave me alone to get on with the job you pay me for, is the first answer that springs to mind. Next question.'

Monica brandished the sheet of paper. 'Let me read this to you,' she said. '"We are outraged at the appalling allegations made against our client, Mr John Featherstone, a.k.a. Flash Jack, by your employee, Ms Maggie Lomax, date, time, etc. We feel, as we are sure you do, that a court case would be detrimental to all our interests. However, unless a full and unreserved apology for the aforementioned remarks is made by Ms Lomax on her programme within forty-eight hours of the date on this letter, we shall have no option but to pursue a retraction through litigation. I remain, etc, etc.'''

Monica put the letter down and looked at Maggie. 'Well?'

'Bollocks,' snorted Maggie. 'Retraction through litigation! Good God, it sounds like something dirty old men do with waste-paper bins.'

Oh lord, thought Monica, sighing. Here we go.

'You're not going to take that shit seriously, are you?' asked Maggie. 'The man's a prat, his manager's a wally, and the solicitor's a crook. The three of them are just trying it on for a bit of free publicity. Here, give it to me.' She leaned over the desk and snatched the letter from the desk, then crumpled it into a tight ball, stood up and hurled it into the litter basket.

'Render unto Caesar that which is Caesar's, and trash goes in the bin,' she said, preparing to leave. Monica took a deep breath and did a pretty good impression of a pissed-off tiger.

'SIT DOWN!' she roared. Maggie stopped dead in her tracks. For a split second, the two women's eyes met in an icy battle of wills before Maggie decided it was too early in the morning to waste energy. She gave a little shrug, retrieved the letter from the bin and sat down again, smoothing out the letter as sarcastically as only she knew how.

'I'm sorry, you're right,' said Maggie, 'I shouldn't have chucked it away like that. A whole tree died for this little gem.' She paused and examined the crumpled paper. 'Well, perhaps not a whole tree. More like a very small weed.' She passed it back to Monica.

'Thank you,' said her boss. 'Now perhaps we can be serious.'

'If we must,' sighed Maggie.

'From your attitude, I can infer one of two things,' said Monica. 'Either you've grown tired of being a DJ on this station, or you were telling the truth on your show and are prepared to stand by it.'

Maggie gave Monica her sweetest smile. 'How could I ever tire of working for you, Monica?'

Monica stared hard at Maggie for a long moment before answering. 'You,' she said, 'are the biggest pain in the arse I have ever met in my entire life.'

Maggie's grin broadened. 'And number one in London,' she smiled. 'Mustn't forget that.'

The day you're not, thought Monica, is the day that you and I part company, my girl. Aloud, she confined her words to business. 'Now then, tell me why you said what you did.'

Maggie considered, all traces of juvenile dementia gone. 'Right. What I said was that I thought white powder was spoiling Flash Jack's career. Now while there may have been the odd nun listening who thought I was referring to self-raising flour, let's assume that most people knew I was talking about cocaine. *I* know he does coke because I've watched him doing it, the guys at the recording studio know it because at least two of them do it with him – and I can name names – and there must be at least half a dozen bits of tail scattered between here and Hendon Central who know about it because it's a well-known fact that flashing is about as much as Flash Jack can actually do, and the tail only follows for the freebie high.'

Monica winced, but Maggie carried on regardless. 'You only have to hear the rehearsal tapes on his last album – and I have – to know what's going on. Half the sodding cost of the thing was down to wasted time and dead brains – the hell with music.' Maggie fished a cigarette from her pocket and lit it, inhaling deeply and blowing the smoke directly, but unintentionally, straight at Monica. 'No,' she continued, 'the only reason you've got that piece of garbage there, is that Jack's conned his manager into believing he's clean, and his manager hasn't got the bloody native wit to follow the thing through in his head. Let them take us to court if they want. It'll be their problem, not ours.'

Monica thought carefully. However much she disliked Maggie Lomax personally, she did have a certain – if grudging – respect for her. 'You're quite sure about that?' she asked. 'You'd go on oath?'

Maggie looked at Monica without the slightest trace of either humour or deceit. 'I would,' she said.

'You do know, don't you,' said Monica, 'that I shan't support you if there is the slightest doubt against you?'

Maggie said nothing. She merely gazed at Monica with an expression of amused cynicism, as if to suggest that she would as soon expect support from a poisonous jellyfish.

Monica lowered her eyes, suddenly unable to meet Maggie's. 'Right,' she said, 'I'll ignore this for the time being, then. Let's just see what goes down. Thank you, Maggie.'

Maggie raised her right eyebrow just a fraction. 'You're welcome.'

Maggie left Monica's office and headed down to reception. She had finished her cigarette, but could find nowhere to put the dog-end. CRFM had been one of the first institutions to be caught up in the new wave of anti-smoking hysteria, and while the public areas of the building contained many receptacles for potted plants and rather nasty items of contemporary sculpture, they contained no receptacles for cigarette ends. It could be argued, thought Maggie, that the sight of the sculpture was far more injurious to general health than the odd cigarette, but that was rather beside the point. She arrived in reception, therefore, holding the smouldering butt aloft in the manner of an Olympic torch-bearer. A small but entertaining fracas was in progress.

Lizzie Stephenson, the receptionist, was deep in breathless conversation with a spotty bass player who had come to be interviewed on the lunchtime show. Their eyes were locked together with the concentration only found in those who are at the bottom of the ladder and willing to climb any rung, no matter how small or how fragile.

Further along the desk, Robin Trower was under siege. His assailant was a flashily dressed young man with a gold chain bracelet, lots of teeth, and a box of records under his arm. He was leaning over the desk and smiling sharkishly at Robin, who was looking confused and bewildered.

'Look, it's all right, honestly,' the flashy young man was saying. 'Maggie Lomax is expecting me. No need to call up. I know the way.'

He was about to go, but Robin stopped him. 'I'm sorry, sir,' he said, 'I can't let you just wander up. I have to call.'

The young man bared his teeth in a reassuring grin. 'Don't worry, they all know me up there – I'm an old friend.'

Robin turned to Lizzie Stephenson for guidance and support, but Lizzie was still riveted to the bass player. With enormous relief Robin spotted Maggie entering reception. The flashy young man also caught sight of her, and his expression lost some of its assurance.

'Miss Lomax!' called Robin. 'This gentleman says he has an appointment to see you.'

Maggie walked over to the desk. 'Oh yes?' she said. 'Robin, let me introduce you. This,' she said, prodding the young man in the middle of his leather jacket, 'is what's called a plugger. In that box are fifty records that he is going to nag me to listen to. As a breed, Robin, pluggers are not a particularly nice species. This particular one is a first-class pain in the butt. They do not get appointments, they leave their goods with you and you will then give them to us.' She turned to the plugger. 'And this,' she said, gesturing at Robin, 'is our new security guard. He may be new but he is a very good security guard, and if I ever find you trying to take advantage like that again, I promise to you that every record you give me will go straight in the bin. Now then' – she took the box of records from the now-crestfallen young man and gave him her cigarette end – 'I'll take these, you dispose of that, and then off you go and annoy someone else, all right?' She took the plugger by the shoulder, turned him round, and shoved him towards the door. 'Bye bye,' she called after him.

Robin looked embarrassed. 'Sorry about that, Miss Lomax, I didn't know.'

'It's OK, lovey, there has to be a first time,' said Maggie. She raised her voice. 'But if a certain receptionist was doing her job properly ...' She left the words hanging in the air. Lizzie turned from her bass player and glared at Maggie with ill-concealed malevolence.

'Sorry,' she muttered.

Maggie was just about to leave when Robin coughed hesitantly, unsure of how to begin.

'Er ... Miss Lomax ...'

Maggie gave him an encouraging smile. 'Yes?'

'I know this is going to sound, you know, a bit silly, but I've got this kid sister, see.'

Maggie was there ahead of him. 'You'd like an auto-graph for her?'

Robin smiled gratefully. 'It's her birthday in a few weeks,' he explained. 'I thought I'd try and get every-one's autograph – make up a sort of album for her.'

'Nice idea,' smiled Maggie. 'Leave it with me. I'll dig up a decent photograph – well, as decent as they ever are. What's her name?'

'Katie.'

Maggie reached over the desk and took the ballpoint pen out of Lizzie's hand and scribbled the name on a piece of paper. 'Don't let me forget about it, Robin.'

'That's smashing, Miss Lomax, thanks a lot.'

Maggie gave the pen back to Lizzie and pulled a face at Robin. 'The name's Maggie, my love. Miss Lomax sounds like a bloody games mistress.'

She turned and walked out of reception, leaving Robin in a warm glow of feeling how nice people were when you got to know them.

Lizzie Stephenson scowled sourly at him. 'Creep,' she said under her breath.

Robin ignored her. She was one of the few people at CRFM who had not proved to be nicer the better you knew them. Much as Robin never liked to think ill of anybody, she struck him as a vain, self-centred little minx, for all her plummy voice and shiny hair. Although pretty in a rather hard-edged way, in repose her face was full of downward-turning shapes: her eyes, heavy-lidded and calculating, her mouth drawn with discon-tent, her nostrils flared as if constantly scenting the air for opportunity.

But now, as Robin watched surreptitiously, her face brightened as if a switch had been thrown. Her eyes sparkled to life, her mouth snapped into a wide smile, and she gave a little toss of the head, ostensibly to shake the chestnut hair out of her eyes, but in reality to show off the delicate turn of her cheekbones. Robin followed her eyes to find the source of this animation.

Brian Callaghan, full and flush with his recent triumphs on Park Lane, was swinging jauntily through the main doors. He approached the reception desk.

'Morning, Tower,' he said.

'Good morning, Mr Callaghan,' said Robin. 'Actually,' he went on apologetically, 'it's Trower.'

But Callaghan was not listening. He had already forgotten the young security guard, and was beaming in on Lizzie. 'Hello, gorgeous,' he oiled. 'When are you going to run away to a tropical paradise and make mad passionate love to me?'

Lizzie looked at her watch. 'About four-thirty?' she replied.

Callaghan shook his head. 'Can't wait that long, I'm afraid. Any messages?'

Lizzie checked the book. 'Miss Hammond said she'd like to see you if you got back before lunch.'

'And so she shall,' said Callaghan. 'Give her a buzz and tell her I'm on my way up to perform unnatural acts upon her luscious and unsuspecting bod.' He swung jauntily out of reception, leaving Lizzie giggling as she pressed the button on the intercom, and Robin feeling uncomfortable and embarrassed. He wasn't used to that sort of witty and urbane repartee.

Monica leant her elbows on her desk, fingertips spread and touching, as if in prayer, and studied her thumbnails as she listened to Callaghan's account of the morning's deal. In essence, it was a deal she was well familiar with: the bartering of advertising for goods instead of cash; but at this point in the financial year, and bearing in mind the forthcoming negotiations concerning Cornwall and Dundee, it was not a deal that she was happy about. Callaghan finished his tale and looked at his managing director. He had expected some congratulation, but none was forthcoming. Instead, Monica continued to study her fingers and merely said, 'Hmm. I see.'

Callaghan was nonplussed. 'What's the matter? I thought it was a good package.'

'In terms of what we've been doing up to now, I'll agree, it is,' said Monica. She picked up the paper that Callaghan had given her. 'Five ex-factory new model BMWs for – what – a year's air-time. No, as a deal it's up to your usual diabolic standard. I only hope the poor chap at BMW won't go home and shoot himself.'

Callaghan grinned, mollified a little.

'The problem is,' she went on, 'that's the best part of a hundred thousand pounds that won't appear in the cash-flow. That's a lot of money.'

Callaghan's eyes narrowed.

Monica looked at him and read his thoughts with unnerving accuracy. 'No, we do not need the hard cash desperately. At the moment.' She wondered how much to tell her sales director, and decided that discretion was the better part of most things. If Callaghan had half the brains she credited him with, he would go away and draw his own conclusions. It would be interesting to see what he then did with them.

'Over the last couple of years, we've been accepting a great many contra-deals like this,' she said, 'and I'm not saying they're wrong *per se*. What I am saying, is that I feel it's now a good time to make the transition from kind to cash. Over the next couple of months, I want to put our house in order. I want our books to be like Caesar's wife.'

Callaghan looked puzzled.

'Beyond reproach,' explained Monica. 'I want to be able to show our books to the world, and I want the world to see a highly successful station with lots and lots of money and not the slightest stain on its character. Contra-deals, however good, however advantageous, do tend to carry a slight air of pollution with them. I want them stopped.'

She studied Callaghan's face to see the effect of her words and had to look away to stop herself smiling. However accomplished an actor he was in front of a punter, Monica could read Callaghan like a book. Interest, glee and horror all flashed across his face in quick succession. Interest because the fortunes of Brian Callaghan were closely aligned with those of CRFM, glee because he obviously felt he was being let in on something no one else knew about, even if he wasn't quite sure what it was, and horror because Callaghan felt about straightforward dealing the way most people felt about mugging old ladies.

'So,' said Monica, 'we're all clear on that score, are we?'

Callaghan stood up to go and gave Monica his most confident smile. 'You call the shots, ma'am, and I'll line up the targets for you,' he said.

'Thank you,' said Monica.

Brian Callaghan left Monica's office to go and unravel things by himself, looking a great deal more poised than he actually felt.

CHAPTER 3

John Thorne was being chased by a tiger. It was a huge golden beast with huge white fangs and right now it had him cornered in the newsroom, his back pressed hard to a tape machine and his feet slithering in something that looked and felt like black treacle. The tiger reared on its hind legs to savage him, and suddenly assumed the face of Monica Hammond. This was more than John could take. He screamed, throwing out his arms and finding them entangled in miles of crackly recording tape which snaked round his neck and threatened to strangle him.

'Daddy,' mumbled a small voice close to his ear, 'stop snoring.'

The tiger and tape faded, and John realized that it was his six-year-old daughter Louise who was trying to strangle him. She had crawled into his bed beside him, and was using all the strength in her small arms to snuggle up to the overnight stubble on his neck. He turned over and held her close. 'I'm not snoring,' he muttered, 'I'm screaming at tigers.' With deep relief, he gradually realized that all the international power struggles and domestic politics he reported every day, not to mention tigers with the face of Hammond, were still a million miles away.

John Thorne loved the middle of the week. On Mondays, Tuesdays and Fridays he had early starts, but on Wednesdays and Thursdays he could sleep in until eight o'clock – a rare and precious treat for anyone who presented news on a twenty-four-hour station. This was his time. No reporters, no radio, no pressure, just that lovely feeling of vague and twilight consciousness with the ones he loved around him. It would be nice if some of them didn't strangle quite so hard, he thought, but it was a trivial complaint.

Patricia Thorne entered the bedroom just as the radio alarm pierced the calm. She deposited a cup of coffee on the bedside table, switched off the alarm and turned the volume down until the background music was just audible. She looked affectionately at the two figures curled beside each other. 'You, young lady,' she said, 'are in my place. Go and get dressed or you'll be late for school.'

The small girl nestled deeper into her father's neck. 'Shan't,' she said as her father fought for breath.

Patricia started to count, slowly and deliberately. 'One . . . two . . .'

Louise sprang out of bed with amazing agility and disappeared towards the bathroom. In this ritual last warning system she had never discovered what happened when her mother got to three, and had no intention of finding out now. Patricia mimicked her daughter's agility and leaped into the empty space beside her husband. 'Anything I can do to help you get up?' she whispered in his ear.

'When did I ever need help?' he replied, slipping his hand inside her nightie.

'Not that kind of getting up, clot,' she said, kissing his ear. 'Getting out of bed getting up.'

John made a grab for his wife, but she was too quick for him. 'Uh-uh,' she said. 'No chance. You've got two minutes; I'm timing the eggs.'

Even though he knew his wife was kidding, John scrambled through a shower and into his clothes in record time, and arrived at the breakfast table looking smarter than Patricia had seen him for some time.

Louise started to giggle over her egg, but Patricia silenced her with a look. 'Three-piece suite, eh?' she said. 'Who's the lucky lady?'

John sliced the top off his egg with Ninja-like accuracy and dunked a toast soldier. 'The new blonde in the newsroom,' he replied, biting the soldier's head off.

'Oh yes? How nice for you,' Patricia smiled and poured herself some more coffee. 'And for her, of course.'

'Bitch,' said John. 'Actually, I've got this Irish bloke coming over today.'

Patricia raised her eyebrows. 'The one you were talking about the other day? Sean whatsit?'

'Sean Hearty,' corrected John, 'head of news for Downtown Radio Belfast. He's coming to look at the new equipment we've got at CRFM.'

'Could be interesting,' said Patricia. 'Have you met him before?'

'No, just spoken on the phone, that's all,' answered John. 'But I know his reputation and you're right, it could be interesting for both of us. I'll be taking him to lunch, by the way, so I won't need much feeding tonight.'

'OK.'

John finished his breakfast and got up from the table, noticing that both his wife and daughter were grinning at him.

'What's the matter with you two now?' he asked.

Patricia laughed. 'I'm sorry, darling, it's my fault, I shouldn't have hurried you so much.'

Louise pointed at his face gleefully. 'You're all stubbly!' she cried. 'You forgot to shave!'

John felt his still-bearded chin. 'Oh, sod!' he muttered as he walked back to the bathroom, leaving his daughter to explode happily into the remains of her boiled egg.

★

Sean Hearty had arrived at Belfast airport well over an hour before take off, partly to give himself ample time to clear the tight security now an everyday feature of Northern Ireland's life, and partly to make sure he got a seat in the front of the plane. He was a nervous flyer and hated having to sit behind the wings. The vibration and noise always made him feel ill, and besides, they always started serving the coffee from the front.

As he strapped himself into his seat, it crossed his mind that it was a bit, well, Irish, to serve coffee from the front when the galley was in the rear, but he came to the conclusion that it was yet another hangover from the British class system. Even on single class flights such as this, they had to start serving where the first class used to be – either that or nobody had told head office that first class no longer existed on flights of less than two hours' duration.

These days, time demanded that Sean fly everywhere, but he didn't like it. He much preferred the days of his childhood, and as the great lumbering aeroplane roared off the tarmac in the most illogical way, Sean comforted himself with memories.

There had been days when he and his father, Patrick, would start out at 4 a.m. to catch the 6 a.m. ferry to Liverpool; from there they would catch the train on to Manchester to watch their beloved United vanquish yet another vastly inferior foe. Those were the glory days of George Best and Bobby Charlton; and it was a wonderful feeling to watch an Irish lad turn the Brits inside out week after week, no matter what kind of fouls they perpetrated on his £1 million legs. He would watch George leave the field at the end of the game, bleeding and bruised, having scored at least twice, and his national pride would be flying higher than the flag standard at the Stretford End.

But that was a long time ago. Now his father tended to stay behind the counter of his tatty betting shop in East Belfast, laboriously counting out the day's takings. Sean had tried to persuade him to 'go computer' but the old man would have none of it. 'I'm too old to change now, son,' he would say whenever Sean raised the subject. 'I've had the old comptometer for thirty years and the day it makes its first mistake is the day I'll think about your high-fangled technology.'

But Sean loved and understood the old man, so he only ever had a go after the third pint of stout in order to wind him up, and would always burst out laughing as soon as the old fellow rose to the bait.

Patrick Hearty's betting shop occupied a unique position in Belfast; because of its location, it had always been a staging post for both republicans and loyalists alike. Every Irishman likes to drink and bet, and as the Hearty family were Irish Protestants as opposed to the English variety, both communities had used the little shop as a half-way house in which to pass messages and set up deals with each other. Both sides respected the family, and the old man never took advantage of his position, except for the odd excursion into the West Belfast totter pubs where all the best stout and the occasional bottle of poteen could be had.

Patrick was as proud of his son as only an Irish father can be. Sean had decided, early on in life, that the best means of mediation lay in the media, and in five short years had raised himself from a humble trainee reporter to head of news at Belfast's Downtown Radio. But last year had been his real year of triumph, when he won the highly prestigious 'Newsman of the Year' award for his coverage of an uprising in the Falls Road.

Sean was justifiably proud of the award, but could not forget the moment he felt a piece of shrapnel piercing his shoulder, and the horror of the thought that he might not see tomorrow. He could not fully accept that he had got the award for journalistic merit, and not for being wounded in the line of duty. Nevertheless, he had accepted the accolade, and the £2,000 that went with it, feeling that at least he had been able to report the truth; and noted with a certain amusement that the award had done wonders for his status, both professionally and in the eyes of the opposite sex.

Once the Tristar had cleared the grey clouds that covered Belfast and levelled out, the prohibition lights went off and the stewardesses started serving coffee, from the front. Sean relaxed in his seat but kept his seat-belt fastened, and accepted his coffee gratefully. Despite what some people called his irrational preference for boats and fear of flying – which Sean didn't think were irrational at all; after all, if the worst came to the worst, he could swim but he couldn't ruddy well fly, could he? – Sean settled down to happier memories. He leaned back, sipped his drink, and thought about the happy day when Georgie Best had scored seven against Northampton in the cup.

He was awakened from his sleep by the voice of the pilot telling him that the time was 9.35 exactly, the weather in London was fine and sunny, and hoping they had all had a very pleasant flight. Sean had. He had slept all the way through it which was by far the best way.

In the arrival lounge, Sean spotted his name on a card held high in the air by a small leather-jacketed gnome. He approached the man.

'Are youse Sean Hearty for CRFM?' inquired the gnome in his sharp Irish brogue. Sean smiled and said he was. 'Well, come along then, I've got the cab outside and I'm bloody double-parked.'

Sean settled into the mini cab and prepared for the inevitable all-Paddys-together routine of expatriates, but to his relief, it didn't happen. Instead, the driver offered him a cigarette. 'Youse coming to work there, are you, at CRFM?'

'No, just visiting,' replied Sean.

'Oh, they're a great bunch of people, I can tell you,' said the cabbie. 'No side to them at all.'

'You do a lot of work for them, do you?' asked Sean politely.

'All the time. Me and Maggie Lomax, we're like that.' He crossed his fingers to demonstrate intimacy and narrowly avoided hitting a Pan Am coach that was pulling out.

'Oh really?' said Sean, wondering what was coming next.

'Sure. Me and Maggie Lomax, we play snooker together,' replied the cabbie proudly as he roared off into the fast lane and away from the airport towards CRFM.

Through the double-glass doors and into the main reception area flowed the teeth-brushed and hair-washed tide of CRFM's daytime people. Lizzie Stephenson spent ten minutes tidying her eyebrows in the ladies' loo before deciding that, as the first representative of the staff that outsiders would meet, all in all she was not bad looking. In actual fact, Lizzie was not the first person outsiders met, Robin Trower was – but she didn't count him. What on earth could a security guard have to offer anyone?

Lizzie was looking decidedly 'convent' in her knee-length grey pleated skirt, neatly pressed white blouse and navy blue Pringle sweater as she settled down behind the Victorian partners desk which housed the station's switchboard. The only visible clue to the fact that her virginal appearance was *only* an appearance, was a pair of black patent stiletto shoes, which left most male employees under fifty fantasizing on whether the school she had just left was St Mary's or St Trinian's.

Anthony Parkin, head of commercial production, arrived a good five minutes after the receptionist had taken up her post. He alone was fully aware that what lay beyond Lizzie's double-stitched hem was not a pair of navy-blue school knickers. Navy blue they were – sensible elasticated wool they most certainly were not. He tried not to smile as he asked Lizzie for his messages, but couldn't resist giving her a surreptitious wink as she handed him two letters and a dog-eared tele-memo.

Lizzie Stephenson and Anthony Parkin were in the throes of a torrid, but top-secret, affair. The reason for this secrecy was not so much that either of them had any other emotional commitments – they didn't – but that affairs were so very much frowned upon by Monica Hammond that she had made it company policy that there would be no interdepartmental hanky-panky on pain of instant dismissal. No one was quite sure why this was; the more charitable members of staff said it was to protect the station's reputation in a generally squalid business; but the less charitable, like Bernie Bonelli, said that it was just sour grapes. If Monica wasn't getting it, then nobody else was either.

Monica did know about the affair, of course – Monica knew everything – but as long as Lizzie and Anthony were so discreet, there was precious little she could do about it, except to file the information away for possible future use. Right now, Monica was filing away yet another, but not dissimilar, snippet of information.

She had finished her usual early-morning meeting with Callaghan, who had obviously spent a troubled night trying to make sense of the previous day's information, and had spent the entire fifteen minutes this morning groping and pleading for more, in as subtle a manner as he knew how. Which, thought Monica, was about as subtle as a Sherman tank.

She sat at her glass and chrome desk, looking out of the window over Stanhope Place. In the street below, Nigel B. and Samantha were leaving the building hand in hand. The girl leaned into him and said something into his ear, and the DJ threw back his head and laughed. He disentangled his hand from hers, and draped his arm around her shoulders. A wry smile came over Monica's face. Well, well, now there's a thing! she thought, as she watched them disappear into Connaught Square.

She knew nothing about the girl who was having such a dramatic and beneficial effect on her star DJ, so made a mental note to find out more. All in all she was quite pleased. Nigel was sounding brilliant since he'd met this girl, he was obviously very happy, and her sheer beauty would ensure a good deal of press coverage when and if the story became public. The trick was to make it public when it suited CRFM, and not at the convenience of some reporter who happened to see them involved in a heavy clinch at Tramps. She would have to trust the gods on this one and pray for good timing. That was the only thing that really worried her. Monica hated trusting anyone, especially gods.

More and more, Nigel was falling under the spell of his new girlfriend, and he wasn't entirely sure that he liked the feeling. It was Samantha who made all the running; she said when they should make love, sleep, eat, go out, stay in, call it a day. In the past it had always been Nigel B., superstar, superstud, who had used women like so many matches, used them to light a brief fire and then chucked them in the bin, but now, for some strange reason, Nigel seemed powerless to stop this woman in her wild rampage across his life, perhaps because he'd never met anyone like her before: so changeable, so unpredictable, so skilled in the art of suspense. Nigel reflected anxiously that it was rather like jumping out of an aeroplane with a new design of parachute that looked suspiciously like a small tea-cosy. It would probably be all right but he didn't really trust it.

Samantha had been in yet another new mood this morning. Ever since she had met Nigel outside the station she had been edgy, excited, dangerous. They reached the flat in Maida Vale and as always, Samantha leapt up the stairs ahead of him. No stockings today, he noticed. She turned and smiled down at him, telling him to hurry up, and then continued up the stairs. Good god, thought Nigel, looking after her, no knickers either.

No sooner had he entered his flat and closed the door than she attacked him. Winding one arm round his neck, she pulled him towards her and covered his mouth with her own in a passionate kiss that allowed no escape. With her free hand she slid the straps of her sleeveless T-shirt down around her waist and unhooked her skirt, letting them both fall to the floor. She tore at Nigel's shirt, regardless of buttons, and wrenched it down round his shoulders, scratching them with her nails and kissing the red weals as they appeared, lowering her head to his chest and biting his nipples painfully. Gone were the soft loving touches of the previous evening, gone was the humour of last weekend. Only savagery remained.

Detached, as if on another planet, Nigel looked over her head at their reflection in the long hall mirror: the lean brown body twined snake-like around his own; the curve of the spine showing white through the skin as she bent to kiss his stomach; the spread of the buttocks as she squatted in front of him; the whirl of golden hair thrown back from her face so she could see to undo his jeans. Nigel freed himself from his clothes and plunged his hands into her hair, winding long strands around his fingers and using the grip to push her head lower.

But she gave him only the most fleeting caress. Kneeling spread-kneed on the carpet, she looked up at him, face flushed, eyes glittering. Like a bitch on heat. 'Do it to me! Now! Come on, do it!' she hissed. She grabbed his hands and pulled him down to the floor beside her, but she was not about to let him make love. With surprising strength she pushed him on to his back, and climbed astride him, pinning his arms to the floor, riding, writhing, heaving, shouting obscene endearments that he would much rather not have heard. Nigel could neither understand nor cope with this side of her nature – all he could do was let her have her way and pray he didn't lose his erection.

He needn't have worried. It was all over in a few seconds. Howling and panting, Samantha reached a shuddering climax that tore at him and made him feel he was being eaten alive from the inside. She lay on him for a minute or so till the shuddering subsided, and then levered herself upright, pushing her hands on his chest. She sat there, head back, eyes closed, and Nigel watched a small bead of sweat roll from the depression in her collarbone, down the swell of one breast, and fall from the softening nipple to his stomach. Tossing the damp hair away from her face, she rolled off him and lay spreadeagled and exhausted on the hall carpet.

Nigel lay where he was and gazed at the ceiling. He felt used and abused; in a rare moment of insight, he suddenly understood the look he had seen on the lovely, anonymous faces of so many of his previous one-night and one-hour stands.

Samantha propped herself up on one elbow and smiled at him. Leaning over, she planted the softest, gentlest kiss on his cheek. 'Love you,' she whispered.

Nigel was stunned. He couldn't believe his ears. The raging demon of a minute ago had been transformed into an angel. He looked at her expectantly. 'That was *love*?' he said.

She lowered her eyelashes and stroked his chest with her fingertips. 'I'm sorry, darling. I know I got a bit out of hand.' She paused and looked at him shyly. 'It's just that I want you so much. I want you all the time.' She suddenly grinned and Nigel saw a last lingering flicker of the demon. 'Next time,' she said, 'you can do all the things *you* want.'

Oh you wicked, wanton bitch, thought Nigel to himself, you really know how to stitch a man up, don't you. Aloud, he said, 'I've got half the sodding carpet stuck to my back. Let's have a bath. You go turn it on, I'll get us some champagne.'

John Thorne arrived at CRFM just after ten, and braced himself for the hurly-burly of the newsroom. On a good day, if all was going smoothly, he could expect to find an air of highly controlled chaos, punctuated by a very occasional wail of dismay from one of the juniors, and all the various items of news slotting themselves as if by magic into their appropriate places. On the other hand, if all was not so smooth, he would be greeted by the sight of several haggard journalists accusing each other of cocking up the tape-machine, two broadcasters with nasty attacks of psychosomatic laryngitis and at least one typist in tears behind the filing cabinet. He took a deep breath and pushed through the swing doors.

True, there was a slight tension in the atmosphere, and true, James Grey was a little white around the lips, but as nobody was actually committing ritual suicide in the corner, John assumed that things were going fair to moderate. He answered the greetings of his colleagues and headed straight for the safety of his small but precise office. Indicating to his secretary that he wanted no calls or interruptions, he settled down and proceeded to read the *Financial Times*, *The Times*, *Guardian*, *Mirror* and the *Sun* in order to acquire as good a general knowledge of what was going on in the world that morning as anyone else had.

When the buzz came from Lizzie that Sean Hearty had arrived, John headed for reception with unusual speed. He observed Hearty through the one-way mirror in the door that separated the green room from the main reception area and realized that in his three-piece suit, he himself was somewhat overdressed. The lanky Irishman's only concession to the importance of the meeting was a neatly knotted tie. In all other aspects of his attire, he looked as if he had just come hot-foot from covering a spot of tribal strife in Botswana. John quickly loosened his own tie and undid the top button of his shirt, before opening the door and advancing towards Hearty with his hand outstretched. 'Sean Hearty, I'm John Thorne. Welcome to CRFM – did you have a good trip?'

Sean took the proffered hand and shook it firmly. 'Not bad, thanks. Except for the coffee. When will airlines get it right?'

'When hell freezes over, I expect,' said John. 'Want a cup of the real thing?'

The two newsmen walked without speaking into the

studio complex. As they passed, one of John's reporters questioned him about the government unemployment figures that had featured in the morning news. John's first reaction was to tell him exactly where to put his statistics but, reluctant to be that rude in front of his guest, he decided against the tactic. Instead, he excused himself, and spent a couple of minutes explaining to the novice reporter how, in real terms, the figures were only conducive to a second-line story as the overall yearly statistics did not relate to a thirty-day sample, especially when forty per cent of the population were on holiday during the summer months, and that a suspected rape would be far more newsworthy, even if the government PR man had offered a slap-up lunch at Trader Vic's as an inducement to broadcast.

He could see that Sean was amused, and added as a further appendix that the trick was to run the story with a funny ending to round off the bulletin, thus achieving a light-hearted ending to the news, while keeping Maggie's hounds sweet and still gaining a free nosh.

Sean grinned at John as they left the reporter gazing after them in adoring amazement and headed towards John's office. 'I see you get the green ones as well as the pros down here.'

'All part of life's rich pattern,' replied John. 'Now, let me sort that coffee.'

Eddy McLeod, general manager of CRFM, watched the two newsmen enter John's office with a certain amount of suspicion. Eddy was suspicious of anything he did not have prior knowledge of, including his wife's menstrual cycle and partial eclipses of the moon, both of which he viewed as part of God's very personal vendetta against him.

A forty-four-year-old, five foot two Glaswegian,

Eddy had graduated to radio through six years of fence-sitting at a leading London advertising agency, a tactic he employed with limited success in his present position. He fooled almost everyone except Monica, who had realized early on that this diminutive Scottish slug had little talent for anything except possibly licking the parts of other people's anatomies that were relative to his own height. The other person who refused to be fooled was Sir Peter French, although this was not actually Eddy's fault. Peter French regarded *anybody* hired by Brian Callaghan as highly suspect, regardless of height or ethnic origin.

Eddy stood outside John's door trying to eavesdrop on their conversation and look nonchalant at the same time, which he managed for at least four minutes until he saw Callaghan appear from the green room. He broke into his best and most calculated smile, and waddled over towards the sales director. 'Brian my boy, how did you get on with BMW?'

A lesser man might have taken this for an inquiry of genuine concern, but Callaghan was not fooled, not for a second. 'None of your business, Eddy, but since you asked – bloody well.'

'Come on, Brian,' wheedled the plump Scot, 'I used to handle that account at B.B.D. & O. I'm just curious as to what they're doing with their budget, that's all.'

'Not spending enough with us is the short answer to that,' said Callaghan.

Every time the word short was mentioned in conversation, Eddy's face assumed the look of an angered Jack Russell terrier. Brian laughed as he pushed past Eddy and carried on towards his office. 'Don't concern yourself, wee fellow, any cars we get from Park Lane will not be coming your way.'

As Callaghan disappeared down the corridor, Eddy's

face contorted into an angry snarl. Screw you, Callaghan, he thought. One day I'll have your balls for bookends.

By the time Sean finished his first real cup of coffee he was beginning to warm to the ebullient Englishman who, despite his zealous attitude to work, seemed to have a natural warmth that Sean found very likeable. There was nothing wrong with enthusiasm as long as it wasn't phoney, and so far he had not been able to find fault with the way John handled either himself or other people. Satisfied that he was among at least reasonably friendly natives, he sat back into the black leather sofa. 'Now then,' he said, 'what's so special about this new portable tape-machine of yours?'

John handed him the Sony 850 operation manual. 'Well, it's small, light, has a 360-degree sound possibility in the microphone, which is adjustable down to 10 degrees, and the quality is comparable with any of the professional studio recorders.'

Sean leafed through the manual. 'Is it easy to transfer?'

'Standard metal tape. Fits any player.'

'What about operation?'

'Nothing to it. Top loading, through the cover, and the real beauty of this little gem is that it has a built-in volume limiter and a full graphic equalizer.'

Sean studied the picture and dimension measurements on page two of the manual. 'You mean all this in a machine six inches by eight by two? What's the catch?'

John pulled a sour face. 'Price, I'm afraid. They're £850 each basic, plus another £400 for extras and casing.'

Sean thought for a moment and then replaced the

book on John's desk. 'That's not too bad. When can I see it in operation?'

'Now, if you like.' John beckoned to the Irishman as he headed towards his office door. 'We use nothing else these days. Come on, I'll show you our news set-up at the same time.'

As the two men walked down the tile carpeted corridor towards the news room, Sean looked at the many concert posters that lined the walls. The Supremes, Jackson Brown, The Eagles, Bob Dylan, Stevie Wonder: all co-promoted by CRFM. He regretted the fact that the troubles in his own country were not conducive to that type of talent playing there, and hoped that one day it would change. The first concert in Belfast by a major star, he thought, would herald the start of many things – and the end of a lot as well.

John noticed Anthony and Lizzie in a tight conversational huddle at the end of the corridor. A sneaky thought crept into his mind, and a sly grin crept over his face. He turned and spoke to Sean in a low voice. 'If we hurry, I can show you how good the long-range pencil mike is for getting the goods on somebody,' he said as they scurried through the heavy soundproof doors.

John collected one of the Sony 850s from the four on the news desk, along with two sets of headphones and an L.R.P. He loaded the recorder and gave Sean a set of headphones before leading him back to a quiet corner in the corridor. 'Don't say a word ... just listen.' He pointed the L.R.P. round the corner in the general direction of the two people at the end of the hall. They were at least thirty feet away. John adjusted the equalizer and volume control. To Sean's amazement he could hear them as clearly as if they had been beside him. It was Anthony who was speaking.

'Look, Lizzie, you *are* doing a great job on the commercials I give you, honestly, but you have to move slowly. A couple of months and you'll be good enough to move on to other things, I promise you. Just don't rush it, sweetheart.'

A deep sigh of frustration and exasperation hissed through the microphone. 'Oh, all *right*!' came the woman's voice. 'It's just that I'm totally, utterly pissed off with reception. Being nice to everyone all the time. All those creeps who come in looking for a star to bother. Bloody Bonelli's groupies. I've been doing it for six months and I'm sick of it.'

Anthony's voice was soothing and wheedling. 'Come on, love, you'll have to be nice to people no matter how high up you get.' There was a short laugh. 'As a matter of fact, the higher up you get, the more people you do have to be nice to. Besides, it doesn't cost anything.'

'Oh no?' The voice was curdled with discontent. 'At least if you're a jock or a producer you get the rewards. And another thing – I hate having to sneak around here pretending I don't know you.'

Sean and John looked at each other and winked, then turned their attention back to the illicit conversation.

'Lizzie, I don't like it either, but it would mean both our jobs if Monica found out, then where would we be – bloody nowhere.'

'What she needs is a good fuck,' spat Lizzie. 'Then perhaps she'd leave the rest of us in peace.'

Sean Hearty couldn't help himself. A great shout of laughter exploded from his lips, quickly followed by a sharp gasp of alarm from the mike. Sean and John turned in unison through the open door and ran for safety. Taking his headphones off, John switched the recorder to 'pause' and tucked the machine under his jacket, and both men slowed to a walk as they headed down the corridor to John's office, speechless with the effort of keeping straight faces. Once inside, they both collapsed laughing on the sofa. Sean was the first to gather himself together. 'Christ, that was close! Just like the Falls Road without the bullets.'

'It may be shit that flies around here rather than bullets,' replied John as he put the recorder on his desk, 'but it can do you just as much damage.'

'No, it can't,' said Sean quietly.

John looked at him, his face suddenly grave. 'No, you're right, it can't. Sorry.' He switched the Sony off and removed the cassette, lightening his voice once more. 'I think I'll hold on to this, however, never know when I might need a favour.'

Sean took the cue. He stood up and stretched his arms above his head. 'One thing you can say for bullets, mind you. At least you can hear the fucking shots.' He looked squarely at his English counterpart. 'I like you, John Thorne, and I like your machine. So where are you taking me for lunch?'

The hours between noon and three are very special in all forms of media, but mean different things to different people. In Fleet Street, it means the pubs have been open for at least an hour and a half and what are we wasting our intellect behind this hot typewriter for when we could be downing a pint of real ale at the Rose; and by the way, it's your shout.

In television, it means a re-affirmation of the laws of social status. Technicians eat chips in the canteen, reporters and presenters eat wholemeal tuna sandwiches in the pub, and executives go to the most expensive restaurant for which they can get someone else to pay.

In radio, it is a precious time of relaxation. A certain amount of business *is* done, but the overwhelming drive is to get the hell out of the race for a couple of hours with whoever your friends are that day.

One person who did not enjoy the pleasures of media lunches was Trevor Jones, Programme Controller of CRFM.

A programme controller, in radio terms, is very different from a programme director. A director usually has a seat on the board and is totally responsible for the output of the station. A controller tends to be under the thumb of the managing director, has a token say on what goes on the playlist, tries (with only moderate success unless he has a great deal of respect from his fellow DJs) to control the other 'on air' personalities, and is, in nine out of ten cases, the first to go if there is any serious screw-up in programming or if the MD thinks he is getting too big for his boots. As a job, it is not so much like walking a tightrope, as hanging from a spider's web over the Grand Canyon.

Trevor had been in the business for twelve years and had sussed the game completely. He kept his nose clean, was basically loyal to Monica, did the best he could with the likes of Bonelli and Nigel B., and lived and died for his noon to three slot. The small weight of the two jobs was easy for him to carry and the extra money made his lifestyle better than he could ever have hoped for had he stayed at the BBC.

He sat in the studio and watched the rest of the staff embark upon their various lunches. There went Lizzie and Anthony, walking close but never touching, pretending no one knew about their sordid affair; Eddy McLeod, with no one to eat with as usual, bringing in boxes of pizza and pastries which would not get offered round and which would make him fart all afternoon; Maggie Lomax, wearing the sort of rampant designer clothes usually seen on Japanese peasants mourning the death of the shogun, off to the pub with a feminist newsreader from Radio 4, and never a smile for himself; John Thorne and the flak-jacketed Irishman laughing and friendly, off to do damage to the wine cellars of whatever expensive eatery they chose to patronize.

Monica, however, was contemplating lunch with some enthusiasm. She had just finished a tedious hour with John Reeve, the head of religious affairs at the IBA. In a monotonous drone he had made several points regarding the lack of 'real' religious content within the programming structure of the station, and had said that it was Monica's duty as a responsible executive to ensure that the moral state of the nation did not fall any lower than its present level.

Monica regarded him as a useless bureaucrat who only had his job in the first place because of the unfair amount of levy placed on all the ILR stations in order to support the seven floors at Brompton Road, and knew that in 'real' terms, he couldn't give a toss about the moral behaviour of a sewer rat. But she refrained from telling him that, in the same way that she refrained from telling him that she would much rather not open up her station to the charges of hypocrisy that would arise from playing music about sex and drugs and rock 'n' roll on the one hand, and preaching hellfire and damnation on the other. Instead, she looked gratefully inspired in response to his helpful comments about rock-gospel, while inwardly wishing she was on favour-asking terms with a practising Satanist.

In Spiritus Sanctimonious, Amen, she thought to herself as she showed him to the office door. She smiled sweetly and thanked him for taking the time and trouble to see her, knowing full well that she would not only disregard his suggestions but would try her hardest to forget them before he had reached the foyer.

She sat behind her desk and kicked off her shoes, feeling wonderfully sinful at the sight of her naked toes. Her private phone rang, and as always, she let it ring at least three times before answering. 'Monica Hammond.'

At first there was no reply, just the sound of close conversation and distant phones ringing. She tried to hear what was being said but to no avail through the ambient hubbub. She felt a moment of extreme annoyance and was about to slam the phone down on its cradle when Frank De Wolf's voice came through loud and clear. 'Monica, hello, I'm sorry. There are people all over my office. Hold on a sec.'

She listened intently as the lawyer dismissed the people in his office in no uncertain terms. The way he handled people was very impressive, and she absently jotted down one or two of the more colourful phrases. At last he was back. 'Monica, are you still there?'

'In flesh if not in spirit.'

'That'll do. I can never get a moment to myself. How are you?'

Monica relaxed her tone. 'I know how you feel and I'm fine,' she said, hoping she knew what was coming next.

'I know it's short notice, Monica, but I've just had a cancellation and I wondered if you would be free for lunch.'

'I'm never free for lunch, Frank, I'm bloody expensive. Especially when you make me feel like a spare airline seat. Nothing short of the Savoy Grill will make me take one step out of this office,' she lied.

Frank chuckled down the phone. 'Savoy Grill it is, then – say half an hour?'

Monica smiled to herself and replaced the phone without any further conversation. She knew he would be there and she also knew she would arrive ten minutes late. I like this game, she thought as she pressed the intercom to her PA's office. 'Suzie, no more calls, no more people, no more work. I'm off to lunch. Tell McLeod I want to see him at four rather than three; cancel my two o'clock and take an extra hour yourself.'

Suzie's startled voice came back over the intercom. 'Gosh! I mean, thanks, Monica.'

'You're welcome. If the place burns down – let it, then call me at the Savoy. But it'd better be that important.' She turned the squawk box off and stood up. She stretched to her full height and then from left to right. Good god, she thought, how can Jane Fonda do this for a living? She made a quick calculation and decided that walking down Park Lane and round by the Palace would give her a nice breath of fresh air, as well as making her a very acceptable eleven minutes late.

Robin Trower was the only person left on reception as John Thorne and Sean Hearty passed through.

Thorne had booked a table at La Loggia, a fashionable Italian bistro on the Edgware Road. It was owned by a Signor Biaggi, a Paddington Tuscan who had always been more than pleased to show him all the elaborate courtesy due to his most valued customers. La Loggia was a spacious place with the tables set out in booths, perfect for quiet business conversations. A doe-eyed Florentine beauty met them at the door, and gingerly took Sean's flak jacket in as few fingers as possible before showing them to their table.

Lizzie and Anthony left the delicatessen arm in arm and strolled cheerfully towards the park. At least, Lizzie strolled cheerfully. Anthony was thinking that if he'd wanted to spend that much on Loire wine, Westphalian ham and English strawberries, he could have gone to a restaurant and saved himself the future pain of getting grass stains out of his trousers.

Monica arrived at the Savoy twelve minutes late. That'll do, she thought as she crossed the marble entrance hall and entered the Grill bar. She saw Frank sitting at a table for two with a bottle of champagne in an ice bucket to his right. Two full glasses were on the table. She sat down slowly and greeted him with a nod of her head and a small smile. Fifteen-love to you, dear, she thought. 'Couldn't wait, eh?' she said. Fifteen-all.

He handed her a gold Asprey swizzle stick. 'It's been on the table for ten minutes, you'll need this.'

Monica took the ridiculously expensive bauble and fizzed her drink with it. Thirty-fifteen, she thought. Aloud, she said, 'Not the kind of thing I would expect you to carry about your person.'

'I bought it as a little present for you,' said De Wolf. 'I had a feeling you'd be late.'

Oh, game, set and match, thought Monica. Congratulations, you bastard. She nodded her head again slowly in amused recognition of the victor. 'Just what I've always wanted. How *did* I manage before?'

They both looked at the gleaming little rod with its golden tentacles protruding from one end. There was a moment of silence, and then both burst into laughter.

'Thank you,' said Monica, 'it's lovely. Absurd, but lovely none the less.'

Several heads turned, but they didn't care.

Lizzie and Anthony were not so pleased at the way their picnic was going. It had started to fall apart when a low-flying pigeon had scored a direct hit on Anthony's bowl of strawberries. But that wasn't the real problem and both of them knew it. Lizzie had been uptight for days, and nothing Anthony could do seemed to please her. He knew this couldn't go on. God knew there was enough pressure at work, he didn't need this. The one thing that made it work for him was Lizzie being there every night, loving him and fading the day into peace. He topped up their plastic cups with Loire wine and studied the grass. 'OK, what's the matter, Lizzie? Want to talk about it?'

Lizzie retreated into a sulk. 'Nope.'

Anthony kept his irritation in rein and his voice gentle. 'Come on, girl, this is me. If we can't talk – we can't – anything.'

She looked up at him, tears gathering in the corners of her eyes. 'Well, that's about it, isn't it,' she whimpered. 'You've just said it all. We can't do anything. It's ridiculous, medieval. All this sneaking around behind people's backs.' She pouted, taking care not to let the tears fall over the rims of her eyelids and spoil her make-up. 'We've been together for six months now; we work together every day and we still have to creep round the station pretending there's nothing going on. It's so *unfair*. Sod Monica and her crappy rules. If we can't be honest about our relationship I want to stop it now!'

Shock waves of horror ran down Anthony's spine at the thought of her leaving him. 'Lizzie, calm down, darling,' he said, reaching across the paper gingham tablecloth and taking her hand firmly in his. 'We both need the job and the station is successful now. It's the right thing for us both to be associated with for the next year or so. Who knows where it can lead? Not just for me. For you too. Be smart, this is no time to rock the boat.'

Lizzie studied his face. She could see his concern. She could see how much he loved her. She could also see that he would do anything for her if she really pushed the point. She smiled. 'Anthony, do you love me?'

'Of course I do.'

'Then let's live together.'

Anthony looked at her in shock that turned from horrible to ecstatic. 'Live together?'

'Why not? It would solve everything. Monica can't say anything if we say we're planning to get married, we don't have to pretend anymore and we cut our over-heads by half. What do you think?'

Anthony didn't know quite what to think. 'Are you saying we should get married?' he said slowly, hoping she would say yes.

'All I'm saying is let's live together. If that works out then we'll think about marriage. As far as everyone at work is concerned, we're engaged.' Lizzie picked a daisy and ever so gently dismembered it. 'It's either that or we call the whole thing off right now.'

Anthony thought all his Christmas Days had come at once. With a single, clumsy leap, he cleared the food, wine and tablecloth and tackled Lizzie waist high and together they rolled down the gradual slope towards the Serpentine. They came to rest about twenty feet from the picnic with Lizzie on top, panting, laughing, success-ful.

'I love you,' said Anthony. 'Let's do it.'

They embraced for at least three minutes, blissfully unaware that their passion was being given marks out of ten by a wayward group of giggling schoolgirls.

John and Sean were well into their coffee when Signor Biaggi brought the telephone over to the table and plugged it into the wall socket. 'Do please excuse, signori,' he said in an accent that owed a lot to *The Godfather*. 'For you, Signor Thorne.'

John took the phone, grunted his hello at the intruder and listened intently for about thirty seconds. 'Right,' he said, in a somewhat dismissive manner. 'Tell James to stop what he's doing and get on it right away. I want a flash as soon as you have some reasonable audio and give me at least four minutes for the six o'clock.'

He replaced the receiver before the caller had a chance to utter any sort of protest and turned to Sean. 'I'll have to go back soon. There's been some sort of drama at Heathrow. A plane overshot the runway. Nasty business.'

Sean took a small sip of his recently arrived, on-the-house brandy. 'How do you get your information about things like that?'

'Police mainly,' replied John, 'but we've built up a fairly good network of stringers who feed us first . . . for a price. How do you get yours?'

Sean gazed into space. 'We have a different set of problems. The police try to slow all the information down as much as they can unless it's one of their own that's been done. All we can do is rely on good will and fair play with all factions of the community – and of course my Dad's betting shop is a hive of activity as far as first-hand info goes. I just have to be very careful not to go to air too early. I sometimes sit on a story for a couple of weeks after I get the original word. In our province the name of the game is not being first, it's getting the timing right.'

John was more than a little surprised to hear from a top-line journalist that being first was not the driving force behind his stories. In his world, people disembowelled each other to be first. He considered his brandy glass for a moment before choosing his next words with care. 'For example?'

Sean looked at the Englishman and also considered. Not his brandy, but whether he could, in any way, trust this newly acquired friend. He decided he could. 'OK. Over the last two weeks there has been a rumour going around that the RUC and prison officers have decided that they're going to cut visiting rights to the high security prisons. It seems that a lot of command information is being passed from the prisoners to their wives etcetera, mainly in code, during visiting hours. Now, one of the main reasons the HighSec run the way they do is to block the chain of command within the IRA. If messages are getting through it obviously defeats the purpose. On the other hand, the majority of the visits are perfectly harmless, and so both sides of the prison inmates are creating hell about it. Our problem is to know what to report and, much more important, when to report it. You have to understand, it's only rumour at this moment, so we don't want to fuel the situation and force the police to move when there is still hope for negotiation. But if they bring in actual legislation, then Belfast will erupt in unholy smoke, and we have to be ready to cover that. Again, trying, however vainly, to promote the middle ground.'

John looked taken aback. 'How good is your information?'

The Irishman shrugged. 'The best. My Dad runs the shop and I live at home. I get it all. The other problem I face, you see, is that I can't put my Dad in danger. Both sides confide in him knowing perfectly well that it'll get to me. So if I'm seen to favour one faction we'll both end up with a bullet for breakfast.'

'Makes my plane story seem like a village fête, really,' said John.

'It is a fucking village fête,' replied Sean, finishing his brandy in one gulp. 'And you be grateful for it.' He looked at his watch. 'I have to phone the airport and check on my flight. Your story might just mean an overnight for me.'

John passed him the phone. 'Call from here, there's no rush, have another brandy.'

CHAPTER 4

Monica slept alone in her private room that night, feeling hot, sticky and restless. Shortly after five o'clock she gave up all thoughts of real sleep and allowed the thoughts that had been swirling fitfully in the back of her mind to come to the front. Predominant among these thoughts was the situation concerning Radios Cornwall and Dundee. She had heard nothing since the Frenchs' dinner party and that concerned her. Even if Lady Isobel wouldn't say a thing until it was a *fait accompli*, she would have thought that Peter would have said something. Perhaps it was her fault: all she had to do was ask.

Trevor Jones had asked for a meeting and Monica had agreed to ten o'clock this morning. An event strange enough in itself, as it had always been Monica who called meetings with Trevor. All he ever did was agree with her and do as he was told. He didn't actually initiate anything. It was very peculiar. Her thoughts flicked quickly from Maggie Lomax to Bernie Bonelli and finally on to Frank De Wolf and his veiled invitation. She stretched luxuriantly and pushed the sheet away from her body, allowing the perspiration to dry in pleasant coolness as she remembered his words.

'London's a pit at this time of year. People moan all winter about the cold and then whine when the weather turns hot. Paris, now, that's different. People enjoy themselves in Paris.'

Monica admitted she didn't know Paris that well. She had spent some time there years ago but ... De Wolf laughed and teased her about the gaps in her education. 'You must let me show you Paris. Please let me show you Paris.'

Monica had not said yes instantly, but she had not said no either. Both of them knew her eventual answer, but where was the fun in spoiling the game for the sake of directness?

Ignoring the squalor of her private nest, Monica bathed and dressed, automatically switching on the radio between courses. Bernie Bonelli was going through his predictable farewell-and-good-morning routine, making, thought Monica, every young woman who was listening in the capital feel slightly soiled. As his closing words crawled through the speaker, Monica was suddenly reminded of long tall Samantha. She made her way downstairs, put the kettle on for coffee, and mentally booked a phone call.

At 7 a.m., Nigel B. made the news dead on time, preceded by the now familiar Timeprice advert. After patching up their brief squabble of the previous day, he had at last persuaded Samantha to stay the whole day and through the night, and the memory of falling asleep in her arms was still fresh in his mind. What puzzled him was why she was not there at four this morning. Just a note in the hollow of her pillow. 'Dearest Nigel,' it read, 'I couldn't sleep so I went home. I'll meet you at the studio after the show. Love you. Sam.'

The red phone light flashed on his console. Nigel answered it. 'Studio one.'

He didn't recognize the caller for a second or two; Monica's voice fairly lilted down the phone. 'Good morning, Nigel, I just called to say the Timeprice spot sounds very good now you've got used to it. As a matter of fact the whole show sounds good.'

Nigel could not believe what he was hearing. Monica

being complimentary at seven in the morning? Monica being complimentary at all? He held back the desire to be sarcastic and ask if this was the same Monica Hammond who was MD of CRFM, and instead thanked her and asked if there was anything else he could do for her.

'No,' replied Monica casually, 'I just wanted to say well done. Oh, yes, while I think about it, there is one thing. This new girlfriend of yours – I saw you leaving with her yesterday.'

The hairs on the back of Nigel's neck stood on end as he waited for the scathing reprimand. What the devil had he done wrong now? But Monica continued smoothly, 'Terribly glamorous. Is she a model or something? You must introduce me to her. You know I like to keep tabs on what you lot are up to. Bring her up for a coffee one morning.'

Nigel was relieved. Monica's tone, while still friendly, was back to its old imperious self. This was the Monica that Nigel understood. 'OK, Boss, I'll talk to her today and ask her.' He stressed the word ask. After all, Monica might have the right to organize him but she didn't own Sam. 'Must go, I'm on in fifteen seconds.' He put the phone down without waiting for a reply, leaving Monica with a dialling tone. Monica studied the phone for a moment and gently replaced it on the cradle.

Taking her coffee from the table she wandered over to the kitchen window and surveyed the beautifully manicured garden in Cadogan Square below. A sparrow alighted on the windowsill. 'Well now, we know all about imitation and flattery, but one of these days we shall have to teach Mr Beresford-Clarke some manners, shan't we,' she said to the sparrow, who promptly flew away.

*

Robin Trower arrived at Stanhope Place five minutes before he was due on duty. He hung his tunic carefully in his locker and transferred his name tag to his shirt pocket. He knew Sam Farrow, the night security man, would be anxious to leave, so he gave up the idea of a coffee and headed directly to the front desk. 'Morning, Mr Farrow. Quiet night?'

Sam smiled at the young boy looking so polished with his crisp new shirt and clean face, and wistfully remembered the days when he had his first uniform and no beard.

'Fine, thanks, Robin. Looks like another scorcher today. I'm going home to water my flowers before it gets too hot.' He gathered his few bits together. 'It's the geraniums, see. I'd have 'em in the ground properly, but the wife insists on having 'em in little pots all over the place. They don't half dry out like that. I keep telling her, but she won't have it.'

'Anything I should know?' asked Robin, not wishing to hold up the good deed Sam Farrow was about to do.

Sam looked puzzled. ''Bout geraniums? No, not really, except to bring 'em in over the winter if you want to keep . . .'

Robin couldn't help laughing. The older man's face cleared. 'Oh! See what you mean! No, no, not really. The man from head office is due at about noon to change the matrix on all the studio doors, so be sure to leave me the new numbers before you go home tonight. And those blokes over there,' he said, pointing at two rather scruffy-suited men standing by the notice board, 'they're waiting for Monica Hammond. They don't want anything to drink so don't bother asking.' He paused for a moment as Robin picked up the ring of keys from the desk and clipped them on to his belt. 'If you ask me,' he continued, 'they're from some charity and they're going to ask Her Ladyship for sponsorship, or even worse, money. That'll put her in a good mood for the day.'

Sam picked his coat off the back of the chair, scooped up his food box from the desk and headed towards the front door. 'Have a good day, Robin. Keep it all safe till I get back tonight.'

'Bye, Mr Farrow,' replied Robin as he watched the patron saint of geraniums disappear down the steps. 'I'll do my best.'

Robin had several jobs to do between eight and nine o'clock when most of the staff began to arrive, and he set about them with joyful diligence. He checked all the outside doors, took down all the messages from the night answering-machine, sorted the first delivery of mail, dispensing each letter into its appropriate cubbyhole, and turned all the monitor speakers on to the same volume. He had just returned from the green room with a cup of coffee when Monica strolled through the door. He slipped the coffee cup under the desk and glanced around quickly making sure everything was shipshape. 'Good morning, Miss Hammond,' he said, beaming a broad smile from his spotless face.

Monica walked across the reception area and stopped in front of him. 'Good morning . . .'

'Trower,' said Robin, feeling a little hurt that he was not known.

Monica sighed and smiled at the same time. 'Yes, I *know* it's Trower, you haven't told me your first name.'

Robin glowed. 'Robin, as in Hood.'

'Yes, of course, Robin. I did see it in your file but I'd got it into my head it was Robert. Do forgive me.' She returned his smile for no more than a second by which time Robin had not only forgiven her but would have walked barefoot over burning coals for her. It was a technique Monica had used many times in the past with great success. Her face stiffened into a businesslike expression. 'Do you have my post?'

'Right here,' answered Robin handing her about a dozen letters. 'By the way, those two gentlemen are waiting for you.'

Monica turned in the direction Robin indicated. The two men came towards her. One of them was holding a brown envelope. Monica realized there was no escape. She was sure she didn't have any appointments until ten o'clock, but as the men got closer she began to invent one. 'I'm terribly sorry,' she said, 'I have an urgent meeting in five minutes, I'm afraid I can't possibly see you now. If you leave your name with Mr Trower, I'll . . .'

The man with the envelope interrupted her brusquely. 'Miss Monica Hammond?'

Monica was not used to being interrupted. Her voice came like ice through a cheese-grater. 'Whatever it is, leave it with . . .'

'Are you Miss Monica Hammond?' the man repeated patiently.

Monica stared at him angrily. 'You know perfectly well who I am or you wouldn't ask. What do you want?'

The man took a deep breath and started an obviously well-practised spiel. 'Monica Hammond, I serve this writ on you as managing director of this radio station at these the registered offices of City Radio Ltd.' He pushed the brown envelope into Monica's hand, and then both men turned abruptly and made towards the door.

'Now just one minute,' hissed Monica. 'What the hell is this all about?'

The man reached the door before turning back to face the furious Monica. 'Don't ask me, lady, I've no idea. I just deliver them.' So saying, both he and his silent mate were out the door and away.

Robin stood open-mouthed, watching the drama unfold and not quite believing what he saw. Monica turned slowly to face him. Never had he seen a face so full of cold fury. The hand that held the envelope was white-knuckled and trembling with rage, and try as she might, she could not keep the shake out of her voice. 'I will kill her,' she said, more to herself than to Robin. 'I will hang, draw and quarter her. I will –' She became aware of Robin watching her in startled fascination. 'I bloody well *know* what this is! Trower! Wake up that stupid bitch Lomax and tell her to be in my office in *one hour*. Is that clear? ONE HOUR!'

Robin stood frozen to the spot. Monica realized that the last thing she needed was a security guard's gossip running like wildfire round the building so, summoning all the control she could muster, she softened her face. A wry smile started to form in the corner of her mouth as she observed the petrified youth. 'For god's sake, Robin, close your mouth, you're not at the dentist.'

Robin did as he was told and tried to return her smile. Monica had a quick look to see how many other people had witnessed the proceedings. To her relief she saw no one. She leaned over the desk confidentially. 'Look, Robin, I'm sorry, I shouldn't have lost my temper. This is all most unfortunate. It's terribly important that no one should hear about this until I say so . . . you do understand, don't you?'

The tacit threat in the soft voice went unnoticed. Robin was proud to be confided in. He stood to attention.

'Yes, Miss Hammond, of course. Absolutely no one.'

Monica smiled. 'Good lad,' she said. 'Now off you go and phone Maggie for me.' She turned and walked towards the green room. As Robin watched her, she seemed almost happy.

Freddie French opened one eye very carefully, and finding that it didn't hurt too much, decided to open the other one. He turned his head slowly and stared at the bedside clock until it came into focus. Even when it did so – more or less – Freddie was confused. If he had gone to bed around eight-thirty, why was it only eight-twenty now? Was time going backwards? Was it his fault? His eyes began to join forces with his brain, and his ears reluctantly joined them. There was light seeping in through the curtains, and there were birds singing outside. It was morning. Well, that's a relief, thought Freddie. One more day scuppered into oblivion. All he had to do was cope with this one.

He shambled out of bed and tried to stand upright, taking a deep breath in order to bump-start his lungs. He held the breath for about ten seconds before collapsing in a foul bronchial chorus of coughing and wheezing. Clenching all the muscles that would obey him, he staggered to the basin and spluttered out a huge wodge of phlegm. He stayed slumped there until he was sure there would be no repeat performances, and then slowly made his way to the window. He started to part the curtains when a shaft of morning sunshine flooded into the room. He jerked them shut again with surprising speed. The bedroom door opened unceremoniously, and Freddie saw his mother standing in the doorway, her nose wrinkled as if the whole room constituted an offence against humanity – which it did.

'Freddie . . . you're up. Good. Get downstairs as soon as you're decent.'

Before Freddie could answer she was gone, slamming the door behind her. Cow, thought the hungover aristocrat. Not good morning, how are you? It's a lovely day. Just come in, shout orders and leave. One of these days, I swear, I'll booby-trap that door with an axe and chop your udders off. He hated being at Eaton Square. He wouldn't have to be there at all if his bitch of a wife hadn't slung him out and changed the locks. On his house, for god's sake! His! They were both cows. All women were cows.

Lady Isobel entered the breakfast room just as Peter was about to leave. 'Morning, Mother. Simmons is just bringing fresh coffee. I destroyed the last lot.'

Lady Isobel took his arm and ushered him back into the room. 'Don't go just yet, Peter, I want a word with you.' She went to the sideboard and lifted the lids on the dishes, inspecting the contents. 'When did you last have kidneys for breakfast?'

Peter raised his eyebrows. 'When I was about nine, I think. Is that what you wanted a word about?'

'They appear every morning and no one ever eats them. Simmons is obviously overindulging his cat. Sit down.'

Peter snaffled a sausage from one of the dishes and sat down. Lady Isobel helped herself to scrambled eggs and toast and took her place at the head of the table. 'Use a fork, Peter, not fingers.'

Peter crammed the whole sausage into his mouth and licked the guilty digits as Simmons entered bearing fresh supplies of coffee. 'Gone now,' he mumbled.

'Good morning, madam,' purred Simmons as he set the coffee pot beside Lady Isobel. 'The radio tells me it will be another fine one.'

'Good morning, Simmons,' replied Lady Isobel. 'We shan't have kidneys at breakfast again, thank you. Tinned food is quite good enough for the cat. We're not made of money.'

Simmons's eyelids flickered imperceptibly, but his voice remained firm. 'Very good, madam.' He left the room, pretending not to notice Sir Peter choking on his sausage.

Lady Isobel waited until the door had been closed before she continued. 'Now then, Peter. Several things. First of all, about your brother. The time has come to do something.'

Peter poured himself more coffee and sighed. It was riddle time. 'Which particular bit of Freddie are we going to do something about? His wife? The salvage concession in Hong Kong? His toenails?'

'His drinking. It's far beyond the pale.'

'Oh, he's all right. It's only this divorce business that's getting to him. Got the constitution of an ox, has Fred.'

Lady Isobel munched on her toast and eyed her son coldly. 'That's beside the point,' she said. 'As far as I'm concerned he can kill himself in any way he chooses. As long as he does it privately, which is very much the point. We couldn't have taken him along last night, which is ridiculous. His concerns in South Africa would have been highly relevant to the conversation. I know you put the issues very clearly, but it would have been preferable to have one of the principals present. He's a laughing-stock among his friends, and it won't be long before he's a laughing-stock in the press.'

Peter gazed out of the window and asked the hopeless question. 'Have you tried talking to him?'

Lady Isobel looked blank and bewildered. 'Me? Whatever for?' she said.

Because you owe the poor bastard, thought Peter. Because if you'd given him one word of concern over the last thirty years, he wouldn't be in this rotten mess. Because if you hadn't bounced him from nanny to governess to headmaster he might know who the hell you are. Because if you'd let him marry that nice little secretary instead of forcing him into bed with a well-bred tart he'd be sitting in the garden playing with his kids right now; instead of which he's drowning his humiliation at watching his wife spend his money on any pimp that comes along. Because if you'd stop pretending that the sun shone out of Father's arse and see him for the feeble hypocritical crook he was, you might appreciate how well Freddie's done in covering up the mess. Because – 'Just a thought,' said Peter. 'Leave it with me. I'll sort him.' The coffee had gone sour in his mouth. He got up to leave, but his mother stopped him.

'I haven't finished,' said Lady Isobel. 'Have you heard from Harry yet?'

'Concerning what?'

'Cornwall and Dundee,' she snapped. 'The deadline for bids is noon. Harry was playing golf with John Longshore yesterday. He said he'd try and let me know the Aylford figures.'

Peter sighed deeply as he sat down again beside his mother. Us, Mother, he thought. Harry said he'd try and let *us* know. 'I'll call him as soon as I get to the office and then call you. Where will you be?'

Freddie came into the room, washed, nearly shaven and still in his dressing gown. Peter poured him a cup of coffee and pushed it across the table to him with a little smile.

Lady Isobel ignored him and carried on. 'I shall be here till lunchtime. I have a meeting at LWT at two. What did we decide? Two twenty-five for the remaining forty per cent?'

Freddie rubbed a hand across his face as if to remodel it. 'Two twenty-seven on forty per cent,' he said, 'unless Portland Industries accepts my bid on their electronics division, which I shall know in about' – he consulted his watch – 'forty minutes. That being so, it only leaves thirty-two per cent of Cornwall and Dundee on the open market so I think we could go to two seventy-five on the remainder – two ninety at a pinch.' He sipped noisily from his cup and grimaced as the hot liquid flowed over his furry tongue.

Peter grinned at him. 'God's breath, Fred. I didn't think you'd pull that one off. Very nice indeed.'

'Nothing's certain till it is,' said Freddie, 'but I didn't leave them much option.'

Lady Isobel finished her scrambled eggs and dabbed fastidiously at her mouth with her napkin. 'Next time,' she said icily, 'I would prefer it if you didn't leave it quite so much to the last minute. I would have liked to examine the details.'

Peter patted his mother's hand and assumed his P. G. Wodehouse voice. 'I say, steady on, old girl. Us boys have got it all in hand, eh, Fred?'

Despite himself, Freddie could not help smiling. His mother withdrew her hand from Peter's as if from a toad. 'Stop that!' she cried. 'Behave yourself and tell me about Hammond.'

'Monica? Oh, five foot six, blonde hair, nice eyes . . .' Peter checked himself as Lady Isobel slapped the top of the dining table with the palm of her hand.

'How much does she know?'

'Only what we told her at dinner.'

'Good. Make sure it stays that way. She's too clever for her own good, that one. Or at least, she thinks she is. Can't think why Harry Connaught speaks so highly of her. Can't bear the woman.' And having thus damned Monica Hammond to the outer wastes of social unacceptability, Lady Isobel French swept out of the room.

★

Monica's day was continuing the way it started. Suzie had phoned in at nine o'clock to excuse herself for the day on account of serious stomach cramps, an excuse Monica had come to expect every month from her somewhat fragile personal assistant. Trevor Jones had told her, in the strictest of confidence, that the word on the street was that Flash Jack was going to sue and that she should prepare herself. Oh thank you very bloody much for telling me, thought Monica. I know loyalty is terrific, but fast loyalty is even better. There was still no sign of Maggie Lomax.

She was leaning back in her chair contemplating phoning Frank De Wolf to accept his Paris offer, when her private phone rang. Thinking it was De Wolf himself, she let it ring for the customary three times before picking it up. 'Monica Hammond.'

'Hello, old thing, Harry Connaught,' came the jovial voice.

Monica tried not to let her disappointment become evident. 'Good morning, Harry. What a nice surprise.' The reasons for the call raced through Monica's mind. He couldn't know about the writ, it was too early. Cornwall and Dundee, perhaps. Maybe it was just social. 'To what do I owe this honour?'

Harry continued cheerfully. 'Listen, dear girl, I know this is terribly short notice but HM is chucking one of her garden bashes tomorrow afternoon. I've got to go and wave the IBA colours, Jessica refuses point-blank to come with me, and frankly, I'm not safe to be let out on my own. Do you think you could escape the massive media pressure for a few hours and hold my hand?'

Monica knew within a split second that there really was a fairy godmother. Amid all this legal embarrassment, none of which she remotely considered to be her own fault, came the invitation she had dreamed of ever since she had started in this business as Harry's junior PA twelve years ago. 'Why won't Jessica go with you?' she laughed.

'Can't bear cold tea and fairy cakes,' growled Harry, 'at least, that's what she says. Personally I think it's because she had a nasty experience with one of the gardeners last year. Caught her taking a cutting of a royal begonia or something. Threatened to send her to the Tower. Do come. It's a miserable boring thing to do on your own.'

'I'd love to go, Harry, thank you,' she said casually, wondering if the day would ever come when she could describe a Palace garden party as a miserable boring thing. She doubted it.

'Fine, wonderful,' said Harry. 'Saved my life. Must dash, see you tomorrow.'

'OK, Harry. Bye.' She held on to the phone until Harry Connaught hung up, her heart beating well over the legal limit. Screw the lawsuit, she thought, screw Maggie Lomax. She, Monica Hammond, the newsagent's daughter from Rickmansworth, was going to Buckingham Palace. She'd wear the cream Dior suit – no she wouldn't, it needed cleaning. The white Monsoon then, with that pink blouse that – oh god, nothing on earth would match and no one made shoes that colour anymore and, oh shit, why didn't she think of that at the time? The grey silk dress, that was it. If it clouded over there was a jacket that went with it, and those pearl-grey sandals looked great and, oh Christ, she didn't have a hat.

The internal phone broke the spell and brought her crashing back to reality. She snatched it off the cradle. 'Yes!' she yelled, thinking, I don't have a hat!

'Miss Hammond,' came Robin Trower's voice, low and conspiratorial. 'Security here. Maggie Lomax has just come in. I've sent her right up.'

'Thank you, Robin.' She was just about to put the phone down, when something in the boy's tone stopped her.

'Miss Hammond . . .' His voice was hesitant. 'Could I possibly see you sometime today? I think – I mean – I might be able to help regarding what happened – you know, this morning. Our little problem.'

Our little problem? thought Monica. *Our* problem? Although she liked the way he had been discreet, be it ever so clumsily, she wondered what a baby security guard could do to help her. Only one way to find out. 'I can give you five minutes at three o'clock.' She put the phone down as her office door opened.

Maggie Lomax stalked defiantly into the room, her enormous handbag tucked under her left arm, and a plastic cup of coffee grasped firmly in her right hand. Although nothing had been said and no explanations given, Maggie had a pretty fair idea of what was going on. Without invitation, she marched over to Monica's desk and sat down in front of it, clearing a space on which to stand her cup. 'OK, what's so important that you have to drag me out of bed at this ungodly hour? Or do I really need to ask?'

Monica remained serene, even though she didn't have a hat. 'Do sit down, Maggie. I'm afraid I have to tell you the worst has happened.'

Maggie sipped her drink and looked at her boss. 'You mean Eddy McLeod has been voted on to the board?'

Monica's expression remained constant. 'I mean we've been served with a high court writ over this Flash Jack affair.'

Maggie relaxed into the full comfort of Monica's Roche Bobois chair. 'Do you want my resignation?' she asked. 'It'll take me ten minutes to write. If I use long words.'

'No I don't,' replied Monica, pausing for just a second to reflect on the tempting possibility of tipping the hot coffee over Maggie's arrogant head, and getting rid of her once and for all. 'I just want to make sure that what you said the other day was true. Every word. If you're making any of this up, or even exaggerating by the tiniest degree, I'll make sure you never work again, either here or any other radio station in the world, and believe me, Maggie, I can do just that.'

She looked at Maggie's face, stricken and impressed, and thought that this time she had made her mark – until Maggie spoke.

'Gosh, Monica, you're so masterful.'

Monica ground her teeth in silent fury as Maggie continued. 'For christ's sake, what d'you think I am? I've been in this business for twenty years. People were trying to sue me when you were pickling peanuts in Domestic Science. I may be daft but I'm sure as hell not stupid. Of course I was telling the truth!'

Monica leaned forward and studied the mean little print on the writ. 'Where did you get your information?'

'I told you before. On the street, in the clubs, from the punters, from the musos. From your ruddy audience!'

'Will it stand up in court?'

Maggie shrugged. 'If they can, it will,' she replied. 'Depends whether you have the guts to let it go to court. One thing is for sure, you can threaten till the cows come home, but I'm not going to apologize.'

'I don't threaten, Maggie,' said Monica calmly, 'I promise. So don't push me. I need some time to work this out, so from now on there will be no mention of Flash Jack, cocaine, or anything remotely connected with it . . . is that understood?'

Maggie's first reaction was to rebel against any hint of censorship, but as she studied Monica's face she wondered if she saw a certain moral obligation to stand by her people no matter what. She was sure this was just an act but at this stage she was willing to give Monica the benefit of the doubt. 'Are you going to fight it?' she asked, looking Monica straight in the eye.

'I'm going to look into the possibility of fighting it, Maggie, but you have to promise me that you will stop this assault on Flash Jack as of now. I will not tolerate any more attacks on that man until this thing is settled. For the second time, do I have your word?'

Maggie thought out her options. She didn't believe for a moment that Monica would support her if it meant that anything could, in any way, rebound and spoil her untarnished record. But as the writ had already been served, her options were severely limited. She could fire her, but she had said she wasn't going to. What the hell, Maggie knew she was right and now would be as good a time as ever to find out what Ms Hammond was really all about. 'OK. Brownie's honour.'

Monica relaxed backwards into her chair. 'Fine. Now go and make yourself scarce for the rest of the day, I don't want you talking to the press. They should have the story by noon and I want to handle anything that comes in today. If they do catch up with you tonight you're to tell them nothing.'

Once again Maggie felt herself bridle at the prospect of her freedom of speech being curtailed. Monica sensed her irritation and revelled in it. 'I know this goes against your usual method of operation, Maggie, but if we have any chance of winning this, it has to be done my way. Don't even play his records. As far as you're concerned, Flash Jack does not exist. If anyone corners you on it, you simply tell them it is now *sub judice* and you can't comment. If they persist, give them one of your famous expletives and walk away.'

Monica looked across the desk to study Maggie's reaction. She was sitting very still, her eyes fixed firmly on Monica's face.

'It's not going to be easy for me,' Maggie replied. 'I don't like running away from things.'

Monica leaned forward and placed both her elbows very deliberately on the edge of her desk, enjoying herself. 'My dear Maggie, this is not going to be easy for any of us. All I'm asking of you is that you keep your head down. I don't think that is too much to ask – given that it was you that caused the mess in the first place. However, if you feel it is beyond your capability, say so now and I will accept your resignation, wash my hands of the whole affair and you can face this alone.' She paused long enough for the statement to take effect. 'And you do know, don't you, that it states in your contract that you will not bring this station into disrepute, so I'm perfectly within my rights to disclaim the whole bloody thing.'

Maggie got up from her chair and made for the door. As she opened it, she turned and spoke quietly to Monica. 'There's a little shop off the Tottenham Court Road that sells very good quality sandpaper, you know. You should go there.'

Monica looked puzzled, but Maggie explained, 'Sit on fences all your life and you'll die with splinters up your arse.'

She shut the door gently behind her, and Monica noticed with hideous, cold hatred, that Maggie had left her empty coffee cup on top of the writ, thereby leaving a little circular stain as a memento of her visit.

*

In the boardroom of Aylford International, Wallace Pike tipped forward in his chair so fast that several members of the board jerked backwards involuntarily, thinking he was about to go for their throats. He would have liked to have done, but instead merely stared at them. Their faces were paralysed like those in the losing dressing-room at Wembley after a cup final. Nobody spoke. Bruce Hamilton played with the corners of his report. Lord Longshore sat back in his chair and studied a fly crossing the neon strip light. He was the only man there not in a state of acute shock and embarrassment.

Pike went for him. 'What the hell do you mean there's only forty per cent left? Those stations are up for grabs. I talked to both chairmen last week. They assured me their boards would sell all the shares, even told me what price they'd accept. And here you are drivelling about forty per cent? What damn good is that to anyone?'

Longshore pressed his spread fingers together as if in prayer and looked at the Australian over the rim of his half-moon glasses. 'Actually, old chap, I think you'll find that as of ten minutes ago, we're only talking about thirty-two per cent.' He smiled benignly at the chairman. 'Sorry.' There was a nasty silence round the table, so Longshore continued. 'Look,' he said, sounding con-solatory while secretly wishing the entire antipodean population of the world would drown in vats of their own despicable lager, 'there's no use getting upset. What you were told was right – as far as it went. The boards are willing to sell, but they only hold forty per cent of the shares. Thirty-two, I beg your pardon. The rest are simply not for sale. Shareholders don't want to know.'

Pike eyed Longshore with suspicion and then extended his glance to the other expressionless men seated around the table. 'Why the blazes didn't we know about this before? What the hell do I pay you prats for, apart from sitting on your fannies and getting fat?' he shouted, sliding his steely-grey eyes from one side of the table to the other and back again. 'What other shareholders? Who are they? What approaches have been made? Of course they'll fucking sell if the price is right!'

Longshore continued after a moment's hesitation, just enough for Pike to be fully aware that the rest of the board was picking its collective fingernails. 'I have looked into it, and you're not necessarily right this time, I'm afraid. I had an idea that something was going on, but as I say, up to ten minutes ago I wasn't sure what. But I think I have gathered the gist of things now.'

'And just what have you gathered?' sneered Pike. 'Except bloody moss, that is.'

Longshore was starting to get very upset indeed. He had a quick look around the table and saw that everyone, including Hamilton, was doing ostrich impressions and realized that if any sense were to come out of this he would have to make the running. The idea appealed to his colonial sense of values; seeing that he didn't consider that Pike had enough clout to run a car wash, let alone a media conglomerate, the thought of riding to the rescue on the white charger of privileged information and flapping the Union Jack all over this pompous Australian's face was rather appealing.

'It was old Harry Connaught put me on to it, actually,' said Longshore in slow deliberate tones, savouring Pike's impatience. 'Played golf with him yesterday. Didn't know what he'd said, of course, but it started me thinking. Mentioned in passing that Porton Industries were hiving off their electronics division. Well, I thought it was strange I hadn't heard about it – as you know, Porton's financial man is on the board of

Cornwall. So I made a couple of calls.' Here he stopped, took out his favourite briar pipe and fiddled with it quietly, hearing the gratifying sounds of gnashing teeth as he did so. 'Porton Electronics sold out to Webb Communications. Papers changed hands at ten this morning.'

Pike was controlling himself with great difficulty. 'What the bloody hell has that got to do with us? Who the devil is Webb Communications?' he said through clenched teeth.

John Longshore lit his pipe and puffed calmly, working out how far he could go before Pike actually came round the table and hit him. 'Webb?' he said. 'Oh, just a small outfit. Deals mainly in Europe. Operating company. It's the parent company that's interesting.'

All eyes were now on Longshore. He smiled at Pike like a genial grandfather and sucked on his pipe. 'French Enterprises.'

The silence that filled the room was suffocating. Wallace Pike rose to his feet and leaned on the table. His face went from red to white to grey and back to red again and his words came in a strangled whisper. 'French Enterprises? As in Isobel, Peter and Fred? As in CRFM?'

Longshore beamed approvingly at him. 'That's the one. So having found that out, I had your girl run a check on all the other shareholders.' Longshore opened his folder and produced a computer print-out from it. 'I haven't had a chance to do more than glance through it, but it's pretty much as I thought.' He gave the paper to the man on his left, and watched it pass down the table to Pike, each man handling it as though it would bite him.

'It's a common enough practice,' he went on, 'I'm surprised you weren't on the look-out for it. Small investors buy shares just below the amount where they have to declare an interest, then sell to the same major investor who does declare his interest, by which time it's too late to do anything. All the major investor has to do is bid openly for the outstanding shares – which he gets at a very good price because there's not a lot left, and there you have it. Total control.' He paused for a second. 'Can't think why Aylford didn't do the same thing,' he added slyly, but Pike was too busy scanning the print-out to rise to the bait.

'Waterside Studios, 4.9 per cent, City Links, 4.9 per cent, Porton Industries, 8 per cent, Amalgamated Engineering, 4.9 per cent.'

'All operating companies for French Enterprises,' said Longshore.

'Shit!' said Pike, throwing the print-out on the table. 'Isn't there a law against that sort of thing, for Christ's sake?'

''Fraid not,' replied Longshore, 'all perfectly legal. Nasty, but legal. The only option we have left is to outbid French on the remaining thirty-two per cent. At least that will give us a foothold – a minority one, but quite respectable all the same.'

Pike sat down and considered his options. The various members of the board relaxed a little and rubbed their necks. Pike picked up his pen and rolled it round in his hands like a set of Arabic worry beads. He surveyed the assembly, slowly moving from one board member to the next until his eyes met Longshore's. A small smirk started to form on his lean face. 'The great British compromise, eh? Oh no, my dear Lordship, that's not my style. Why pay for something I can get for nothing? They have something we want – but then again, we have something they want.' Pike grinned unpleasantly at Longshore. 'Information may be harvested by effete aristos on the high-class golf courses of this fucking country – too late for use, I may add, but deals are done by businessmen.' He jabbed the table with his forefinger. 'Right here.'

At eleven fifty-five, Harry Connaught called Peter French and told him there were no other significant bids for the remaining shares in Cornwall and Dundee. At eleven fifty-six, Peter called his mother and passed the information on, and at eleven fifty-seven, he gave Freddie the go-ahead to bid at whatever price he liked. At eleven fifty-eight, Freddie bought the outstanding shares for two pounds and twenty pence each. At eleven fifty-nine, Lady Isobel French opened a bottle of champagne all by herself, and at twelve noon, Monica Hammond became chief executive of three radio stations – and nobody even bothered to tell her.

CHAPTER 5

Badedas was a simple joy in the life of Nigel Beresford-Clarke. With his first breath of success, which paid a handsome £15, he bought a giant-size plastic bottle of the thick green liquid and soaked in his tub for two hours, slowly adding hot water and planning his take-over of world media.

Some years down the line not much had changed.

Maida Vale had replaced Acton and his bath would now fit two, but it was still the same N. B.-C. Sometimes it had been a rough ride, but Nigel found out early how to smooth the bumps. He had two things in his favour. A perceptive mind and a voice like a mink-lined raincoat. His perception of how media constantly changes to fit the needs and tastes of its audience led to his first job as a freelance sports reporter in Kent, the year before Maidstone won promotion to the football league. Within three months he presented weekend and holiday relief shows. His second anniversary celebrations included his own weekday afternoon programme; five years later, here he was, a weekday breakfast on London's number one, a 911 in the garage and on a good week another two thousand spending money for 'opening' this and 'voicing' that.

Nigel's bathroom, described recently in the *London Evening Standard* as 'Tastefully Male', was definitely his favourite room. A double tub, shower, sauna, jacuzzi, two basins and a large eighteenth-century Spanish cadenza seemed nonchalantly scattered over the carpeted and tiled 20-by-25-foot room. He spent far too much money on a full-size reproduction of Roy

Lichtenstein's *Whaam* which occupied most of the only free wall opposite the sauna and shower.

The scent of Badedas filled him with security.

He finished his soak and his glass of Moët and smiled to himself as he stepped from the bath and into his Missoni bath robe. Ten-thirty in the morning and the rest of the day was his. No Samantha, no voice-overs, no hassle from Monica and the temperature outside a warm seventy-one degrees. He wandered over to the cadenza and felt around the back of the centre drawer. He withdrew his hand clutching a small plastic bag and a package of king-size cigarette papers. Nigel wasn't a regular smoker – he kept a small supply of grass handy, mainly for his female guests – but today he needed to mellow out without getting drunk, today he needed dark glasses to make him anonymous. The only problem was choosing a hat to complete his disguise.

Monica never wore hats. She hated them. Wide-brim hats affected peripheral vision and she kept wanting to brush them away, pill-box hats made her feel like a performing monkey, and cloche hats reminded her of 1920s racing drivers and their phoney, newsreel smiles. But here she was going, at last, to meet the Queen and that occasion required a hat.

She decided that Harrods would be the only plausible place to shop for this evil garment; after the events of this loathsome morning, a lunchtime spending spree would go at least part of the way to redressing the balance.

The station was uncommonly quiet as Monica made her way down the corridor towards the studio complex and green room. Only Eddy McLeod was to be seen hovering near the newsroom chatting up a junior secretary. As Monica approached the couple she could see the girl was very uncomfortable with the situation and was trying her best to stave off the aggressive Scotsman without much success. Eddy was using the 'arm around the shoulder' technique, making any escape virtually impossible. Monica loathed seeing sexual harassment in any form, and coming from this objectionable half-pint, it was unforgivable. 'McLeod,' she snapped in a tone that would make a drill sergeant jealous.

Eddy instantly removed his arm from the girl's shoulder, spun on his heels and stood to attention in front of Monica. The relieved secretary took her opportunity, smiled thankfully at Monica and scurried off down the corridor to the safety of the ladies' loo. Monica fixed her gaze on the very upright general manager until she heard the loo door shut.

'Don't,' she said, through clenched teeth.

McLeod tried to make light of the whole matter. He relaxed his body and grinned his answer 'I was only showing some fatherly concern. Charlotte's only been here a few weeks and she feels a bit lost.'

'Charlotte,' said Monica coldly, 'has been here for three months. She is a highly competent young lady who has a very bright future with this company and doesn't need any help, fatherly or otherwise, from the likes of you. Do I make myself clear?'

Eddie's instinct for self-preservation took over. 'Yes, Monica,' he whimpered. 'Very clear.'

'Good.' She turned and continued towards the studio, leaving the defeated manager with his head bowed and his hands clasped together in mock prayer hoping that one day that pious bitch would come unstuck and that he would be there to see it.

She passed the studio, smiled at Trevor Jones who replied with his usual thumbs-up gesture, and as she went through the door into reception she wished that all her staff were as loyal and dependable as her pro-gramme controller.

Lizzie was changing places with Robin Trower as Monica walked across the foyer. It was her lunch hour, and Anthony had promised something extra-special in the form of a moving-in present. Her mind pondered the possibilities. A real slap-up lunch at a quiet, roman-tic restaurant would be her first choice, or maybe he would take her for a ride on one of those funny rowing boats on the Serpentine. Whatever it was she would enjoy it because Lizzie loved surprises, and since their showdown picnic in the park Anthony had been so will-ing to please that she sometimes wondered if this was the same person. Gone were her moods and tantrums. No more sneaking around the station pretending they were not sleeping together; best of all she was now the proud owner of a £2,000 diamond ring, which Lizzie wore with some considerable pride and which, no matter how things turned out in the end, she had no intention of ever giving back.

Monica reached the front door and stopped, turned around, and beckoned to the receptionist. 'Lizzie,' she said, before continuing in a tone that was more a com-mand than an inquiry, 'are you busy for lunch?'

Lizzie instantly forgot about the lunch, the rowboat and Anthony's surprise. 'No, Miss Hammond,' she said. 'Is there anything I can help you with?'

'If you would be so kind, yes, there is. I have a little shopping to do and I would value a second opinion.'

Lizzie leaned in close to Robin Trower. She took his hand in order to get his undivided attention and spoke to him in a very low whisper. 'When Anthony shows up tell him I had to go out with Monica. I'll see him after lunch with all the details. Thanks. You're a sweetie.'

Without waiting for a reply she turned to face her managing director and pushed her thirty-four-inch bust out to is full frontal position. She always did this when she wanted to be noticed.

Lizzie was as happy as a just-fed praying mantis as the two women walked down Stanhope Place towards the Bayswater Road. During the last nine months she had done everything in her power to get noticed by Monica, all to no avail. Then here, out of the blue, comes this invitation to shop, the one thing that Lizzie knew about. Even more than surprises Lizzie loved shopping. The only thing that kept Lizzie from being a 24-hour-a-day, 7-day-a-week shopper was the finance it required; the one thing she had going for her was that she had *very* good taste. Even on her limited budget she always looked a thousand pounds more than she was worth, and here was the opportunity to put her skills to work for the one person at CRFM she wanted to impress.

Monica hailed a cab and Lizzie opened the door. Monica sat back into the seat and straightened her dress. The cabby waited for a few seconds before inquiring about the destination. Monica looked surprised, as if he should instinctively know. 'Harrods,' she said, 'and close the partition.'

The cabby thought: how rude.

Lizzie thought: how wonderful.

It was a very quiet lunch hour at CRFM. By 12.45 Robin had only answered three phone calls and nobody had come to call for anybody; in fact, it seemed that the whole world had gone out to some warm pasture to spend a couple of hours soaking up the welcome warmth of what was turning out to be the hottest day of the year so far, and left poor Robin to be the lonely guardsman of the entire castle. The one thing that consoled him was the thought of his three o'clock meeting with Monica. He felt that what he had to offer was going to be of invaluable use to the radio station and that made him feel very important. The information he was going to give Monica was a name.

Joe Mace.

Joe was a private detective who had called on Robin two weeks previously at his home in Deptford while 'pursuing a line of inquiry regarding a missing teenager believed to be living with a known drug addict somewhere on this council estate'. Robin had invited him inside and for the next two hours and over endless cups of coffee Joe Mace had unfolded his entire casebook to the young man, who took every word as gospel and was, on the whole, very impressed. Joe looked at himself as a sort of Mike Hammer figure. In fact he was more like Lonely from the *Callan* series. He lived with his overweight wife and equally overweight teenage daughter in a large tumbledown Victorian house in Muswell Hill, drove a ten-year-old Citroën XL and, through no fault of his own, had the most horrendous sinus problem. His wife had given up supplying him with handkerchiefs the day after they were married, so everywhere Joe went he had a box of Kleenex mansize as a constant companion.

Despite his problem and his somewhat shabby appearance Robin was convinced that if anyone could help Maggie Lomax and get the goods on Flash Jack, it was Mr Mace, and he felt sure that Monica would agree with him.

At this moment Monica had other problems to solve. She surveyed the roomful of hats in Harrods millinery department with growing trepidation. How could she possibly decide when all her instincts told her to run away and forget the whole idea? Lizzie, meanwhile, was very busy picking up various creations, looking at them from different angles, even trying a few on and admiring herself in the counter-top mirrors. Monica watched her closely and was impressed by her air of self-confidence. Suddenly Lizzie found what she was looking for. A red, medium-brim, flat-top hat which instantly reminded Monica of a Spanish bullfighter. 'I can't wear that,' she said. 'My hair is far too long and besides, I've nothing to go with it.'

Lizzie walked towards her, hat in hand, and smiled at Monica in a way best described as controlled innocence. 'This is Harrods,' she whispered. 'You can get everything you need here, and this will look beautiful on you. Let me show you.' She handed Monica the hat and in one sweeping movement gathered Monica's shoulder-length hair and scooped it up to the top of her head. 'You should wear your hair up with this, it will be stunning.' Monica placed the hat slowly over Lizzie's hands. When the hat was in place Lizzie removed her hands without letting one strand of hair escape. She stepped back to admire the effect. 'See for yourself,' she said. 'It's perfect.'

Monica looked nervously into the counter mirror beside her. Lizzie was right. It was perfect, and the thought of having to buy a complete new outfit to complement this new acquisition appealed to Monica enormously.

Ninety minutes later Monica was one outfit richer and £850 poorer. Lizzie Stephenson was very pleased indeed.

Brian Callaghan, on the other hand, was not pleased at all. Timing was the all-important thing to Dirty Harry.

Timing in sales, timing in lovemaking, timing in squash: all of his successes were attributed to good, if not impeccable, timing. He had expertly arranged a lunch at the flat of one of his most valued clients, knowing full well that the client would be in the North of England leaving his wife to do the entertaining. There had been several phone calls that morning trying to postpone the lunch, all of which Brian had dodged with the help of that expert timing. He arrived at Number 5, Northumberland Avenue, just after noon, clutching a dozen roses and a bottle of Bollinger. When Mrs Client answered the door it was apparent that she was well ahead of the sales director's game and, what's more, was about to take over the leading role.

They had both gone through the customary display of sensuous politeness as they hurried the smoked salmon and emptied the bottle of champagne. The main course, thought Brian, will be in the bedroom. And so it was.

By half past twelve, Brian Callaghan was lying naked on a king-size bed waiting with great anticipation for his 'best client's wife' to 'finish in the bathroom'.

But alas, the best-laid plans, let alone best-laid clients' wives, can sometimes let you down through some silly little mistake, and Brian was about to make his. In his rush to get all his clothes off as quickly as possible he had forgotten to turn off his telephone pager; just as Mrs Horny came into the room wearing a silk basque and a smile, the damn thing went off.

Brian jumped from the bed to silence the offending machine, tripped over his black Gucci loafers and fell flat on his face. Mrs Client went to help, stubbed her foot on the bed-corner and landed on top of Brian, thus winding him and exposing the message on the accursed machine for both to see. It read 'Call me – I miss you – Charlene'.

Brian became embarrassed, Mrs Horny became Mrs Uninterested and Dirty Harry cursed the day Alexander Graham Bell was born.

The afternoon passed without a hitch for Monica. She felt wonderfully satisfied with her shopping spree and more than a tinge of warmth for Lizzie Stephenson. She had never regarded her as anything more than a pretty receptionist until today, but the way she had handled herself at Harrods showed Monica that there just might be more to this lady than met the eye. At three o'clock she had had her meeting with Robin Trower and promised to see Joe Mace later in the week. Robin left her office feeling he was doing the station a great service and Monica chalked up fifty Brownie points for staff relations. The four o'clock sales meeting produced no awkward moments, mainly due to Brian Callaghan's uncharacteristically quiet mood. Monica knew something nasty had happened to him. She didn't know what, but whatever it was, it pleased her to see at least half his sails flying at half-mast.

At the Aylford offices things were far from quiet. The Frenchs' moves to acquire Cornwall and Dundee had been deciphered in detail, and to say the board were feeling somewhat embarrassed could rank as one of the great understatements of the decade. Several members were employing various excuses in order to extricate themselves from this farce and possibly save their jobs.

The only person not affected by the neurosis at Millbank Towers was Wallace Pike. He was enjoying an effortless ride through London's hectic afternoon traffic in the passenger seat of Lord Longshore's 1968 Bentley Continental. He loved riding in hand-built British cars.

'So what we're dealing with, in this little corner of the British media, are the Frenchs – correct?'

Longshore attended to the business of missing a speeding London cab. 'Only thing about driving oneself, Wallace, it requires concentration.' He stopped at the traffic lights leading to the Embankment. 'If you can deal with the Frenchs you can bypass most of the problems you now face in one hop. The problem is – dealing with the Frenchs.'

Pike smiled and turned slowly to face the aristocrat. 'Anyone –' he paused to ensure the driver's full attention '– can be dealt with – it's just a matter of how.'

Longshore returned his smile. 'Give me a week, Wallace, I'll go door hunting.'

Nigel hunted his front door for five minutes. The marijuana filled him with confusion and goodwill towards not only mankind, but also Samantha and the noisy dog next door; even Monica, he was sure, had her good side.

He decided, wisely, not to drive.

Today he would use the underground. Confident in his disguise, he took the Bakerloo line from St John's Wood, changed to the Victoria line at Green Park and emerged into the sunlight again at Brixton station. He loved this High Street. No pretence here, just real life with real people. Two black girls turned and looked in half-recognition; he ignored them and walked the two hundred yards to Coldharbour Lane. Turning left at the Pizza Hut he saw the faded wooden sign that marked his destination.

The Coach and Horses was a grubby little pub nestled between a minicab firm and a laundrette. The entrance door hung loosely on its hinges and the red and gold paint was peeling off all but one of the window frames. The one new window was to the left of the door. Nigel wondered who had been thrown through it to necessitate the repair.

Inside, a pool table dominated the small smoke-filled room. A dozen wooden tables covered with plastic gingham tablecloths circled the perimeter. The wall furthest from the door housed the makeshift bar.

Nigel stood in the entrance and removed his sunglasses. The bass notes from the reggae jukebox vibrated through his body. A large black man with shoulder-length dreadlocks looked up from the pool table. The serious look of important shot play disappeared from his face. 'N. B.-C., Blood . . . Wa gwan, ma bredrin, I na see ya face in too long, ma man.'

Nigel walked over to him and the two men embraced. The man pushed Nigel to arm's length, holding him firmly by the shoulders. 'Let me see ya, man . . . Jah . . . ya still look white to me.' They both laughed and embraced a second time.

The man's opponent broke the moment. 'Ya goin' ta play ya shot, Dread . . . or ya ganna quit?'

The smile disappeared from the man's face as he turned back to the table. He potted the two remaining yellow balls and the black in what seemed to be one continuous movement. Before the black ball had sunk he turned away from the table, put his arm around Nigel's shoulder and ushered him towards the door. 'Ya no wanna stay in dis company, ma man . . . no class, Nigel, no class at all.'

Outside, the day's heat was reaching its zenith. The two men walked with a lively step along Coldharbour Lane towards the High Street.

They had first met in the late seventies during Nigel's first visit to Jamaica. The man was just plain Tony then, living the Rasta life in the Blue Mountains and selling corn by the roadside. Nigel had rented a car with a view to driving across the mountains to Montego

Bay. Like most things in Jamaica at that time, the car broke down thirty miles out of Kingston. Nigel was stranded, lost and scared. As he sat in the car trying to decide his next move there was a tap on the window and there stood Tony, big, black and with a smile that seemed to cover his entire face. Nigel felt a warmth from him that dispelled his fear. They sat by the road, ate some corn, smoked some herb and within an hour Nigel had forgotten Montego Bay, the broken car and most of his previous life. He spent the next three weeks with Tony and bonded a friendship he knew would last. Tony's musical talent astounded Nigel to the point of disbelief. He could make music with anything and everything around him. Before he left, Nigel promised his newfound friend he would get him started in England; within six months he had kept his promise. A decade later Tony was now Stompy Dread, musician, writer, producer, leader of Britain's number one reggae band, Rasta Spear, and London's top-paid session percussionist.

They walked across the square and headed up Brixton Hill.

'I'm sa glad ta see ya,' said Tony, his smile as big as Nigel remembered on their first meeting. 'Where ya bin, ya no come see ma face fa so long?'

'I'm just *so* busy. I did a dozen commercials last month and that breakfast show means bed by nine latest.'

'Ras man . . . someting else g'wan. Ya naw phone me *tree weeks*, man.'

'Well, I must admit I have been a bit preoccupied for the last little while.'

'Ya say . . . Ras clot . . . Tell me 'er name.'

'Samantha.'

'Jah bless 'er name . . . She good to ya, man?'

'She blows me away . . . that's just it, my friend, I'm not in control of this one. She seems to be calling all the shots.'

Tony stopped dead in his tracks. Nigel carried on for a couple more steps, stopped and turned to face his friend. Tony's face grew hard as he squinted into the sun and tried to see into Nigel's eyes. Nigel stood firm and said nothing.

Tony threw both his hands in the air. 'Ma man . . . I do believe ya in love.' He started to dance in front of Nigel. 'Jah be praised . . . de Ras boy in love.'

Nigel felt embarrassment begin to fill his cheeks as people started to stare at Tony's dancing. 'Come on, man. Cool it.'

'Ah . . . ya white boys all de same . . . scared ta let it out . . .' Once again he put his hand around Nigel's shoulder. 'Come, me bredrin . . . come to my place . . . we ave some tea and lick a spliff . . . I wanna know all about dis woo-man.'

Maggie's day didn't seem to start at all. She overslept by four hours, her favourite blouse had a huge wine stain down the right side from a small contretemps the night before, and it was now four o'clock and still no sign of the cab she'd ordered at three. If I ever get rich, she thought, the first thing I'll do is hire a maid. An English one, who looks like Monica, and I'll make her do everything twice.

Her cab arrived at ten past four. She was in the middle of trying to find more space in the largest handbag she owned. She leaned out of her kitchen window to confront the fresh-faced driver on the street two floors below.

The young man shielded his eyes from the sun with

one hand and waved to Maggie with the other. A broad Glaswegian accent cut through the hot afternoon haze. 'Miss Lomax, do nae hurry, I'll park the wee car and wait.' He didn't know, but that accent had saved him from a broadside of abuse. Maggie held up both hands to signal 'ten minutes' and ducked back inside.

She arrived at CRFM just before five o'clock. Robin Trower greeted her with his usual warm smile and a handful of mail. 'I thought you weren't going to make it, Miss Lo . . . er . . . Maggie. I was about to phone to see you were all right.'

Maggie grabbed her mail with one hand and Robin's now empty hand with the other. 'You are, without a doubt, the most thoughtful person here,' she said. 'Oh, wait a minute.' She rummaged through her handbag and produced one signed picture of Trevor Jones and a piece of headed paper with 'Best Wishes – John Thorne' written on it. 'Here's a couple more for your collection, young man. We'll soon have them all accounted for.' Robin's smile was all the thanks she wanted. She carried on before he had time to speak. 'Save your thanks till we get them all,' she said. 'Then you can buy me a *very* large Scotch.'

'I sure will,' he replied and diverted his attention to the telephone switchboard with its five flashing red lights.

Maggie shuffled through the green room, stopping briefly to replenish her stock of Silk Cut, wave hello to Kenny Parker and treat herself to a Diet Pepsi. John Thorne saw her disappear into the library and hurried after her. 'A word in your ear, Maggie,' he said. 'If you've got the time.'

'I've always got time for harassed-looking news editors, they look like I feel first thing in the morning.'

'Maggie, I need your help to test the water.'

'I never test water, John, nasty, polluted stuff. Fish fuck in it, you know.'

'Oh, Maggie, I'm surprised at you, that is a *very* old joke.'

'My dearest John, I'm a *very* old broadcaster.' She put her arms around his neck and kissed him lightly on the earlobe. 'Fancy a quick fish?'

'Maggie, be . . .'

'Don't you dare say serious,' she said, breaking the embrace and gathering a pile of CDs from her cubbyhole. 'What can I do for you . . . MISTER Thorne?'

'Do you ever do any items on prisoners' wives and girlfriends, etcetera?'

'About a month ago, when that report came out about Brixton being such a shit hole. Why?'

John ignored the question. 'What kind of reaction did you get?'

'Not much really. Ex-cons supported the report. Said beatings were more commonplace than reported and the wives said they missed getting laid. What is this about, John?'

'Just a hunch, my little haggis.' John's pager started to flash and he immediately headed for the door. Looking back over his shoulder he called out to Maggie, 'If you get a chance hit the subject again and let me know what happens.'

'Will do . . . and John . . .'

'Yes.'

'Thanks for the "little".'

She stuffed the day's assortment of promotional CDs and records into her already overloaded handbag and headed for the studio.

Monica breezed past her in the hall, they smiled and nodded to each other but not a word was spoken.

Monica had meant to speak to her about the Flash Jack affair, but right now her mind was on other things. Tomorrow was her big day. Tomorrow she was going to meet the Queen and she was going to start preparing for it right now. She walked through reception without seeing anyone and into her waiting cab. She was carrying her two green Harrods bags and she couldn't wait to try the whole outfit on in the privacy of her own room.

The maid had been in to clean so the flat was spotless. She went to the kitchen to pour herself her customary vodka but stopped before reaching the cabinet. Not today, she thought, today I deserve better than that. She went to the fridge and found a bottle of Moët D.P. 1974. 'And why not,' she said as she carried it into the sitting room in search of a flute glass.

Opening champagne bottles was not something Monica did. That was men's work. The little wire bit could so easily break a nail, or the cork pop out without a moment's warning and shower your clothing with wet bubbles. She went in search of an instrument to safeguard her nails, found a small cocktail pick and proceeded to attack the wretched wiring, keeping it at arm's length to avoid any sudden disaster. To her immense relief the wire detached itself from the cork with consummate ease. The cork started edging its way up the neck of the bottle. She grabbed the hem of her skirt and covered the top of the bottle, gave it a quick twist and heard the 'pop'. She immediately placed the bottle on the coffee table and watched a small stream of bubbles trickle over the neck and down across the shield-shaped label. Her right hand was still holding the cork under her dress. She let it drop and noticed a small wet patch six inches above the hem. A small price to pay, she thought.

She filled the flute glass slowly, savouring every bubble. She wiggled her toes in the carpet. Just one more thing, she thought. Must have a quick look at the dip poll. She opened her briefcase and removed the computer print-out. Her professional survival depended ultimately on the results contained within these documents and Monica had learned to read above, below and in between the lines. The dip poll was not a major survey like the BARB, or JICRAR, which were used not only to advise programming but also as a basis for setting the stations' sales rate-card and therefore its profitability. The 'dips' were a continuous eye on the trends and swings, as they happened, on a weekly basis. Monica knew that like the 'penny and pounds' theory, if you got it right on the dips, the JICRARs would look after themselves.

She unfolded the survey on top of the glass-top coffee table and put her champagne glass over the figures for Radio One. The top line pleased her. Nigel B. was number one at breakfast by twelve per cent and the rest of the day was holding up very well behind him. Capital FM was running a close second, as usual, and their new Gold AM channel was starting to make inroads, especially in the afternoon. She put that down to the television exposure Kenny Everett was getting through the repeats of his Thames series. She briefly entertained the thought that it could be due to Kenny being better than almost anything on the air including Nigel B., but she dismissed that theory out of hand. Monica believed that if Kenny was that good he'd be working for her. Radio One was still third overall, Radio Two was going up and down like a yo-yo. Confusion there, she thought. Long may it continue. Radio Four was peaking at eight a.m. and one p.m. Heavy news – nothing she could do about that. LBC was fluctuating between third and fifth, also a pretty standard showing, although it did surprise Monica that the big names they were now using were not pushing them into the top two. The new London stations KISS and JAZZ were starting to show, but only down with Radio Three and GLR. Monica refilled her glass and did some more toe twiddling.

After the second glass of champagne she felt she was ready to try on her new clothes. She poured a third glass and walked across the hall towards her private door. The phone rang. She let the answerphone do its job. She waited for the incoming message. 'Hello, Monica, Frank De Wolf. I tried your office and they told me you left early. Could you give me a call . . . I've got some champagne to go with the swizzle stick.' Click.

So have I, thought Monica, as she headed up the stairs to where she knew she was safe.

At Eaton Square the Frenchs had just finished their evening meal. Simmons had finished clearing the table and Freddie had finished his third brandy. Peter was reading the city page of the *Standard* while Lady Isobel looked daggers at her younger son and suggested it was time they bought at least one French vineyard before the entire family fortune was wiped out by Freddie's drinking.

Peter folded the paper in front of him and looked lovingly at his mother. 'As it happens, old girl, we do own, I think – correct me if I'm wrong, Freddie – four vineyards. All of them acquired, at a very reasonable price, by the man you so hastily scorn.'

Lady Isobel sat upright in her chair. 'Poppycock! You could have bought them for that price if you hadn't been busy with important matters like running the property and media side of things.'

'We all work as a team, Mother, everyone is important.'

'How can you trust someone who is drunk by lunch and absolutely blotto by tea? I ask you, we must do something . . .'

Freddie replaced his brandy goblet on the table in front of him and glared at his mother. 'If I may be allowed to schpeak . . .'

Lady Isobel turned back to Peter. '. . . see what I mean, he can't even talk anymore.' She turned back to Freddie. 'The word is S-P-E-A-K, not schpeak or whatever it is you are trying to say.'

Freddie stood up, knocking the chair backwards on to the floor. 'I've had enough of this,' he snapped. 'Peter, if you can bear to tear yourself away from this talking pronunciation book I would like to see you in the study before I get really drunk.' He picked up his glass, half-filled it with numbered Napoleon and stormed out of the room, slamming the door.

Lady Isobel sank into her chair. 'Really, Peter, we must do something . . . and quickly.'

Peter left his chair and crossed the room to his mother's side. He gave her a hug and a small kiss on her grey hair. 'You mustn't taunt him so. He loves you, as I do.'

The old lady caressed Peter's hand. 'Go to him,' she said. 'I feel nothing but anger.'

As Peter entered the study on the second floor Freddie was pouring another brandy from a crystal decanter. 'One day, Peter, I swear, I'll kill that woman.'

'Fred, I won't let you talk that way about our mother. It's causing her great distress to see you drink so much.'

'She's the bloody reason I drink! If she just gave me credit for one tiny thing I've done I'd . . .'

'That's not true. You know it isn't. Your drinking has very little to do with Mother. You started drinking heavily, Freddie, when you got married.'

'And it was Mother who made me marry that soppy cow. She couldn't stand the thought of me being happy with Jennifer just because she was an employee, so she sent her away when my back was turned and set me up with Miss Bovine from Bridgewater.' Freddie flopped into the leather settee. 'Don't try and tell me it wasn't her fault.'

Peter poured himself a brandy, swirled it around the goblet and inhaled the bouquet. 'You have a point,' he said.

Freddie smiled and a love passed between them that only brothers know.

Peter straightened his tie, Freddie tried to straighten his mind.

'I've come across an opportunity which is too good to pass up and will also help us get established financially in the Far East.'

'I don't know if I can take all this in just now, Freddie. Couldn't we talk first thing in the morning?'

'In the morning I need the deal complete, at least between us. Just sit down and listen. You know the Kin Won bank of Korea?'

'Yes. One of the last private family banks in the world.'

'Not for much longer.' Freddie allowed himself a smile. He knew his brother would be surprised.

'Good lord,' said Peter. 'Don't tell me the old boy has finally capitulated to the pressure of the open market.'

'Not only that, my old stiff, there is dissension in the ranks and we can make a quick ten million before they have time to draw breath.'

'Pounds or dollars?'

'Dollars.'

'Shame.'

'Are you complaining?'

Peter sank back into the soft leather chair. 'Not in the slightest, old chap, please, do continue.'

'The youngest boy, Kwan, has a problem near and dear to my own heart. He is in love with a lovely French girl and the family, of course, insist on him marrying some little Korean moneybags who he met once when they were both five years old. Kwan holds three million shares he inherited direct from his grandfather and he's willing to sell them to me at two dollars fifty, take the money and the French lady and spend the rest of his life sailing the world and living off the interest.'

'This all sounds very romantic, Freddie, but I don't understand how that makes us ten million dollars.'

'The last thing the old man wants is "trouble at t'mill". If the flotation goes without a hitch the family stand to make around two hundred million. A scandal of any kind, let alone one this close to home, could cost them at least a third, maybe more.'

'Go on.'

'Try this scenario . . . We buy the shares from Kwan at two dollars fifty. Ten days for the money to clear and Kwan to make himself scarce. That still gives us five days before they announce the flotation. I go and see the old man and offer him the shares at, say, six dollars on the understanding that we say nothing publicly and we keep the profit deposited in his bank. He'll make at least another four dollars per when the institutions are let in, our money is hidden until we need it but still delivers ten per cent on the capital.'

'How much capital . . . exactly?'

'If I get six, and I'm sure I can, ten point two-five million.'

'Finance?'

'We've got three liquid. Mr C. in Geneva will lend us three at five per cent for thirty days using the Monet as collateral and I need your help for another one point five.'

'In what way?'

'I need to short-mortgage some of the property, but I don't want to leave any trails.'

Sir Peter stood up, wandered towards the door and assumed his best Bertie Wooster pose. 'When do you need the money?'

'Assurances by noon tomorrow, money in seven days.'

Peter smiled at his brother as he slowly opened the study door. 'Goodnight, Freddie.'

Freddie looked at his brandy glass and placed it, still half-full, on the table. 'Goodnight, Peter.'

CHAPTER 6

Monica sat at her breakfast bar eating bran flakes and drinking freshly squeezed orange juice. She looked at the dial on her kitchen radio to make sure she was tuned to CRFM. A Jerry Jeff Walker love song on the eight-fifteen 'free-choice' spot. He's playing that because he wants to, she thought, and made a mental note to find out a lot more about Sandra ... Sarah ... Samantha! that's it ... and find out rather sharpish.

In Monica's plan of things the fifteen past the hour free-choice spot played an important part. It made the DJs feel they were part of the programming process, it showed their skill in making a programme flow and, most important, it let Monica know their frame of mind on an hourly basis. Nigel was usually David Bowie, Bob Marley, Dire Straits or the occasional classic rock or soul track from the sixties. Country love songs were a new addition to his repertoire. She underlined her last mental note.

Today was her big day and she was going to savour every moment, but first there was the problem of the Weekend dip survey. She adjourned to the sitting room and spread the report across the coffee table and started to study the 'top lines'. Weekend shows are different to weekday slots. On the weekend, people listen through choice as opposed to companionship. They want to be entertained rather than have a nice source of background music and information. Monica produced a lot of speciality shows with high-profile presenters over the weekend and they were subject to sudden and violent popularity change.

The other bee in her bonnet was sport. She had fought the board and, it seemed, the entire male staff over her objection to sport. She argued that the BBC did it very well and now that Capital Gold had entered the arena with a top-flight sport team, the production budget required to launch a service that could compete with those two heavyweights would not be worth the kind of revenue it could generate. She also knew seventy per cent of her weekend audience were female and that one brown, sexy male voice was worth two dozen loud-mouthed lager louts screaming two-one . . . two-one in vocal disharmony.

Her answer to Saturday afternoon sport was Washington Blake and the Soul Survivor show. Blake was a six foot two black man from New York City. He sounded like Barry White after elocution lessons and his music ranged from George Benson to George Duke via Aretha Franklin. He sometimes slipped in tracks by people Monica had never heard, but they always sounded right and *always* made her toes twiddle, even when there was no deep-pile carpet.

Monica looked at his overall 'reach' figure. Down nine points . . . not good . . . not good at all. Where are they going? Gold sport . . . up two. Radio Four . . . up one. Jazz FM . . . up six! She made a note in her diary: Sat./2 pm/Jazz/listen. She never went into battle without knowing the strength, and weakness, of the opposition.

The smile quickly returned to her face when she read the next piece of information. His audience profile was eighty-seven per cent female. 'You can afford to lose ten overall, my lovely music man, if eighty-five per cent of what's left is a prime target,' she said as she made another note in her diary: Sales/food/fashion/mags/baby prods/ to Sat. 2–6 pm @ 10% prem.

The rest of the weekend held the line. No real

changes. A few bits of lower-line information concerning performance profiles that Monica filed away for future bargaining power, but in the main, the station was holding well.

She phoned Harry Connaught's office and left a message on the answer-machine. 'Monica Hammond calling. Please tell Harry I'll not be in the office this morning and could he pick me up from Cadogan Square. Thank you.' She made one more call, to Vidal Sassoon. 'Steven, can you fit me in at eleven . . .? Thank you so much, see you then.'

Monica mused on the two-hour bath and dressing session that lay ahead. Heaven. Today was a major toe-twiddling day.

It was turning out a major dosh day for Nigel. On his arrival this morning he picked up an overnight message from his agent that McDonald's were going to use his voice for their winter campaign. With repeats, that was ten grand for his Christmas stocking. Anthony Parkin arrived early, at half past eight, for the express purpose of offering him three commercials at £200 each. Could he do them at nine o'clock? They were on air at eleven.

He could and would . . .

Anthony's office was a celluloid jungle. Tape reels seemed to be falling out of every nook and cubbyhole. Old commercials, new commercials, background music, voice-over audition tapes and various F/X libraries were crammed into every available inch of space. Nothing seemed to be labelled or filed but Anthony could find almost anything in the time it took to ask for it.

Nigel strode into the cluttered closet and burst into a slightly off-key rendition of 'Semi-detached Suburban Mr James': '*So you finally named the day . . .*'

Anthony smiled the warm glow of the loved. 'We're

not getting married yet, we're just moving in together. Anyway, who are you to talk? I hear that tall blonde has got you playing love songs on your free-choice spot.'

That took Nigel back a bit and he wondered if anyone else had noticed. 'Samantha? . . . yeh, she's a . . . very nice lady. Nothing serious though . . . I'm too busy to get serious. I get this dickhead who keeps coming in first thing in the morning and offering "loadsamoney" so I'll do his poxy local scripts. I'd tell him to piss off but I feel sorry for the guy.'

Anthony gathered an assortment of tapes and scripts together from the disaster area he called a desk and the two men walked down the corridor to the production studio. 'Nigel, you are, without a doubt, a beautiful human being.'

'Well thank you, Anthony.'

'Has anyone else told you that today?'

'I don't think so . . . no, you're the first.'

'So you didn't get a call from Monica then?'

'Anthony.'

'Yes.'

'I don't feel sorry for you anymore.'

The large double soundproof doors of the production studio slowly closed behind the two men, leaving only their aftershave to replace the laughter.

The subject of their joke was having an absolutely wonderful time. She was washed, powdered, preened and sitting comfortably in one of the soft brown leather chairs that adorn the Salon Sassoon. Monica brought 'the hat' with her, so there could be no mistakes.

Steven was about to work his magic.

Nigel's next appointment was at four in the afternoon. He left the station at eleven and started contemplating a few hours' sunbathing. Reality struck. Last night, he and Tony had somehow ended up at Maida Vale. The place was now a tip and with far too much of the wrong stuff lying around to leave for the cleaning lady. This was a job for . . . 'Cleaner Man'.

He opened his apartment door. Stale everything surged up his nostrils. Starting with the kitchen, he opened every window in the place. The bedroom smelled vile. There's a dead person here, he thought, and went in search of the body. It didn't take long to find it.

Balancing half off the bedside table, on the pillow side, was a silver carton which contained what can only be described as vindaloo in a state of reproduction. Nigel grabbed the end nearest the pillow. Of course, the liquid had somehow found its way to the bottom of the carton and his hand was now yellowish-brownish and *wet* . . . He looked skyward. 'Thanks a whole bunch.'

The doorbell rang.

'Thanks a whole bunch again!' he shouted, feeling certain the carton was now glued to his hand. He shuffled into the hall slamming the bedroom door behind him. 'I'll bet it's the jerk with the dog from next door,' he mumbled to himself. He smiled. 'I'll give him the vindaloo, no dog could survive that.'

Nigel opened the door. 'Hel– *Samantha* . . . I . . .' He was getting that frontal-lobotomy feeling again. 'I . . . thought you were on a modelling job . . . you . . . said you wouldn't be back till Friday . . . I . . . I'm in the middle of cleaning the . . . I . . .'

One step and Samantha was next to him. 'Give me a kiss, not excuses.'

Nigel was without the use of his right hand and the right side of his brain. 'Let me just . . . get rid of this . . .'

Samantha placed her mouth over his, blotting out his excuses.

Too late, he thought, as he kicked the door shut.

They made love in the kitchen, on the hard, cold, tiled floor. She removed his clothing with expert ease, while not allowing him to reciprocate. She pushed his bare back on to the cold tiles, her mouth darting from left to right as she bit his neck and shoulders, her hair gently whipping his face as she moved. Her silk floral dress rubbed against his chest as she twisted and turned on top of him like a snake trying to shed its skin. Her hand caressed him, holding his erection, pushing it between her legs and rubbing it against the folds in her dress. She felt so soft to him, so warm. The different textures and temperatures made him shudder with delight and pain and he was, once again, transported to fresh coital fields.

They lay in each other's arms, Samantha stroking the side of his neck and up behind his ear. She gently twisted the hair on the nape of his neck around her first finger. 'Did I do right coming back two days early? . . . Or shall I go home and come back Friday as we planned?'

Nigel let himself drift for a few more seconds. Suddenly, propping himself up on one arm and looking at that lovely face he said, 'Do you mean to say that no one knows you're here till Friday?'

'No one.'

'What happened?'

'I'd finished by last night. They offered double fee to stay and shoot some lingerie for a mail-order firm, but I thought lingerie . . . Nigel; Nigel . . . lingerie . . . and here I am!'

Nigel kissed her again, stood up and offered her his

hand. She took it and rose from the cold floor in one smooth movement. Nigel felt so overjoyed he didn't even try to speak.

She afforded him a quick curtsy and a slow smile. 'My bag is outside the door. You run a bath and I'll make sure we're out of soap.'

'Pardon?'

'So I can lick you clean . . . silly.'

Nigel retrieved the suitcase from outside the apartment wondering, once again, why he became so slow-witted in her company. A lady down the hall took a sharp intake of breath while she waited for the lift. It was then Nigel realized he was naked.

The suitcase was much heavier than Nigel anticipated. He dragged it into the living room where Samantha was sitting on the right-hand settee, her clothes remarkably straight considering the previous twenty minutes, sifting through the pile of debris from last night. 'For heaven's sake, sweetheart, what *didn't* you eat?'

Nigel felt embarrassed by both his nakedness and his gluttony. 'My friend Tony and I met up for lunch yesterday,' he said. 'Somehow it seemed to go on till midnight.'

Samantha picked through the bits in the ashtray. 'I can see why,' she said in a tone sharper than he had known before.

Nigel's thoughts spun out of control. 'I . . .'

She lifted her eyes from the table, stared into Nigel's face and spoke in a tone that would make every mother proud. 'Put some clothes on, Nigel, you look ridiculous.'

As he dressed, the guilties had a field day. Why didn't I tell her before . . . what if she's *really* anti-drug? . . . I'll bet she thinks we had women here last night . . .

She probably thinks I do cocaine, LSD, heroin . . . all at once . . . Shit, how could I let this happen? . . . She's on her way out the door right now . . . Yes . . . she's had time to write a note . . . any second now I'll hear the door . . . All I had to do was clean it up last night . . . taken five bloody minutes . . . FUCK THIS!

He strode as manfully as he could down the hallway and into the living room. 'Sam, before you do anything, hear me out. Tony and I have known each other since . . .'

Samantha was sitting cross-legged on the floor expertly attaching the third paper to a three-skin roll-up. She looked at him as if he were totally mad and revelled in his bewilderment. 'Don't tell me you've nothing left.' She did a stunningly good impression of Bart Simpson. 'You can eat my shorts if you can't deliver.'

Nigel now had a heart attack to go with the frontal lobotomy. He collapsed beside her. 'I'm not even going to ask . . .'

Samantha pressed her hand to his mouth. 'Don't.' She threw her hair over her shoulder in a perfect arc. 'Just get the grass.'

'Yes, ma'am.'

Sir Peter French was using the company car today. A twenty-year-old, long-wheel-base James Young Phantom Five. One-hundred-and-seventy-thousand miles of service and still the loudest noise was the clock. He had ordered a new Turbo Bentley sixteen months ago and he looked forward to delivery sometime before Christmas. As he sat back into the leather luxury of the rear seat and closed his eyes, he pondered the wisdom of giving up such a magnificent piece of British craftsmanship.

The ring of the car phone broke his trance. He carefully lifted it from its cradle in the centre partition. 'Peter French ... Freddie, how are you, old chap? ... Yes ... That will be fine ... I'll have the paper on your desk within the hour ... You're welcome ... Pardon ... no, I'm lunching at the club ... Pardon, look, I am sorry, this line is dreadful ... Think nothing of it, old boy, it's the least a brother can do ... Fine, see you then ... Goodbye.' He replaced the phone with equal care and sat back to finish his power-nap.

Monica returned home with a new hairstyle and a hat that fitted perfectly over it. She stepped into her newly acquired Conran creation, found the zipper at the first time of asking and even managed to do up the little hook and eye at the top of the dress without too much difficulty. She stood in front of the full-length mirror for a final inspection. The dress made her shoulders look much slimmer than they were (two points). The line of her breast was perfect (two points). It fell away from her hips at just the right place and cascaded into a fusion of small pleats which seemed to move slower than her body when she turned (five points), and Lizzie was right, the hat looked stunning.

'Ten out of ten,' she purred. Monica loved her little games.

She practised her elegant walk while descending the stairs. She was a naturally elegant person but a bit of practice, specially before such an important occasion, never hurt. The phone rang and she nearly jumped out of her Clive Shilton shoes. She let it ring three times so she could regain her composure. 'Hello. Monica Hammond.'

'Monica, it's Harry, what a lovely day.'

'Harry! Yes it is, quite magnificent. How are you?'

'Top ho, my dear, top ho.' Monica knew there was more. She kept silent. 'Listen, Monica, I'm just off for a quick bite at the club with Sir Peter. Would you care to join us?'

'If you don't mind, Harry, I'd rather not.' She hated that 'club'. They allowed women in, but only just. A small lie should be enough to win the day. 'I've just got back from the hairdresser and I'm not dressed yet.'

Harry Connaught accepted Monica's statement without reservation. 'I quite understand, my dear, it was just a last-minute idea of mine, not to worry. One more thing before I let you go. I'm afraid timing is at the head of the agenda today. We have to hit our slot, you see.'

Timing, like elegance, was natural to Monica. She didn't understand his concern. 'Our what, Harry?'

'Well, you see, we have to arrive at a certain time, I suppose to keep all the paperwork straight. Our time is two-fifty. We have to arrive at the Palace at two-fifty or they might not let us in.'

For paperwork read security, she thought. How exciting! 'What time do you want me ready?'

'If I pick you up at two-forty, that should do nicely. I'll phone when we're nearly to you and maybe you could come down and meet the car.'

Some Prince Charming, she thought, no rushing up the stairs with a huge bunch of red roses. No spreading his cape over the bald patch in the hall carpet. Oh well . . . maybe not, the stairs might kill him. 'That will be fine, Harry, see you then. Enjoy your lunch.'

'Thank you, my dear, I'll give Peter your love. Goodbye.'

Monica placed her finger on the telephone 'R' button. She heard the dial tone and punched in a familiar number: 730 1234. It rang twice.

'Good afternoon, Harrods.'

'Food Hall, please.'

'Thank you, madam, connecting you now.'

'Food Hall.'

Monica recognized the voice. 'Hello, Eduardo, Monica Hammond.'

'Miss Hammond, how nice-a to hear from you. How can I help?'

'What is nice today, Eduardo?'

'I've got some lovely gravad lax, just in, not too much dill, just right, with some special sauce I made myself. I've got to sell, Miss Hammond, my wife, she get fat from too much ... I got nice salad to go with and maybe some carrot cake for after.'

'That sounds perfect. Eduardo, could you be an absolute sweetheart and pop it in a cab for me? I'll pay the driver for everything.'

'No problem, Miss Hammond. It's Cadogan Square, isn't it?'

'Yes, Eduardo, Number Twenty-nine. Thank you, you've done me a great favour. Goodbye.' She replaced the handset *very* slowly, glided across the kitchen, sat on her favourite chair next to the window and gazed out on to the square. She must remember to remove her Conran before lunch. A sauce spot on her new dress was the only disaster she could foresee.

Everyone seemed to be having a play day today. Monica and Harry were going to visit the Queen. Sir Peter had decided that raising one and a half million pounds and suffering lunch with the IBA was enough work for one day. A slow round of golf with Longshore sounded perfect for such a hot afternoon, although he was somewhat surprised at the sudden invitation. Nigel and Samantha were about to land back on earth any minute now for a refuelling stop and Maggie Lomax was just waking up.

She felt across to the other side of the bed, making sure he was still there. He was. Now she put her mind on fifteen interesting ways to wake him up. HE was Bradley Thompson, male model, very heterosexual and Maggie's lover, on and off, for the last two years. He had brown eyes and large hands. He loved women for themselves. Last night Maggie had told him most of her problems. He listened intently and even offered one or two possible solutions. That was half the turn-on with Bradley, that and his large hands. Maggie felt adored all night and lost count at orgasm number eight. Today she was going in search of numbers nine through twenty.

The exception that proves the rule was Brian Callaghan. Dirty Harry was working his little *tuchas* off with no thoughts of anything except how to improve his sales percentage, reorganize the department for maximum efficiency and show the board that it was he that should be in charge of this company and not that snooty Monica Hammond. It was a MAN's job anyway, and there's the truth of it, he thought.

The truth of it was that Mr Callaghan could not stand working for *any* woman, snooty or otherwise.

He, too, was having lunch sent in, but not from Harrods. His was coming direct from the canteen and served in the boardroom along with four identical copies for the directors of ATS.

Air Time Services was a sales company that sold national advertising to local stations. They would negotiate, with the advertising agencies, for large international accounts, such as Coca-Cola or Lever. They then passed on the campaigns, tailored and complete, to the stations they represented, minus a fifteen per cent commission, of course. Everybody wins. The stations get heavyweight advertisers, which makes them look good and it pays well, at no man-hour cost except logging. The advertiser has only one person to deal with for a good chunk of his media cake and as, in England, where there were only three companies playing the game, the advertising executive can cover the whole country's radio in three meetings and slither off down to the closest wine bar.

ATS was the biggest of the three. They represented only nineteen out of the possible sixty-two stations on the network, but they had the big ones.

ATS didn't bother with the small community outfits or the lame ducks.

ATS was owned by Aylford.

The purpose of Callaghan's lunch was to restructure his deal with ATS. They had represented CRFM for twelve years, long before Aylford took them over, long before Callaghan was any kind of executive at all. Last year they put fourteen point five million into the station coffers minus the usual fifteen per cent, of course. Now that Callaghan controlled the sales on three stations, he thought it time to reduce that percentage.

He'd done his homework. Cornwall and Dundee added another thirty per cent to his overall reach. Bums on seats. With his new thirty and their old fifteen, a new deal was possible. Now his ace card. CRFM was the ATS flagship, with two brand new guns. Aylford, or no Aylford, ATS would rather eat chicken droppings than lose CRFM as a client.

Callaghan didn't get on with Australians, and these four were getting right under his toenails. He couldn't bear the accent for a start and their humour made him think Bill and Ben were sophisticated.

He suffered the food, the beerstains on the tablecloth, the stupid jokes and the accents for over an hour. Finally, the last spillage had been mopped up by a disgruntled Mrs Purvis from the canteen and Dirty Harry could get down to business. 'The way we see it, gentlemen, we now have thirty per cent more to offer, and possibly a lot more to come within the next twelve months. Our profiles are the best of any station on the network and our prime time for the next three months is already ninety per cent sold. We feel that a reduction in your commission rates is called for to offset the increased revenue you can expect. I therefore propose that we look to end this present agreement, which I'm sure you know has only six months to run, and think about a new agreement to cover the next, say, three years.'

The Australians showed nothing in their faces. That's another thing about them Brian didn't like. The large one with blond curly hair leaned back in his chair and started scratching his chest. 'Well, Bri . . . I'm afraid we don't quite see it that way. We're happy with the present set-up . . . I mean, you get us tickets for Lords, we go and watch England get thumped . . . What could be fairer than that?' The Australians all laughed and slapped their hands on the table.

Brian tried a smile, but couldn't. 'Gentlemen, I'm serious. If I don't put something much more imaginative to my board by this time next week, I think they will look long and hard before renewing with your company.'

The Australians stopped laughing. The blond one spoke again. 'You have an agreement with us, which already covers any new acquisitions, and, as you say, runs for another six months. We will honour that contract and we expect you to do the same. As for what happens in six months from now . . . I guess your board will have to do what they think fit.'

Callaghan couldn't believe what he was hearing. The blond continued. 'If you would like to discuss renewing for a further period at the same rate, I'm sure we can hammer something out, but ATS is not prepared to consider any fundamental changes in structure at this moment.'

Callaghan was about to explode. Arrogant, pushy bastards! He kept the lid on it . . . just. 'Well gentlemen, we seem to be at an impasse. May I suggest we talk to our respective boards and talk again, say, two weeks from now.'

'That's fine by me, Bri, I'll look forward to your call.'

Brian Callaghan stubbed his toe, crashed into a running newsman and swore at his secretary, all before reaching his office.

The blond was driving around Hyde Park Corner on his way to Millbank Towers when the car phone rang. He touched the button that allowed hands-free operation. 'Ian Mathews here.'

'It's Wallace Pike, Ian, how did you get on?'

'Bloody great, Mr Wallace. You were right, it was a shot at a cut in commission. I told him to piss off and that we'd worry about renewal when the time comes.'

'Good, bloody good. Are you on your way back?'

'Yes, sir, about ten minutes away.'

'Drop in and see me.'

'Will do, Mr Wallace.'

Monica was standing outside her front door as the IBA Daimler Princess turned into Cadogan Square. A Princess, she thought, how appropriate.

The car stopped beside her and Harry Connaught opened the back door from the inside. 'Monica, my dear, you look *absolutely stunning*. You'll be the talk of the party.'

I will, I will, I will, she thought, as she glided into the seat beside him. 'Thank you, Harry, how nice of you to say so.' Monica had a little toe twiddle inside her shoes. 'Will we make our time slot?'

'Oh, I should think so.' Harry nodded at the driver, who immediately took off at just above funeral pace. He pressed a button beside him and the glass divider slid up quickly, separating them from the driver. He turned to face her. 'There is just one thing I'd like to mention before we get overtaken by the events of the afternoon. As you know, I've just had lunch with Peter and he's concerned about this too.'

I wish I'd gone to the lunch, thought Monica. She summoned up her most interested look. 'Do go on, Harry.'

Harry lowered his voice, even though they were completely alone. 'Brompton Road feel that Aylford will take your acquisition of Cornwall and Dundee very badly.'

Tough shit, thought Monica. 'Do you think they'll try and blow us up, Harry?'

'If they thought they could get away with it I wouldn't put it past them. They put a lot of work into their applications and they are desperate to get into British media.'

Monica saw a small opening and shot through it. 'I thought the IBA was making sure that wouldn't happen, Harry. From what I gathered from our dinner at Eaton Square, the IBA would rather see the whole network sold to the French family than see one piece of it fall into Aylford hands.'

Harry Connaught fidgeted slightly in his seat. Monica always had a knack of disarming him with some small gem of reverse logic or slight misquote. When she worked for him it was hard to resist, but now she could get nasty with it. 'The IBA does what it can, my dear, but I do think you should watch out for anything coming from their direction. They're a bit hot under the collar about the method Peter used and are liable to start fighting dirty. I don't want you getting hurt.'

Fighting dirty is all right by me, she thought, it would match the state of their collars. She smiled at Harry and caressed the side of his face. 'Bless you, Harry, you always do look out for me, and I appreciate it very much.' She removed her hand and turned to face the front. 'Now tell me what I'm supposed to do at the Palace.'

Nigel and Samantha had cleaned each room in the flat and then made love in them to 'purify the vibes'. It was just before three as they entered the bathroom.

Samantha surveyed the room. 'Not much damage here.'

Nigel nodded agreement. 'We only came in here for a pee.'

'In that case,' said Samantha, flicking her hair in another near-perfect arc, 'why don't you roll another one and I'll get the champers. No good wasting a perfectly good room, just because it's clean.'

Reality struck Nigel for the second time today. 'Shit . . . I've got a voice to do at four o'clock and the studio is down in Soho . . . I've got to go.'

'Go?' said Samantha. 'Are you serious . . . GO?' She grabbed him in a headlock with remarkable speed and then sat down.

'Ouch!' shouted Nigel.

'I'll give you OUCH!' she shouted back before dropping her voice to a menacing whisper. 'Listen to me. It cost me treble what you make to be with you. The least you can do is cancel one lousy gig.' She squeezed a little harder around his neck. 'Besides, O stoned one, you're too trashed to work. You go into any studio in town and they'd have the drug squad there before you get to take three . . . No, my lad, you're only good for two things right now, and one of them's feeding.'

Nigel was starting to choke. He clutched her arm and eased it off his windpipe. 'I've got to phone . . .'

Samantha released him. He fell the rest of the way to the floor, she stood up straight. 'Let me do it,' she said. 'What's the number?'

'Up there.' He pointed at the Spanish cadenza. 'In my organizer, Delane Lee, studio B, Mr Stockman.'

Samantha found the book and dialled the number. 'Hello, is Mr Stockman there, please? I'm calling for Nigel Beresford-Clarke . . . Yes, hello . . . Mr Stockman, I'm calling for Nigel . . . yes . . . well, there's been a terrible accident. Nigel got his head trapped behind the loo in his flat . . . Yes . . . I don't know, he was doing some house cleaning and somehow he got stuck . . . I know it sounds funny but it's not for him, Mr Stockman, we've had to call the fire department to come get him out . . . No, I don't think he'll be free by four . . . can he phone you tomorrow? . . . That'll be fine, thank you. Goodbye, Mr Stockman.'

Nigel had held back hysterical laughter before, but this time, when Samantha replaced the phone, his lungs nearly burst.

Maggie Lomax lost count again at seventeen.

Monica was counting the seconds as the Princess circled

the Wedding Cake and came to a measured stop outside the visitors' gate. The driver opened the rear door. Harry got out and immediately turned around and offered Monica his hand. She swanned out of the limousine to the flashes of twenty cameras. The fact that the paparazzi did this to everyone didn't faze Monica in the least. At this second in time they were for her. She smiled at them and enjoyed every millisecond. Harry offered his arm which she gratefully accepted and they walked across the courtyard to the right-side archway which led directly to the garden. Monica had hoped to go through the centre archway, but Harry told her that was only for what he called 'regulars' and, of course, collecting knighthoods.

The garden looked beautiful. Beautiful everything. Beautiful flowers, beautiful people, beautiful sunshine, beautiful Harry, beautiful royalty. Oh ... twiddle, twiddle, twiddle, twiddle ...

She was sure Harry was speaking to her but she heard not a word. He squeezed her hand lightly with his arm. Monica blinked. 'Oh, Harry, I'm so sorry. I was miles away.'

'That's quite all right, my dear, that's easily done. Let's move over towards the small marquee.'

'See someone you know?'

'Good lord, I know most of this motley crew.' He glanced around the full three hundred and sixty degrees. 'Except that bunch over there.'

Monica looked to where he was pointing. For a split second she thought she saw Frank De Wolf, but dismissed it out of hand. She didn't think they allowed lawyers on this lawn.

Harry kept staring. 'They look New Zealanders to me. Most likely part of some Commonwealth club or other.'

Monica didn't care if they were the rugby-bloody-All-Blacks, she had come here to see the Queen, and as she wasn't due for another ten minutes, Monica just strolled along beside Harry feeling very pleased with herself indeed.

At five to three there was a lot of shuffling around; everybody, somehow, seemed to form themselves into straight lines with corridors down the middle. Some man in a grey suit beckoned to Harry and he moved, with Monica, to the front of the first line. At three o'clock precisely, as Big Ben was chiming, Her Majesty the Queen walked through the door right next to Harry and Monica. With her were Charles, Diana and Margaret. The Queen gave the briefest of smiles to the assembled masses and walked down the four steps to lawn level. The other royals dutifully started walking down the other people-lined corridors.

The Queen was wearing a plain blue dress and a white hat with matching handbag and shoes. The last of Monica's nightmares disappeared. She knew it was impossible, but the thought of the same-dress fiasco had passed through her mind more than once in the hours leading up to the party.

Monica's mind stood to attention as the Queen stopped in front of Harry Connaught and held out her right hand. 'Connaught, how nice to see you again. Are you still looking after our media for us?'

Harry took her hand very gently. 'Yes, Your Majesty.'

She glanced toward Monica. The Queen's escort spoke. 'Ma'am, this is Monica Hammond. She's the managing director of CRFM here in London.'

The Queen moved her attention and her hand towards Monica. 'How nice to meet you.'

Monica fought her nerves with every ounce of her

strength. She smiled and did as Harry had coached her, a medium-sized curtsy which made her the same height as the Queen and the words, 'Your Majesty.'

The Queen gave her hand the smallest squeeze as if to reassure her and returned the smile. 'We do enjoy your station, Mrs Hammond. We especially like that chap in the morning, Nigel . . .'

'Beresford-Clarke, Ma'am.'

'Yes, that's it. We like to listen to him for a time after the news on Radio Four. He has a lovely voice.'

'I'll tell him you said so next time I see him, Ma'am.'

The Queen detached her hand from Monica and moved to the next person down the line.

Monica let the moment wash over her like a thousand tides. When Her Majesty had moved a respectable distance down the line Monica tugged on Harry's arm and gave him a slow gentle kiss on his cheek. She also made a mental note to tell Nigel nothing about her conversation with the Queen and underlined it twice.

'Come on, my dear,' said Harry as he started to walk away, almost dragging Monica after him. 'Let's get to the small tent and scoff some tea and bickies before the rest of the rabble get stuck in.'

'What is in the big tent?' asked Monica as they walked at the accepted pace towards the refreshments.

They had walked into the middle of the antipodean contingent. Harry realized the problem and reverted to his diplomatic roots. 'Well, my dear, the Queen takes tea in the *small* tent.' He bumped shoulders with a very large black man in a long multi-coloured jelabba. 'I do beg your pardon,' he said, and expertly manoeuvred both himself and Monica away from the throng.

As they found a piece of open space between the rose beds and the large tent Monica suddenly stopped dead in her tracks. Straight ahead of her, no more than four feet away, stood Frank De Wolf. It *was* you, she thought. He was facing half away from her and hadn't seen her yet, but she knew a meeting was inevitable.

Harry was quick to notice. 'Someone you know, my dear?'

Monica blinked for the second time today. 'Yes . . . a friend.'

'I'll leave you to say hello then. I see old Jimmy over there, must have a word with him. Back in a trice.'

Monica reflected on how wonderful the élite were at knowing exactly what to do.

De Wolf turned and saw Monica. Without a second's hesitation he walked over to her and gave her the politest of embraces, kissing her lightly on both cheeks. 'Monica.'

She decided to steal some of the Queen's script. 'Frank, how nice to see you.'

De Wolf seemed genuinely glad to see her. His body language was all plus and his face was radiant. 'What a lovely surprise, I didn't expect to see you here.'

'Nor I you,' she said.

The smallest tinge of embarrassment crossed Frank's face. 'I'm only making up the numbers with some clients of mine. How about you? Are you here with Sir Peter?'

She knew he was hiding something. Nobody 'makes up numbers' at these sorts of functions. 'No, I came with Harry Connaught from the IBA.' She decided to have mercy on him – after all, it was lovely to see him. 'His wife couldn't make it, so in a way, I suppose, we're both making up the numbers.'

'Will I see you inside for tea and sticky buns?' he asked pointing to the big marquee.

'I think Harry said we are supposed to go over there,' she said, pointing to the little marquee with its two guardsmen standing neatly at ease on either side of the entrance.

Frank felt the wind rapidly removing itself from his sails. 'How splendid for you,' he said.

Monica felt a change of subject was called for. 'I got your message yesterday.' A quick white lie now, to regain the advantage. 'I didn't get in till late so I thought it best not to disturb you.'

'You can disturb me anytime.'

It's the way you disturb me that I'm finding hard to deal with, thought Monica, as she smiled her reply.

De Wolf briefly looked behind him and saw that his 'clients' were slowly moving towards the unguarded marquee. 'I must get back,' he said. 'Call you this evening?'

'After eight would be fine.' Monica now knew that not only was there a fairy godmother, but she was also, in fact, directly related.

The moment De Wolf left, Harry was back at Monica's side. He offered his arm and drew Monica close to him. 'All right, my dear?'

Monica felt the tension leave her. 'Fine, thank you, Harry,' she said. 'Shall we sample some royal bickies?'

Bickies were also on the menu at Maida Vale. After the cleaning, the cooking. Samantha sent Nigel to the shops with a list, a kiss and a promise. She promised him the best chocolate chip cookies this side of New York City and after a day of sex and marijuana he felt he could eat the lot ... and New York City. Samantha also had a surprise for Nigel. She poked around in her suitcase, found what she was looking for and danced off into the bathroom.

Maggie Lomax had given up counting. Bradley Thompson had left for a photo session some half hour ago with a promise to phone later that evening. Maggie had no doubts he would, he always did. She lay in her bathtub, soaking away the minor bruises she had acquired over the last seventeen hours and gently rubbing her ample body with a bar of Dior soap. She washed her neck, breasts and stomach. She closed her legs on her hand and the bar of soap and felt a shiver of pleasure pass through her body. She thought briefly of masturbation but couldn't summon the strength. 'That's enough for now, my little precious,' she said, wishing that every man on earth could be as good as Bradley Thompson.

By eight o'clock that evening Maggie had floated through two hours of her show without the slightest hint of discourse to anyone. She had beamed into the station at half past five spreading peace and goodwill to all before her. John Thorne was the only one not fooled by Maggie's mood. He found her pulling 'Time In a Bottle' out of its sleeve in the library. 'Bradley coming to pick you up tonight, Maggie?'

She tried looking coy, but failed. 'My, my, we are observant, aren't we,' she said. 'Right fella, wrong day.'

'Good on ya, Maggie, it's nice to see you smiling.'

'You're a wee gem yourself,' she said, as she skipped out into the hall.

When the news ended at three minutes past eight Maggie continued her 'joy to all' programme. She answered line four. 'Good evening, CRFM, you're on the air.'

An East End accent attacked her. 'You're going to get yours, you slimy Scots sow.'

Maggie wasn't fazed in the slightest. 'You mean I'm going to win the pools?'

The attack continued. 'You know bloody well what I mean. If you don't stop having a go at this country's number-one rock singer, Flash Jack, we're going to come up there and cut your tits off.'

'I'll make a wee note of that. What was the name again – Flash who?' The phone clicked dead. Maggie pulled down the phone fader and punched up line eight. 'Obviously not a real doctor, but God knows I could afford to lose a few inches. Good evening, CRFM, you're on the air.'

Monica was listening to the radio in her kitchen. She passed the last call off as some ardent Flash Jack fan having a go. He certainly sounded thick enough. The phone call she wanted had not yet materialized. She looked at her watch: a quarter past eight.

Monica listened more intently, she knew the 'free-choice spot' was next. Maggie introduced Jim Croce and 'Time In a Bottle', calling it one of the best love songs ever written. 'Good God, they're all at it,' Monica said to herself as she turned the radio off and reached for the vodka.

Her phone rang.

One . . . two . . . three . . . four rings. She lifted the handset off the cradle. 'Monica Hammond.'

'Hello, Monica, it's Frank.'

Twiddle, twiddle. 'Hello, Frank, I see you survived the big tent.'

'Thank you, yes. How about you?'

Monica could feel a good game coming on. 'Fine, Harry is such a wonderful escort. He makes one feel so relaxed.'

'Monica, do you remember the other evening we talked about Paris and your apparent ignorance regarding that beautiful city?'

Monica remained silent.

'Well, I wondered if you would allow me to complete your education on that subject next weekend.' (Ace serve: love–fifteen.)

Monica bubbled inside but kept calm. 'Do you mean next weekend as in the twenty-first or next weekend as in Friday?' (Fifteen–all.)

'Oh, next weekend as in the twenty-first.'

I'm glad you said that, thought Monica. (Let call: first service.) She left as long a gap as she dare before answering, 'What a lovely idea. Yes, Frank, I'd love to.'

'Wonderful, just wonderful. We can stay at the George V.' Monica could hear the delight in his voice and hoped hers was not giving as much away. 'Do you think we could have dinner before then?' he said. (Double fault: fifteen–thirty.)

Monica allowed herself a small laugh down the phone. She knew this game was hers. 'Not a chance, Frank.' (Fifteen–forty.) 'But I *will* accept roses.' (Game to Miss Hammond.)

There was silence from the De Wolf end of the conversation.

Monica thought she'd be kind to him for the second time today. 'Balls please . . . my service,' she said, and gently replaced the handset back on the cradle.

Frank De Wolf replaced his phone, laid back on his bed and grinned at the ceiling. He now knew what game he was playing, he just had to figure out how he had lost.

Within the hour, two dozen long-stemmed, scented, red roses arrived at Monica's flat.

The card read 'One Game All – First Set'.

CHAPTER 7

While Monica and Frank were just starting their match, Anthony and Lizzie were into the third set, with Lizzie leading two sets to love. She had been very busy, or at least the estate agents had been very busy, finding a suitable love nest. Lizzie knew what she wanted: two bedrooms, one with en-suite bathroom, two receptions, one to be used as a dining room and, if possible, a nice-sized garden. After surveying several possibilities, she finally settled on a lovely little flat in a converted Victorian house near Swiss Cottage that met all her requirements and had its own covered entrance at the side of the building.

Anthony was somewhat concerned that this was costing him more than an arm and leg-over, but Lizzie persuaded him that all property was money well spent, that with the twenty thousand of his money she was about to invest in furniture and decoration, she would add fifty thousand to the value and that, if they decided to sell, say in two years' time, his half would be worth much more than it was costing him now.

She also persuaded him to make her his production assistant at CRFM, which finally got her off that damn switchboard and doubled her wages, to say nothing of advancing her career

First game, third set – Miss Stephenson.

To be fair to Lizzie, she did contribute considerably to the game. She spent one lunch-hour at the Roche Bobois showroom in Baker Street, found a three-piece suite that was perfect for the flat, then went to John Lewis and bought almost the same thing for half the price. She listened intently to the discount sale ads on the station, waited for the 'Last twenty-four hours – final reduction', and bought enough fourteen-pounds-a-yard carpet to do the entire flat for just under four pounds a yard. She persuaded a friend of her mother's to build her a six-thousand-pound kitchen for under three, and a friend of his to re-lay the back patio on his day off for three cups of tea and a leg show. Lizzie knew how to get what she wanted.

Anthony watched, smiled a lot and signed the cheques. He was very much in love.

The day after the Palace garden party they arrived at the station entwined around each other like a Japanese root tree. Anthony still had a few blobs of paint on his face and arms from last night's decorating. Lizzie was squeaky clean. Robin Trower greeted them as they crossed the foyer. 'Hello, love-birds, another lovely day.'

Lizzie saw no reason to be friendly to 'junior staff' anymore so ignored his greeting. 'Any mail for us?' she said.

Anthony's manners had not diminished. 'Good morning, Robin, I never thought I'd see the day when I would like to see some rain in London, but I must say we could do with some now.'

Lizzie grabbed the mail and Anthony's arm. 'Come on, dearest, we can't waste time with idle chit-chat.'

Lizzie was a lady in a hurry.

Brian Callaghan was also in a hurry and mightily pissed off to boot. Yesterday's meeting with the Aussies had not only got under his toenails, it had ripped them out down to the quick. He had been at his desk since seven o'clock this morning trying to plot some way to sink those Aussie bastards once and for all. His much-abused secretary arrived at nine o'clock, made him a strong, black coffee and sat down, notebook in hand, beside him. She was used to him looking rough, usually after one of his 'client evenings', but not *this* rough. 'What's the matter, Mr Callaghan, are you not feeling well?'

Brian was glad to have someone to talk to. He talked over the events of the previous day sparing her no details of his feelings, ending with what he would like to see happen to the entire antipodean race.

She listened intently and, when she was sure he was finished, delivered her solution. 'Why don't you set up on your own? We've got three stations now. I'm sure there are others who are as unhappy as you with ATS. Why not band together and form your own media-buying service? Capital have done it and I believe they're making a packet.'

Brian cupped both his hands behind his head and leaned back in his reclining, black leather desk-chair. He flashed a smile that only very expensive dental surgery could produce. 'Phone Monica, see if she's around, and Sally . . .'

'Yes, Mr Callaghan.'

'Stand by your desk, there could be some fast work to do this morning.'

Sally stood up and walked to her adjoining office. A thank-you would have been nice, but she knew Dirty Harry too well to expect one.

Monica was around, albeit walking two feet above her deep-pile carpets. In her mind, memories of the Queen, De Wolf, Harry, the Princess limousine, the Conran dress, the hat that fit, fused with the anticipation of Paris. She hadn't felt like this since . . . she had never felt like this . . . and it felt *wonderful*. The ringing broke her fantasy. 'Monica Hammond . . . Sally, good morning

'. . . That's fine . . . Right away, if you like . . . fine, goodbye.'

Within a minute Brian Callaghan was in Monica's office and busy repeating his Aussie story less some of the more colourful adjectives. He also put forward 'his' solution to the problem.

Monica listened and nodded in all the right places, while trying to keep her mind off Paris. 'Have you any idea who would come in with us?' she asked.

'Not at the moment, I only thought of it a few moments ago.'

'In that case I suggest you find some likely candidates and sound them out.'

'I'll get on it right away. Have you got any thoughts on who?'

Monica felt a red light flash inside her head. 'I thought everyone was quite happy with A T S. I'm afraid you'll have to dig around on your own with this one. After all, you know all the sales directors.'

'You're right, Monica, I think a few quiet lunches or maybe a quick round or two of golf might do the trick.'

Brian got up to leave. Monica felt another red light. 'One more thing, Brian. You know, of course, that I can't sanction this officially, not until we have board approval.'

Brian spun around on the deep-pile carpet. 'What do you mean?'

Monica noticed his irritation and was having none of it. '*Exactly* what I said.'

Brian breathed a sigh of defeat. 'You mean you don't like the idea?'

Monica wondered why so many men still had the temperament of little boys. Today, however, she could handle anything, including little boys. 'I think it's a splendid idea, Brian. Handled in the right way, it could solve a lot of problems. But you must know we can't go around enticing other people to break contracts with a powerful company like ATS without having our board solidly behind us, especially when we've been doing business with that company since Pontius was a pilot. What I'm saying is, go ahead and do some groundwork and find out who the likely players are, and when you've put the package together we'll go to the board and see if they agree. In the meantime, not a word to anyone . . . This is a covert exercise, Brian, and it will have to stay that way until *the board* wishes to go public.'

The word 'covert' struck Dirty Harry like an invitation to join MI5. He now thought of himself as the Captain Kirk of the media business. He gave Monica a crisp salute and 'went boldly' from her office to make his first phone call.

Monica phoned Harry Connaught and thanked him for yesterday. She also wanted to find out more about possible Aylford moves. Harry repeated what he said in the car but could add nothing more. She called Eaton Square. Simmons told her both Sir Peter and Frederick were not at home but Frederick had mentioned he would drop in and see her sometime today, and would she like a word with Lady Isobel? Not likely, she thought, made a quick excuse about being late for a meeting and hung up.

There was a knock on her office door. Monica straightened herself behind her desk and cursed Suzie and her damn cramps. 'Come.'

The door opened and there stood Robin Trower with one of the grubbiest human beings she had ever seen. He wore a very drab corduroy suit which was at least two sizes too small – Monica could only guess that its original colour was green – a close-checked shirt with one end of its collar turned up and a garish, striped tie.

He carried over his right arm a dirty brown raincoat. Monica was sure she saw movement inside one of the pockets and was convinced there was some life form lurking there.

Robin beamed at Monica from the doorway. 'This is Joe Mace,' he said. 'He's come to help with . . . the little problem.'

Not in *my* office, she thought. 'Mr Mace, thank you for coming. Robin, will you show Mr Mace to the conference room? I'll be along directly.'

Robin nodded and shut the door. Monica made sure there were no dirty footmarks on her deep-pile carpet.

After a few minutes' conversation Monica started to warm to Joe Mace despite his appalling appearance. His constant sniffing reminded her, for some inexplicable reason, of Eddy McLeod but he seemed to know his business, and since nobody except her and Robin knew of his existence, he just might be the perfect person to get the goods on Flash Jack. She told him as much as she knew about Flash Jack and his nasty habits, offered him a five-thousand-pound retainer to be reviewed on a monthly basis and suggested, in a somewhat direct manner, that he should invest some of his first month's fee in a new tailor; that is, if he wanted to be let in to the types of places frequented by the rock-and-roll circus.

Joe Mace not only wanted to be let in, he wanted to become a permanent member. Most of his life was taken up by the DHSS or following some poor nobody, hoping to catch him *in flagrante* with anything other than his tiresome spouse. To be part of 'rock and roll', part of 'showbiz' was something he spent sleepless nights dreaming about. He tried to convince Monica he only looked this way because he was 'under cover' on a job concerning diamond theft, but he wasn't very convincing and Monica wasn't fooled, even for a split second.

Monica gave him her personal cheque to cover the first month so that no record of his employment would show up on the company books, and also gave him her private phone numbers so he wouldn't have to go through the station switchboard. To complete the deception she gave him a code name, Mr Smith, with instructions never to use the name Mace in connection with this case.

Joe Ma – Mr Smith was very impressed.

Monica Hammond was just a tiny bit apprehensive.

The Honourable Frederick French was just a tiny bit hung-over. He was at home, but still asleep, when Monica called. Last night faded into this morning so smoothly that he hardly noticed the join. The slamming of the front door woke him at ten thirty-eight. He had missed breakfast and the usual morning lecture from his mother; it was she, in fact, who slammed the front door. He watched from the window as Lady Isobel and Simmons drove off in the Range Rover to raid Fortnum and Mason or whatever it was those two got up to on Tuesday and Thursday mornings. The maid didn't get past the second floor until after lunch so, at last, Freddie was alone. He danced a little jig, or two steps of one until his thumping head told him to stop. Even if he couldn't handle the physical part, for a moment, his spirit was free.

The radio in his bathroom was always tuned to Radio Three. He turned it on and heard the beginning of Elgar's *Enigma Variations*. He was strong in the faith that for once the gods of timing were on his side.

It took Freddie half an hour to get showered, shaved and suited. He intended to drop in on Monica today and see how she was progressing with the restructuring of Cornwall and Dundee. Although Freddie still held a small but festering grudge against her because she was given the job he so badly wanted, he knew it wasn't her fault and he did find her an exciting woman. He also thought his mother's treatment of her at dinner the other week was so shabby that maybe he could find another recruit for his cause.

He put on his favourite tie.

Monica was progressing very nicely with the restructuring of the two new satellites. After her interview with Joe Mace she stayed in the conference room and continued to build. The sales were not only bad at Cornwall, they were wasteful. She looked through the sales reps' dossier. There were no sales progress reports, no post-campaign reports, no profiles on clients and no daily call sheets. The only things that proved they could write were their expense sheets, which Monica noted was the only up-to-date file in the entire dossier. Dundee was better organized but their results were just as bad.

As Brian Callaghan was going to be very busy 'coverting' around the industry, Monica thought this would be a good opportunity to give David Westbury an outing. She scribbled a handwritten note to her sales director.

Dear Brian
Re: Cornwall & Dundee

In sales terms, we have very limited time to put a good rep team in the field. I know you are very busy just now, so I think it a good idea we send David Westbury down to Cornwall, to at least make a start on the training. I want him in place next Monday. Please ensure he has all the software and sales aids

*he requires and I would like a twice–weekly report
from you as to his progress.*

Monica Hammond

In programming terms, Monica had no doubt as to her
course. When dealing with stations this far down the
rating scale there is only one viable option. Top Forty.
She didn't like it. She never listened to stations that
played it, but it would guarantee a base line of listeners
she could build on. Monica ran a very tight Top Forty
format. Two of the Top Ten played every hour so they
rotated within five hours. All the rest, eleven to forty,
played in order with no leave outs, and the oldies, four
an hour, were former Top Five records. The DJs hated
it, but any one of them worth their company car would
never admit it. It was lowest common denominator, it
was incredibly boring to work, but it was successful
and, right now, that's what counted.

Her capital investment was a grey area. She wanted
at least one hundred thousand pounds to do a proper
job, but she knew she would settle for fifty. She could
gain some advantage here by cutting staff. In Cornwall's
case that was not hard. She could trim eleven from that
staff list without even setting foot in the place, but
Dundee was already down to the skeleton, in fact,
Dundee was a very efficient little outfit, they just didn't
have an audience.

The phone rang. Monica ignored it. She kicked off
her shoes. The conference-room carpet was dark-brown
tile with no pile whatsoever. She put her shoes back on.

There was a quick knock on the door and it opened
before she could reply. There stood Robin Trower for
the second time today.

Monica really didn't have time for more staff Brownie
points. 'Robin, I'm extremely busy at the moment,' she

said, looking at this smart young man over the rim of her glasses. 'Whatever it is, please see me later.'

Robin looked slightly embarrassed but realized why she hadn't answered the phone. 'I'm sorry, Miss Hammond, but it's Mr French. He's downstairs looking for you.'

Monica knew her priorities. 'Which one?' she asked.

'Not the chairman, ma'am, the rather large one.'

'I wouldn't say that too loud if I were you,' she said. 'He is the Honourable Frederick French MBE, and I don't think he'd take too kindly to being called "the rather large one".' She paused long enough for the message to sink in, stood up, gathered her papers together and passed Robin in the doorway. 'Give me three minutes and then send him to my office,' she said, and hurried down the hallway to where the carpets fitted her style.

She knew what Freddie would require to entertain civilized conversation; as he entered her office she had a cup of black coffee and a large brandy waiting for him on her glass-top coffee table. Freddie smiled at her as he downed the brandy and took a sip of coffee. 'My dear Monica,' he said as he flopped down on the settee. 'You have an absolute knack of producing the right thing at the right time. Something I have tried all my life to achieve, with very limited success.'

Monica was not too sure of Freddie. Unlike Sir Peter, whom she worked with on a daily basis, Freddie seemed a stranger and that bothered her. She knew he was probably, in business terms, the smarter of the brothers, and that it was his drinking that kept him hidden away at Eaton Square while Peter did all the public relations. She sat behind her desk with her toes slowly gripping the carpet and waited for him to open the conversation.

Freddie placed the half-empty coffee cup on the table

beside the empty brandy glass. 'I thought I'd just pop in to see how you were getting on with Cornwall and Dundee,' he said.

Monica had put the sales and programming files on the coffee table in anticipation of Freddie's request. 'The files are in front of you,' she said, pointing to the brown folders.

Freddie looked at the folders but did not pick them up. 'I want you to tell me,' he said. 'I can never make head or tails of all that computer printout rubbish.'

Oh, what a liar, Monica thought, as she adjusted her position in the chair. She started by telling him the current financial status of the two stations and within ten minutes had covered all the bases from sales to programming. He should know as much as her about Cornwall and Dundee – after all, he was a director of the company, he was responsible for putting the deal together.

Freddie listened, taking in every word. He picked up his empty glass and looked pleadingly at Monica who pointed to the cabinet on the right-hand wall. 'Help yourself.'

He poured himself another 'small' one and turned to face his managing director.

'When Peter first told me you were going to be MD of Cornwall and Dundee I was mightily pissed off.' He returned to the settee, bumping his shin on the table corner on the way. 'But I must admit, from what I've just heard, we definitely have the right person doing the job.'

A compliment was the last thing Monica expected. She expected rejection, additions to the plan, subtractions, advice, anything except a compliment and a carte blanche to carry on. The astonishment must have shown on her face although she tried very hard to conceal it.

'Why thank you, Freddie, what a lovely thing to say. Could you stay around all week and recharge my ego for me?' She thought a small joke might hide her embarrassment.

Freddie laughed and finished his brandy. 'I mean it,' he said. 'There's not another MD on the network who goes about their task with as much preparation and forethought as you, Monica, to say nothing of natural talent.'

Monica loved what she was hearing but wondered if there was another reason for his flattery. She decided a change of tack was called for. 'I may run my little radio stations, but I can't put together multi-million-pound deals the way you do, Freddie, and that, to me, is the real talent in this business.'

Freddie's mind scanned the Korean Bank deal with the ease of a forty-megabyte hard card and made a mental note to phone Kwan within the next hour and advance the situation. 'I suppose we all have our parts to play,' he said. 'Isn't it funny how the grass is always greener?'

'In what way?'

'Well, here I am, wanting to run two tiny bits of media, while you want to make million-pound deals.'

Monica walked, albeit barefoot, on the side of caution. 'As you say, Freddie, we all have our parts to play.'

Freddie relaxed his body stance and sank back into the folds of the settee. 'Monica, can you spare me a few days of your time next week?'

Monica's toes stopped moving.

Freddie beckoned to her. 'Come and sit over here, next to me. Let's have a little chat.'

Monica fought to keep her mind clear. So many possibilities, so many wonderful scenarios. She bought some more time. 'I think I'll join you in a brandy,' she said.

'One thing, Monica.' Freddie had raised his voice just enough to ensure her complete attention. 'Is this room bugged?'

Monica decided instantly to continue with the truth. 'It can be.'

'Will you please neutralize it?'

'Right away, Freddie.' Monica opened the bottom right-hand drawer of her desk, removed a cassette from a small tape recorder and placed it on the desktop in front of her. She took the brandy decanter and another goblet from the cabinet and sat next to Freddie.

'How do you activate it?' he asked.

'From the lock switch on my intercom.'

Freddie laughed and nearly spilt his brandy. 'Good Lord, so do I.'

Monica poured herself a brandy, but didn't drink.

Freddie told Monica about Korean banks, Swiss banks, old men who can't afford scandal, his friend Kwan, and all without revealing, exactly, how much money was involved. He also mentioned travel arrangements, and that was where Monica would be a great help.

Monica took a sip of brandy.

She was to go to Miami on Monday. Reservations would be made for a villa at the Key Hotel in Biscayne. She would await instructions from him as to where to pick up travel documents, legal papers, money and Mr and Mrs Runaway. She would return to the hotel and wait for delivery instructions, making sure that Kwan and Mrs Froggy, as he had now taken to calling them, were afforded every courtesy. She would return on Thursday with a new package of jingles from a Miami production company to stave off any questions.

Monica concerned herself briefly about committing CRFM to a jingle package she had never heard.

Freddie noticed the small frown appear and guessed the reason. 'Don't worry, you won't have to play the silly things, just change your mind in two weeks' time.'

Monica finished her drink.

Freddie poured her another.

'We need someone we can trust, Monica. It's very important to both Peter and myself. All you have to do is babysit these two and guard them from any outside interference. I don't foresee any trouble but if it comes you will have to use your initiative to get them out. If Kwan's family hears about this and manages to stop them we could lose millions.'

Her star was rising and Monica was thrilled. One small red light flashed in her head. 'Of course I'd be more than willing to help in any way I can,' she said. 'What does Lady Isobel think of my involvement?'

A cloud appeared in Freddie's face like a sudden summer storm. He scratched the side of his forehead. 'Mother knows nothing of this, nor must she until it is over.'

There was menace in his voice. Monica was sure it was directed at his mother. She decided to test the water. 'Is there anyone else I should know about?'

'You deal with no one except Peter or myself.'

'In that case, Mr French,' she said, delivering her best smile and hoping that the thousands of tiny thrills that she felt surging through her body were not finding their way to the surface. 'I am . . . at your service.'

For every action there is a reaction, and today, Maggie was the prime candidate for Monica's down side. Maggie's boiler broke producing a lukewarm shower, she ran out of toothpaste and butter, her milk was off and she'd just received a phone call from Bradley cancelling next Tuesday as he had to go to New York to film a

Ford commercial. She told him it would be wonderful and that he was bound to have a great time, but inside, Maggie knew that she wouldn't be as nice to the people on the phones tonight. A quick trot to the corner shop replaced her toothpaste, butter and milk. She stopped at the hardware store and persuaded the kind Mr Goldstein to fix her boiler in ten minutes, and not next Wednesday as he first suggested. On her arrival home she went through the 'find the key' ritual. She was about to vent a very loud scream when Mrs Hopkins from downstairs arrived, key in hand. Once inside, Maggie stopped at the table in the front hall to collect her mail. A gas bill, two advertising blurbs, a letter from Texas and a plain white envelope with her name typed on the front. She scooped the lot unceremoniously into her handbag and started up the two flights of stairs.

Mr Goldstein duly arrived. Maggie made him a cup of coffee and he set to work on the boiler. The letter from Texas was from her friend Louise. Lots of gossip and news, just what Maggie liked. She read it twice. The gas bill got filed with the telephone and electric statements with a sly promise to do them *all* next week. The advertising got binned. That left the white envelope. She opened it, and pulled out what seemed, at first, to be a blank piece of paper. On closer inspection Maggie saw one sentence typed in the middle of one side.

We know where you live!

She threw the paper on the desk. 'You bastards ... you scaly-back, parrot-nosed BASTARDS!'

Mr Goldstein ran into the room. Maggie was standing by her desk, fists clenched, seething with rage. He ran to her and stood between her and the desk. 'Whatever's wrong, Miss Lomax? What's happened here?'

Maggie looked into Mr Goldstein's cratered face and

tried to regain her composure. 'Nothing to worry about really. Something just caught me by surprise.'

Mr Goldstein picked up the paper from Maggie's desk, read the message to himself and carefully replaced it.

'Come and sit down,' he said, ushering her away from the desk. 'I'll make a nice cup of tea and you can tell me all about it.'

'I'm fine . . . really . . .'

Mr Goldstein had known this kind of persecution before. He stood beside her as she sat in the chair. 'Do you know who they are?'

She could feel his sympathy. 'I've got a pretty good idea . . . but on the other hand, with my job, perm any one from a hundred.'

'What are you going to do about it?'

'I don't know . . . nothing I guess. What can I do?'

Mr Goldstein walked to the desk and examined the paper and envelope. 'This was hand delivered . . . means they've been here this morning. Did you see anyone outside the house this morning?'

Maggie laughed and reached for a Silk Cut. 'Are you kidding? I didn't even see this morning, this morning.'

'Is there someone you can call, a police friend maybe? Someone like PC Campbell. He's our local bobby and a good customer of mine. I could have a word . . .'

Maggie lit her cigarette and took a deep drag. 'OK, Mr Goldstein, thank you, thank you very much . . . if you think it will do some good . . . I must say, receiving a letter like that, out of the blue . . . it did twist my knickers, just a wee bit.' She got up and walked towards the kitchen. 'I'll make the tea . . . by the way, Mr Goldstein . . .'

'Yes, Maggie?'

'Would you like a little touch of the light fantastic in yours?'

The old man smiled and all the cracks in his face turned upwards. 'I don't mind if I do,' he said.

If today Monica and Maggie were two sides of the same coin, Nigel was the edge. Getting up alone, the show, the swim at the Swiss Cottage Holiday Inn were all average. He was meeting Samantha for lunch. Things were bound to get better.

Trader Vic's was always the right temperature, regardless of the weather outside, thanks to a very good heating and cooling system. Nigel felt the cool engulf him as he descended the red spiral staircase which led to the reception area. A lovely Eurasian girl greeted him at the bottom of the stairs. 'Good afternoon, Mr B., your young lady is waiting at the bar.'

Nigel entered the lounge and saw Samantha at the far end of the glass and bamboo bar. She was wearing a simple white dress with no sleeves, her hair was tied on top of her head with a long pony tail flowing down to her shoulders and over her left breast she wore the gold dolphin brooch he had given her last weekend. She slid off the bar stool and put her arms around his neck. 'I've reserved a table round the back so we can be alone,' she whispered in his ear and led him down the three steps to the part of Trader Vic's reserved for people who are camera shy.

They had a superb lunch. Titbits to start, followed by Indonesian Lamb Roast with peanut sauce and peaches. When Nigel ordered coffee the waiter appeared with two goblets of brandy and a gift-wrapped box which he placed in front of him. Nigel looked at the waiter, who showed no expression at all, and then at Samantha. 'What is going on here?' he asked, with a devilish grin on his face.

Under the table Samantha rubbed her bare foot against his leg. 'Happy birthday, sweetheart.'

'Sam, you're crazy, my birthday's not until March.'

Samantha's foot progressed to his upper thigh. 'This is for last year.'

Nigel was glad the waiter was leaving. 'You didn't know me last year,' he half whispered across the table.

'That's why the present. I hate missing birthdays for any reason.' Her foot came to rest on Nigel's chair and her toe twiddling left Monica's efforts in an altogether different class. 'Go ahead . . . open it,' she said, her eyes dancing.

Nigel carefully removed the ribbon and then the wrapping, trying hard not to tear the paper. He took a sharp intake of breath as the label on the box revealed itself: Pentax Zoom 105 Super Camera. He knew this camera very well. Two months ago he did the voice-over for its commercial when it won European Camera of the Year. The 'average' had certainly left Nigel's day.

She gave him a slow, soft twiddle. 'Do you like it?'

'I think it's the best camera in the world. Thank you . . . it's wonderful.'

Samantha signalled to the waiter who came instantly, bill in hand. 'I'm paying for lunch too,' she said. 'It's all part of the prezzy.'

Nigel felt a mixture of love and lust run through his mind. 'I . . .'

'Don't say a word,' she interrupted. 'Let's go home and see if it works.'

The sun was streaming through the living-room window when they arrived back at Maida Vale. With one smooth movement Samantha removed her dress and left it where it fell. She opened the glass patio door, stepped on to the balcony and lay, face down, on the army cot Nigel used for sunbathing. He went directly to the kitchen fridge and extracted the last bottle of cold champagne along with two glasses from the freezer compartment. He restocked the fridge with two more bottles from the wine rack before joining Samantha on the sundeck. He stood beside the door and basked in the beauty of her body. Her hair cascaded over her right shoulder and hung in a fan over the side of the cot, the sun picked out highlights and made them shine like diamonds. Small beads of perspiration were beginning to form on her slender back.

'I love you, Sam.'

She opened one eye, the side of her mouth curled in a half smile. 'What did you say?'

'I love you, Sam.'

She turned over, her right hand shielding the sun from her eyes. 'You must be drunk, sweetheart,' she said as she sat upright, 'you've only known me a few weeks. I would say you're in lust, which is fine by me, but love . . . I doubt that.'

Nigel sat down beside her still holding the cold bottle of champagne and the frozen glasses. 'I know what I mean, Sam.'

For the first time since he'd known her she looked alarmed. She pulled her legs up in front of her and clasped both hands around her knees. 'I don't think I'm ready for this.' She seemed suddenly unsure of herself, fighting for each word before speaking. 'I didn't think DJs fell in love . . . I thought you were all much too busy worrying about your image and didn't have time for anything else.'

Nigel put the champagne and glasses on the small table beside the sunbed and gently held Samantha by the shoulders. 'I just want us to be together,' he said.

She slowly raised her head and looked at him. He could see small tears welling up in her eyes. 'It's not that easy for me,' she said. 'I just can't stop everything and live with you ... My family would never allow it ... I'm half-way through things I must complete ...'

Nigel realized how little he knew about this woman. He had never met her parents, he didn't know exactly what she did for a living ... he didn't even know where she lived. 'Sam, slow down. I didn't say anything about moving in, I don't want to change your life. I'm just in love with you and I thought it was time I told you ... that's all.'

She suddenly became in charge again. 'In that case why don't you open the champagne and put some film in the camera? I feel like having my picture taken.'

CHAPTER 8

Monday mornings were usually an effort for Monica but not this week. This week she was going to Miami on a megabuck deal for the Frenchs, and if all went according to plan, she would be back in time for a weekend in Paris with Frank.

She knew that if she was to stand the slightest chance of becoming part of the heady world of high finance or possibly even be invited to join the French brothers as part of their parent company she would have to change her attitude towards an awful lot of things. There could be no more petty power games with wayward disc jockeys, no more mini manipulations of junior executives just to see them squirm. No, from now on she must save her games for a much higher level. She must be sweetness and light to all around her and she must ensure the confidence of her subordinates. It would not be easy, but the rewards would be worth whatever it took.

There was a lot of smiling and toe twiddling going on at Cadogan Square.

She had worked through the weekend on Cornwall and Dundee; by Sunday night her battle plan was complete. She also wrote her quarterly finance report for CRFM, dictated several memos ranging from breaches in music format to overspending on the promotional budget and cancelled the maid and the milk. As John Thorne started the eight o'clock news she completed her final task, informing Eddy McLeod that she would be away for a few days to look over a new jingle package and could he please make sure that the completed staff expense forms were on her desk for signature by Thursday noon.

She had been awake since five o'clock, partly through excitement and partly because her 'dip' figures had shown the two Capitals were taking large chunks out of Bernie Bonelli and she wanted to find out why. She spent half an hour switching between Clive Warren on FM and Dave Cash on Gold. At half past five she tuned to CRFM and within two links she knew why Bernie was losing his audience. The crassness of his presentation slimed from the radio with every sentence. His contract was up for renewal in three months and Monica comforted herself with the knowledge that she would not offer him a day's work after that date.

At quarter to six she turned the radio off in favour of the CD player and Vivaldi's *The Four Seasons*. She packed her two matching Gucci suitcases with great care, deliberately leaving out any evening wear. Monica always left herself at least one 'shopping opportunity'.

Following her phone call to Eddy she made a large pot of fresh coffee as she listened to John Thorne hand back to Nigel at 8.04. Nigel sounded so good. He was warm, friendly, mature, witty, in fact everything Monica wanted in her front-line presenter.

She would definitely renew *his* contract.

The kitchen phone rang. She answered it after the first ring. 'Monica Hammond.'

'Good morning, old chap . . . sorry . . . Monica.'

'Peter, good morning. I thought you'd forgotten me.'

'Not at all, dear lady, we're a little behind ourselves this morning. Had a rough time getting Freddie awake.'

'Is he all right?' she asked.

'Fine, thank you.' Peter stopped to clear his throat. 'Monica, I have your tickets and itinerary. May I drop them off to you in, say, ten minutes?'

'That will be fine, I'll see you then.'

She poured herself a large mug of coffee and topped it up with a small measure of brandy to calm her nerves.

Peter arrived in exactly ten minutes. Monica opened the outer lift door and they greeted each other with a polite peck on each cheek. Peter walked into the living room and put the travel documents on the table. He looked so elegant in his pinstripe Savile Row suit. Monica watched him closely and wondered if Frank De Wolf would ever look that good.

Sir Peter turned to face her. 'Freddie and I are very pleased you are able to help us in this little venture,' he said.

Monica tried, unsuccessfully, to give the impression that this sort of thing happened to her on a daily basis. 'I think it's jolly nice of you to give me a three-day holiday in Miami,' she said.

Sir Peter understood about soldiers on their first mission. 'It's only a holiday if it all goes to plan,' he said. 'If something goes wrong you're going to have to fly by the seat of your pants . . . I'm sorry, hem of your skirt.'

Monica felt quietly confident. 'Freddie has briefed me well, I think I can handle the task.'

'I'm sure you can.' His face took on a sterner look as he sat down on the settee. 'There is one more thing I would like to discuss with you before you leave,' he said. 'Please sit down.'

Monica's confidence turned to apprehension. She concentrated on Sir Peter's face. Not the slightest hint of anything. He was so polished and she was such a novice. She dutifully sat down and waited for him to continue.

'Monica, in the near future there may be some changes at CRFM and as we have a few moments alone, I would like to put your mind at rest in case you hear anything from a third party.'

Changes ... third party ... Monica didn't like that. Put your mind at rest ... that was better. 'What changes, Peter?'

'We've been approached by Aylford with a view to a stock swap.'

Monica felt her world quake. Aylford on the board! What about the IBA? She must have heard wrong. 'Did you say Aylford?'

Peter saw the shockwaves hit her. He reached over and held both her hands as a form of reassurance. 'Don't worry, Monica, this won't affect you in any way. There is no question of them wanting, or getting, a seat on the board. In fact, it might not happen at all.'

'What about the IBA, what about Harry Connaught?'

Sir Peter smiled and patted her hands. 'This doesn't concern them at this time, it's purely a financial arrangement.' He gave her hand a little squeeze. 'Both Freddie and I are anxious to have you work closely with us, but you must trust me, Monica. I would *never* compromise your position, either personally or within the company. You must believe that.'

Monica thought back to all the times Sir Peter had stood beside her when she needed help. He had never let her down. But everything was moving so fast. She had to make a choice. 'What if I'm asked . . .?'

Sir Peter was two steps ahead. 'You deny all knowledge. I will keep you informed of developments on a strictly confidential basis and you'll discuss it only with Freddie or myself.'

Monica's confidence began to return. Now was the time for the big question. 'And Lady Isobel?'

Sir Peter's mouth became soft but his eyes remained firm. 'Just Freddie or myself,' he said.

All doubt removed itself from Monica's mind. She knew, in business terms, she would follow Sir Peter into the jaws of hell, so the jaws of Aylford would be no trouble at all. One small question remained. 'When you say stock swap, do you mean CRFM for ATS?'

'Broadly speaking, yes. Why do you ask?'

Monica permitted herself a small chuckle. 'Brian Callaghan has asked me if he can set up a consortium to go against ATS.'

Sir Peter looked concerned. 'What did you tell him?'

'I told him he could dig on his own but I could not support him without board approval.'

Sir Peter stood up, walked to the window and surveyed the pristine gardens of Cadogan Square. He turned and smiled at his managing director. 'Of course, you're absolutely right.' He clasped his hands behind him and walked slowly back to the settee. 'And the way things stand at the moment, I wouldn't give him a snowball's chance in hell of getting it.'

Eddy McLeod thought he hadn't a snowball's chance of anything this morning. Monica's phone call meant hours of boring work gathering expense forms from all the various departments, checking them through and putting them in date order so 'Her Majesty' could sign them on her return. On top of that, Brian Callaghan had sent David Westbury down to Cornwall to do a training programme, thus leaving all the sales department organization to good old Eddy.

His wife Judy entered the kitchen wearing the nylon bathrobe, her hair done up in pink and green curlers and carrying last night's hot chocolate mug. 'Good morning, Eddy,' she mumbled.

The tiny Scotsman grunted.

'What's the matter, dear, got a headache?'

'Headache, stomach-ache, backache, you name it, I got it.'

Judy came to him and started rubbing his shoulders. 'What's the matter, Eddy?'

Eddy spent the next five minutes holding forth about the unfairnesses of life, the universe and CRFM in particular. He called Monica every kind of bitch and moaned about how no one understood or helped him in that God-forsaken dung-heap of a radio station.

Judy stood behind him, rubbing away, and nodding her head from side to side in time with each new complaint.

'If it wasn't for the mortgage and the kids' education,' he said, 'I'd tell them to shove their station down the nearest drain.'

'Don't worry,' she said, stopping her massage and shuffling towards the door. 'I hear that Brian is setting up a new sales force. Maybe you can be part of that.'

Eddy had heard nothing about any new sales force and as he rubbed his head and drank his cold coffee he wondered where the hell Judy got her information.

In Muswell Hill, Joe Mace was sifting information faster than an IBM 2000. On Friday he spent four hundred pounds at the Next sale getting a complete new outfit, and thirty pounds at David Gale remodelling his hair. A visit to the Woolworth photo machine completed his new image. He cut off the best of the four small pictures and carefully pasted it on the back of a blank Stringfellows celebrity membership card along with his new name, Joe Smith. At midnight he slipped into the fashionable club in Upper St Martin's Lane in search of his prey. He felt horribly out of place. As he descended the stairs to the lower floor a balding man in his fifties with a giggling girl on each arm walked past him. He felt jealous, but it gave him confidence. He stopped at the bottom of the stairs to let his eyes adjust to the disco lights. In the round banquette in front of him sat the man he had come to see. Flash Jack, in the flesh. Joe studied his face discreetly and wondered what it was that women found so attractive.

Joe spent half an hour standing at the bar nursing a very expensive orange juice and gathering information. There were two older men with Flash and six much younger girls. He saw lots of champagne, trayloads of nibbling food and the odd breast fondle, but no evidence of any kind of drug. He followed Flash into the toilet and was well miffed when all he did was pee. He stood behind the pillar next to the banquette in hopes of eavesdropping on the conversation but the music was too loud. At one-thirty he left and took a cab home, the music still ringing in his ears.

It had taken him the weekend to get over the experience and here he was, Monday morning and still no closer. He looked across the breakfast table at his wife and thought of the balding man from Stringfellows. At least he had the guts to go out and party with the bimbos once in a while and to hell with the cost.

He regurgitated Friday's information over and over in his mind. There was not a single snippet that was any comfort to him. Only one thing for it, he thought, as he headed up the stairs towards the shower, I'll go out again tonight, tomorrow night, and, if needs be, the night after. Sooner or later Jack would slip off the wagon and Joe would be there when he did.

Joe Mace had worked on drug heads before. He knew their form and he was sure this puffed-up pop star was no exception.

Nigel's weekend was, in a word, glorious. Samantha stayed with him Friday night, and waking up with her Saturday morning was something he knew he wanted to repeat on a regular basis.

On Saturday they drove to Oxford and spent the day taking pictures of each other and messing around on boats. Since Nigel's confession of love, Samantha had become the perfect lover. She was constantly tactile, listened intently to all his plans and dreams and made love to him in the car, on the boat and beside the river. They spent Saturday night at Maida Vale. Samantha cooked a shepherd's pie which they demolished in the jacuzzi along with two bottles of champagne. They spent the early hours of Sunday morning watching Marx Brothers videos, taking more pictures and generally having a great time.

On Sunday morning Samantha complained about her lack of clean clothes. A problem quickly solved by Nigel's suggestion that they go to Camden market and buy some new ones. The market was hot and crowded. They didn't seem to notice, as they clung to each other and were buffeted between the stalls. By four o'clock they were back at the flat sunbathing in the nude, the newly acquired clothing, still in the carrier bag, lying in the entrance hall awaiting the sunset.

Monday's breakfast show went without a single hitch. Nigel felt strong, smart, warm and witty. His eight-fifteen free-choice record was Rod Stewart and 'You're In My Heart'. He got the voice-over dead right. When you're in love, everything is possible.

Monica Hammond was not in love but she also thought everything was possible as the stretch Volvo came to a stop outside Terminal Three at Heathrow airport.

She usually travelled in jeans and a sweatshirt to ensure maximum comfort but this time she chose a dark-blue two-piece Dior suit. This time her arrival was more important than her travel comfort. She intended to make the best possible impression on everyone, and travelling first class, both in ticket and in dress, was her first step towards achieving that goal.

The seat was large and luxurious, the food superb and the film was funny, Tom Hanks playing an overgrown child. It reminded her of Freddie and his tantrums with Lady Isobel. Poor Freddie, such an acute brain that could be rendered childlike by the temper of an old lady. She hoped that one day he would be able to break free from her and realize his true potential.

It was mid-afternoon, local time, when Monica's plane approached Miami. She looked out the window and saw the sun hanging like a large orange balloon through the haze of cloud cover that engulfed the city. Her mind crystallized on the task ahead.

The customs official inspected her visa, stamped her passport and instructed her to 'have a nice day'. She could never understand their cold politeness or their overstated uniforms. A cold blast of air-conditioning made her shiver as she pushed her trolley along the cold marble floor towards the exit. She saw a tall, Hispanic-looking man holding a card with the name 'Hammond' printed in Letraset. She introduced herself and watched a surprised expression appear on his face. He was obviously expecting a man. Monica chalked up a fifteen–love score.

'Welcome to Miami, ma'am,' he said, as he held open the back door of the long-wheelbase Cadillac limousine.

'Thank you,' she replied, stepping into another air-conditioned environment. 'Do you know where we're going?'

'Yes, ma'am, the Key Hotel, Biscayne.'

The car moved effortlessly through the rush-hour traffic as it headed towards the myriad of bridges that separate the keys from the mainland. The glass partition was down and the driver kept Monica informed of all the landmarks they were passing. They had stopped at a red light approaching the Biscayne turn-off when the driver turned and looked at Monica. 'If there is anything you need while you're here, just let me know.' He gave her a smile and a wink. 'Anything at all.'

Monica did not expect such familiarity from a driver, but she did appreciate a good game. She put on her most English accent.

'What, precisely, do you mean by anything?'

The driver laughed and turned around, watching Monica in the rear-view mirror. 'Come on, ma'am, you may be English but you don't look stupid. Anything means anything. Coke, grass, men, a good time . . . you know . . . anything.'

Monica refused to be shocked. She was in the big league now and no one was going to get the better of her today, or any other day for that matter. She just might have use for a man who was native to the city and would do anything that was profitable. 'I have no use for the things you mentioned,' she said. 'But I will be needing a driver who knows the city and can be discreet.'

'Then I'm your man, Miss Hammond. I can be as discreet as a Hershal curve ball.'

'I beg your pardon?'

'Sorry, ma'am, it's a baseball term. By the way, I can also get tickets for all the sports events in town at very reasonable prices.'

Monica hunted around in her bag for a pen and then realized she was in America. 'Do you have a card?' she asked.

'I'll make sure you have one before I leave.'

Monica pushed the button marked 'Part' and a tinted

glass window separated her from this 'helpful' young man.

Her villa was the height of luxury. Two bedrooms with en-suite bathrooms, a large reception area complete with well-stocked bar, a walk-in cloakroom and toilet next to the front door and a lovely balcony that surrounded the whole villa with views over the private beach and tennis courts. She chose the bedroom with the best beach view and set about unpacking her suitcases. She called Eaton Square and told Freddie she had arrived safely before abandoning her travel clothes and soaking in her double bath for half an hour to eliminate the last traces of the flight.

Back in London Maggie was also having a bath, albeit a single, and she was just as happy as Monica. Bradley phoned her private line while she was on the air to say his plane left at ten-fifteen on Tuesday morning, so if Maggie could get him to the airport by nine-thirty he could spend Monday night with her. She said yes without a moment's hesitation and was very nice to all her callers for the last hour of her show.

She stepped out of the bath, towelled herself dry and put on her favourite woolly nightdress. Another thing she adored about Bradley was that he was not into, what she called, costumes. She didn't have to put on stockings and suspender belts or expensive underwear and equally expensive perfume. Bradley was into skin-to-skin sex. Nothing added, nothing hidden, nothing taken away. She knew that he would arrive on time, bring a bottle of excellent French wine, listen to her talk through the events of the day, and at the right time take her in his arms and make love to her.

She set her bedside alarm for six o'clock and had just

finished drying two long-stem wine glasses when the door bell rang.

She would get him to the plane on time. She would also do her best to pick him up on his return in ten days.

Freddie was also making travel arrangements.

Lady Isobel was dining with a friend at Chester Place and Peter had given Simmons the night off, which meant the brothers could finalize their Korean deal in the relative privacy of their own home. Freddie had stayed remarkably sober today, just the odd bottle of wine with lunch and a couple of brandies to help wash it down.

The front-door chimes echoed through the empty house. Peter answered the door and escorted Kwan and his beautiful companion into the drawing room.

Freddie had placed a black leather briefcase on the large oak table that dominated the far side of the room. The Korean and his lady seemed apprehensive. Peter offered them a drink and engaged in small talk in an effort to ease the tension. Freddie looked at his watch and realized his mother could be home in less than half an hour. He poured himself a large brandy and addressed himself to his Oriental friend. 'Kwan, everything we discussed has been arranged. The papers are in the briefcase ready for you to sign.' He saw a small flicker of panic in Kwan's face. 'I know this is a big step for you both to take, but let me assure you, everything will go according to plan. The money is in Miami and we have one of our best people in place over there to make sure there are no slip-ups. I'm very envious of what you're trying to do, I only wish I had had the guts to do it when I had the chance.' He saw a slight smile cross Kwan's face. 'If you have any doubts about what you are doing, however small, now is the time to speak, because from now on there is no turning back.'

Kwan released his lady's hand and seemed to stand almost to attention in front of the brothers. 'We have thought long and hard on this matter, Mr French, and there is no way we can live without each other. As long as you can assure me that my family will not be subject to ridicule or, in any way, held to ransom, I will proceed as we agreed.'

Sir Peter answered without a second's hesitation. 'You have our word.'

'In that case, tell us what we must do.'

Freddie retrieved the briefcase from the table. Inside were two British passports, two airline tickets and several formal documents. Freddie handed Kwan the passports. 'This is your new identity. You are Mr and Mrs Bernard Chang from Edgware, you were both born in England and have been married for five years. Kwan . . . I'm sorry . . . Bernard, you are an executive of Colby Electronics in charge of satellite research. Inside the passport you will find identification to prove your status. There are also Visa, Access and a gold American Express card under the name of Bernard Chang. As we own Colby Electronics all bills will be paid by us and your identity will be secured. Tonight you will stay in a suite we have reserved for you at the London Hilton and catch a flight tomorrow for Miami. Upon your arrival you will be met by a Miss Monica Hammond. She will have travel documents and visas for Rio along with bank drafts for the full amount agreed.'

Kwan carefully studied the documentation. 'You have done an excellent job, Mr French,' he said. 'Which of these papers do I sign?'

Meanwhile, in Miami, Monica signed her restaurant bill and took a slow stroll back to her villa.

Tomorrow would be a very busy day.

Brian Callaghan's day was getting better by the second. His morning meetings with the Anglia and Birmingham stations proved more fruitful than he originally hoped. It seemed there was more than slight discontent with both the way ATS handled their national sales and the apparent lack of promotional campaigns for any station north of Watford. Birmingham's sales director, Peter Bradshaw, was a hardened Yorkshireman, and shared Brian's inherent dislike of anything Australian. He had offered to seek out other potential defectors and report back to Brian within a week.

His lunch was profitable on two fronts. The sales director from the Kent station pledged support and suggested that a London orbital sales force could be set up with CRFM at its nucleus. The idea held great appeal for Brian, as did the director's beautiful blonde personal assistant. He waited patiently until the call of nature overtook the Kentish man and then, within the space of two minutes, he had address and phone number logged together with a promise of dinner for next Wednesday.

Two more successful late-afternoon phone calls from his friends in advertising agencies nicely rounded off his business day and, as Big Ben struck nine, he struck another blow for chauvinism by convincing the newest CRFM director, Jemima Stewart, that only by going to bed with him would she *really* start to get the feel for what media is all about.

Whether she believed him, or was simply in need of a lustful excursion, was something between her and the small leatherbound diary that was her constant companion.

The noise of the air-conditioner woke Monica at five

o'clock on Tuesday morning. Her exposed shoulders felt icy cold and she reflected on how lucky she was to live in England where people didn't have the American preoccupation with climate control. She pulled the blankets over her head and curled up into a tight ball in an effort to get her shoulders warm.

There was a chirping sound filtering through the blankets. She pulled them tighter around her body. The chirping continued. She pushed out her right arm, felt around on the bedside table and dragged the offending chirp back under the covers. 'Hello.'

'Monica, good morning, it's Freddie.'

'Freddie . . . what time is it?'

'Time to wake up, dear lady, time to shake a leg. I can hear you've not surfaced yet. I'll call you back in half an hour.'

Monica didn't like air-conditioning or 'have a nice day' but she adored American power showers. This was going to be a powerful day from shower to sunset.

She ordered scrambled egg with smoked salmon, pineapple juice, toast and coffee. She was pleasantly surprised when it arrived within ten minutes.

Freddie's second call came as she finished her second cup of coffee.

'Monica Hammond.'

'Ah, that's better. Have you finished your breakfast?'

'Thank you, yes, your timing is perfect.'

'Is everything to your liking at the Key? I find it a splendid place. The service is very good.'

'Wonderful, and the views across the beach are heavenly.'

'Do you think our love-birds will be happy there?'

'How could they not be?'

'Quite so . . . well, let's see if we can help them on their way. Do you have pen and paper?'

'Go ahead, Freddie.'

Her instructions were simple and precise. She was to visit a downtown law firm at half past nine and collect a briefcase from a Mr Parkinson. She would return to the Key and deposit the case in the hotel safe. At noon she would lunch at the Cape Florida Room, where a table would be reserved under the name 'Richardson'. Mr Richardson would join her for lunch and give her further instructions along with travel documents and airline tickets. She was to meet 'Kwan and Mrs Froggy' off the seven o'clock flight from London, take them back to the hotel and phone Eaton Square.

'Have you got all that?' asked Freddie as he finished dictating the London phone number.

'Every word,' replied Monica.

In London, the French brothers drank a toast to Kwan and Mrs Froggy. They were very pleased with the day's work.

In Miami, Monica let the thick towelling bathrobe fall slowly from her body and stepped into the cubicle for another power shower.

In Korea, Mr Chin Wan phoned his son Kwan at their house in Belgravia. There was no reply.

Lizzie Stephenson put the finishing touches to a special cake she had baked for Anthony's pre-awards dinner. He'd been nominated for Best Radio Commercial – household division, and Lizzie thought it appropriate to invite a few of his closest 'Friends' from the advertising agencies for a quiet nosh-up and possibly to lay some groundwork for future voice-over and production contracts. The dinner was set for tomorrow night and Lizzie was ready, with twenty-four hours to spare.

Anthony was ready for bed. He had worked all evening on the Staybright scripts. He had to finish by Wednesday and so far not one decent idea would crytallize in his head. Monica was due back on Thursday with a new jingle package and that meant the production studio would be tied up for at least two days while they were transferred from the master tape to the carts needed for studio operation. He wondered why Monica was buying another package now. The last set was only six months old and they sounded great on air. He thought the main reason for her sudden decision had more to do with spending a lazy week in Miami than her determination to improve the station sound.

Tuesday in Miami was far from lazy for Monica Hammond. Her first task was to solicit the services of yesterday's driver. That done, she spent an hour concentrating on herself. Her hair was her first victory. It dried well and fell into place with the minimum of brushing. Make-up fine, just a slightly lighter lipstick than usual to blend with the suit. She chose one of the Pierre Cardin creations she favoured for board meetings and important client lunches. His cut was tailored but still retained enough flowing lines to preserve her femininity. She thought how well the dark grey and pink two-piece would blend with the black interior of her transport and was confident of success as she stepped out into the Florida sunshine.

Monica wanted to keep the advantage of home territory. She was sure Mr Parkinson was a totally trustworthy ally, but the thought of exposing herself to maybe half a dozen strangers in order to get to him did not appeal. She called him from the car. 'Mr Parkinson, good morning . . . Fine, thank you, the hotel is lovely . . . I'm about five minutes away . . . Mr Parkinson, I wonder if you would do me a great favour . . . I have another appointment at nine forty-five and I would be most grateful if you could meet me downstairs in my car to save me coming to your office.' It was at times like this when Monica proudly used every ounce of feminine charm at her disposal. 'If that creates a problem, I do understand, but I would be most grateful . . . Thank you, Mr Parkinson . . . I'll see you in five minutes then, goodbye.'

The brown-suited Mr Parkinson looked a touch apprehensive as he stepped into the back of the Cadillac. Monica greeted him with her warmest smile and her firmest handshake. They exchanged pleasantries about the weather, the summer in general and the well-being of the French brothers.

When Mr Parkinson was sure he had the right Monica Hammond he handed her a silver Samsonite briefcase. He produced a business card from his jacket pocket and wrote two sets of numbers on the back. 'This is the combination to the case and my private phone number,' he said. 'If you have any trouble at all, call me.'

Monica accepted both items and offered her hand for another firm handshake. 'Thank you, Mr Parkinson,' she said.

She deposited the case in the hotel safe at nine-fifty. At ten-fifteen she was sunbathing on the villa balcony.

At half past eleven Monica finished her third power shower, slipped into a light yellow summer dress and prepared herself for Mr Richardson.

*

The Cape Florida Room sparkled with brightness as she arrived, five minutes late, and sat down opposite her latest contact. She thought him to be in his middle to late fifties, probably still an active sportsman and, from the cut of his suit, very successful. They ate seafood and salad, and drank two bottles of mineral water. The conversation proved her last two assumptions to be correct. He talked of his love of deep-sea sport fishing and showed her pictures of marlin and shark he had caught off the coast of Florida while cruising with the lady in his life, a sixty-foot Chris Craft named *Miko*.

The business part of lunch was over in a trice. Just before the coffee arrived, Mr Richardson slid a brown manila envelope across the table. He explained that inside were two first-class tickets for Mexico City on the noon flight tomorrow and that he had no further instructions. Monica was surprised at how easily it was going, almost too easily. Mr Richardson invited her to spend the afternoon on the *Miko* for a short cruise of Miami harbour. She declined in favour of the hotel solarium where she had already booked a four o'clock massage.

By half past seven 'Bernard and Suzanne Chang' had cleared customs at Miami airport. Monica waited in the car while the driver collected them and their newly acquired matching Harrods luggage.

They seemed nervous, but too much in love to care. Suzanne was a strikingly beautiful woman. Monica felt no jealousy, just a slight tinge of envy at the way Suzanne beamed with excitement as she held on to Kwan's arm with the strength of a tigress.

Once inside the villa, the couple started to relax. Suzanne asked Monica how long she had been here, what was it like working for the Frenchs and didn't Sir

Peter have a nice smile, while Kwan wandered around the villa checking out mod cons and studying the various *objets d'art* that filled every free corner of the white stone building.

Monica gave the stock answers, but did agree sincerely about Sir Peter's smile. She took a bottle of Krug and three champagne glasses from the well-stocked bar, and handed the bottle to Kwan. 'Would you please do the honours? I'm hopeless at this sort of thing.'

Monica sat down opposite Suzanne and waited for Kwan to join them. 'I think it's very courageous of you to run away like this,' she said.

'Not so much courageous, as necessary,' replied Kwan. 'My family forbade me to see Suzanne again and neither of us could live with that situation. We have no choice.'

Oh, I hope you make it, thought Monica. 'I'm going to phone Freddie soon, is there anything I should tell him?'

'Yes, there is one thing,' replied Kwan, nervously fingering the top of his glass. 'My butler will think I'm missing if I don't come home tonight and he just might phone my father.'

Monica stood up and walked towards the phone. It was a hitch, albeit a small one. She began to feel useful for the first time.

Monica phoned Freddie's private number.

'Monica, how lovely to hear your voice. Is everything all right?'

'Just a small hiccup regarding Kwan's butler. Could call the father this evening or tomorrow if Kwan doesn't get in touch.'

'Oh dear, no, we don't want that. Could tip the whole damn apple-cart. Just a minute, let me think.'

Monica waited.

the effort of doing that at this moment was far too great. She suspected Ian wouldn't be very accommodating towards her either as he was Roger's best friend. Still, at the moment none of that was important. The fact she hadn't heard from Eddie was. It was all she could think about and as the days passed his bewildering absence was having a terrible effect on everything she did.

All sorts of excuses to justify his absence raced around her head. He'd had a dreadful accident; been called away urgently on business; a member of his family was ill – but never once had it crossed her mind that his lack of contact could simply be because Edwin Taylor was a selfish man who hadn't given her another thought since he'd said goodnight to her seven nights before after making arrangements to meet her outside the Belgrave Cinema two nights later. He would have met her sooner, he had said, but he'd to go away to finalise a big business deal. They'd celebrate his success when he returned.

She had been so excited and had dressed particularly carefully to look her best for Eddie, buying herself a new frock which she could ill afford, and nervously waited outside the cinema at ten minutes before the appointed time. And she had waited and waited. Finally at nine-thirty she had tearfully accepted the fact that Eddie wasn't coming and had returned home where she had sobbed herself to sleep.

A loud crash, followed by a thud then a scream jolted her out of her stupor and her face screwed up in disgust. Her parents' row was turning violent, which was nothing unusual. Why didn't they just kill each other and be done with it? she thought unkindly. No wonder her brother had been jubilant to get that job digging the foundations of the new M1 motorway. If nothing else it had got him away from here, albeit temporarily, and she felt her brother was lucky.

Suddenly the four walls started to close in and she jumped up as an overwhelming desire to be out of this house overwhelmed her. Creeping down the stairs, she deftly unhooked her coat from the wall rack just inside the front door and left.

Across town Eddie Taylor was a very worried man but he did not let this show one iota as he gave his elderly landlady one of his charming smiles as she placed a plate of egg and chips down in front of him on the frayed, stained tablecloth. The egg was swimming in fat, the yolk broken, spreading out all over the undercooked white, and the chips were burnt. It looked disgusting but was regardless better than anything he could remember his own mother putting before him. And most importantly to Eddie this meal, the same as all the rest his landlady had served him since his return to Leicester after his fateful trip to Coventry, was free to him, although the aged dirty creature who had cooked it wasn't aware of that yet. He had only five pounds left of the ten he had stolen from his mother of which in truth he owed all but a few shillings to Mrs Herbert for his board and keep, but he had no intentions of giving it to her. He knew in order to survive he'd need to lift a wallet or two and pray the cops didn't spot him.

'My lodgers don't normally eat in,' Mrs Herbert cackled as she fussed around, passing him the salt and pepper. I'm not surprised, he thought, as he began to tuck in. 'So it's nice for me to cook a meal fer a lovely gentleman like yerself. I don't get many like you, yer know. Yer'd never believe how some of 'em leave their rooms, and the state of the sheets . . . well, I'll leave that to yer imagination. A slice of bread and butter?' she asked.

The bread would be stale and the butter was in fact cheap margarine. 'Two would be lovely,' he said giving her a suggestive wink. 'And another cuppa?'

She gave him a broad, rotten-toothed grin. 'Comin' up.'

Surprisingly the food was quite palatable and he wolfed down the lot and eyed her expectantly when he had finished, hoping for a pudding. He was disappointed then alarmed as, clearing his empty plate, she gingerly lowered herself down on the rickety chair opposite and he instinctively knew she was expecting a cosy evening of chatter. Sitting in his dire room alone or traipsing the streets was a far better prospect than listening to her going on all night. He quickly chose traipsing the streets, aware of his urgent need to make definite plans for his future, which so far since his return from Coventry had eluded him. The thought of going back to legitimate work held no appeal. Besides, he doubted very much that he'd get a job without a reference.

Hurriedly scraping back his chair, he rose. 'Well, that were grand, Mrs Herbert, but I must dash, I've a business appointment.'

'Oh, business appointment, eh?' she said, impressed.

If only I had, he thought ruefully as he made a quick exit.

Hands dug deep into his coat pockets, mind churning, he walked aimlessly until he spotted a deserted children's playground – a black tarmac area with a few rusting swings and a frail-looking roundabout, closed in by metal railings – at the end of a run-down terraced street. Slipping through the gate, he gratefully sank his weary body down on a swing, absently rocking it backwards and forwards as he continued deep in thought.

Damn and blast Kelvin Mason, he fumed. If it wasn't for his double dealing Eddie would be well on his way to making a fortune by now. His hard work in getting all those backstreet garage owners desperate to do business with him had been a total waste of time. And all for the lack of a paltry twenty pounds! There was no getting away from it, he was at the bottom of a black hole with no apparent means of climbing out. To use one of Kelvin Mason's expressions, he was up the Swannee without a paddle, but worse still he had a hole in his boat and was sinking rapidly.

A great hatred consumed him for all the people he felt had ruined his life: Kelvin, Amanda Sutton and her father, his mother. What were they all doing now? he wondered. All sitting pretty, he guessed, with not a care or a thought for what they had done to him. His resolve to deal with them grew in intensity until it burned so fiercely it felt as if it was branding his very soul. He made a solemn promise to himself. He didn't care how long he sat on this swing, he wasn't getting up until he had thought of a way to revenge himself on those responsible for his dire situation.

A desolate Stella suddenly realised she was very cold. It was dark and she stopped abruptly to get her bearings. A surge of horror filled her when, looking around, she realised she was the other side of town. She guessed she had been walking for at least three hours, possibly more, and every second of that time her thoughts had dwelled on one thing or one person alone. Edwin Taylor. She had a dreadful feeling she was never going to see him again. She had made a complete fool of herself over him and through her own stupidity had lost everything she had

'Yes, I've got it,' continued Freddie. 'I'll send Simmons to fetch his evening suit and a shooting outfit. He'll tell the butler Kwan is going to Gloucester with us for a few days, that should do it. Now, there's a few things you need to do at that end. Do you have the brief-case?'

'No. It's still in the hotel safe.'

'Fine, leave it there for now. Do you have the air tickets?'

'Yes.'

'Good. Phone the airline tomorrow morning and change the reservation to the day after.'

'Is there a change of plan?'

'Not in mine,' Freddie said. 'At noon tomorrow Mr Richardson will pick you all up from the hotel and take you to a small airfield to the west of Miami. You will put Kwan and Mrs Froggy on the plane along with the briefcase and drive back to the hotel with Richardson. Are you with me so far?'

'Yes.'

'On Thursday morning you phone the airline and change the reservation again, this time to the Saturday evening flight. You then phone me and tell me which flight *you're* on and I'll meet you from the airport.'

Monica was impressed. 'That sounds foolproof, Freddie.'

'Don't tempt the gods, Monica.' Freddie knocked three times on his wooden desktop. 'How are the happy couple?'

Monica looked across the room and saw them looking out the window towards the beach, their arms wrapped tightly around each other and their heads touching. '*Very* happy.' She lowered her voice so they couldn't possibly hear. 'She is charming, Freddie, and he is so determined, I do hope they make it.'

Freddie laughed. 'So do I, Monica, but maybe not for those reasons.' He sat up straight in his chair. 'How are you coping? Is everything all right with you?'

She was touched by his concern. 'I'm fine,' she answered.

'Then look after them well and I'll see you Thursday evening.'

Monica replaced the phone and joined Suzanne and Kwan at the window. 'Everything is just fine,' she reassured them. 'Now, where would you like to have dinner?'

Wallace Pike was eating alone in his oak-panelled office at Millbank Tower. Longshore arrived as he washed down the last mouthful of chips with some Foster's lager, straight from the can. 'Come in, me old mate, wanna beer?'

Longshore made his way to the drinks cabinet. 'I'd like a stiff Scotch, if that's all right?'

'Sure thing, help yourself. How are things going? Have you cracked the French problem yet?'

Longshore poured himself a large Bell's and sat in the wing-back chair opposite his chairman. 'I think there could be a gap in the armour, so to speak, but it will be expensive.'

'It can't be worse than what we're doing. I spent a hundred grand on those two little piss pot stations and we ended up with diddly squat.'

'I have a feeling the French brothers are moving into television.'

'How d'ya know?'

'I don't for certain.' Longshore took a long slow mouthful of whisky. 'Peter asked me if we had any electronic interests in the Far East.'

Pike's mind snapped to attention. 'What did you tell him?'

'I think he knows perfectly well that we have considerable holdings in that area. I think he was asking if we want to sell.'

'OK, OK, but what did you tell him?'

'That it was not my area and he would have to talk to you.'

'Good,' said Wallace Pike, throwing his empty Foster's can with Exocet accuracy into the paper bin. 'How do you reckon that's a crack in his bloody armour?'

'Because when I wasn't forthcoming on the Far East he jumped right in and offered us a deal for ATS.'

'Jesus H. Christ! D'ya mean he wants to buy the sales outfit? Good God, man, that's not what I'm after. I wanna buy . . . not bloody sell.'

'Not sell, Wallace, swap. He wants a stock swap, CRFM for ATS.'

'Get away . . . How much?'

'Twenty-five per cent of ATS for five per cent of CRFM, and here's the expensive bit, Wallace, he wants a quarter of a million cash, with no seat on the board.'

Pike slapped his hand on the desk and slumped back in his chair. 'That pommie bastard knows when he's in the driving seat, I'll give him that. How much per share does that work out at?'

'Close to fourteen pounds, almost twice the market value.'

'That's highway bloody robbery!'

'Only if you take it at face value, I think this is part of a much bigger French plan. Getting them to deal on anything they have that much control over leads me to believe there's more to this than making a fast profit.'

Pike studied Longshore with reserved admiration. 'Go on then, what's your scenario?'

'I've thought for some time that Peter and Freddie

would soon sell out their interests in British radio. Freddie's ambition is more far-reaching than domestic media. For the last two years I estimate they have made at least a hundred million on their property and industrial interests which means they don't need the cash. Therefore, they are just testing the water with this deal. If we bite, it will stop the squabble between us, and will also make us the natural successor should they wish to dump the lot, which in my opinion will be within the next two years. Even sooner if we help them acquire Far East electronics firms.'

Pike opened another Foster's and took a healthy swig. 'You could be right, but it would cost us a bloody bundle if you're not.'

'Well, Wallace, you pays your money . . .'

'And you takes your choice . . . I know. I'll need some time to mull this over. When does he want an answer?'

'No hurry. This one is not on view to the general riff-raff.'

Wallace Pike swigged his beer and thanked the good Lord he had the wit to have Longshore on his board in the first place.

Monica had turned off her bedroom air-conditioning before retiring on Tuesday night, so Wednesday morning was considerably more comfortable.

She phoned the airline, moved the reservation, retrieved the briefcase from the hotel safe and by eleven forty-five had Kwan and Suzanne preened, packed and waiting in the lobby.

Mr Richardson arrived driving a blue Mercedes station wagon. He was very jolly this morning. Monica was pleased for the help. She joined in the merrymaking and by the time they cleared downtown Miami, all four were having a very loud belly-laugh about Monica's story regarding the 'dos and don'ts' of living in America.

Just before one o'clock they reached what seemed to be a military establishment to the west of the city. Mesh wire with a barbed topping surrounded the perimeter and there were armed guards at the gate. All but Mr Richardson looked worried. 'Don't concern yourselves,' he said. 'This is one of my factories. We do some government work here, that's why the security.' He waved at the first guard, who whipped off a snappy salute and raised the barrier. 'We have to go through here to get to the airfield.'

Monica was intrigued by the neatness of the establishment. A dozen or so buildings of different shapes and sizes were all painted in two-tone green and grey. All had neat white interconnecting pathways with herbaceous borders and the grass surrounding the buildings was cut and edged. She saw three people in white coats standing on a pathway comparing clipboards.

'Electronics,' said Mr Richardson.

'I beg your pardon?' said Monica.

'We make electronic parts here. Mainly computer bits, hard cards, rams, high speed motors, things like that.'

And the rest, thought Monica.

Mr Richardson stopped at the last green and grey building before another armed gate. Beyond the gate Monica could hear the whine of jet engines. Mr Richardson asked for Kwan's travel documents and trotted off into the building. Monica turned to face the back seat passengers. 'Not much longer now.' She squeezed Suzanne's hand. 'Almost there.'

The gate was already opening as Mr Richardson returned to the car. He smiled and waved to the guards as they drove through, turned right and motored up a slight incline. From the ridge Monica could see a tarmac runway and a huge green and grey building with a small green and grey executive jet parked alongside.

Monica made sure the couple were safely on the plane before handing over the Samsonite briefcase and a small card on which she had printed the combination. There were hugs and handshakes all round, a little tear from Suzanne and a little lump in Monica's throat.

She stood beside the Mercedes and waved as the jet roared overhead on its way to Rio.

'What are you doing for the rest of the day?' asked Mr Richardson.

'A little shopping, a little swimming . . . you know, the usual working day of your average busy executive.'

Mr Richardson laughed. 'Can I persuade you to take me up on my offer to show you Miami from the sea? I can supply shopping and swimming and add some lobster and champagne for good measure.'

Monica had a quick toe twiddle. 'Mr Richardson, I do believe you've talked me into it. May we stop by the hotel first?'

'Sure thing, and please, call me John.'

In London it was late breakfast time for Joe Mace. He was sifting more information and making a few phone calls, following another uneventful night at Stringfellows. When Flash Jack did finally crack, Joe Mace would be ready for him.

Lizzie and Anthony finished the Staybright commercials and contemplated an early lunch. Last night's dinner had been a roaring success. The 'Friends', always on the lookout for potential award winners, became 'Best Buddies'. They told Anthony he would be, without a doubt, one of the hottest copy writers of the decade and how lucky he was to have such a beautiful lady to support him during this time of fame and pressure. Anthony agreed, and Lizzie smiled as she served her special home-made cake with the coffee.

Maggie crossed the threshold of CRFM just before noon. An early-morning message on her answerphone from John Thorne sounded urgent, and Maggie was not one to let a friend down. She walked, unannounced, into his office. 'Now then, my little turnip, what has got you sounding like a ruptured goat this early in the morning?'

'Maggie, sit down, help yourself to coffee.' He spoke at his intercom. 'Brenda, no more calls, no nothing for ten minutes, I am temporarily dead to everyone except God.' He sat back in his chair and watched Maggie as she tipped four teaspoons of sugar into her coffee. 'That stuff will kill you,' he said.

'I'm having a race to see what wins: sugar, tobacco or booze.'

'Are you giving odds?'

'Not on bets I can't collect,' she said. 'Now tell auntie Maggie all about it.'

'Have you done anything about that prisoner story yet?'

She hadn't, neither did she particularly want to in her present frame of mind, but her journalistic instinct took over. 'What is this all about, John? I don't think you're giving me the whole story here.'

'I don't even know if there *is* a story here.'

Maggie slurped her coffee and lit a Silk Cut. 'I'll be the judge of that. Run it by me.'

John struck a 'confidential' pose, his shoulders forward and his hands clasped together on the desk top in front of him. 'Do you remember I had a visit from the head of news at Downtown radio?'

'You mean the camouflage kid, what's-his-name?'

'Sean Hearty.'

'That's the one. Yes, I remember. An expensive lunch on the company and you sold him some of our old machines.'

'They were new machines, but that's not the reason.'

Maggie dragged on her cigarette. 'Go on.'

'He mentioned, in passing, that the Brit police were thinking of cutting off the visiting rights to the high security blocks.'

'Serves them bloody right. Anyone who goes around blowing up other people should only have one visitor as far as I'm concerned. The one that puts the rope around his neck.'

'That's not the point. If this story is true, it will push on through all the way to the government and if I start running it now we will be weeks ahead of everyone else.'

'What's stopping you then?'

'I can't substantiate. The Northern Ireland Office won't comment, there's nothing on the wire and I can get piss-all out of IRN. The only angle I have left is to pick up something from your show. If you can get someone from Kilburn to say she's been refused permission to visit her husband in Ireland, at least I'll have a bullet in my gun and I can go back and fire it at the NIO and see if it hits a nerve.'

Maggie studied the newsman. 'You really want a Sony award, don't you?'

John's frustration flickered in his face and Maggie knew she was only half-right. 'OK, sweetie, now finish the story.'

'I don't think it's right that the last remaining link that these men have with real life should be stopped because the coppers can't get their security right. I'll grant you that a large percentage of them couldn't give a flying fuck if they ever see their old girl again, but it's not like that for all of them. If their wives and children have the courage to visit them, we should not take that privilege away.'

Maggie slowly stubbed out her cigarette in the freebie IRN ashtray. 'As I said, one terrorist, one visitor.' She sat back in the chair. 'But I see your point.' She dipped into her bag for another Silk Cut. 'I'll tell you what, rude boy. You take me out for one of those Sean Hearty-type lunches and I just might consider your request.'

John let his shoulders drop. 'You're a friend beyond reproach,' he said. 'Biaggi's?'

'That'll do me, Jimmy.'

Eddy McLeod was having no lunch at all. He was hard at work behind a stack of paper and cursing Brian Callaghan, David Westbury, Sir Peter French, God, and especially Monica Hammond, who, he was sure, would be lying on a beach in Florida sipping a pina colada.

Almost right.

She was lying on the stern sundeck of the *Miko* sipping champagne.

John called up from the cabin. 'Do you mind if I stick a line over? I think there might be the odd barracuda out here.'

'Of course not,' replied Monica. 'Will I be able to watch?'

John walked up the stairs, closely followed by two crew members carrying assorted poles, lines and tackle. 'You sure will, lady.' He crossed the spacious cockpit and stood with his arms folded on the sundeck next to Monica's feet. 'You can have a go, if you like. You might snag a big one.'

Having a go, snagging a big one, that sounded like broken finger nails and torn muscles. 'Thank you, John, but I think I'll just stay here, out of harm's way, and watch the experts.'

Much to Monica's relief, they caught nothing. The thought of a 'big one' being hoisted up on deck in front of her and ceremoniously gutted nearly put her off the iced lobster claws.

By sunset, the *Miko* was cruising at five knots through one of the many neat-sided canals that weave their way around the southern coastal side of Miami. The crew moored her perfectly into a berth, which seemed to Monica far too small for such a graceful lady. John helped her ashore and extended an invitation to dinner.

'You've been far too kind to me already, John. I'd like to go back to the hotel, freshen up and collect my messages. I feel I should call London before I make any plans for this evening.'

'I quite understand. My driver will take you. I'll call you in an hour.'

Monica felt safe with John Richardson. He was kind, courteous and generous to a fault, with none of the usual half-hidden sexual undertones. He seemed to be what he said he was, a successful businessman with a love of the sea, but there was a danger that lurked somewhere behind those steel-grey eyes that Monica found irresistible. She matched his friendly stare as he helped her into the back seat of the company Cadillac. 'I hope to see you later,' she said.

Monica let the bubbles from the jacuzzi tickle around every crevice of her body for an extra five minutes and gave serious thought to installing one of those marvellous machines at Cadogan Square. She patted herself dry and rubbed extra moisturizing cream on her shoulders and legs where the sun had done a small amount of damage. There were no messages from London – she didn't think there would be – but she called Eaton Square just to touch base. She told Freddie the events of the day and asked for more information on John Richardson.

She heard Freddie's laugh resound across the distance. 'Don't tell me he's tried to pick you up, old girl.'

Not so much of the old, thought Monica. 'Not at all, *old chap*, he's been a perfect gentleman. I'm having dinner with him tonight and I would like something, other than deep-sea fishing, to talk about.'

'You be careful, Monica. He has quite a reputation with the ladies.'

'I will, Freddie. Now tell me about him.'

'He's divorced with three grown-up children. His main business is computer parts and, as you know, he loves fishing. I know, to my cost, that he plays a good hand of canasta, if that's any help.'

'Hardly,' she lied, knowing full well that tonight she just might be learning a brand new game.

CHAPTER 9

The comfortable first-class seat securely enveloped Monica as she fastened her belt. The flight back was effortless; as the huge jet began its approach to Heathrow she reflected on her memories of the last four days. She hoped Kwan and Suzanne were safely tucked away in Rio. She remembered the Key hotel with its beautiful views and horrible air-conditioning and, most of all, she relived last night and the lovely John Richardson trying to teach her canasta. He was not really her type, in a physical sense, but she was hard pressed to remember when she had been treated more like a lady by someone that much of a gentleman. She was sure Freddie's warning was made from jealousy and not from any real first-hand information.

She cleared customs and was surprised to see Sir Peter waiting for her at the exit to the green channel. 'Peter, what a surprise, I thought Freddie was meeting me.'

'I've just dropped him off. He's on his way to Korea,' he said, taking control of Monica's luggage trolley. 'With any luck we'll have a result by Monday.' He moved quickly towards the main entrance of Terminal Three. 'We must hurry – Simmons treble-parked the car in a bomb zone.'

The familiar lights of London reflected on the shiny black Rolls-Royce as it glided across the elevated section of the M4. Peter inquired about Monica's trip, carefully avoiding any mention of boat rides or card games. When he was satisfied there had been no major problems he handed her a square flat package. 'The new jingles,' he said. 'Remember, that's why you were in Miami.'

They both laughed and he poured more champagne.

'Could I tempt you to a morsel of food at the Savoy?' asked Sir Peter.

'That's very kind of you, but I think I should drop by the station and catch up on a few things,' replied Monica. 'I'm going away for the weekend and I don't want to come back to a mountain.'

Maggie Lomax was busy climbing the mountain of prisoner reform as Monica passed the studio on her way to the deep-pile carpets. Only two callers had anything remotely interesting to say on the subject and neither was Irish. She had promised John Thorne she would do her best, but this was becoming ridiculous.

Monica's interest was nil in both Maggie Lomax and prisoner reform. She set about the expense sheets, internal memos and four days' mail like a woman possessed.

Maggie gave up on prison visits and was chairing a lively debate on wife-beating when Monica passed the studio again, some two hours later, on her way to Cadogan Square. On her arrival home she poured herself a very large vodka before unpacking, then repacking her suitcases, this time with much more La Perla than Pierre Cardin.

Friday morning was uncommonly cool for the summer of 1990. Monica had slept with her window open and for a brief moment she thought she was back in Miami with that terrible air-conditioning. A warm bath and a quick blast from the fan heater soon remedied the situation. She made a small bet with herself that Frank would phone at half past nine. When the phone rang at twenty to ten she doubled the bet and went for gold.

'Good morning, Frank. Did you sleep well?'

There was silence and then laughter from Frank De Wolf. 'Good God, are you clairvoyant, or have you hidden a camera in my house?'

Oh what a lovely day, thought Monica. 'Not at all, Frank, I've answered my phone that way all morning.'

More laughter resounded down the phone. Monica just smiled and wished she'd been to the betting shop.

'I must say,' said Frank, trying hard to regain his composure. 'I do like to wake up to a good laugh. Thank you, Monica.'

Her mind flashed on various one-liners regarding waking up, a good laugh and full-length mirrors. 'I'm pleased I could be of help,' she said.

Frank was finally in charge of himself. 'Have you had breakfast?'

'Just some toast and coffee.'

'I was thinking of sending out for some croissants and hot rolls. Would you care to join me?'

Frank had obviously planned the whole weekend down to the first and last detail. Monica didn't care, as long as she stayed in charge.

'I don't even know where you live,' she said.

'I'll have you picked up in an hour.'

De Wolf had hired a VIP car from his local mini-cab firm and at eleven o'clock the Granada Scorpio stopped outside a small but fashionable house in a narrow street off the Fulham Road. Monica stepped into the sunshine and instructed the driver to deposit her suitcases beside the steps. Frank's appearance at the door was somewhat of a shock. She only knew him in pinstripe suits and smartly cut jackets; to see him standing barefoot, in a pair of old jeans and an oversized T-shirt, made her feel a little overdressed.

'Come in, come in. You're just in time,' he smiled. 'Everything's hot and waiting.'

He stored the luggage in the hall and escorted her to the kitchen. Monica liked this kind of house. The colour scheme was a little dark for her and the kitchen was where the dining room should be, but converting old houses was not the easiest of tasks, and from what she could see he had made a reasonable effort to get things right. Frank piled the hot croissants and rolls on a blue and white Victorian serving dish and placed it beside the butter and various jams on the kitchen bar. The smell of fresh coffee filled the room. He gave her waist a little squeeze as he passed behind her. 'You look lovely.'

Monica let her head fall back on his shoulder. She felt his warmth against her back. 'You look as if you're ready for Blackpool beach,' she said.

He slid his arms around her waist and whispered, 'You have a knack of catching me off guard.'

Monica turned in his arms and gave him an oblique kiss on the cheek as she broke his hold and moved with sylphen ease to the other side of the bar. She didn't want to be that close to him, not yet. Even dressed in grubby clothing his touch made her nerve-ends tingle. She was determined to stay in charge.

He buttered and ate a croissant in the most erotic way. Coming from him, she liked this kind of sexual innuendo and thought briefly about strawberries. 'What time does our flight leave?' she asked.

'When we get to the airport,' he blurted, through a mouthful of pastry. 'I've borrowed a friend's plane for the weekend.'

Monica raised her left eyebrow. 'Nice friends.'

As Frank now knew about her little games he chalked up a fifteen–love score, poured himself a coffee and buttered another croissant. 'Make yourself at home,' he said. 'I must finish off upstairs and put on some shoes.'

Monica sipped her coffee and surveyed the surroundings. The kitchen was fitted with dark oak units and white tile worktops. The double sink, oven, hob and microwave were ergonomically correct and spotlessly clean. She opened one of the cupboard doors. 'Smallbone . . . very nice,' she said, quickly closing it, in case he returned. She buttered herself a croissant and added more than a small dollop of blackberry jam.

The sweet taste gave her courage to explore. She walked down the narrow hallway and into the living room. Two deep, black leather sofas, each side of a smoked glass table, dominated the room. The walls were painted white and virtually covered with various paintings and prints, mainly of a Victorian military theme, although Monica did notice the odd water-colour depicting scenes of tranquil beauty. An antique writing desk with matching chair took pride of place next to the 'real gas' fireplace. To the right of the desk a large book-rack covered the rest of the wall. At last, she thought, a clue. She walked to the desk and picked up a paperback copy of *Henry and June* by Anaïs Nin. She opened the book and started to read.

The powerful descriptive prose made her feel uncomfortable, at the same time sending her imagination into a dream of expectant fantasy. Monica raised both eyebrows, closed the book and swiftly replaced it on the desk. She scanned the bookshelf in search of the same author. Between the law books and the National Geographics she found *Delta of Venus*, *A Spy in the House of Love*, and *Under a Glass Bell*.

She was reading the foreword to *Delta of Venus* when Frank walked into the room. He was wearing a light grey Armani suit, a blue silk shirt, and a pair of black Italian loafers.

'Is this more to your liking?' he asked, doing a quick turn in front of her.

'Very smart, Frank,' she said, placing the book on the desk.

Frank looked at the book. 'Have you read any Nin?'

Monica felt slightly more uncomfortable. 'As in?'

'Anaïs Nin.' He stood alarmingly close to her. 'She wrote the book you were reading.'

Monica felt very uncomfortable indeed. 'That, I'm afraid, like Paris, is another glitch in my education.'

'You must read her. She is one of the most descriptive writers of her time.' Frank picked up *Henry and June* from the table and handed it to Monica. 'Take this with you,' he said.

She accepted his gift and, for the first time, took a good, long look at *Mister* Frank De Wolf.

The 'friend's' jet was bigger than the one in Florida. At least she could stand up in this one. The feeling of speed during take-off made her pulse race and, as they cleared the coast of Dover, she began reading *Henry and June* while Frank talked to his office on the two-way telephone. She eavesdropped on his conversation long enough to hear his opening remarks. 'I don't care whose knickers are in a twist. I told you yesterday, no work this weekend, and that's final.'

Paris was emptying for the summer. The broad streets gave everything a feeling of space. Frank and Monica sat in the back seat of a Paris taxi and held hands. Monica didn't usually 'hold hands' with anyone, but today, with Frank, in Paris, it seemed the natural thing to do. She gave his hand a squeeze. 'Do we get to pass . . . oh, there it is.'

The taxi swung around the Arc de Triomphe and

into the Champs-Élysées. Frank stroked her hair as she turned to look at the Arc through the rear window. 'It's beautiful,' she said.

'This is the Champs-Élysées,' said Frank. 'It means field of dreams.'

'What does?'

'Champs-Élysées.'

'Of course it does!'

'Monica, you're incorrigible.'

She held his hand a little tighter. 'Oh, I do hope so, Frank.'

The taxi parked at the entrance to the George V Hotel. Frank organized the luggage and paid the driver. They checked in and the porter showed them to their suite on the eighth floor.

Monica stood in the centre of the drawing room and tried to take in all the regal splendour in one swoop. It was as she imagined Napoleon would have lived: the ornate tables and chairs scattered over an embroidered room-size carpet which, in turn, covered a marble floor; baroque paintings, in carved gold frames, hanging on panelled walls; two sets of french windows leading to a large tiled balcony which seemed alive with fuchsias cascading down from several hanging baskets.

Frank tipped the porter and closed the door. 'What'cha think?'

'It's magnificent, just magnificent.'

'I want to make some arrangements for tonight. It would spoil the surprise if I made them from here, so I'll nip down to reception . . . OK?'

Monica placed her right index finger under her chin and lowered her head. 'Why, Monsieur De Wolf, are you thinking of sleeping somewhere else tonight?'

He held her face with both hands and kissed her firmly enough to allow no escape. The initial shock rooted her to the spot, but as he continued, she felt the tension ease. She put her arms around his neck, pressed her body close to his and returned the kiss. He was tender and loving. No hands thrusting their way between her legs or down her cleavage. He just held her tightly and kissed her, then whispered in her ear, 'Only if you lock me out.'

Monica held her head back and laughed her first real laugh in years.

Frank released her and walked backwards towards the door. 'I won't be long,' he said.

Monica walked to the window and looked out over Paris. Too late now, she thought.

Eddy McLeod was having the same thoughts in London, only he was thinking it's too late in the day to be working when he could be lying out in his back garden catching a few rays. He left the station by the side door to dodge reception and bundled himself into his Ford Sierra. However, with his usual bad luck, most of the other working inhabitants of London decided to do the same, and within five minutes he found himself near Shepherd's Bush, caught in the most horrific traffic jam, both he and his car engine badly overheating. He took a side road to avoid the mess and promptly found eight sets of road works and as many traffic lights. At one red light he saw Callaghan's shiny new BMW parked outside a small hotel. That in itself was just another minor irritation. What was a *major* irritation was the subsequent sight of Callaghan emerging from the hotel in the company of Eddy's wife. Irritation turned to rage as Callaghan gave Judy the keys to the BMW and asked her if she would like to drive. He now knew where she got her information, but he needed the job, so there wasn't a damn thing he could do about it.

He felt a bump and the hiss of escaping air. The Sierra had a flat tyre.

Frank De Wolf knew surprises like Lizzie Stephenson knew shopping. He returned to the suite, room service in tow, with a bottle of Krug, and assorted peeled and sliced fruits artistically placed on a bed of crushed ice. Monica finished unpacking and was about to test the bed when she heard the cork pop.

'Frank?'

'Right first time.'

They sat opposite each other as they demolished the fruit and sipped the champagne. Frank tipped his head back and let a slice of pear slide into his mouth. He squeezed open a fresh fig and slowly devoured the inside until the juice ran out the corners of his mouth.

How wonderfully rude, thought Monica.

Frank's thoughts exploded as he watched Monica do extraordinary things to a very large strawberry.

The second part of Frank's surprise was dinner. He changed into his tuxedo and watched the news on television while Monica finished getting ready. When she really wanted to impress, there was only one colour to wear. Black. The silk, knee-length Yves Saint Laurent dress slid over her La Perla underwear with consummate ease. She pulled her long blonde hair from inside the dress and watched in the full-length mirror as it cascaded over her shoulders. She added diamond earrings and her mother's rose-shaped diamond brooch to complete the outfit.

She stood in the bedroom doorway and waited for Frank's reaction. He came to her and held both her hands. 'You look beautiful,' he said.

'And you look very handsome,' she replied.

Dinner was a gastronomic delight. The George V dining room was full, but Frank's earlier excursion had secured the one table that was cut off from the rest of the room. He ordered the meal when he made the reservation and Monica was pleased that the embarrassment of deciphering a French menu had passed her by.

The first course of *Flan de cresson aux cuisses de grenouilles* served with a Pouilly-Fuissé wine, was followed by *Châteaubriand à la moutarde* accompanied by a superb bottle of claret. For dessert, Grand Marnier soufflé with demi-sec blanc Monbazillac. Coffee and a small goblet of numbered Napoleon finished the meal.

Monica reshuffled her priorities and put John Richardson in second place.

They strolled arm in arm through the lobby, up in the lift and into suite 804 without speaking.

Frank took her right hand and held her in a waltz position. 'We haven't danced,' he said. 'Our first night in Paris and we haven't danced. That will never do.'

'Shall I turn the radio on?'

Frank would not let her go. 'No work of any kind, remember. We'll make our own music. What's your favourite slow number?'

Monica fought to remember just one tune, any tune. Her mind wouldn't focus. Once again her shining knight rescued her.

'"I'm Not in Love", 10 cc – that will do,' he said.

They started to dance to the silent music. *I'm not in love* – Monica removed his bow tie and let it fall to the ground. *So don't forget it* – Frank carefully took her earrings off and put them in his jacket pocket. *It's just a silly phase I'm going through* – she kissed his neck and smelled the slightest scent of expensive aftershave. *I'm not in love ... Oh no* – as they reached the bedroom door he unzipped her dress, but did not remove it. *You wait a long time for me* – she slid both hands over his chest and shoulders, removing his jacket in one flowing movement. *You wait a long time for me* – he kissed her lightly on the lips as she loosened his belt and undid his top trouser button. *I keep your picture* – they fell together on the bed – *On my wall* – and took each other's love without reservation – *It hides a nasty stain that's hanging there* – until the music ended.

Monica was first to wake. She felt his arm around her waist, his hand resting on the swell of her stomach, the warmth of his body against her back. She turned over slowly and gently rubbed her breast against him. He put his arms around her, but did not wake. She felt between his legs and smiled in sweet surprise. In a single movement she sat astride his body and took him inside, swaying gently like a riderless rocking horse.

He opened his eyes. His hands moved up her body, caressing her breasts before locking together behind her neck. She lowered her head, her hair falling down to cover both their faces. She felt her senses focus and gripped him tight inside her. He responded in an instant; then relaxed and held her face. 'Well, good morning, Monica Hammond.'

'Well, good morning, Frank De Wolf.'

Room service was impeccable. They sat cross legged on the bed, wrapped in the hotel's thick, white, monogrammed bathrobes, devouring eggs scrambled with cream, caviare, small pieces of decrusted toast and large bowls of freshly made coffee. Monica felt happy and free, and that was the difference.

She hated relationships almost as much as hats. Not

that she didn't want one – but her ex-husband, and every man who went out with her more than twice, wanted to put a piece of her in prison. Not physically – she sometimes enjoyed a bit of prison after a good day at the races – but mentally, that's when she ran away. Monica preferred her games. They were safer. It was not like that with Frank. He just gave, sure of his own strength and politely confident. She watched him trying to put a tablespoon of caviare on a teaspoon of toast. She reached over the silver tray and pushed the lot in his face.

'You little vixen!' he said, trying with both hands to scoop as much caviare into his mouth as he could manage, before giving up and letting the majority tumble over his bathrobe. 'I have ways of dealing with errant females who dirty my clothing.'

Monica lifted the tray slowly and deliberately off the bed and on to the bedside table. She turned back to him. 'Promise?'

Freddie promised himself never again to drink sake, as he woke up alone in his suite at the Seoul Sheridan Hotel. What with the time change and the late night, he hadn't a clue what time of day it was and cared even less.

His first encounter with the old man had achieved reasonable success. Old Chin was a wily campaigner. He nearly caught up with Kwan in Miami. The false reservations to Mexico City threw him off the trail just long enough to allow Kwan to escape; when Freddie walked into his office the only question left in the old man's mind was 'how much?'

Freddie told his story and the old man offered four dollars a share.

Freddie opened at eight and settled for six.

The old man offered him more tea.

Today Freddie was a happy man, despite his hangover. He phoned his brother and woke him up.

'Good lord, Freddie. What time is it?'

'Haven't a clue, old thing. I'm totally disorientated in that department, but I've done the deal with Chin and I thought a phone call was in order.'

Sir Peter became fully awake in a millisecond. 'I say, well done, Freddie. Did you get the six?'

'I certainly did, and what's more, I think the old boy sees the scope of our business and is looking to us to be one of his best clients. He said he saw this as a deposit on future dealings.'

'Be careful, Freddie, after stinging him for ten million, you can bet he'll try for his revenge.'

'He can try all he wants. He wouldn't dare for a year after going public and by that time we could be elsewhere.'

Peter relaxed back into his bed. 'That's wonderful news, many congratulations. When will you be coming back?'

'I don't know.' He squinted at the window. 'It's daytime here, so as soon as I arrange the formal transfer I'll be on my way. I'll call from the airport and leave word of my flight.'

'That's fine, I'll see you at Heathrow. Goodbye, Freddie, and once again, well done.'

Lady Isobel pushed open Peter's door and stumbled into the room. 'Who the blazes was that, phoning at this ungodly hour?'

'It was Freddie. He's just been most successful with a deal in . . .'

'That drunken reprobate. It had to be him. Where is he? In jail . . . No, don't tell me!' Lady Isobel stomped from the room and slammed the door.

★

Freddie opened the door of his mini-bar, took out two brandy miniatures and did his best impression of Tommy Cooper. 'Brandy ... headache, headache ... brandy, aha ... ha ... ha.'

Monica and Frank sat holding hands and sipping brandy Alexanders at the hotel bar.

'Where would you like to go today, Miss Hammond?'

'Well ... I don't want to be a typical tourist, so I think we should start with ... the Eiffel Tower, then the Left Bank, Notre-Dame, Montmartre and the Arc de Triomphe.'

They giggled like schoolchildren.

'And, I suppose, you want to do all this before lunch?'

'Yes, most definitely, and ... oh yes, the Louvre. I must go there, I want to see the *Mona Lisa*.'

'She's not as good as they say, you know, and she's covered in bulletproof glass and surrounded by little Japanese men taking pictures.'

Monica laughed aloud. The barman turned and looked. She pulled Frank close to her and whispered in his ear. 'I don't care if she's giving birth. I ... want ... to ... see ... the ... *Mona Lisa*.'

'And so you shall, you sweet old-fashioned thing,' he whispered back.

They did, indeed, see the *Mona Lisa*, Notre-Dame and the Left Bank where they stopped to have lunch at an outdoor Parisian café. In the afternoon they had planned for the Arc and the Tower, but their plans went a bit astray once Monica saw the shops along the Champs-Élysées. By half past four they were back at the George V loaded with six carrier bags.

They struggled into the suite and flopped, exhausted,

on the bed, lying still while they regained their strength. They turned to face each other and exchanged a tender kiss. Frank was the first to speak. 'Bath?'

'Bath,' said Monica, jumping to her feet. 'Perfect!'

Monica loved that bathroom. She thought the marble would be cold and inhospitable, but although the en-suite was marble from floor to ceiling, the under-floor heating made it feel warm and cosy, and more than a bit erotic. Frank filled the bath and added some bubbles from the courtesy bath pack. Monica jumped in at the non-tap end.

Frank stood naked beside the bidet. 'That's not fair, I ran the bath, I should get the good end.'

'Whoever said anything about fair?' said Monica, turning to face him, both hands cupped under her breasts. 'I didn't hear fair. Did you hear fair?' she said, addressing her remark to her left breast.

Frank held his nose and jumped, bum first, into the tub. The water splashed everywhere, on the floor, in the bidet and, to her complete shock, right over Monica's head.

'Now look what you've done,' she said. 'My hair is ruined.'

'Fits your reputation,' he replied.

Monica swung her fists at him with all her might. He grabbed her wrists and stopped her dead in her tracks. They sat, soaking wet, staring at each other, both of them trying very hard not to laugh.

'Do you mind if I fall just a little in love with you?' he asked.

She gently slid her hands around his neck. 'No, I don't mind, Frank . . . I don't mind at all.'

They had dinner at a small restaurant in Montmartre. They ate mussels in tomato sauce, lamb casserole and freshly made ice-cream. They drank far too much house wine, but compensated by not having any brandy with the coffee. The view from the restaurant was magnificent. The whole of Paris stretched out below them. They tried to spot the George V. Frank found the Arc de Triomphe and pointed to a spot just south of it. 'I think that's us,' he said. 'Just there, the orange light.'

'Is that the hotel or the suite?' They laughed. Monica stroked the back of his head. 'By the way,' she whispered, 'I love you too.'

Frank turned, very slowly, and kissed her forehead. 'I think we should go back to the orange light and discuss the consequences of that last remark,' he said.

There was no view of the outside from Stringfellows, but Joe Mace was getting more than an eyeful from all the assorted bimbettes on the dance floor. This was his third visit and the home crowd thought he must be some big record-company executive or business manager to be frequenting their watering hole on such a regular basis. A few of them tried to start a conversation and a couple of them brushed against him trying for nipple contact, but he ignored them all and kept his attention on the job at hand. Jack was there tonight, as usual, with his constant bevy of beauties, but he seemed uninterested in the company; Joe was getting more frustrated by the minute.

Jack excused himself and headed for the toilet and Joe dutifully followed. Jack went into the first cubicle while Joe washed his hands and kept an ear cocked for any telltale sniffing. They both ended up at the same hand-drier, Jack looking at himself in the small mirror and Joe sniffing away to try and clear his sinuses.

Jack stopped admiring himself and looked across at the sniffing detective. 'Have you got any more of that stuff or is it all up your nose?' he asked.

Joe's years of experience allowed him to keep a straight face. 'I've got lots of it,' he said. 'Who's asking?'

Jack's face lit up like a Christmas tree. 'John Featherstone,' he said. 'Also known as Flash Jack. Singer, writer, producer, all-round good guy and at this moment, bored to tears.'

Joe held out his hand. 'Pleased to meet you. I'm Joe Smith, all-round bad guy and purveyor of just about anything you like.'

Jack shook his hand and had a quick look around the room to make sure they were alone. 'Listen, what are you holding? Got any coke? Can I score off you right now?'

Joe started the hand-drier, as if to cover the conversation. 'I don't travel with it . . . you understand . . . but, as it happens, I'm off to a party with a couple of ladies who have just received a shipment of fine Peruvian Flake.'

Jack's eyes glazed over. He grabbed Joe's arm like a man about to drown. 'That sounds brilliant. Can I come with you or can I meet you there?'

'What about your friends? I can't invite the whole world. These ladies are very selective, to say nothing of horny when they've done a gram or two. I don't want a gang-bang on my record. Bad for business . . . you understand.'

Jack held Joe's arm even tighter. 'Give me five minutes. I'll meet you outside the Hippodrome.'

Oh how easy you are, thought Joe, as he pretended to think. 'OK, Mr Jack, you're on. Give me ten minutes. I'll meet you outside the Hip and we'll go party.'

Jack left to sort out his hangers-on.

Joe made a quick phone call.

★

At just past midnight they arrived at the Water Gardens off the Edgware Road. Jack was nervous and twitchy, Joe was quietly smiling. It wasn't often he got laid and paid on the same job.

Janet and Sally occupied the top left penthouse in the first tower of the Water Gardens. It didn't belong to them, it came with the job. They were high-class hookers who had crossed Joe's path on a previous job and tonight they were on a grand each plus expenses to show this rock star a good time. Janet answered the door holding a small mirror and a McDonald's straw, and wearing a very low-cut dress. Joe knew he would have to participate in all the goodies in order to prove his credibility, but as the alternative was Muswell Hill and his wife, the prospect was far from repulsive. They snorted coke, smoked joints and, as Sally gave Joe a wild and frantic hand-job on the kitchen table, he blessed his luck and hoped the tape recorder was still working.

In suite 804 at the George V, Monica held her sleeping lover close to her and gently kissed his cheek. 'So much for staying in charge,' she said softly, and slowly closed her eyes.

Frank woke early on Sunday morning and got quietly out of bed leaving Monica asleep, clutching the duvet around her waist. He walked tiptoe from the bedroom so as not to wake her and closed the door gently behind him. He called room service from the drawing room and made his request. The service manager reminded him it was Sunday, but assured him he would do his best.

Twenty minutes later there was a quiet knock on the door.

Frank helped the waiter pull the serving trolley over the door sill. Camembert, Brie, Pont l'Eveque, Roquefort, Epoisses and St Marcellin cheeses were neatly arranged on a large wooden board on top of the trolley. The board was surrounded by croissants and alongside, four warm baguettes stood smartly to attention in their wicker holder. At one end of the trolley a ceramic coffee pot stood shoulder to shoulder with a glass jug full of freshly squeezed orange juice. On the lower deck was an ice-bucket containing a bottle of Dom Perignon 1978 and two crystal glasses.

The waiter went out of the room and returned a few seconds later with a large silver vase containing two dozen long-stemmed roses.

Frank gave him a hundred-franc tip and closed the door quietly behind him. He pushed the trolley into the bedroom and parked it on Monica's side of the bed. He placed the roses on the table beside her. She was still asleep. Frank watched her breasts rise and fall with her steady breathing. He studied the angular beauty of her face and the silhouette of her legs under the covers. Even in repose, Monica was a very stunning lady. He removed the bottle of Dom Perignon from the ice bucket, removed the top wire and started to ease out the cork. It left the bottle with considerable speed and a loud bang, denting the ceiling just to the right of the chandelier.

Monica sat bolt upright in the bed.

Frank was smart enough to keep the trolley between himself and Monica, just in case her reaction was the same as yesterday's bath splash. 'Good morning, sweetheart, did you sleep well?'

'Frank! You . . .' She focused on the trolley loaded with goodies and then the roses on her bedside table. 'You wonderful, wonderful man.' She held out her arms to him. 'Come here.'

He was reluctant to move from behind the safety of the trolley.

'This instant!'

Joe Mace woke up with a runny nose and a king-size headache. He didn't remember getting back to Muswell Hill, in fact, he didn't remember much past two a.m. He looked over to his bedside table and saw three cassettes neatly stacked beside the phone. He forced a smile. He looked at the snoring wife beside him and thought of Sally. He knew the job was done. He knew he'd got Flash Jack. He rolled over and went back to sleep.

CHAPTER 10

At six o'clock Monday morning a personal best was being achieved by the Honourable Frederick French MBE.

He was showered, shaved, suited and sober. The time change, East to West, had something to do with this phenomenon, but it was not the whole story. He walked, with a certain determination, down the main stairs of Eaton Square towards the entrance hall. He stopped halfway down and looked up at the picture of his great-grandfather the Brigadier General Sir Reginald French KBE, DSO and Bar. 'I wonder if you would approve of what I've done, Sir Reg,' he said, giving the old boy a jaunty salute then changing it into a two-fingered gesture. 'Nossir, you would have started a war, killed thousands of people and then invested in the funeral business.' Freddie continued his lively step and called back to the picture, 'Sorry, old chap, things don't work like that any more.'

He walked down the hall and into the kitchen. Simmons and company were not due until half past six and Freddie took full advantage of the empty kitchen. He made coffee, scrambled eggs, fried bacon and burned some toast. His manner was relaxed as he sat at the large pine table and ate his breakfast. Simmons appeared at the kitchen door, bade him good morning and inquired if he was all right.

'Bloody marvellous, thank you, Simmons. And your good self?'

Simmons reacted as if he had found the 'Honourable' in this situation every day for the last twenty years.

'Very well, thank you, sir. Will you be lunching at home today?'

'No, I won't,' replied Freddie. 'But I will be driving the Aston Martin. Would you please bring it round from the mews.'

'What time will you be needing it, sir?'

'Right away, please.' The butler turned to leave. 'One more thing, please let it warm up for a couple of minutes before you drive it. It's not been run for a while.'

Freddie drove on to the M4 just before seven o'clock. The traffic was building up on the town-bound side, but Freddie was heading out and the road was relatively clear. He hadn't driven the Aston for a good few months. It was a DB 4 Vantage, sage green with red upholstery, and Freddie's favourite form of transport. As he passed the Heston service area he opened the throttle and clocked a quick ton before the Hayes turn-off.

He didn't know if it was the thought of Kwan and Mrs Froggy making their getaway to a better life, or the ten million dollars' profit that made him feel so good, but today Freddie French was a winner. Much more than that, Freddie French was a winner on his own terms. As he geared down for the M25 interchange he pondered on what would be the most appropriate reward to give Monica Hammond for her part in the affair.

In Paris, Monica's weekend affair was coming to an end. They woke up at five o'clock and made love until half past six. De Wolf had an appointment in London at ten, so they scrambled from the hotel by half seven and arrived at Charles de Gaulle by eight. Frank dropped her at Cadogan Square at half past nine with a kiss and an invitation to dinner at Fulham.

She unpacked her suitcases and felt a mixture of sadness and joy. Sadness because the weekend was over and already she was missing Frank; joy for the realization that maybe, just maybe, Frank De Wolf could offer more than sexual gratification and a gold Amex card.

Monica arrived at CRFM just before eleven o'clock and went straight to her office. She blotted out all thoughts of Frank, Paris, the George V, and strawberries from her mind. Her first business thought was of Freddie and the Korean deal. Had he returned? Did it all go according to plan? She was sure he would be in touch. Cornwall and Dundee occupied her mind only briefly, she was confident her outline would be acceptable to the board in its present form.

Her private phone rang. Sure it was Frank, she picked up the phone with some excitement. 'Monica Hammond.'

'Monica, good morning, Harry Connaught.'

Monica's heart sank just a little but she didn't let it show. 'Harry, how lovely to hear from you. Are you well?'

'In a manner of speaking, Monica. I have a small problem with your news this morning.'

Monica knew she was totally unarmed. 'I'm terribly sorry, Harry, I've been away for the weekend. I just arrived at the office ten minutes ago, I'm afraid I haven't heard the station all morning. What seems to be the problem?'

'Your news carried a story regarding Ireland. From what I gather, it was unsubstantiated and could have breached the code in more than one place. Do you think you could look into it for me and ring me back?'

'Right away, Harry, I'll call you straight back.' Monica replaced the phone and gritted her teeth in anger. She pushed her station intercom button. 'John Thorne to my office . . . NOW!'

John dutifully arrived within a minute. He took one look at Monica and guessed the situation. 'This must be the IBA complaining about the Irish story. Am I right?'

'You certainly are.' She pointed at the seat opposite her desk. 'Sit down, John, and tell me the whole story, and I mean the *whole* story.'

John told her of the jail visits, the government's reluctance to talk, Maggie's phone-in, his thoughts on the subject and concluded by telling her that if the IBA were sounding off so early, it must mean that there was something to hide.

Monica listened intently to the entire saga. When John had finished she sat back in her chair, crossed her arms in front of her and stared at him over the rim of her glasses. 'I cannot believe that a man with your experience could even entertain letting a story like that go out without, not only substantiation, but also a clean bill of health from the IBA,' she said. 'Have you any idea what they could do to us?'

John had an idea, all right. He knew the ground beneath him could turn to jelly at any time. He knew he was bending the rules. He also knew Monica was away for the weekend, so he took a calculated risk this morning. A calculated risk that had just come back on him like a ton of Irish peat. 'I have it on very good authority that this story is happening now, just the way I reported it,' he said.

'Where did you get your information?'

'I have a very good source in Belfast.'

Monica took a deep breath, held it for a few seconds and slowly let it out in John's direction. She spoke in a slow, deliberate and very menacing way. 'What you have done, Mr Thorne, is break every rule in the book and you have put this station in the gravest jeopardy. Unless you tell me *immediately* who your informant is and what, if any, his or her connection is in this matter, you may consider your contract with this station terminated as of this second.'

John decided attack was the best form of defence. 'I have it on good authority that . . .'

Monica slammed her hand down on the desk. 'Damn you, Thorne, I don't give a shit if it's the Pope. I want a name, and I want it now!'

John saw unemployment staring him in the face. He hated Monica for being so damn . . . Monica, and he hated himself for being such a coward. 'Sean Hearty,' he said.

'As in Downtown Radio?'

'Yes.'

Monica relaxed in her chair. 'That's better,' she said. 'Now go away and find me some good *local* stories and leave the world of international politics to those who understand it.'

John fought against the urge to tell her just where to put her job, station and the small statue of the Eiffel Tower that adorned the top of her desk. He said nothing.

'Well, what are you waiting for?' she asked. 'There's no story here except your imminent departure if you don't get out of my sight this instant.'

John stood up and walked towards the door.

'Another thing,' spat Monica. 'We are an entertainment station. We also supply a news service of local interest. If you have a problem with that, I suggest you apply to the world service, although I doubt they would give you a second chance.'

John Thorne neither recognized, nor answered, her

last statement. He walked out of the office and slammed the door.

Monica phoned Harry Connaught and relayed the source of the story.

'Thank goodness this is not a regular occurrence,' said Harry, in a very official tone of voice. 'CRFM have such a good record, I would not like to see this sort of thing happen too often. Maybe it's time you got your newsroom to re-read the rule book.'

Damn you, John Thorne, thought Monica. She did not relish being told off like a schoolgirl who had not done her homework, especially when she had nothing to do with the crime. 'Thank you for being so understanding,' she said. 'I can assure you this will not happen again.'

Suzie bounced into the office. 'I've brought you a fresh coffee,' she said. 'And here is the rest of your mail.'

Monica received both with thanks and watched her fragile secretary leave the room. She thumbed through the messages until she found the one she was looking for. *Ring Mr Smith – Urgent*. She phoned Joe Mace and arranged to meet him at Cadogan Square, four o'clock that afternoon. Her intercom buzzed. She flicked it on. 'Yes.'

'Miss Hammond, Mr Freddie French called while you were on the phone. He wants to know if you would be so kind as to feed him lunch today.'

Monica quietly cursed her timing. 'Did he leave a number?'

'Yes, Miss Hammond, a mobile phone.'

'Then please call him right away.' Monica switched off the intercom and waited. Her phone rang within a minute. 'Freddie. How are you?'

'Top of the world, thank you, Monica. How was your weekend?'

Honesty to one's directors is one thing, but Monica had no intention of showing her real feelings regarding Frank De Wolf. 'Very pleasant, I'm afraid I overdid the food just a bit, but then, a little over-indulgence every once in a while is good for the soul, don't you think?'

Freddie had a master's degree in 'reading between lines'. He guessed Monica must have a lover but what he wanted to find out was who and how serious. If she was to become part of the French inner sanctum, security was the number-one priority. 'I'm in Bond Street at the moment,' he said. 'Why don't we meet at the Ivy, say, half an hour?'

'I look forward to it. Goodbye, Freddie.'

Monica and Freddie picked their way through Dover sole, new potatoes and a mixed salad. Freddie told her most of the details about the Korean trip and thanked her for the part she played in Miami. 'Now then,' he said, folding his napkin and placing it beside his empty plate. 'Tell me about Paris.'

Monica felt awkward and wanted to change the subject, but she knew that, in the end, Freddie would get the answer to his question. Anyway, there was nothing to say she couldn't have a lover, a boyfriend, a bloody social life. Just because Freddie hid his love inside a bottle, didn't mean she had to hide her happiness. 'I went with Frank De Wolf,' she said. 'He's a lawyer, I don't think you know him.'

Not yet I don't, thought Freddie. 'Is he good to you?'

Impertinent, thought Monica, as she took a sip of mineral water. 'He's good *for* me, is the way I would put it, Freddie.' She decided to lighten the tone of the conversation. 'He gives a good back-rub.'

'That's wonderful, my dear, a good back-rub is the basis for a good marriage I always say.'

'Good Lord, I don't think marriage is an issue here, I've only known him a short while.' Monica realized she must wrap this up before it got out of hand. 'How's your love life, Freddie, did you find a nice little Korean lady to rub your back?'

Freddie had the information he wanted. 'I'm afraid not. Chin has a few lovely granddaughters, but he keeps them well hidden.' He smiled at her. 'I didn't mean to pry into your private life, I just wanted to find out if he was the jealous type.'

'I don't think so,' she said. 'Why on earth do you ask?'

Freddie opened his briefcase and took out a square, flat box with the name Cartier embossed on the top. 'I've bought a little thank-you present and I wouldn't want it to cause any embarrassment,' he said.

Monica took the box and slowly opened it. A look of utter astonishment filled her face. Inside the box was an emerald and diamond necklace. Five square-cut, matching emeralds surrounded by diamonds, set in a plain gold chain. The light of the restaurant danced in the gems and reflected in Monica's eyes. 'Freddie, I don't know what to say. It's beautiful.'

'It's me that has to say, and I say, thank you,' he said. 'There is one stipulation, however.'

'Name it,' she said.

'You must let me take you to dinner so I can see you wearing it.'

She felt relief, happiness and a touch of real warmth for this pudgy aristocrat. 'It will be my pleasure.'

'Friday evening at the Gavroche?'

Monica looked down at the necklace and, once again, watched the lights dance inside the stones. She looked up at Freddie and for the first time noticed that he was not drinking; in fact, he was cold sober. 'Mr French, you have a date.'

Freddie smiled and made two mental notes. Frank De Wolf and Dun & Bradstreet.

Monica was far too elated to consider returning to the station. She accepted Freddie's offer of a ride to Cadogan Square where she stood in her kitchen and admired the exquisite piece of jewellery. She thought she would get some reward for her Miami trip but this was far beyond her wildest expectations. She closed the lid of the Cartier box and put her treasure in the safe, behind the Hockney original in the living room.

Maggie gathered her treasures from the desk top and dumped them into her handbag. They consisted of a tube of lipstick, a Parker pen, a packet of Silk Cut and a birthday card Bradley had given her some three months ago. A quick beer and maybe a game of pool at the Grapes was uppermost in her mind as she walked down the hall towards reception. John Thorne seemed to appear from nowhere and, grabbing her arm, practically frogmarched her out of the building and into Stanhope Place.

'Just a wee minute,' she said. 'I don't mind being abducted if it means outrageous sex or at least a large Scotch, but do you have to be so rough?'

'I'm sorry, Maggie, I must talk to someone intelligent before I throw myself off the nearest tall building.'

Maggie retrieved her arm and turned to face the newsman. 'Somebody has obviously had a field day in the newsroom,' she said. 'Don't tell me . . . you've been lumbered with another one of Lady Isobel's relations, who is even more of an idiot than the last one.'

'I've been lumbered by the IBA and Monica over this damn prison story.' He lowered his voice and spoke close to her ear. 'She nearly fired me this morning.'

'Don't be daft,' replied Maggie. 'She fires me at least twice a week and I'm still drawing a pay cheque.'

John continued in his low tone of voice. 'Don't you see what this means? If the IBA are getting jumpy over a last-in news item that I said was only a possibility, we must be on to something really big. I need some more help. You must run some more prisoner phone-ins. There's bound to be someone out there connected with this mess. All you have to do is find them. I'll do the rest.'

Maggie pulled back and put her handbag in front of her, guaranteeing a safe distance between them. 'Listen, my hyperactive friend, I ran that for you last week and I got as much reaction as a sand sale in the Sahara. Now, why don't you let the whole thing drop for a while; maybe you'll see another angle that doesn't incur the wrath of Brompton Road?'

'I don't need another angle, I need true freedom of the press.'

'You need a good kick in the ass,' said Maggie, walking off towards the pub and calling back to him over her shoulder, 'and I need a drink. Are you coming?'

John thought for a moment about high buildings, but decided against it in favour of a large gin and tonic.

Joe Mace gratefully accepted a large vodka and tonic from Monica and handed her three cassettes. 'This is it,' he said. 'There's enough on there to sink Mr Flash Jack for good.'

Monica took the tapes and walked over to the music centre. She couldn't help thinking that even with his new clothes, Joe Mace still made a designer suit look like it had been slept in for three days. She loaded the second tape into the player and turned it on.

'Just put the mirror on your ass so I can do a line and then lick you.'

'Sure thing, Jack. God, you've got a big prick. I want you to fuck me . . . now!'

'Just stay still till I snort this line.'

'Sally, give his prick a good suck, I want it juicy and hard when he fu–'

Monica turned the tape off and spun around to face the detective. Joe sat expressionless on the settee, sipping his drink.

'Well, it would seem we have him,' said Monica, trying to conceal the embarrassment she felt. 'Do you have signed affidavits from the ladies?'

'I will have by tomorrow noon.'

'And the master tapes?'

'In my safe.'

'In that case,' said Monica, raising her glass, 'I believe we have successfully concluded our business, Mr Mace. I would like copies of the affidavits as soon as possible and because you have been so quick, I will arrange a small bonus on receipt of the papers.'

Joe thanked her, finished his drink and left.

Monica poured herself another large vodka and turned the tape back on.

When Frank phoned to confirm dinner he noticed a little unsteadiness in her voice. 'Is everything all right?'

'Yes, I'm fine. Are you about to leave the office?'

'In about five minutes.'

'Why don't you pick me up from the flat.'

'About half an hour?'

'See you then.'

Monica put the phone down and walked up to her private room in search of a suspender belt and a pair of matching stockings.

Wednesday was a board day and Monica chose to sleep

alone on Tuesday night. The sex games she'd played with Frank on Monday night left her bruised and sore. She enjoyed every second, but she needed time to recuperate and put this whole thing into perspective. She also wanted the bitter joy of missing him; it made her feel in love. Peter called at half past eight to tell her he was going to announce the ATS deal at the board meeting and to offer her a ride to the station the next morning.

The meeting started on time at half past ten. Jemima Stewart didn't seem as interested in the sales director's report as she was at the last meeting. Her attention was focused on Monica and Sir Peter, which Monica found more than a bit disturbing. Brian Callaghan was focused on himself. His report ended with the revenue forecast for the next quarter; he sat down to subdued applause. The chairman stood up, thanked Brian and congratulated him on the excellent revenues produced by his department in the last quarter. Peter removed his half-moon glasses and slowly studied the board members from underneath his eyebrows. His gaze rested on Monica.

'Before we hear from Miss Hammond with her plans for Cornwall and Dundee,' he said, 'I think it wise to interject a piece of business that will go some way towards paying for the improvements that I'm sure she will recommend. I have been approached and have accepted, subject to the board's approval, an offer from ATS for five per cent of this company in exchange for twenty-five per cent of ATS plus two hundred and fifty thousand pounds cash. They will receive non-voting shares and will not seek a seat on this board. We will have voting shares of ATS and one seat on their board for which I would recommend Brian Callaghan.'

There were quiet murmurs of approval from around

the table, not that many of them would dare go against the chairman's wishes. Besides, at first reading it sounded like a very good deal for CRFM, to say nothing of the fact that they wouldn't be asked to put their hands in their pockets and fork out money for Monica's new improved satellites. Everyone was happy, except the man who had just been offered a seat on the board of ATS.

Brian Callaghan stood up and slapped his jot-pad down hard on the boardroom table. 'You must be joking,' he screamed. 'You can't do a deal with ATS. I'm working on a consortium to go against them. Within a year we can wipe them off the face of the earth.' He glared at Monica. 'You knew about this. You told me to go ahead and set it up. What the hell do you think you're doing? My ass is on the line with at least four stations. In another couple of weeks I'll have this wrapped up.'

Monica had waited a long time for this moment. She spoke with a mixture of innocence and mockery. 'My dear Brian, I said no such thing.' She paused and watched the horror creep into Dirty Harry's face. 'I *said* you could *not* approach companies that were already contracted to ATS until you had board approval, and in your sales report I heard nothing concerning any consortium whatsoever. If you have contacted directors of other companies with a view to setting up a rival sales force, you have done so without my permission, or the approval of this board.'

Sir Peter interjected to allow Monica time to draw breath. 'We are offering you a seat at ATS, which will mean you still control the sales force and, surely, it would be better to fight them from within – that is to say, if you are dead set against letting them continue in their present form. Personally, I feel they do a good job and I think we are very lucky to be given the opportunity to acquire such a large slice of their equity.'

Brian scanned the table for a friendly face. Everyone avoided eye contact with the exception of Jemima Stewart. She gave him the sweetest of looks, smiled, and reached into her handbag in search of her diary.

'You've stitched me up,' he hissed. 'You bastards have bloody well stitched me up!'

Sir Peter stood up. 'I think that's quite enough, Mr Callaghan. If you would like to see me after the meeting I will be happy to continue this discussion, but the matter before the board at this moment is our stock and cash transfer with ATS, not the setting up of rival sales forces.'

Monica watched Sir Peter with total admiration. His voice was calm, but commanding, and his air of supremacy captured the attention of everyone in the room. She was witnessing the downfall of a horny salesman and she couldn't wait for the final scene.

Callaghan placed both hands on the table and tried, unsuccessfully, to break Sir Peter's stare.

'Fuck the lot of you,' he shouted. So saying, he left the room, and the employ of CRFM.

Sir Peter sat down and surveyed the stunned board members. 'I do apologize for Brian's behaviour,' he said, allowing the faintest smile to cross his face. 'But I can assure you it won't happen again.' There were sighs of relief as his audience readjusted themselves in their seats. 'Now, shall we proceed with the matter in hand. Before I give you details of this transaction, is there anyone opposed, in principle, to the acquisition of shares in ATS?'

Not one dissenting voice was heard. Sir Peter leaned over and spoke softly to Monica. 'By the way, old chap, do we have a replacement?'

'David Westbury?'

'Yes, I like him. Where is he now?'

'Down at Cornwall, training the sales force.'

'I think we should bring him back, don't you?'

Monica smiled and nodded her approval. She didn't mind bringing him back, she didn't mind Sir Peter calling her 'old chap', she didn't mind if the moon was cheese. Callaghan was gone. O Happy Day!

The meeting adjourned just before noon. The ATS deal received unanimous approval, Monica received eighty thousand pounds for the re-launch of Cornwall and Dundee and David Westbury received two phone messages as he finished his morning lecture. He wisely chose to phone Monica first; within two hours his BMW glided smoothly on to the A30, heading for London. He didn't return Brian's call.

Monica fairly skipped down the hallway that led to her office, her mind agog with all the nice things that were happening to her. She tried not to dwell on them too long, as she was very superstitious about tempting the gods. She rounded the last corner before the deep-pile carpets and bumped head on into Nigel and Samantha. Nigel, as usual, was as quick as a whippet. 'Of all the hallways in all the world . . .'

Monica regained her composure. 'That's very good, Nigel, you should work that into the show.'

Nigel changed to Matt Dillon. 'Do ya really think so, Miss Kitty?'

Monica ignored him and looked at Samantha. 'We pay a fortune for that dark-brown voice of his and we can never get him to use it. Do you have that problem?'

Nigel watched as the two most important women in his life weighed each other up. 'Monica Hammond, Samantha Keating.'

Monica smiled at the girl, then turned her attention to Nigel. 'Don't you have some commercials to make? I would like to have a brief word with your friend.'

Once inside Monica's office Samantha felt at ease as she accepted an orange juice and sat down on the sofa.

'I'm sorry I whipped you away from Nigel like that,' said Monica. 'But I've been meaning to talk to you for some time now and I didn't want to miss this opportunity.'

Samantha met her eyes full on. 'Have I done something wrong?'

'Good gracious no, as a matter of fact, you seem to be doing everything right.'

Sam sipped her orange juice and placed the glass on the table.

'Since he's known you,' Monica continued, 'his show is sounding better and better. I just wanted to say whatever it is you are doing to him, please keep it up.'

Samantha relaxed and smiled at Monica. 'I must admit, I was scared of meeting you. You have an awesome reputation among the DJs.'

Monica returned her smile and walked over to her desk. 'Tell me something: has the press been around you two asking questions?'

Samantha answered directly. 'Not really. We don't go out much, we tend to stay at home and . . . amuse ourselves.'

Monica knew she had nipped this one in the bud. She leaned against her desk and adopted the most confidential voice she could muster. 'You realize, we have a lot of time and money invested in Nigel.'

'I'm sure he gives you excellent value.'

'Without a doubt. It's just that I wouldn't like some grubby reporter from the tabloid press printing a hastily worded story about the two of you that would put this station in a bad light and, most likely, cause you both a great deal of embarrassment.'

Samantha thought for a moment before replying. 'What are you suggesting we do?'

'We both know that Nigel will do nothing to help or hinder any press story that might break, so it is up to you to make sure nothing untoward happens in that area. What I'm suggesting is that, if possible, we should control any press from this office. We have a large department that does nothing all day but feed stories to the press as seen from our point of view. If anyone approaches you for a story, or even a quote, all you have to do is refer them to me. I will take care of everything and you two can get on with enjoying yourselves.'

Samantha smiled and straightened her dress. 'That's most kind of you, Miss Hammond, I'll most certainly do that if anyone should ask.'

Monica pushed the station intercom button. 'Nigel B. to my office please.' She turned to face Samantha. 'I'm glad we had this little chat.'

Nigel and Samantha walked into the cool of the underground car-park.

'Whatever did she say to you?' asked Nigel.

'Mainly bullshit about selling our story to the press.'

'Our story. What does she mean, our *story*?'

'You know ... DJ porked me eight times a night against my will ... that sort of thing.'

Nigel unlocked the Porsche. Samantha slid into the passenger seat and studied his face.

He read the concern in her eyes. 'What's the matter?'

'She scares me, sweetheart. There's something about her.'

'She scares me too, but she also pays the mortgage. Sunbathing?'

Sam slipped her hand between his legs. 'Eventually.'

Brian Callaghan was in the middle of clearing his desk when his secretary returned from an early lunch with Lizzie Stephenson.

'What's the matter, Mr Callaghan?'

Brian looked up from his desk, his face ashen with anger. 'I've told Sir Peter-fucking-French what he can do with his two-bit radio station.'

Sally stood in the doorway for a few moments as his last statement resounded in her head. When a company director goes, that usually means his secretary is also out of a job. She decided to take this one step at a time. 'What happened?'

'You know the sales force I've been putting together?'

She knew all right. It was her idea in the first place. As her mind raced forward, she had fleeting thoughts of poetic justice.

'The bastards stitched me up and did a deal with ATS,' continued Brian. 'Monica-bloody-Hammond said nothing about it. French just sprang it on the board and I'm left with my ass on the fucking front burner.'

Best place for it, thought Sally.

'I've got lots of friends in the agencies, I'll have another job by close of play today.' He slammed his briefcase shut and stomped towards the door. 'And another thing' – he turned to face his astonished assistant – 'this place is on the skids. If I were you, I'd get out quick before you become a staff cut.' He slammed the door so hard the glass nearly broke.

Sally sat down in Brian's comfortable leather chair and did some rapid calculations. Self-preservation was the order of the day. She decided to phone Monica.

'I'm sorry to bother you, Miss Hammond, but I wonder if I could have a word with you this afternoon.'

Monica was expecting her call. 'Come and see me now, if you like,' she said. 'Why don't we have some lunch?'

'That would be lovely.'

'Reception then, say . . . ten minutes?'

'Thank you, Miss Hammond, I'll see you there.' Sally replaced the phone, sat back in Brian's chair and felt much better about herself, her job and her managing director.

Monica ate while Sally talked about Callaghan, CRFM, how it was her idea for the sales force and how she was frightened of losing her job.

'This company does not work like that,' Monica reassured her. 'You don't get fired unless you break the rules.'

'Or set up alternative sales forces,' said Sally.

'Correct,' said Monica.

The two women laughed aloud and decided to order a large dessert.

Monica returned to the office and informed Suzie that Sally would be joining her to help out with Cornwall and Dundee, so could she arrange with Eddy McLeod to have an extra desk, filing cabinet and computer terminal delivered this afternoon. The station was buzzing with stories of Callaghan's departure and Suzie was desperate to get the real story. 'What happened to Brian Callaghan?'

'Brian Callaghan is no longer with us,' replied Monica. 'David Westbury is the new sales director. He'll arrive back from the West Country later today. I would like to see him first thing in the morning. Please arrange it.'

Monica swept into her office, sat behind her desk,

removed her shoes and had the most enormous toe twiddle. Brian Callaghan is no longer with us . . . God, that sounded good.

The intrigue of office politics was the last thing on Nigel's mind as he held Samantha in his arms and pondered her last remarks. 'How long will you be away?' he asked.

Samantha snuggled up closer to him and stroked his face. 'Only a couple of weeks. I tried to cancel but the trip's already paid for.'

'Who is this Daphne Bowles person?'

'She's an old school friend of mine.' She rolled over him and off the other side. 'I was going to tell you earlier, but I thought I could get out of it. I promised her I would go before I met you. You know what it's like, you have to book these things months in advance. Anyway, it's only two weeks.'

'I'll pay the cancellation fee,' said Nigel, willing to try anything to make her stay. 'I've got some time off soon. We can go on holiday together, anywhere you like.'

Sam propped herself up on one arm and looked sternly at Nigel. 'I promised her I would go, she doesn't have that many friends and I don't want to let her down.' She relaxed and kissed him lightly on the cheek. 'I promise, I'll write every day and if you miss me, that shows you love me. It's probably good that we have a break from each other. I'd like some time to sort out how I feel. This has been a pretty fast ride for me as well, you know.'

'I miss you already,' said Nigel.

Samantha played with the belt from Nigel's bathrobe. 'You could always tie me up so I couldn't leave,' she said, pulling the end of the belt from under Nigel's back.

'I've never tried that sort of thing.'

'Think of it as educational,' she said, grasping the brass bedhead with both hands.

CHAPTER 11

Thursday, 26 July was a very important day for the creative personnel of CRFM. It was the day or, to be more precise, the night of the annual advertising awards. Independent radio survives on advertising, some would even say because of advertising. Whichever theory you subscribe to, the annual awards are the most important event of the year, not to mention a fabulous excuse to put on the glad rags and party till dawn.

Anthony was up for two awards – Best Radio Commercial (household) and Best Promotional Commercial. Lizzie celebrated the nominations by spending what little money he had left on a gownless evening strap that she felt sure would attract all the photographers. 'It's no good winning the award,' she said to Anthony, 'unless people get to hear about it, and that means publicity.' Anthony couldn't care less about publicity, but he did care about Lizzie, so he just smiled his agreement and had his evening suit dry cleaned.

During the day the station was alive with gossip and snippets about who was going with whom, what everyone was wearing and if anyone would disgrace themselves like last year, when a slightly drunk Trevor Jones fell head first into the punch bowl. Most people agreed on the starting line-up: Nigel and Samantha, Trevor and Mrs Trevor, Bernie Bonelli and some tart, Kenny Parker and Sally (they're just good friends, you know), Maggie and John from news, Eddy McLeod and Judy, Monica and . . . good God, it has to be David Westbury, because she always goes with the sales director, Washington Blake and probably that gorgeous model he goes out with – what's her name? – Pippa, that's it, Pippa, and, of course, the stars of the evening, Anthony Parkin and Lizzie Stephenson. There were also a lot of side bets floating around regarding the finishing line-up, at three to one, bar Bernie Bonelli.

Most participants packed up work at three o'clock to give themselves time to prepare for the event. For most, three o'clock coincided nicely with the end of lunch, so, all in all, it was a very laid-back day at London's number-one station.

David Westbury, however, had no lunch at all. He was far too busy trying to make sense of the mess left by Callaghan. During his meeting with Monica that morning, he requested the services of Sally Preston. Monica explained Sally's change of duties, but was sympathetic to David's cause and didn't want to see him get off to a bad start. She agreed to split Sally's time, half and half, as long as Monica had first call and on the understanding that David found a new secretary as quickly as possible.

This was to be Nigel and Samantha's last night together before she went on holiday, so there was a sombre feel floating around Maida Vale. Sam tried to keep things light and breezy, but Nigel was just not his usual perky self. She tried jokes, sex, TLC, even anger; nothing worked.

She finally cornered him in the jacuzzi. 'Listen here, shit face, you've got to snap out of this. We have to present ourselves to your adoring public tonight and your face is so long you need coasters on your chin.'

'I just think it's stupid to go on holiday with somebody you haven't seen socially for, what, three years, when all you have to do is tell her that you have met a man and you're very sorry, but he comes first.'

'I can't do that, Nigel. I said I'd go and I'm going, and that's that.'

Nigel looked down at the bubbles that surrounded him.

Samantha slipped the shoulder straps over her arms, the dress slid effortlessly to the floor and she stood naked in front of him. Her body seemed to shine in the dim light of the bathroom, her long blonde hair fell down across her breasts. She stepped into the jacuzzi and pressed herself against him. 'I will come back,' she said. 'I love you.'

Nigel held her so tightly he almost squeezed the breath out of her. She grabbed at his hair, pulled his face up to her level and kissed him with great ferocity. There was no escape from her passion. She dragged him under the water, grabbing his penis and using it as a handle to turn him on his back. He felt he was drowning and tried to loosen her grip. She held him tighter. He felt his back touch the bottom of the tub and the jetstream rush by his head. He put both hands against her ribcage and pushed as hard as he could. She released him. He struggled to the surface, gasping for air. When he finally regained his senses he saw her on the other side of the jacuzzi, laughing.

'What the fuck was that?' he said.

'If you can't live without me I thought we'd try dying.'

Nigel shook his head. 'You could have done some serious damage.'

Samantha stopped laughing. 'Oh, for Christ's sake, Nigel, lighten up.' She turned to get out of the tub. 'Find another sucker to throw tantrums with, I've had enough.'

Nigel grabbed her and pulled her back into the water. She landed, back first, in the centre of the tub. She struggled to her feet and swept the hair from her face. 'I gather you don't want me to leave,' she said.

'I don't want you to leave,' replied Nigel.

'Then lighten up and let's enjoy what should be a great night.'

Nigel felt foolish, childish, inadequate and in love. 'OK, anything you say.'

'That's better,' she said, turning away from him. 'Now rub my back . . . Start at the top and work your way down till I say stop.'

Monica treated herself to Pauline Brightman, a young, talented masseuse who made house calls. She carried a wide range of oils and powders and today Monica chose jasmine oil to complement her mood and because she loved the smell. Pauline worked on her for an hour, rubbing, stroking, pummelling, digging into muscles and dispersing the last of the Monday-night bruising. They had a friendly working relationship, Pauline telling Monica all about her Terry and how he sent her roses yesterday to celebrate the fact it was Wednesday, took her to see the new Kevin Costner film last weekend and generally being an all-round nice guy, and Monica telling Pauline absolutely nothing about Frank De Wolf.

After the massage, Pauline saw herself out of the flat so as not to spoil Monica's relaxation time, which she regarded as an essential part of the treatment. Monica lay face down on the bed, drifting into half sleep and feeling wonderful. The sound of the phone broke the spell. 'Monica Hammond.'

'Sweetheart, you sound asleep,' said Frank De Wolf.

'I nearly was,' replied Monica. 'I've just had a massage and I was drifting away.' She looked at the bedside clock. 'It's a good thing you phoned, I've got to get going or I'll be late.'

'You've got the awards tonight, haven't you?'

'Yes, and Freddie French tomorrow. It's a busy couple of nights.'

'Can you find time for your lover somewhere over the weekend?'

Monica smiled to herself and turned over on her back, slowly rubbing her stomach with her free hand. 'I could do with you here right now,' she said.

'Sorry, darling, no can do. I'm up to my balls in corporate legality.'

'Lucky old corporate legality,' said Monica. 'How about Saturday morning until Sunday night?'

Frank laughed. 'You are such a brazen hussy, you should be taught some manners before it's too late.'

Monica stroked her stomach. 'Saturday morning then, about elevenish?'

'I'll call you after ten. Enjoy the awards. Goodbye for now.'

'Goodbye, Frank.' She dropped the phone on the pillow beside her and drifted for an extra ten minutes.

Eddy McLeod took his preparation very seriously. He was still euphoric over the dismissal of Brian Callaghan and now viewed Judy with contempt. Judy had farmed the kids out to her mother for the night, hoping that she could have a pleasant evening with her husband. She bought a new green and white evening gown from the small dress shop in the high street and was adjusting the shoulder straps when Eddy walked into the bedroom.

'Can you give me a hand with this damn collar stud? It's driving me crazy.'

Judy let go of her straps and tried to help him. 'I don't know why you don't buy a one-piece shirt, these things went out with the ark,' she said.

'I might not be as "with it" as your fancy friends,' he replied, 'but I happen to think formal means traditional and that, to me, is separate collars and wearing braces.'

'Suit yourself, but nobody knows the difference once the jacket is on.'

'I know the difference,' snapped Eddy.

'Well, that's all right then,' said Judy, with just a touch of sarcasm.

They finished dressing without speaking another word. No further help was asked for or given. There were no mutual compliments, no kiss when they left the house; as the warring couple stepped into the warm evening air, Eddy handed her the keys to the black BMW. 'I've got this car for the night,' he said. 'I believe you know how to drive it.'

Two dozen photographers waited outside the Grosvenor House Hotel for the procession of celebrities that were about to arrive. Chris Tarrant was the first and, as host for the evening, he received particular attention. He was followed by other Capital folk and they, in turn, were followed by minor celebrities from the out-of-town stations and production companies. The first to arrive from CRFM were Nigel and Samantha. She looked stunning in a full-length black evening dress with a black velvet choker. The boys from the press snapped away and shouted the usual questions: 'Who's your lady friend, Nigel?' 'How long have you known her?' 'Are you getting married?' Nigel ignored them all and ushered her inside and away from the flashing lights. Monica and David were next to arrive. They were greeted with much less fuss, just the odd flash and no questions. However, when Lizzie stepped out of the hired limousine in her gownless evening strap the lads went wild. 'Over here!' 'This way, miss!' 'Show us some leg, dear!' 'That's fabulous! Just once more!' 'Who's your boyfriend?' 'What's your name?' Lizzie was in paradise and she knew it was only a matter of time until they all knew her name. Anthony smiled politely and opened the big glass entrance door, so she could glide into the hotel without breaking her stride.

Judy parked the black BMW in the underground car-park and she and Eddy took the lift to the ground floor. There was not one photographer to greet them.

The social part of the evening progressed without much incident. Monica didn't know David Westbury very well; as he was now only one place behind her in the executive pecking order, she was not about to give him any ammunition he could use against her in the future. He seemed nice enough, but Monica knew, only too well, that the nice guys cause the most damage. Eddy and Judy spoke to everyone except each other. Bernie Bonelli, tart in tow, was louder than ever. Maggie and John kept each other company and slowly realized they were the only 'news' people in the place. Nigel was a real star and Samantha complemented him perfectly. Anthony was his usual well-mannered self, lovingly watching Lizzie try to exude the star quality so natural to Nigel Beresford-Clarke.

At half past ten Chris Tarrant walked on stage and performed a very funny five-minute monologue about commercials, production assistants, the IBA and the state of radio in general, before announcing the winners of the twenty-two awards that were on offer. There was a hush at the CRFM tables as he announced the nominees for the Best Promotional Commercial.

'And the winner is,' he said, opening the gold and white envelope and leaving a big enough pause to accommodate a double-decker bus, 'Capital Radio for The Coca-Cola Music Festival, producer: John Burrows.'

Massive applause erupted around the room.

Polite applause could just be heard from the CRFM contingent.

Lizzie held Anthony's hand. 'Don't worry,' she whispered. 'You'll get the big one.'

The Big One was next. Chris Tarrant loosened his tie and cracked a joke about pressure and toilets. When the laughter subsided he continued. 'The next award is for the Best Radio Commercial for a household product . . . and the winner is . . . CRFM for Staybright, producer: Anthony Parkin.'

Everybody jumped. Monica clapped and let out a very uncharacteristic 'Whoopee'. Nigel turned to face Anthony, both fists clenched like Gary Lineker completing a hat trick. Eddy banged both hands on the table and shouted 'Bravo'. Bernie Bonelli stuck two fingers in his mouth and let go a deafening whistle. Lizzie hugged her Anthony with all her might, while the recipient of the award smiled gently and seemed somewhat embarrassed by the whole affair.

By half past eleven the ceremony was over and the disco was in full swing. A steady stream of well-wishers filed past Anthony's table, offering congratulations and promising to 'phone him soon and have lunch'. Bernie was on the air at midnight and, to everyone's relief, left just after eleven. Nigel and Samantha 'slow danced' to 'Jive Talkin'' which got everyone's attention. Monica was glad she had had her little talk on Wednesday.

Monica arrived home just after one o'clock. There was a message from Frank on her answerphone. 'Good morning, Golden Goddess. Could you wake the one who loves you, just to say goodnight?'

She called him right away. They talked until half past two.

Nigel and Samantha spent what was left of the night together and after his show he drove her to the airport. Driving back along the M4 he noticed even the Porsche was sounding rough.

Monica was feeling rough as she walked into her office. Last night had been a lot of fun, but there was always a price to pay for too much champagne. She studied the rating sheets for last week and noticed a considerable dip in the mid-morning show. Nick Glover was usually as reliable as rain in summer, but something was coming adrift with that time slot and she had to find out what was wrong. She glanced through the music list, the competitions, the mail count and the features. They all seemed solid and nothing had been changed from the successful formats that worked for the past two years. She looked at Capital, LBC, Radio One, Two, Three and Four. No increase in any of them. This could just be a blip in the survey; she would keep a close eye on next week's chart.

Her private phone rang and she cursed herself for being there. She thought about leaving it, but Monica was not that kind of person. 'Monica Hammond,' she said abruptly.

'Monica, Harry Connaught.'

Oh God, she thought, this is the last thing I need. 'Harry, what can I do for you?'

'It's what you've done to me that needs discussion.'

In all the years she'd known him, he'd never used that tone of voice. 'What on earth's wrong, Harry?' she asked, touching the red switch on her intercom.

'I hardly think you have to ask.' His voice was quaking with anger. 'I'm just astounded you didn't even have the courtesy to at least inform me of what was going on.'

Better late than never, thought Monica, as the penny finally dropped. 'Do you mean the ATS deal?'

'Of course I mean the ATS deal. You've not only let the Australians in, you've held the bloody door open.'

Monica needed time to think. 'Harry, I was sure Peter told you about it. I assumed you both talked at lunch, the day of the garden party.'

Harry's anger was unabated. 'The first I heard was this morning, from my ruddy secretary!'

'Harry, that's awful, I don't know what to say. It's all been a terrible misunderstanding. I was not involved with the negotiations and when I heard, I assumed one of the Frenchs had already sought your advice as a matter of course.'

His voice softened. 'Do you mean to tell me you were not a party to this travesty of justice?'

Monica crossed her fingers as she replied. 'The first I heard was at Wednesday morning's board.'

There was a pause at Harry's end of the conversation. Monica hoped her lie had worked. 'If I had known anything beforehand I would have called you right away,' she said cautiously.

Harry now knew she was lying, or at least not telling the whole truth. 'There will come a time,' he said, 'when you will have to decide where your loyalties lie, Monica, with me and the IBA, or with those unscrupulous multinationals who don't give a fig about real broadcasting, and if this little deception is anything to go by, that decision is not that far away.'

Monica's answer was immediate. 'With you, Harry, of course. I owe you everything, I wouldn't knowingly do anything to compromise your position.' She felt a slight offensive would now be appropriate. 'We have several minor shareholders in this company. Do you really think that five per cent with no seat on the board is going to cause trouble at the Home Office?'

'It's not the five per cent, it's who it belongs to that counts.'

Monica had an idea. 'May I talk to you in confidence?' she asked.

'I wish someone would.'

'From what I gathered from the board meeting on Wednesday, it's not so much Aylford owning five per cent of us, it's more us owning twenty-five per cent of ATS. I feel that Peter and Freddie are thinking of having a crack at the Aussies, and this is their starting point.'

'You mean the French family buy Aylford?'

'Stranger things have happened.'

'Well, well, are you sure?'

'I'm not sure, but from where I sit, it looks a strong possibility.'

'Why the money then? Why did Peter ask for money? That makes it look as if CRFM needs capital.'

'Exactly.'

'What was all that hogwash about Cornwall and Dundee, getting us to drop the levy because you couldn't afford to buy them?'

Monica said nothing.

'Good God, that was all part of it.'

'All I can say, at this moment, Harry, is that there are several million pounds safely placed within the French company structure, to be used as acquisition money at a future date.'

Harry Connaught breathed a huge sigh of relief. 'Thank you, Monica, that makes me feel a lot better.'

Monica wasn't finished yet. After the offensive, the final rout. 'One more thing, Harry. We didn't have this conversation.'

'Of course not, dear girl, of course not. I'll speak to you soon. Goodbye.'

Monica hung up the phone, reached into the lower right-hand drawer of her desk and turned off the tape recorder.

Lizzie heard the phone ring from her nest, deep inside the duvet. She stuck a leg over to Anthony's side but there was no one there. She sank deeper into the covers and let it ring. Anthony came in the front door and reached the phone just as it stopped ringing. He placed the eggs he'd bought on the kitchen counter, broke the baguette in half and put it in the oven and dumped the morning papers on the chair. He scrambled three eggs, adding some finely chopped mushroom and a pinch of nutmeg, arranged them neatly on a plate, placed the warm baguette alongside and put the whole lot on a tray with a cup of tea and the papers and headed for the bedroom.

He stood in the doorway and looked at the lump in the middle of the duvet. 'Come on, lazy bones, it's nearly noon,' he said.

There was a stir from the bed, but no life form appeared.

'Lizzie, the house is on fire.'

Still nothing.

'I've cooked you breakfast, your favourite, eggs, mush and nutmeg.'

Still no movement.

'We're in all the papers.'

The covers flew off and a wide-awake Lizzie sat upright in the middle of the bed. 'Let me see, where are they? Did we make all of them?'

Anthony dropped the papers beside her. 'All the tabloids,' he said. 'Most of them are of you, but I get a mention in the copy.'

Lizzie opened the *Mirror* first. Sure enough, on page six, was a picture of Lizzie in her gownless evening strap, showing lots of leg and smiling from ear to ear. Underneath was written, 'Lizzie Stevenson, fiancée of award winning producer Anthony Parkin, arriving at the Grosvenor House Hotel for last night's annual advertising awards dinner.' She looked disappointed as she handed the paper to Anthony. 'Look at that,' she said. 'They've spelt my name wrong, with a *v* instead of *ph*.'

'It doesn't matter, you look beautiful.'

Oh yes it does matter, thought Lizzie. She thumbed through all the papers. They all carried pictures of her and they all spelt her name wrong.

Maggie walked into CRFM at four o'clock, bleary-eyed and in no mood to talk to anyone. Her head hurt every time she moved it. She shuffled up the stairs, trying to keep her throbbing cranium as still as possible. She passed Monica half way down the hall.

'Maggie, I would like a word with you.'

Maggie cringed as the words sledgehammered into her brain. 'Can you possibly whisper?' she muttered. 'I'm having a hangover.'

Monica was sympathetic, which came as a great surprise to the suffering Scot. 'I won't keep you long. I've had some good news regarding Flash Jack.'

'Don't tell me, he's topped himself and saved us all a lot of trouble.'

'Not quite, Maggie, but he has strayed from the path of righteousness, so to speak.'

Maggie felt better already.

'It is most important that you say nothing about him

or his music on the air at this time,' commanded Monica. 'One slip could cost us the entire situation.'

'Anything you say, boss lady.'

Monica nodded, turned, and continued walking towards reception without saying another word. She had far more important things on her mind. In a few hours she would be dining at Le Gavroche and she had to choose a dress that would complement her necklace.

The wardrobe in her private bedroom was crammed with all manner of clothing. Saint Laurent mixed with St Michael, Monsoon with Jean Muir. Monica bought things on instinct and then hoarded them away for future use. After careful consideration she knew what she wanted, a three-quarter-length cerise silk dress by Givenchy she had bought a few months back at the Harvey Nichols sale. She brushed her hair in a simple style, off her forehead and held by two matching black grips just behind her ears. She added diamond stud earrings, wandered down to the living-room safe and completed her outfit with the most beautiful piece of jewellery she had ever owned.

She stood in front of the mirror and studied the finished product. The colours in the dress danced through the emeralds and seemed to make the diamonds move around their centre stones. She smiled with satisfaction as she reached for the final touch, her black Mappin & Webb lizard handbag, the one big enough to hold her small dictaphone recorder.

The Phantom V pulled up outside the unassuming brown wooden door in Upper Brook Street which is the entrance to Le Gavroche. Freddie looked very handsome in a dark navy, two-piece suit. He had not raided the car's cocktail cabinet on the way to the restaurant, but Monica was sure that would change once they were inside. Silvano greeted them like long-lost cousins and showed them to the banquette just to the right of the large glass cockerel that dominated the upstairs bar. The customary glass of champagne and silver tray of Amuse Gueules, consisting of caviare on thin toast, small lobster claws and crab in pastry, was delivered with almost invisible ease. Freddie commented on how beautiful the necklace looked and how well Monica's dress blended with the dark reds and soft greens in the room. Monica replied that she hoped she didn't blend too well, as Freddie might have trouble finding her, come the end of the evening.

'I'm slowing down,' said Freddie. 'I will not let my mother get the last word, even if it means going on the wagon.'

Monica didn't think for a second that he could ever give up the demon drink, but she did admire him for trying.

The second glass of champagne was delivered accompanied by the menu. Freddie noticed a slight flash of horror cross Monica's face. 'I think you should consider French lessons,' he whispered. 'If only to understand what food you're eating.'

Monica was grateful to Freddie for a lot of things, but she was not going to let him get away with that. 'I understand enough to know what I want,' she replied. 'Tonight I want soufflé, fish and assorted desserts.'

And so she had soufflé Suissesse, a fillet of sole with saffron and, for dessert, Assiette Gourmande, consisting of lemon tart, ice-cream in a biscuit tulip, rich chocolate truffle cake, blackcurrant mousse and poached fruit with vanilla cream. Freddie started with a slice of fresh foie gras with wild mushrooms, followed by three small fillets of lamb, beef and veal, each in a different sauce with appropriate garnish and, for dessert, he helped Monica with the Assiette Gourmande. Coffee and brandy were served in the downstairs lounge; as Monica watched the waiter pour the second cup, she was more than impressed with Freddie's sobriety.

'Are you really giving up the juice?' she asked.

Freddie was more alert than she had ever seen him, and more than a bit cheeky. 'Only if you give up wearing low-cut dresses,' he replied.

Monica dropped her head in false modesty and did a fair to middling impression of Scarlett O'Hara. 'Why, Mistah French, I do believe you have embarrassed me.'

Freddie tried for Rhett Butler. 'Gosh no, ma'am, I wouldn't do that for all the cotton south of Memphis.' Freddie continued in his normal voice. 'You have a rare beauty and a rare talent.'

Monica's mind went on red alert. Two compliments in one sentence could mean either death of glory. She took a sip of coffee and smiled as he continued, 'Peter and I feel you are somewhat wasted at what you are doing.' He stopped to let the waiter light his cigar and to allow his last remark to register. 'I would like you to consider joining the board of French Enterprises.'

Monica had waited over three years to hear that request, but she knew, even with the invitation, there was still one major obstacle to overcome. 'That would be wonderful, Freddie, but, with the best will in the world, I can't see your mother agreeing to that. She doesn't even like me on the board of CRFM.'

Freddie moved from the chair opposite and sat beside her. He spoke in a low voice. 'There comes a time when everyone outlives their usefulness. Mother has been the matriarch of our family for over thirty years. Her judgement on business matters is not what it used to be. Peter and I have been handling the day-to-day running of the companies for over five years now and we have reached a point where we have to do something about Mother, before she becomes a liability.'

Monica was dumbstruck. Here was a member of one of the oldest families in England talking, to a relative stranger, about performing a *coup de grâce* on the head of that family, and offering her the job of replacement. She didn't trust any of this. All of a sudden, she didn't trust Freddie French. 'It all sounds wonderful,' she said. 'But I'm afraid I couldn't accept at this moment, not until Lady Isobel has left. Don't you see, she would make it impossible for me to function in any role of which she had ultimate control.'

'I understand completely,' said Freddie. He started to laugh. 'Good God, don't tell me about her ultimate control. I've been subjected to it for nearly forty years.' He lowered his voice again and held Monica's hand. 'What I'm saying is, Peter and I have no direct heir. There isn't anyone within the family that could, or even wants to, get involved with the business, so we have to look outside. You did a sterling job for us in Miami, you run the radio stations like clockwork and we both know you. When the time comes that Mother is no longer with us, Peter and I would like you to take her seat on the board.'

Monica got her trust back and cursed herself for doubting. 'I'm speechless, Freddie. Of course, under those circumstances, I'd be more than happy.'

'Good,' said Freddie, emptying his brandy goblet and beckoning the waiter for a refill. 'And now, if you'll allow me, a little present to mark the occasion.'

Monica was beside herself with joy and expectation. She knew that life sometimes walked right through the doorway of expectation, but she was sure it would not be tonight. Trips to Miami, beautiful jewellery, seats on the board. Whatever next? The waiter brought the brandy and placed it in front of Freddie, then placed a green leather book beside the brandy.

Freddie handed the book to Monica. 'This is for you,' he said.

Monica opened the book and read the ornate inscription on the inside cover. 'This edition of *French Country Cooking* has been specially hand-bound in a limited edition of 250 copies, each volume signed by the authors and numbered.' It was signed Albert and Michel Roux and numbered 26. Monica opened the book and found, to her great relief, it was written in English.

'Freddie, you are a poppet,' she said. 'Does this mean you expect me to cook on board days?'

'It would make a nice change from what Simmons dishes up.'

'One surprise deserves another,' laughed Monica. 'I had a call from the IBA today – Harry Connaught is not very happy with you two at the moment. He thinks you've dumped on him from a great height.'

Freddie studied the tablecloth. 'I suppose we have, in a way, but that's not a surprise.'

'I'm coming to that,' said Monica. 'I made up a terrible lie on your behalf and the more I think of it, the more I'm not sure I did right.'

Freddie viewed Monica with some suspicion. 'Is this a joke, dear girl? Are you having one over on old Freddie? I fear you are.' He decided to give her the benefit of the doubt for a little bit longer. 'Where's the surprise?'

Monica produced the small dictaphone recorder and a mini pair of headphones from her handbag. 'The surprise is . . . I recorded the lot, so you can make up your own mind.'

'How wonderfully devious,' said Freddie as he pushed the small headphones into his ears and turned on the machine. Monica watched as his facial expressions changed as the conversation progressed. A little serious, a small scowl and a robust laugh as it finished.

'Machiavellian,' he said.

'In a good sense?'

'Most definitely. You avoided the truth with expert precision.'

Monica remained serious. 'I wasn't sure.'

'You haven't, in fact, told any lies at all. There is money in the cookie jar, it's just not for Aylford.' Freddie handed her the tape machine. 'You couldn't have done any better, even if you knew all the facts. You're either very intuitive or very lucky.'

'I'm very full,' replied Monica. 'That was a lovely meal.'

Lizzie was full of confidence as she cleared away the supper dishes and gave Anthony a big hug. 'Well, dearest,' she said, 'we did the business. One award and all the papers, that's not a bad day's work.'

'It's better than losing a fortune at Ascot, I'll give you that,' replied Anthony, holding his Lizzie tightly and slipping his hand down the inside of her dress.

Lizzie manoeuvred on the couch so he could only reach halfway down her back with his exploring fingers. 'I think it's time we had our own show,' she said.

Anthony pushed his other hand inside her dress. 'If it was television, we could sell your ass for a fortune.'

'I'm serious,' snapped Lizzie. 'We could produce a double-hander for a weekend slot. Music and advice about setting up first homes.' She became gentle and allowed him to move his hands further down her body. 'We could call it Anthony and Cleopatra. It would work, I know it.'

Anthony stopped groping and looked at Lizzie. 'You could be right,' he said. 'A show like that just might make it. There must be, what, two million people who are in that position and we could target the advertising to fit the format.'

Lizzie pushed herself against him. 'Let's make a pilot,' she said.

'You're on, baby, we'll start tomorrow.'

Lizzie smiled to herself and let Anthony put his hands anywhere he wanted.

Maggie Lomax was having a rough night. Her hangover wouldn't go away, her timing was out by a second and the 'fast rapport' section of her brain had gone into retirement. She was into the final half-hour of her show and was cruising towards the news. The private phone light on the console started to flash. Please don't let it be Monica, she said to herself as she lifted the handset. 'Good evening, this is Maggie Lomax in an unwell state. What can I do for you?'

'Good evening, this is Bradley in a drunken state and lost in New York City.'

'Thank God it's you,' she sighed. 'How's life in the Big Apple?'

'Boring.'

'I can't believe that.'

'It's true. The only thing that will save my sanity is if you let me talk rude to you on the phone.'

Maggie's record was coming to an end. 'Hold on, Bradley,' she said, switching on the microphone. 'This is CRFM, news is ten minutes away. To take us there, the Allman Brothers band, live at the Fillmore East.' She turned the monitor down and picked up the phone. 'Now then, big boy, you have nine and a half minutes to do your worst.' There was silence from the New York end. 'Bradley ... Bradley!' she shouted. 'Wake up, you bastard!'

CHAPTER 12

The weekend continued the way it had started for Monica Hammond. Frank picked her up for lunch on Saturday. In the afternoon, he somehow persuaded her to help him polish the Bentley. It was something she would never have considered a week ago, but today she found herself enjoying the sensation of watching the shine appear from under her polishing rag, even though it did cost her the index fingernail of her right hand. Frank was very sympathetic and rushed her to Harrods, just before it closed, for a repair and rebuild. On Saturday night they 'roughed' it at the Texas Lone Star Café, eating lots of hot Mexican food. Frank drank a little too much Budweiser and Monica drank far too much red wine. Sunday was a day of rest in more ways than one.

On Monday morning Monica awoke alone, but happy. Frank was such a change from the men who had drifted in and out of her life over the past ten years. Most of them couldn't live with her power, or her ambition. First of all they tried to change her and when that didn't work, they tried to dominate. She compiled a list of stock phrases they always used: 'Don't you ever feel like giving it all up and having babies?'; 'Come and work for me'; 'I can afford to support us both'; 'A woman like you doesn't need to work for a living'; 'You could find satisfaction running the country estate'; and the one that really pissed her off, 'It's not natural for a woman to be a managing director.' Frank was different. He was pleased she was successful, he encouraged her without being pushy or arrogant. He let her spirit run free instead of trying to cage it and, most important, he made love to her with the understanding of what a woman needs. On Saturday night they listened to the Joe Mace tapes and played wild sex games all over Frank's house; on Sunday morning he was soft and loving, kissing all the little welts and bruises from the night before, rubbing her back and legs with scented oil and serving her coffee and hot croissants as she lay soaking in the bath. Monica knew it was early days, but she felt that, if Frank asked her, she would be willing to make a commitment to this stylish lawyer, or at least, show him her private bedroom.

She had done one piece of business on Saturday. She phoned Flash Jack's lawyers from Frank's place and made arrangements to meet them at the station on Monday morning. Frank had suggested Monday morning, he said that would give Monica an edge as, on the whole, lawyers didn't function until after lunch on Mondays. Monica wasn't really worried how they functioned, she had the affidavits, the tapes and a statement from Joe Mace. She had the goods on that little pipsqueak and she was going to enjoy telling them where they could put their writ.

In Eaton Square, Monday morning was progressing much as usual, except that Freddie was sober. Lady Isobel was holding forth on the injustices of the IBA regulations, Freddie was reading the *Financial Times* and Peter gleefully destroyed a plate of scrambled eggs.

'Will you look at this?' said Freddie, folding the *FT* and handing it to Peter. 'They say the Kin Won bank is set to be the biggest flotation in Korean history.'

Peter scanned the article and handed the paper back to his brother. 'I'm glad it's working out for the old fellow,' he said, 'I would hate to see him come adrift.'

Lady Isobel looked up from her toast and coffee. 'Do you think we could find time to discuss some business that affects this family?' she asked, assuming that such frivolity as Korean banks had no place at her breakfast table.

Peter directed his attention to the old lady and answered in his usual soft voice. 'Of course, Mother. What did you have in mind?'

'I've been looking at the financial report on Piccadilly Radio. I think they are ripe for a take-over.'

'They probably are,' said Peter. 'But don't forget they are a big outfit, not small fry like Cornwall and Dundee. We can't pull the same tricks with them. They would see us coming a mile away.'

'And besides,' interrupted Freddie, 'do you think it wise to get any deeper into radio at this moment?'

The old lady glared at Freddie with a totally dismissive look. 'Just because you show up sober on a Monday morning doesn't mean you've suddenly got a grasp of the media business,' she said. 'Manchester is a prime market and we should be part of it.'

Freddie swallowed his pride with his scrambled egg. 'Peter's right, Mother, I doubt we could buy enough on the QT to take control and that would mean an almighty scramble at the back end, with us having to pay well above the odds.'

'Poppycock!' replied the old lady, addressing her next remark to Peter. 'All we need is about thirty per cent, that will mean six, maybe seven companies, we could do that in a morning.'

Peter stopped eating and considered his reply. 'It sounds good when you say it like that, Mother, but the question we have to ask ourselves is: do we want to buy any more British radio? My feeling is that we should hold off until we know how deep this recession is going to be.'

Lady Isobel would not let go. 'What difference does that make? We can't touch our property because the bottom is out of the market and industry is dying a death. What's left? Media . . . that's what. Media goes on regardless.'

'Quite so,' replied Peter. 'It also survives on advertising, and that is the first thing to be cut when times are bad.'

'Radio advertising is,' injected Freddie. 'Television is a better bet. Maybe we should think along those lines.'

'Television is too expensive,' snapped Lady Isobel. 'If you had an ounce of sense you'd know that. No, I'm going to buy Manchester, with or without your help.' So saying, she swept out of the room, confident they would eventually see her point of view.

The brothers looked at each other in disbelief. Peter took a deep breath and let his shoulders drop. 'We've got to tell her sooner or later,' he said. 'She could spoil the whole plan.'

'Bloody well let her then,' replied Freddie. 'She can't *really* harm us, we're dealing outside the country. The only person she's going to hurt is herself.'

'I don't want to see that happen. I don't want to see her compromised.'

'I'd like to see her well and truly screwed,' laughed Freddie. 'I'd give a year's profit to see that.'

Peter laughed, but shook his head at the same time. 'You two are the eternal antagonists,' he said. 'It would be so much better if you could just bury the hatchet.'

'In her head is where I'd bury it.'

Peter knew it was time to change the subject. 'By the way, did you manage to talk to Monica?'

'I did and she will.'

'Good,' said Sir Peter, standing up and placing his napkin neatly beside his plate. 'At least with her on board, we will be able to have a peaceful breakfast.'

Freddie followed his brother from the room. 'I wouldn't count on that,' he said.

Blissfully unaware of the political connivances at Eaton Square, Monica arrived at the radio station with no more on her mind than the downfall of Flash Jack. She hurried through the morning chores, sorting out expense claims, holiday requests and sales projections with the ease of a hot knife through frozen butter. The contingent of lawyers, managers and interested parties arrived ten minutes late and marched into Monica's office in single file, taking all the available seating plus two chairs hurriedly commandeered from Studio Two.

Monica let them all settle in and offered them coffee. By the time the introductions were completed, she had picked out their leaders. There were only two people who mattered. The manager, Tony Lazer, and his lawyer, John Dillman.

Monica was coldly polite as she addressed her opening remark to John Dillman. 'I've asked for this meeting because I don't think it serves anyone's purpose to drag this into court when the outcome is obvious,' she said. 'I don't wish Flash Jack any harm, but, as you must appreciate, this station has been called to task and I cannot let this accusation go unanswered.'

The lawyer was cautious in his reply. 'Are you saying, Miss Hammond, that you want an out-of-court settlement?'

'What I want, Mr Dillman, is a retraction of all charges and a written apology from either Jack or Mr Lazer.'

There were quiet murmurs around the room. Tony Lazer was the first to speak. 'This is ridiculous. You have libelled my client and I intend to see that his reputation is vindicated.'

Monica sat back in her chair and looked straight into Lazer's eyes. 'Mr Lazer,' she said, 'what Maggie Lomax said about your client is perfectly true. He is a user of cocaine, has been for some time and I am in a position to prove it beyond all doubt.'

Dillman held his hand up to stop Tony Lazer saying anything more. 'I would be very interested in seeing your proof,' he said.

Monica handed Dillman two affidavits. 'These are sworn statements from a Miss Sally Monroe and a Miss Janet Montgomery who participated in illegal drug taking with your client on Saturday, 21 July. I am also in possession of another sworn statement from a third party who was also present at the same occasion, and a complete tape recording of the event.'

Monica sat forward in her chair, crossed her arms on the desk and let the most innocent of smiles cross her face.

The entourage of non-combatants, now deduced by Monica to be friends of Tony Lazer, started to fidget in their seats. Tony jumped to his feet. 'You've conned the lot!' he screamed. 'You've made this up to try and dodge the charges. I know my boy. He's as clean as a whistle.'

'I'm afraid not,' replied Monica coldly. 'Everything in those statements took place. Your "boy" has been very naughty and I think you should be grateful I don't press countercharges against you for the inconvenience you've caused this station and the mental strain you've caused one of my broadcasters.'

John Dillman studied the statements and handed them back to Monica. 'I must say,' he said, 'you seem to have a good defence of justification.'

Monica took back the statements with relief.

'Except for one thing,' Dillman continued. 'I know that this evidence was bought and paid for by this station and would not stand up in court for more than five seconds.'

'Whatever do you mean?' asked Monica.

'What I mean, Miss Hammond, is that these women are professional prostitutes who were paid a thousand pounds each to entrap my client and the third statement you have is from a private detective named Joe Mace, who set the whole thing up.'

Monica felt her stomach turn. How could he know that? Her security had been solid. Nobody knew. 'I hope you can prove that,' she said.

'Yes, I can. The ladies in question live in the Water Gardens, off the Edgware Road, they are known to me and I dare say I could get them to change their statement as long as the price was right.'

'Well, come on down!' shouted Tony Lazer. 'CRFM has just come unstuck.'

Monica was at a loss for words. All her planning had come to nothing. She was facing defeat and probably the sack. How could this be? The chances of this lawyer knowing these prostitutes were a million to one. How did he know about Joe Mace? Maybe the girls told him. This was a nightmare. Damn Maggie Lomax. Damn Flash Jack. She played her last card. 'Whether it was entrapment or not,' she said, 'I have tapes that prove Jack uses cocaine. You may discredit the statements, but you can't fault the tapes, Mr Dillman.'

'They're inadmissible,' said the lawyer.

Monica saw a gap in his armour and plunged her knife in as far as it would go. 'Not to the press,' she said. 'They will fall on this like a ton of bricks. If I release the tapes, your client's reputation is shot, and believe me, I will release them.'

'Go ahead,' shouted Tony Lazer. 'There's no such thing as bad publicity.'

John Dillman slammed his hand down on Monica's desk. 'Mr Lazer,' he shouted at the half-pint cockney. Lazer sat back on the sofa and crossed his arms. Dillman turned towards Monica. 'I do apologize for my client's behaviour,' he said.

Monica nodded and decided to remove the knife, just a little. 'Maybe we should discuss this between the two of us, Mr Dillman. I don't see the point continuing the way we are.'

'Good idea,' replied the lawyer. 'Is there somewhere they could wait?'

Monica called Sally from the adjoining office and told her to show everyone to the conference room and replenish their drinks. Tony Lazer was reluctant to leave. 'This is my client you're talking about,' he said. 'I have a right to be here.'

'You've relinquished that right with your choice of language,' said Dillman. 'Now, please, everyone, wait in the conference room, I won't be long.'

The contingent filed out of Monica's office and left her alone with Dillman. Monica decided to plunge the knife back in. 'Where did you get your information?' she asked.

John Dillman just smiled at her.

'I can't believe you know them, the odds are too great.'

'How I know them is irrelevant, Miss Hammond. The fact is, I do.'

Monica realized that this lawyer was too sharp to fall into any trap that she could think of from the top of her head. Given a day or two and she might catch him, but she didn't have a day or two, she didn't even have a minute. 'What now?' she asked.

'The way I see it, we have a Mexican stand-off. Your evidence is no good, so you can't win in court, but the tape you hold could damage my client quite considerably. What I suggest is a quiet settlement, say fifty thousand plus costs, and we drop all charges.'

Monica's confidence came flooding back. She loved a good fight, but she was about to finish this one as fast as she could. 'I don't see how you can possibly expect us to pay any damages at all, Mr Dillman. We are right. Flash Jack *is* a drug user and we have proved it.'

'I'm afraid my client wouldn't accept any settlement without some damages being paid.'

'The damage, Mr Dillman, will be caused if the papers get hold of tapes of your boy doing naughty things to a couple of ladies while indulging in illegal substances. No, I'm afraid I couldn't even contemplate paying damages of any kind.' She saw his face tighten and thought she would appeal to his greed. 'What I am prepared to do, is pay *your* costs direct.'

John Dillman knew this game and liked it. He could charge Monica anything he liked and still send a bill to that crashing bore Tony Lazer. He gave Monica a knowing smile. 'That would save my client a lot of money,' he said. 'But I still feel he will ask for some kind of clearance as far as the Lomax programme is concerned.'

Monica felt an honourable draw was within her grasp, which was infinitely better than the hiding she was staring at a few minutes earlier. 'I would be willing to voice a complete retraction within forty-eight hours.' She knew she had to wrap this up now, with no chance of a change of mind from either the lawyer or Lazer management. She produced the Joe Mace cassettes from her desk drawer and passed them to Dillman. 'These are copy tapes of the night in question,' she said. 'I'm sure your client will find them very revealing. I will expect your invoice within the next few days.'

John Dillman put the tapes in his coat pocket, stood

up and walked towards the office door. He opened it, then turned to face Monica. 'You're a smart lady,' he said, then turned again and closed the door gently behind him.

Monica gripped the arms of her chair until her knuckles turned white. Her mind raced through every scenario concerning Joe Mace and his bag of tricks. It just didn't make sense. She flicked the switch on her intercom.

'Yes, Miss Hammond.'

'Suzie, you're back. Good. Please get me Frederick French on the phone and Maggie Lomax in my office within the hour.'

Maggie's Monday was progressing great guns until the phone call from Monica's secretary. Mr Goldstein had arranged for PC Campbell to visit her and discuss the hate letter. He asked her how many letters she had received and took the letter away with him. She felt safer just knowing that he was around.

She was just settling down to a daydream and an illicit cream cake when Suzie called. She tried to refuse the appointment, pleading a backache, but Suzie told her that Monica wasn't in a very good mood and that she should make the effort, or everyone would suffer.

Maggie arrived at the station fifty minutes later, stormed through reception, nodded the briefest of hellos to Robin Trower and padded into Monica's office with eight minutes to spare.

Monica looked up from her paperwork and smiled the kind of smile that Maggie neither liked nor trusted.

'Come in, sit down,' said Monica, pointing to the chair on the other side of her desk. 'I have some good news for you.'

'Couldn't you tell me on the phone?' moaned Maggie. 'I thought only bad news was delivered in person.'

'It's a little of both. I've sorted out the Flash Jack problem, but we will have to do a retraction.'

'Bollocks!' shouted Maggie. 'I'm not taking back a single word. You can fire me if you want.'

Monica knew she would still have to do the retraction and she was sure Maggie knew enough people in the press to come up with a stinking article that could stir up enough trouble to put her seat on the parent board in jeopardy. But still, why not, let's have some fun. 'Off you go then,' she said. 'And don't slam the door on your way out.'

Monica had seen that startled look that appeared on Maggie's face before. It was when her ex-husband was kicked in the balls while playing in a charity football match. She thought she'd try a second shot.

'I think I'll get Bernie Bonelli to replace you,' she said, trying hard not to laugh.

Maggie's face lit up. She now knew Monica was not serious. 'You are a sly one,' she said. 'I fell for that hook, line and sinker.'

For the first time since they'd known each other, Monica and Maggie laughed together without a hint of attrition.

'How did you fix it?' asked Maggie.

'It's a long story and one I'd rather not repeat, but we are still faced with this problem of a retraction.'

Maggie stopped laughing. 'Come on, Monica,' she said. 'You can't get me to say it was a lie, when we both know every word was true.'

'I didn't say you, Maggie, I said we.'

'I'm sorry, Monica, I don't follow.'

'You don't have to say anything. I will get Anthony Parkin to voice a retraction and we'll run it at three o'clock in the morning.'

'Can you do that?'

'I most certainly can,' chirped Monica. 'I only promised them I'd do it within two days, I didn't specify when.'

'Ah, Monica, that's brilliant.' Maggie fished around in her handbag for a Silk Cut. 'Do you mind if I smoke?' she asked.

'I don't care if you burst into flames,' replied Monica.

The two women laughed together again. 'God, that's an old joke,' said Maggie. 'You're worse than me when it comes to old jokes.'

'I don't think I want to take this conversation any further.'

'In that case, let me buy you a drink to celebrate the demise of Flashy cokehead.'

'That's a very kind offer, Maggie, but I have another appointment in ten minutes.'

Maggie got up to leave, stood to her full height of five foot three and stuck out her hand. 'I never thought I would do this,' she said, 'but I would like to shake your hand.'

Monica stood up, accepted her handshake and watched her carefully as she left the office. She didn't have another appointment in ten minutes, but she didn't think it wise to take staff relations that far. She walked over to her drinks cabinet and poured herself a large brandy.

Freddie was having a small brandy when Monica called to tell him the outcome of the Flash Jack affair. He listened to all the details and told her that she had handled it very well. He asked her to come to Eaton Square at four o'clock, but did not tell her why.

Nigel B. was feeling like a lonely and forgotten person.

Maida Vale seemed cold and empty without Samantha. The jacuzzi didn't interest him, neither did the pinball machine nor the sundeck. He wandered around the flat remembering all the places they had made love and the little jokes they had shared. He looked through his address book but couldn't be bothered to phone anyone. He finally collapsed on the living-room floor and stared at the ceiling. The doorbell rang and he jumped to his feet. She's come back, he thought, as he raced down the hall. He opened the door and there stood Tony, holding a huge bunch of flowers and looking every inch out of his head.

'Wha say, man, I come ta see de woman o' dis house.'

Nigel embraced his friend and helped him down the hall and into the living room. 'You're too late, she's gone.'

'Ras, man, wha gwan?'

'She's gone on holiday with a girlfriend.'

Tony flashed that famous grin and placed the flowers in the large green vase on the coffee table. 'It good ting I come, bredrin. Ya look as if ya need cheerin' up.'

'I need Sam back, that's what I need.'

Tony reached into his leather bumbag and produced a handful of marijuana. 'Some killer 'erb, man,' he said, dumping it on the table. 'Ya gwan lick a spliff o' dis and she come back in ya dream.'

Nigel held his friend's hand. 'No thanks, Tony, I don't feel like it today.'

'Blood clot, ya got, 'im bad, man.' Tony reached into his bag again and came up with a cassette. 'Look at dis as bidness, man, dis ma new album, you gon 'ear it first.'

Nigel sighed and gestured towards the music centre. 'If anything's going to make me feel better, it's your music. Put it on and turn it up.'

By the end of the first side Nigel was into the music and out of his box. 'You're a real friend, d'ya know that, Tony?'

'Cool, man,' replied the rasta. 'I run outa Rizla.'

Nigel pointed to the writing desk. 'Top drawer, right-hand side.'

Monica dumped her rating sheets into the bottom drawer and closed her desk on the worries of the day. She decided to walk through the park and catch a cab in Knightsbridge to take her to Eaton Square. Freddie didn't say why he wanted to see her, but if the last few weeks were anything to go by she was sure it was good news. She watched the lovers in the park, some walking, some lying on the grass, some just standing together holding hands. For once she felt part of that whole scene. She watched them and remembered Paris, the George V, the house in Fulham and Frank making love to her in the bath. She smiled and walked around the Serpentine with an extra spring in her step.

She arrived at Eaton Square just before four o'clock. Simmons greeted her at the door. 'Good afternoon, Miss Hammond.'

Monica saw no reason to break the illusion. 'Good afternoon. Lovely day again.'

'Indeed, Miss Hammond, Mr French is in the study, on the second floor.'

Freddie was sitting behind the oak partners' desk on the far side of the room, reading the last edition of *Country Life* when Monica entered the study. He stood up and walked towards her. 'Monica,' he said. 'Do come in.' He poured a very large brandy from the crystal decanter on the sideboard and thrust it into her hand.

'I think it's a bit early for me to start on this,' Monica said, as she accepted the drink and sat down on the buttoned leather sofa next to the desk.

'I think not,' replied Freddie. 'You're going to need it.'

Monica felt a sense of foreboding as she settled into her seat and cradled the brandy goblet in both hands. 'Whatever's wrong?' she asked, studying Freddie carefully, trying to grasp a clue as to the source of his concern.

Freddie felt and looked embarrassed. He walked slowly back to the desk, sat down behind it and emptied his glass of brandy in one gulp. 'I know how Dillman got his information about the Joe Mace tapes,' he said.

Monica was now totally bewildered. 'I would think that was good news,' she said. 'I knew there had to be a leak somewhere. It was all too clever for them to work it out on their own.' Her mind flashed on all the possibilities. 'Who is it?' she asked.

Freddie picked up a brown manila folder from his desk. As he opened it Monica could see the name Dun & Bradstreet on the front cover. 'I'm so sorry to have to tell you this,' he said. 'Frank De Wolf is a spy.'

Monica looked at Freddie, but could not see him. Frank's name spun around in her head. Her first reaction was pure anger, not at Frank, but at Freddie French. This must be some cruel joke. How could he do such a thing? She tried to speak, but no words would leave her mouth. She just sat on the sofa and stared at nothing. Freddie stood up and poured himself another brandy.

'I'm sorry, Monica,' he said. 'I would give anything to say it's not true.'

Monica instinctively attacked the closest target. 'What the hell do you think you're doing, Freddie? You've been checking up on me behind my back?'

'I had no choice.' Freddie sat beside Monica on the sofa. 'I'm sorry, I'm so very sorry.'

Monica realized, within that split second, that

Freddie was telling the truth. She started sobbing uncontrollably. She dropped the brandy glass on the floor and covered her face with both hands. Freddie put his glass on the table and put his arm around her shoulder. She felt destroyed. All her hopes, all her dreams, all her memories of the last few weeks flashed through her mind and burst in a bubble of betrayal. She tried hard to control herself. She grabbed for her bag in search of a handkerchief. Freddie offered his. She took a deep breath and blew with all her might. It worked. Freddie removed his arm, picked up her glass and filled it with brandy. 'Drink some of this,' he said.

She drank the brandy and felt the warmth fill her body. She fought her tears and tried to regain her composure. 'God, Freddie, I've been such a fool,' she said. 'How could I have been so stupid?'

'We've all been stupid at one time or another. The main thing to remember is, don't get mad, get even.'

Monica looked at Freddie through watery eyes. 'Tell me the details,' she sobbed. 'I want to know all the details.'

Freddie put the Dun & Bradstreet folder on the table in front of her. 'It's all there,' he said. 'When Peter and I first thought of inviting you to join us, we had to make sure you were safe. The only person we didn't know about was Frank. The occasional lover is entirely your business, we trust you not to talk about our business with them, but Frank was somebody you obviously cared about and we had to make sure he was kosher. We ran a check on him and found his clients were Queensland Properties, Ten Star Investments, Rock Securities and ATS, all companies owned entirely by Aylford. Frank De Wolf works exclusively for Wallace Pike.'

Monica dried her eyes and looked at the report. It

was all there. Her sorrow turned to anger, she threw the file across the room with all the strength she could muster. 'That bastard,' she screamed. 'I was set up from day one.'

'I'm afraid so,' replied Freddie. 'The only good thing to come of this is that he doesn't know we are on to him.'

Monica tried her best to raise a smile. 'This is no time to get mad then,' she said.

'It's a time to get even,' replied Freddie.

Monica felt the waves of emotion about to hit her for the second time. 'Freddie, I need to be alone,' she said. 'Do you mind?'

Freddie walked from the room without saying another word and quietly closed the door behind him. As he walked down the hall he could hear her crying softly in the privacy of her own despair.

Sir Peter arrived home just after five o'clock. Freddie informed him about the events of the afternoon and that Monica had taken it very badly.

'I'm not surprised,' said Sir Peter. 'One could tell she really cared for him. Where is she now?'

'In the study.'

'Is Mother at home?'

'She's spending the evening with Francis and John.'

Sir Peter slapped his brother on the back and moved him towards the stairs. 'In that case, why don't we take the lovely lady to dinner and drown this clandestine love affair in some excellent Château de Rothschild?'

The brothers entered the study and found Monica lying on the sofa. 'Is this what we pay a hundred and fifty thousand pounds a year for?' said Sir Peter.

Monica sat bolt upright and tried to focus her bleary eyes.

'Relax,' said Freddie. 'He's only joking.'

'I must have dropped off,' said Monica, hurriedly trying to compose herself.

'Not to worry,' said Sir Peter. 'We know you've had quite a shock, but now is the time to pick up and start again. Don't you agree?'

Monica stood up and brushed herself down, trying, as best she could, to straighten her dress. 'I do believe you're right, Peter,' she said, reaching deep inside herself to find that final brave face. 'Where do we go from here?'

'That's the spirit,' said Freddie, making a punching movement with his right hand. 'First of all we take you out to dinner and get that magnificent mind back in working order.'

'Simmons will show you to the guest suite,' said Sir Peter. 'You can wash up there and if you need anything from your flat, just tell him and we'll have it sent round.'

Monica smiled at them both and began to feel like her old self again, although she was sure she didn't look it. She took a small sip from the brandy glass, more to rid her mouth of the taste of tears than for any effect it might have, and walked into the hallway, where Simmons was waiting. He followed her up to the guest suite, where she gave Simmons the keys to her flat and a list of things she wanted from Cadogan Square, then locked the door behind him. Nothing she had experienced before compared to the loneliness she felt at that moment. She gritted her teeth, lay face down on the single bed and punched the pillow several times as hard as she could, pretending it was Frank's face. 'Bastard . . . bastard . . . bastard!' she said to herself as each blow was struck. All the sex games, all the tender moments were all lies. They were all part of a *business* deal. He said he loved her and she believed him, and yet all the time he just wanted information. She felt used, betrayed, foolish, vulnerable, but most of all, she felt dirty. Very dirty. She sat up on the bed, her hands clenched tightly in front of her. 'I'll get you, Frank De Wolf,' she hissed. 'You'll know what fucked means when I'm through with you.' She stood up and literally tore her clothes off, ripping her dress in the process. She went into the en-suite bathroom and stood under the shower, turned it on full blast and scrubbed her skin raw with the loofah.

By the time she'd dried herself, she'd worked out several ways to make Mr De Wolf pay for his deception.

Simmons arrived back with Monica's things and placed them neatly outside the bedroom door. He knocked politely. 'I've left your items in the hallway, madam. Will there be anything else?'

'No, thank you,' said Monica from behind the locked door. 'Thank you very much.'

Simmons moved quickly away to attend to his other duties.

Monica started with her make-up, carefully removing all traces of the preceding drama; within thirty minutes she had transformed herself into a vision of total control, with not a hint of disorder anywhere about her person. She walked down the two flights of stairs to the main drawing room. Sir Peter and Freddie were having a lively discussion about the merits of investing abroad to save the ridiculous amount of tax which was now being forced upon them by the government that *they* had helped into power. Peter was the first to notice her appearance at the doorway. 'Monica,' he said. 'You look wonderful. Do come in. May I get you a drink?'

Freddie looked at her with amazement. He had known her for a good few years, but he had never seen her look this lovely. He walked over to her and offered his arm. 'My dear, you look stunning,' he said. 'Say you'll be with me tonight and that you won't even look at my brother.'

Monica felt sure this was calculated flattery, but she didn't care. She took his arm and glided into the room. 'I'll have a vodka and tonic, if you please, Peter.' She turned to face Freddie. 'Have you thought of any ways to execute our revenge?' she asked.

'You being here with us, instead of being somewhere else with him is a good start,' said Freddie. 'How about you?'

'I thought of cutting his balls off and using them as a door knocker,' she replied. 'But I couldn't find a knife blunt enough.'

Peter handed her a rather large vodka and a small bottle of tonic. 'That's my girl,' he said, giving her a kiss on the cheek. 'Where there's a sense of humour, there's a chance of survival, I always say. I thought we would go oriental tonight. How does the Non Ya sound?'

Monica nodded her approval.

'Fine,' said Peter. 'I'll get Simmons to make the reservation.'

Maggie and John drank a few large bevvies before Maggie's show to celebrate the outcome of the Flash Jack affair. John stayed behind to make sure Maggie was OK on the air. He didn't need to worry. She was on top form. By eight o'clock she was steaming. The music was good and the wit was as sharp as a razor. She knew she could not mention Flash Jack or anything about the result, but she couldn't resist just one little dig.

'This is Maggie Lomax on London's Number One. Here's a little tune for everyone who likes good guitar playing and for the odd ones of you who like the title.'

She played Eric Clapton and 'Cocaine'.

As the track ended she picked up line four. 'CRFM, you're on the air.'

'I'm going to blow your ass sky high, you fu–'

Maggie was fast enough to cut the caller off before he finished the sentence. 'Here we go again,' she said. 'Look, if you want to swear on the radio please phone up Capital. We know all those words and we're not impressed.' She punched up a commercial break and sat back in her chair. She knew she mustn't let it get to her, it was all part of the job, but she felt deep down that whoever this was he had a real sinister streak to him that frightened her more than she would like to admit. The commercial ended and she segued into a live Bruce Springsteen track.

The fun had suddenly disappeared and Maggie couldn't wait for nine o'clock when she could run away and play some snooker.

Monica and the French brothers were playing games of a much more serious nature. The food at Non Ya was excellent and they ate their fill of chicken with cashew nuts, ginger beef, jumbo prawns in garlic, and other various Peking delicacies. Monica still felt waves of emotion drift over her, but she was determined to stay strong and the thought of revenge added sweetness to the bitter pill. Coffee and brandy was served as the three of them put their heads together across the round table and started to plot.

'I think we could gain a lot from all this,' said Sir Peter. 'He doesn't know that we're on to him, so he'll accept anything we say.'

'As long as Monica can string him along,' said Freddie.

'Yes, please,' said Monica. 'In fact, I look forward to that part almost as much as stringing him up at the end.'

'What I suggest,' said Peter, 'is that we tell him, through Monica, that we are about to bid for six other stations on the network. Aylford will then try and buy up every share they can get their hands on. We will contact those stations as if we intended to purchase and that will send the price up a bit more. Aylford pay through the nose, we pull out, the share price drops. They lose money and Mr De Wolf is discredited.'

'A plan after my own heart,' said Freddie.

Monica just smiled and ate another chocolate.

'This could also have a knock-on effect,' continued Freddie. 'If we get the timing right, Aylford will be short of cash at the same time as we put our radio interests on the market, thus causing them to sell their satellite holdings to us at a much lower price if they want a swap for our stock. Simple but effective, I would say.'

'I agree,' said Monica. 'But what about De Wolf? There has got to be a way of wrecking his career for good.'

The two brothers looked at each other, and then at Monica.

'I think we can leave that in your very capable hands,' said Freddie.

CHAPTER 13

Anthony Parkin was now an award winner. He had always been one of the top professionals, but now he took an even greater pride in his work. When Lizzie arrived in the production studio to do her voice links for the Anthony and Cleopatra pilot, he had already cut together the theme music, three items on redecorating kitchens, an interview with a local plumber and had contacted the sales department to enlist their help in finding a sponsor.

Lizzie listened to the interview and her face lit up like New York City. 'This is great,' she whispered in his ear, as she hugged him tightly around the waist. 'Do you realize what kind of buzz this will create around the business? I can see the headlines now. The first programme from award-winner Anthony Parkin a brilliant success.'

'Hold on a minute,' replied Anthony. 'We haven't even finished it yet, and besides, there's no guarantee that Monica will even give us a slot. There are hundreds of pilots made every year and only ten or twenty ever see the light of day, let alone get rated.'

'You let me worry about Monica, dearest,' she said with controlled confidence. 'You just work your magic and I'll get us a slot.'

Anthony kissed his Lizzie on the forehead and handed her a script. 'Just pop into the voice booth and read what's written,' he said. 'Until this is put together, we have nothing but good will and hot air.'

Lizzie slid her petite body past him, making sure he got the full benefit of her thirty-four C cups. She propped herself up on the stool, put on the headphones and adjusted the microphone. 'Do you want some for level?' she asked.

'Just give me "Peter Piper picked a peck". I have a feeling you'll need a pop shield.'

'Peter Piper poked a prossy, and paid her half his pension.'

Anthony laughed over the talkback. 'You need a shield, I'll be right back.' He went next door to steal one from studio three and on his return found David Westbury and a rather Germanic-looking gentleman standing at his console. 'Can I help you?' he asked.

'Anthony,' said David Westbury. 'Just the fellow. May I introduce Helmut Von Krugge, chairman of Bellux Home Care, the biggest DIY chain in Europe.'

'Pleased to meet you,' said Anthony, extending his hand.

'Likewise,' replied the German, gripping Anthony's hand with the strength of your average power vice. 'I've heard so many good things about you and your radio place.'

'Helmut is a new client of ours,' said David. 'He's opening five new DIY centres in London over the next six months and he's interested in sponsoring your new programme.'

'In that case,' said Anthony, removing his hand from Helmut's grip and making a fist behind his back to make sure no bones were broken, 'welcome to the fun factory.'

'Do you have the show ready for my hearing?' asked Helmut.

'We've only just started,' replied Anthony. 'I should have the pilot finished by late this afternoon.'

'I will not hold you up by one minute,' said the

German, clicking his heels. Good God, thought Anthony, someone actually does that. Helmut was not at all embarrassed. 'Can we meet for dinner at my hotel and further our discussions?' he asked.

'That would be fine,' said Anthony.

'About eight then, and please to bring the lovely lady voice with you.'

'She's the other half of the show – I wouldn't leave home without her,' replied Anthony, hoping to end the conversation on a funny note.

There was no reaction at all from the DIY man.

As soon as David closed the studio door behind him, Lizzie was on the talkback. 'Who was that?'

'It could be the answer to our prayers,' replied Anthony.

'A sponsor?'

'Could be. He wants us to have dinner with him tonight and he wants to hear the finished programme, so let's get to work. Read me the first line so I can get a level.'

'What about my shield?'

'No time for safe sex, kid, just give it to me straight.'

'Anthony.'

'Yes.'

Lizzie stuck out her tongue and slowly licked the end of the microphone.

'OK, girl, you win,' he said in sweet defeat. 'I'll bring it in.'

Lizzie liked to win, no matter how small the game.

Lady Isobel was another natural winner. For thirty-five years she had been a major influence on French Enterprises and since the death of her husband in 1970, she had run the company with an iron fist wrapped in aristocratic silk. It was true that for the last five years Peter had taken over more and more of the day-to-day running of the empire, but she was still the power behind the throne. He had diversified into foreign markets, built up the media interests and delivered the biggest profits the company had ever known, but she still felt that, ultimately, she had the power to make or break anyone. Besides, if it weren't for her, Peter would still be messing around at some university, trying to complete an arts degree that would have served no useful purpose whatsoever. Today her primary task was to begin her acquisition of Piccadilly Radio; to that end she placed a phone call to Harry Connaught.

Harry was having a troublesome day. He was happy with Monica's explanation about the French/ATS deal, but the Home Office had been on to him with a few questions that were very hard to answer. He fobbed them off with an assurance that the Australians were falling into a trap that could cut their interest in British media by a considerable amount, but at this stage he was unable to supply any more detail. The HO replied that they were sure he knew what he was doing, and that phrase made Harry Connaught a very nervous man.

He answered Lady Isobel's call straight away and went through the customary pleasantries, and ended by thanking her for the kind and generous contribution to the Great Ormond Street Hospital, of which he was a prominent fund-raiser.

'You're more than welcome,' replied Lady Isobel. 'The reason I'm calling you today is that I require some information about Piccadilly in Manchester.'

Harry felt a small warning tremor. 'What kind of information?'

'It's in a mess and we intend buying it. What I want to know is, are there any other interested parties?'

The original tremor turned into something much larger. 'I think you're being a trifle hasty on this one. They seem very stable to us and the major shareholders have a lot of capital between them. I know they wouldn't welcome a take-over bid and a hostile approach would be very expensive indeed.'

'God's breath, Harry, I'm not going to take them over, I'm going to buy them out from under their own noses. The company should be showing at least another thirty per cent profit. It reeks of bad management and I intend to put it right.'

Harry now felt a full-blown earthquake. 'Isobel, you can't do that. It's highly unethical and the company is too big to take on by yourself. It has far-reaching interests outside the radio station, and I believe the lack of net profit is due to their reinvestment programme which, as you know, we support.'

'Poppycock. They're a lame duck, a big duck, I'll give you that, but we make twice as much as them from our London station alone. No, Harry, it all goes to prove what I've always said, management north of Watford couldn't make a penny from a pound if it wasn't handled by the City.'

Harry knew there was no point in arguing with Lady Isobel once she had made up her mind, but he was damned if he would let her go on a wrecking spree through the most successful station on the network outside London. 'I really think you should reconsider,' he said. 'Have you discussed this with Peter and Freddie?'

'Of course,' said Lady Isobel, her voice becoming noticeably irritable.

'And what do they think?'

'What they think is none of your business,' she snapped. 'Look here, Harry, I phoned you up to ask a straightforward question. If you feel it's beyond you to give me a straightforward answer, I'll get my information elsewhere.'

Lady Isobel slammed the phone down on its cradle and left a buzzing sound in the Director General's ear.

Monica's phone manner was as pleasant as a picnic in Petts Wood when she called Frank De Wolf to arrange dinner. She suggested they meet at the restaurant and insisted that tonight was her treat, as he had done so much for her over the past few weeks. She chose Joe Allen's because it was so full of life – Frank said it was noisy and crowded. She said that as she was paying, she could choose and they agreed on nine o'clock.

'Bastard,' she hissed, as she hung up and placed another call to Freddie French. They agreed to start the deception with three stations: East Anglia, Essex and Kent.

'Kent's not a bad idea,' said Freddie. 'I wouldn't mind buying that one just to inherit the sales force.'

'Don't change the game on me now,' said Monica. 'I find it tough enough dealing with De Wolf. I don't need a change of plan to complicate everything.'

Freddie laughed. 'You'll be just fine, Monica.'

The thought of turning that two-faced bastard over and watching him drown in his own lies went a long way towards making Monica feel strong. That's what she needed more than anything else, to feel strong. She dreaded the thought of having to pretend with him, although she had thought of a few very interesting ways to get her own back on the sexual front.

Monica was half an hour late arriving at Joe Allen's. Frank was at the bar and well into his third whisky.

'Darling,' she said, 'I'm so sorry I'm late. Peter kept me talking for hours on this new station deal.'

'Can I get you a drink?' he asked.

The word is 'may' not 'can', she thought. 'Yes please, sweetheart, vodka tonic.'

Frank offered her his seat at the crowded bar and as he brushed by her he kissed the side of her neck. She responded by sliding her hand down the front of his trousers. One good grab, she thought, but not just yet.

They ate chilli and drank ice-cold beer. Throughout the meal Monica noticed little things about him that she hadn't spotted before. The way he looked at other women as they came into his line of sight, how he would check his reflection in a picture glass and flick his hair back if it was out of place. In repose, his eyes turned cold and somehow evil. She was sure she was exaggerating because of what she now knew, but she also realized that the old cliché about love being blind had definite merit and vowed never to let it happen again.

'How was your day, darling?' she asked with the sincerity she was sure could win her an Oscar.

'Just the usual corporate crap,' he answered, spooning a mouthful of red beans. 'How about you?'

'Not bad, very interesting really. The French brothers are such go-ahead people, it's a joy to work with them.'

'What's this about new stations?' he asked. 'I thought Cornwall and Dundee were already put to bed.'

Gotcha! 'Oh, these are new ones. They're making a bid for some more out-of-town outfits that are in trouble.'

'I thought the rest of the network was fairly stable.'

And I thought you loved me. DAMN . . . she could feel herself beginning to crack. 'Excuse me, I must just go to the loo.' She left the table, walked quickly into the ladies' room, and had a good talk with herself. She remembered the garden party and how he appeared from nowhere with the . . . AUSTRALIANS! Of course, she should have suspected him then. The fact that she had caught him out now, albeit a little late, made her feel strong again. The only thing that bothered her now was the thought of having sex with him tonight. She didn't feel that strong yet. Suddenly the answer came to her. She walked back to the table.

'I'm sorry I took so long,' she said, leaning across the table and talking softly in his ear. 'Wrong time of the month.' He bent forward to kiss her cheek, but she moved away and sat upright on her seat. 'Now, where were we?'

'Other stations in trouble,' he replied.

'Yes, well, Freddie thinks Anglia, Essex and Kent are having difficulties, and from what he showed me, I have to agree.'

'Will you buy them the same way as you did Cornwall and Dundee?'

Gotcha again! I never told you how we bought them. 'I should imagine so,' she said sweetly. 'I always say, when something works, stick with it.'

Frank finished his beer and stuck his hand up to order another round.

'Not for me,' said Monica.

Frank turned up his charm to number ten. 'I'm sorry, darling. Do you want to go home?'

Why not, thought Monica. You can phone Pike and start the ball rolling right away. 'If you don't mind, Frank, I wouldn't mind an early night.'

Monica kissed him good night in the Bentley outside Cadogan Square. It was a warm, tender embrace. She caressed his face with her hands and slid her tongue slowly between his lips. She could feel his passion rise and just as he was about to place his hand inside her blouse, she gently slipped away from him and opened the passenger door. 'Good night, darling,' she whispered. 'I'll call you tomorrow.'

As the Bentley turned into Pont Street, she spat the taste of him from her mouth.

Nigel spat his mouthwash into the bathroom sink and realized how much he hated four o'clock in the morning. It was a no man's time, fit only for insomniacs and night workers. It wasn't so bad when Samantha was there. She didn't like it any more than he did, but she always made an effort to make him feel cheerful. One morning she even set the alarm for half past three and made love to him until four-fifteen. That morning's show was one of the best he'd ever done and he wished she was with him now to help him cope with the loneliness of this wretched hour. He shuffled into the kitchen and dumped two eggs, a pint of milk and a spoonful of honey into the blender, then covered his ears to drown out the noise of the motor. He drank his breakfast in two gulps, pausing only to check the date on the Marilyn Monroe calendar that adorned the kitchen wall. Friday, 3 August. Half-way through. This time next week he would pick up Sam from the airport. That thought made him feel better as he wandered back into the bedroom in search of a clean pair of jeans.

He arrived at the station by half past five and forced a smile at Bernie as he passed the studio. Bernie was on his own today, so at least he didn't have to put up with the usual crass sexual innuendo that inevitably occurred when Bonelli had some ugly groupie in tow. John Thorne was beavering away in the newsroom, compiling the first bulletin of the day. Nigel waved at John and made a 'T' sign with his two index fingers. John signed a 'C' back, and within a couple of minutes Nigel walked into the newsroom carrying two large cups of very black coffee.

'Good morning, o king of news,' he said, placing one of the cups on John's desk and taking a loud slurp from the other. 'What's new in the world?'

'The shit's hit the fan in the Middle East,' replied John. 'Iraq has invaded Kuwait.'

'Makes a change from Maggie bashing the Krauts,' sniggered Nigel.

'I think this could be serious, there're more "D" notices flying around than Beecham's got powders.'

'I'm sure Israel will sort them out, they usually do. Anyway, isn't Saddam still trying to kick the shit out of Iran?'

John looked up from his desk and eyed the breakfast jock with guarded suspicion. 'Don't say anything on air, Nigel, the MOD are hot on this one.'

'Calm down, Johnny boy, it'll all be over in a week and let's face it, the *Sun* and the *Star* will have a field day. I can see it now. Sod Off Saddam in four-inch type, all over the front page.'

'Just keep all the Iraqi jokes to yourself, Nigel, the IBA will have your balls for bookends if you make light of this one.'

Nigel studied the newsman's face and could see he was serious. 'OK, boss,' he chuckled. 'I'm only in this for the rock and roll. The three things I've learned in my limited experience of this business are don't argue with news, don't crash a voice-over and *never* fade a Bruce Springsteen record. By the way, does Monica know?'

'The main story broke yesterday, and so far I haven't heard a dicky from the slave driver of Sloane Street.'

'You will, dear boy, you will,' said Nigel, as he gathered his things together and headed towards the studio for his customary spot of unwitty repartee with Bernie Bonelli.

Monica did know, of course, but she trusted her head of news enough not to bother him by stating the obvious; besides, she was much more interested in finding out what Sir Peter and Freddie thought of the situation. She arranged a morning-coffee meeting at Cadogan Square as Freddie had suggested. They wanted to set a few things in motion regarding Aylford. Eaton Square was unsuitable because of Lady Isobel and the station was far too heavily populated to guarantee security, so Cadogan Square was the obvious choice.

The brothers arrived at ten o'clock and welcomed a cup of Monica's fresh brewed Colombian coffee. Peter set his papers out on the living room table and called the meeting to order. At first it seemed strange to Monica that he should go through the formalities of meeting procedure, until she realized that it did wonders to focus the mind.

'First of all,' said Sir Peter, 'I would like Monica to tell us the outcome of her dinner with De Wolf on Tuesday.'

'I'm pleased to report that he is now totally convinced that we are after Anglia, Essex and Kent. I should imagine that Aylford are already sniffing around trying to ascertain whether or not these stations are in as bad a financial state as I made them out to be,' she said, with some considerable pride.

'Good,' said Sir Peter. 'The next move is up to you, Freddie. After this meeting, you must make a few phone calls and pretend to show an interest and you, Monica, should meet again with De Wolf and plant the seed for the next series of acquisitions. I would suggest we go big this time. Any ideas, Freddie?'

'Downtown, in Belfast, would be my next choice. A

good solid PLC, with lots of floating shares and almost impossible to get to the truth as they are too far away, then I think maybe the GWR Group in the West Country, or maybe even Capital.'

'Do you not think we could be stretching the limits of our credibility if we go for Capital or GWR?' asked Sir Peter. 'Everyone knows they are very healthy, especially Capital, where the MD has become the toast of the city with his astute handling of their television and theatrical acquisitions. Monica, what do you think?'

'I think Nigel Walmsley won't be at Capital forever. If Aylford think we have an inside track on him leaving, they could come to the conclusion that we were trying for a major take-over and try and buy everything that's available, with a view to selling it back to us at a much higher price, or at least swap with us, so they get a piece of the cake.'

'Very good,' said Freddie. 'If we could convince them of that scenario, it would cost them dearly to get into the game and what's more, if Monica is right, and Walmsley leaves, the price is bound to drop, so they lose either way.'

Sir Peter looked at Monica over the top of his half-moon glasses. 'Do you think you can convince De Wolf?' he asked.

'I do,' she replied with conviction. 'The other thing to consider is that your mother trying to punch her way into Piccadilly will add credence to our cause.'

'Wonderful,' said Freddie. 'For once the old bat is doing us a favour and she doesn't even know it.'

'I think we can conclude at this point,' said Sir Peter. 'Unless there is any other business?'

'There is one thing,' said Monica quickly. 'What are your impressions of the latest developments in the Gulf?'

'That is a very complicated subject,' answered Freddie.

'It is something we have been aware of for some time now,' interrupted Sir Peter. 'May I say to you at this moment, Monica, that the whole of the Middle East situation has figured strongly in our reasoning for the future development of French Enterprises.'

Monica looked at both the brothers and wondered if she should learn Japanese.

John Thorne finished the nine o'clock news with a light story about a Chinese rock star who was having one hell of a time with the lyric of 'Rock Around The Clock'. He walked into his office and found a hastily scribbled note on his blotting pad. *'Please call Maggie – Urgent.'* He dialled her number and took a sip of his cold coffee. A very shaky Scots voice answered the phone. John sat upright in his chair. 'What's the matter, Maggie? Are you not well?'

'Can you come over to my flat?'

'What's wrong?'

'Just come over now . . . please!'

'Ten minutes,' said John, hanging up the phone and moving smartly from his desk towards the door. He ran through the newsroom, shouting orders as he went. 'James, you do ten o'clock and stand by for eleven. Sara, IRN feed. Bill and Karen, sub-edit. I'll be on the bleeper. Bill, keys to the radio car!' The young reporter took the keys from his pocket and tossed them at the moving Head of news. 'Is it outside?' asked John. Bill nodded.

John drove to Maggie's flat with the headlights full on, at well over the speed limit. She saw him arrive and threw down her front-door key. He let himself in and found her puffing furiously on a Silk Cut. She ran to him and held him in a vicelike grip, her head resting on his chest.

John comforted her the best he could and sat her down on the settee. 'What's been going on here?' he asked.

Maggie looked up at him. She had obviously been crying. She clasped her hands in front of her mouth, her arms together, elbows touching and rocked slowly back and forth. 'I got another phone call,' she said. 'Here, at the flat . . . this morning.'

John did not have first hand experience of this sort of thing, but he could see the effect it was having on Maggie and he knew he had to put a stop to it. 'Do you know who they are?' he asked.

'No, but I can't take any more,' Maggie whimpered. 'I'm afraid to go out and I'm afraid to stay home.'

John studied her eyes. He had never seen such terror, especially in somebody as strong as Mad Maggie Lomax. She could usually deal with anything, both on and off the air. He went over to the window and looked up and down the street. An old lady sitting on a bench and a mother pushing her pram with a mongrel dog following behind were the only things moving in the area. He checked for people in parked cars. He could see nothing. He walked back to Maggie and covered her white knuckles with his hands.

'This is what we do. I'm going to make a cup of tea while you get your things together. Then you're going to come and stay with Patricia and me until we can get to the bottom of this.'

'I can't . . .'

'I don't want to hear another word,' said John, standing up and walking towards the kitchen. 'I don't want to hear what you can or cannot do. You called in the troops and now I'm going to look after you.'

The faintest of smiles appeared on Maggie's face.

'That's better.' John returned her smile. 'Now get enough things together for a couple of days and I'll phone home and tell Pat you're coming.'

On the drive over to the Thornes' house Maggie had a verbal sluice about the mystery phone calls and letters. She talked about Flash Jack, who she was sure was the prime candidate, the regular oddball callers, men who would phone her on air and pretend to talk about the subject on hand, but the only thing they really had in hand were their dicks – she called them out-patients; and worst of all, the yobbos, who would wait for her outside the station and lambast her with crude obscenities, but always at a safe distance, so she could never catch them and give them the kick in the goolies they so richly deserved.

'Have you ever thought that it might be something to do with this IRA story I'm dealing with?' asked John.

'I don't know, John, I haven't got a clue who it is. That's what got me so rattled.' Maggie reached into her bag for a cigarette. 'You know, I think I should tell Monica about this.'

'You're joking. She'll just say it's all part of the job and if you can't cope with it, you shouldn't be doing it.'

'I'm not so sure. She handled the Jack thing very well and, what's more, I found out she even has a sense of humour.'

'I know that, Maggie,' laughed John. 'I've listened to Bernie Bonelli.'

'Very funny, but I mean it. I'm going to call her from your place and see what she has to say.'

'If it makes you happy,' said John, not believing for one moment that Monica would take the slightest interest in anything as obtuse as dirty phone calls or anonymous letters.

Monica was about to leave for the station when Maggie's phone call was relayed from the office. She listened to her story and told her to stay exactly where she was. She organized a recorded snoop on Maggie's phone-in number, police protection when she left the station and a private surveillance on her flat, before calling a cab to take her to John Thorne's house.

Patricia Thorne showed Maggie to the spare bedroom and assured her she was welcome to stay as long as necessary. Patricia was such a warm and loving person and Maggie felt safe in this rambling family home with all the children's toys, worn furniture and scratched paintwork.

'I'll make some coffee,' said Patricia. 'Or maybe you would like something stronger?'

'I wouldn't say no to half a glass of whisky,' replied Maggie.

'I'll have it ready for you in the kitchen.' Patricia hugged Maggie warmly. 'You just settle in and come down when you're ready.'

Maggie unpacked her suitcase and felt not envy, but confirmation, that there was a real life possible in this crazy world.

Monica arrived as Maggie was finishing her second whisky. Patricia put coffee and shortbreads on the living-room table beside what was left of Maggie's whisky bottle. She left the three of them alone and went to pick up her youngest from nursery school.

John watched closely as the two women discussed the details of Maggie's predicament. He was impressed by

Monica's genuine interest. Monica thanked John for taking Maggie into his home and complimented him on his quick action. She also suggested that he have someone pick up the radio car, as it would be needed at the station. Up to now John had known she was a good managing director, but as she talked the fear out of Maggie, his estimation of her as a woman went up tenfold.

Patricia served a light lunch of lasagne and salad with a bottle of Frascati, which Maggie devoured before anyone could grab a second glass. Monica organized the engineering department to collect the back-logging tapes for the past three months and edit out all the mystery calls on to a cassette, so she could pass them to the police while John arranged for the radio car to be collected. By the middle of the afternoon, things seemed to be getting back to normal. Maggie assured Monica everything would be fine for the programme tonight and that in the end, no one was going to get the better of her, be they Irish, perverted, yobbo or just plain sick in the head.

The two women shared a cab to the station. Maggie's impression of her boss had also changed somewhat in the last few days. There was still an underlying friction between them which Maggie suspected would always be there, but Monica had shown an understanding and willingness to help that Maggie had previously thought was bred out of her by her driving ambition to get to the top.

It never occurred to Maggie that Monica could be playing an entirely different game.

Lizzie Stephenson was waiting in Monica's office. She held the Anthony and Cleopatra pilot tape tightly in her hands as she rehearsed her speech. Monica was not that pleased to see her sitting uninvited on her couch, but she greeted her with a smile and asked the purpose of the visit.

'Anthony and I have made a pilot for a weekend show and I'd like you to hear it,' said Lizzie. 'We are meeting a sponsor tonight, so we need your opinion of it right away.'

Monica didn't like being forced into instant opinions, but the word 'sponsor' was always music to her ears, so she listened to the tape and, to her surprise, was very impressed with what she heard. 'This is very good indeed,' she said. 'The only problem is I don't have a slot for it just now, sponsored or not.'

'Thank you, Monica,' beamed Lizzie. 'As long as you like it, that's all that matters.' She retrieved the tape and skipped out the door.

Lizzie had a plan. She went to her office to instigate phase one.

Monica also had a plan. She phoned Frank De Wolf and invited him to dinner at Cadogan Square. She bought two thick fillet steaks and some fresh salad on the way home and prepared the food before having a long soak in the private bath.

Frank arrived shortly before eight o'clock. Monica felt much stronger now. She was charming, witty, and more than a little sexy. She wore a loose, red dress that showed every curve of her body to its best effect. She fed him food and information about the plans of the French brothers and their impending take-over of British radio.

'Do you really think they will try for Capital?' asked Frank, as he nibbled on a very large radish.

'I can't say for sure,' replied Monica innocently. 'All I know is what I hear from the brothers. I doubt if I'm getting the whole story, but it would make sense if their MD was to go into television.' She stood behind him and put her arms around his neck. 'I really shouldn't be telling you this. You don't represent any one who might have an interest in radio, do you?'

'Good heavens no,' said Frank. 'My clients are all in property and securities. I don't move in the heady world of media.'

'That's all right then,' said Monica. 'This is privileged information and I would hate to see you get in trouble with the Bar Council for not declaring your interest.' She let go of him and walked over to her writing desk. As Frank turned his back to pour himself another glass of wine, Monica quietly turned off the tape recorder.

CHAPTER 14

Sunday morning began at noon for Nigel Beresford-Clarke. Tony had visited him on Saturday night and the two lads hit all the pubs on the Edgware Road that sported a pool table, before ending up at Maida Vale, listening to Bob Marley and watching the snooker on television with the sound off.

Nigel had all the Sunday papers delivered each week, so the first thing he did, once he cleared his pit, was to open the front door and pull them inside the flat, before the dog next door decided to use them as a toilet. He bundled them under his arm and headed for the kitchen to blend up some breakfast. The Kenwood's motor seemed louder than usual this morning as he scanned the front pages. Kuwait, Kuwait, Kuwait – every paper had the Middle East all over its front pages. Every paper, that is, except the *News of the World*. Nigel looked at their front page in total disbelief. There was a picture of him stepping out of the jacuzzi, a cigar in one hand and a glass of champagne in the other, with only a small towel airbrushed on to hide his embarrassment. The headline read, 'Britain's Top DJ in Sex Orgy with 17-Year-Old Schoolgirl'. In the top right-hand corner was a picture of Samantha dressed in a blue and white school uniform, with a small caption underneath that read 'Full story and more pictures on pages 4, 5, and 6'.

Nigel went into shock. He turned the blender off and turned to page 4. There were more pictures of him with hardly any clothes on and more of Samantha looking every inch a convent girl. The article began with a quote: 'The first time I met Nigel I knew he would be my undoing. He was so sexy, I just couldn't resist his charms.' It went on to document making love in every room of his flat, their day out at Oxford and how he introduced her to the pleasures of marijuana while instructing her in the art of mutual pleasure. He sat on the kitchen floor and read all three pages. He knew he should feel angry, hurt, betrayed, but he felt nothing at all, just a numbing of all his senses. He poured his breakfast from the blender and drank it straight down. He walked over to the picture of Samantha he kept on top of the music stack. He looked at it for at least a minute, trying to reason why she had done this terrible thing, why she had thrown away everything they were building together. He also wondered why he was so calm, when he should be hopping mad and calling her every foul name he could think of. The only sensation he felt was one of bitter sadness. He just stood and looked at the picture of Samantha.

In desperation he grabbed the photograph and threw it on the floor, shattering the glass. He thought that would make him feel better. It didn't. He kicked it across the room and threw his empty glass after it. He went around the flat in search of all the little bits and pieces that connected them: the photographs, the camera, the heart-shaped badge she bought for him at the market, the menu from the little restaurant in Oxford, the stolen ashtray from Trader Vic's and one stocking he found on her side of the bed. He took everything into the kitchen and jammed it all into the swing bin, pushing it down as far as his arm would reach. His anger was starting to surface. 'You fucking bitch!' he shouted. 'You were the one that showed me. I taught you nothing, except how to work a radio desk, and that was the only thing you never gave me credit for!'

He afforded himself a smile and realized that however

fragile, his sense of humour was still intact. He also realized that he could be in deep trouble with the radio station. He phoned Monica and got her answerphone. He began to leave his message. 'Monica, this is Nigel. I don't know if you've heard, but . . .'

There was a click on the line as Monica cut in. 'I certainly have, Nigel,' she said, her voice cold and detached. 'Where are you?'

'At home.'

'Are there any press outside your building?'

Nigel hadn't given any thought to that. 'I don't know,' he said.

'Well, go and look,' said Monica. 'I'll hold on.'

Nigel peeked through the curtains of his front-facing window. There were eight people standing on the pavement outside the block of flats, some holding cameras. He walked on to the sundeck, which overlooked the garage area at the back of the building. Two people there, one with a camera. He went back to the phone. 'They're here, loads of them at the front, but only a couple near the garage.'

The front doorbell rang. Monica heard it through the phone. 'Don't answer that,' she said. 'Can you get to the garage without them spotting you?'

'I think so.'

'Good. Now this is what you are to do.' Monica's voice was calm but authoritative. 'Get to your car. Drive over to my place, making sure you are not followed. Park your car in a side street away from Cadogan Square and call me from the phone box in Sloane Street. Do you understand?'

'Yes.'

'Listen to me, Nigel. You're in trouble, but I'll try and help you if I can. Do exactly what I say and talk to no one.'

Nigel was surprised at her attitude, but very grateful for her help. 'I should be there within the hour,' he said.

'It doesn't matter when you get here. Just follow my instructions, that's the important thing.'

Monica hung up and Nigel made another phone call to Mrs Turner who lived in the flat below. 'Mrs Turner, Nigel Beresford-Clarke. I've got a little problem I wonder if you could help me with.'

Mrs Turner had read the *News of the World*. 'I don't think you have a problem,' she said. 'Do you give lessons to anyone, and if so, can I put my name down?'

That's just what I need, thought Nigel. He decided to ignore the remark. 'Mrs Turner, I want to get out of the building. Can I go through your flat?'

'How will you get here?' said the woman, trying to sound sexy.

'I'll come in through your balcony. I need you to help me down.'

'Just like Romeo and Juliet,' she said. 'How exciting. I'll be waiting on the balcony. Oh my Romeo, don't be long.'

Nigel felt like throttling the old bat, but she was his only way out. 'I'll just be a minute. Thank you so much, Mrs Turner.'

He dressed in record time, had a quick shave and brushed his teeth. He ignored the doorbell when it rang again and went in search of the outsize cowboy belt he'd bought at the Wembley Country Festival, the one with the double buckle. He found it at the back of his wardrobe, collected his car keys from the hall table and walked on to the sundeck. He looped the belt through the railing and let it fall over the edge.

'I'm here, my Romeo,' said Mrs Turner from the balcony below.

Nigel popped his head over the edge and looked at the reporters in the garage entrance below. They had not heard her and they were not looking up at the flat. 'Please keep your voice down,' he said, as he held on to the belt and slipped himself over the railing. 'Just grab my legs if you can.'

Nigel felt no fear as he dangled in space for a few seconds before Mrs Turner was able to get hold of his right leg. In fact it was the best thrill he'd had since Samantha disappeared. He swung his body into the space between the balconies and let go of the belt. He landed squarely on top of Mrs Turner, knocking her to the floor. 'I'm terribly sorry, Mrs T.,' he said, jumping off and running into the flat before she could regain her composure. He ran out her front door, down the stairs and into the garage. He tried to keep his mind off Samantha and the damn reporters as he fired up the Porsche. He pretended he was James Bond. He knew that was childish, but it helped to focus his mind on the mission in hand.

He opened the garage door with his remote control and laid a strip of rubber the length of the ramp. By the time the reporters realized who it was, he was past them and into the street. He turned right, away from the front of the building, and roared up Hall Road towards Lord's Cricket Ground. He drove to Baker Street, keeping an eye on the rear-view mirror to make sure he wasn't followed. When he was satisfied that he was alone, he drove through Hyde Park and into Sloane Street. He parked the car in Draycott Place and phoned Monica. She told him the coast was clear and that he should walk to her flat right away.

'One more thing,' she said. 'Don't stop along the way for anything. I don't want you getting recognized in some shop. That would lead them straight to me.'

Nigel had thought of buying some flowers in Sloane Square as a thank-you for Monica, but he took her advice, put on his sun glasses and walked around to Cadogan Square.

Monica knew all about this sort of publicity. The IBA would be on the phone on Monday complaining about the moral aspect, she would receive several letters from irate listeners saying they would never listen to the station again, and she would catch a considerable amount of flak from senior members of staff who would like to see her position weakened. She would hold all these points over Nigel's head for some time to come, but would not fire him. She knew the usual result of this kind of story: his ratings would double within a matter of days and ratings meant cold hard revenue in the radio business. Besides, except for the drug reference, the story made Nigel look very good indeed. Mandy Smith had made young girls seem fair game – all that remained now was to control the aftershock and Monica was convinced she could handle any future stories to her advantage.

She opened the lift door to let Nigel into the flat. She handed him a large Scotch and pointed towards the living room. 'Well, Nigel,' she said, studying the front page of the paper. 'I didn't realize you were so . . . muscular.'

Nigel cracked a very false smile and drank the whisky.

'Another?' asked Monica.

'Not just yet, thanks. I just want to sit for a while.'

Monica hadn't expected this kind of attitude. She had been waiting for him to reel off excuses or scream around the place cursing the girl and all her family, but instead found a quiet and defeated Nigel B. She knew that feeling intimately and, although she had no intention of telling him about Frank, she could see the same hurt in him as she was feeling herself. She understood that he really cared for this girl and had been let down with a tremendous thump. She poured herself a vodka and sat on the edge of the sofa. 'Do you want to tell me about it?'

Nigel had expected to be stood up against a wall, and used as a target for Monica's legendary temper. He was too broken up to reason it any further; he was just grateful for a place to be. 'I thought she loved me,' he said. 'We got on so well together. I was ready to make a commitment and all the time I was being set up. Have you any idea what that feels like?'

'It has never happened to me,' she lied, 'but I can imagine how you feel.'

'I doubt that, Monica, but thank you for your sympathy.'

Monica sat beside him on the sofa. 'Nigel,' she said, unsure as to how he was going to react, 'I was once in a similar situation. I had been let down very badly by someone I trusted and a good friend of mine gave me some very good advice. He said don't get mad, get even.'

Nigel kept staring at the coffee table. 'I don't want to get even, I just want her back.'

Oh my God, thought Monica. This is a problem. 'Then you must pretend it never happened.'

'How can I?'

'Not as far as she's concerned, you can't. But as far as the outside world is concerned, you treat it as a great piece of press and get all you can out of it and, believe me, Nigel, this is a *great piece of press*.'

'Do you think so?' asked Nigel, welcoming the first positive statement he'd heard today.

'I know so. Apart from the drug reference, which these days means less than a parking ticket, the article made you look like radio's answer to Julio Iglesias. All that business about teaching her about love-making and doing it in every room – brilliant copy. I bet your ratings double within a week.'

Nigel looked at her and smiled.

'It's me that has to suffer,' she continued. 'I'll have to deal with the IBA and the outraged listeners. You just go on the radio and be yourself, but don't come to me for a raise when the figures go up or I'll do what the IBA will ask and fire your backside out of town.'

The smile disappeared from Nigel's face. 'That won't get her back though, will it?'

'There are some things that you must leave in the hands of the gods, but remember, you don't know all the facts. There might be more to this than you know at the moment.'

'How can there be?' asked Nigel. 'She had to sanction the whole thing. They used her quotes. She had to be in on it. What's more, she's gone away. I can't talk to her to find out.'

'Where's she gone?'

'To Switzerland – Geneva, I think. On holiday with a friend.'

A small alarm sounded in the back of Monica's mind. France, Spain, Italy, maybe, but a holiday, in Geneva, at this time of year, didn't sound right. 'Who is this friend?'

'Someone she knew from school.' Nigel laughed for a second and threw his hands in the air. 'See what I mean, it all makes sense.'

'Not to me it doesn't,' said Monica. 'School trips go to lots of places, but not Switzerland. Switzerland means family, and one with lots of money. I wonder if she was put up to this by someone who has an axe to grind.'

'I don't follow you.'

Monica thought she had said quite enough already. 'It's nothing, Nigel, it's just me rambling on. Would you like another drink?'

'Yes, please. I think I could do with the whole bottle.'

'That's not a bad idea, Nigel.' She spotted the surprised look on his face even before it appeared. 'You can't go back to your place tonight. Why don't I get a couple of bottles and some nice food from the shop in Sloane Street and we can spend the evening plotting our revenge? You can sleep here tonight and sneak into the station via the car-park in the morning. By the time you get off the air, I will have released our story and you should be half-way off the hook.'

'Sleep here!' said Nigel, his mind unable to decipher the implications of her remark.

'On the sofa,' chirped Monica. 'I'm told it's very comfortable.'

Harry Connaught was far from comfortable as he sat down to dinner with his wife Jessica at their town house in Ebury Mews. He had pondered Lady Isobel's phone call. He told Jessica about it on the night it happened and she had advised him to let Lady Isobel go her own way, that she would come unstuck by herself and that no help was needed from either Harry or the IBA. There was just something that niggled away at Harry's mind and would not let him rest.

The leg of lamb was served whole on a wooden carving platter, the broccoli, carrots, french beans and new potatoes were being kept hot under the lids of their serving dishes and the servants had retired leaving

Harry to carve the meat. He cut four slices for each of them, giving Jessica the outside piece, which she loved, and only managed to get when they dined alone.

'You look worried,' she said. 'Are you still concerned about Isobel?'

Harry spooned five new potatoes on to his plate and passed the serving dish to his wife. 'Yes I am,' he answered. 'I can't take the risk of Manchester getting into a pickle over that woman. They are at a very important stage of their development and I don't want to see a French cat among their Lancashire pigeons.'

Jessica swapped Harry's potatoes for her bean dish. 'In that case, why don't you tell them what she's up to? I'm sure it's not necessary, but if it makes you feel easier, call them tomorrow.'

'I feel like I'm ratting on a friend,' said Harry, turning his attention to the broccoli.

'Peter and Freddie have been good friends to you,' said Jessica. 'But Isobel hasn't been much of a friend to anyone since her husband died. Unless I'm reading the signs wrong, I think the brothers will oust the old lady before the end of the year.'

'Do you really think so?'

'Yes. You could be doing them a favour by stopping her before she loses too much of their money.'

Harry ate a slice of lamb with a small dab of mint sauce. 'This is lovely meat,' he said.

'Yes, it is,' replied Jessica. 'While we're on the subject of food, I have a problem that's been nagging at me for weeks.'

'Out with it, my dear, a problem shared, etcetera.'

'Every Sunday we have carrots and we never eat them.'

Harry pondered for a moment as he finished his mouthful. 'You're absolutely right, my dear.'

'I'll tell cook to stop making them,' said Jessica, feeling very pleased with herself indeed.

Nigel and Monica were becoming more pleased with each other as the evening progressed. She found a packet of chicken Kiev in the freezer along with mixed veg and some potato skins stuffed with mushroom and topped with cheese. She went to the shop in Sloane Street and bought a bottle of Scotch, a bottle of vodka, two bottles of wine and a sort of chocolate gateau that looked far too good to resist.

They ate and drank, and talked and drank and polished off the chocolate gateau and drank; by ten o'clock they were both two sheets to the wind. Monica didn't let anything slip about either business or Frank De Wolf. She had made sure that Nigel knew his place as far as the sleeping arrangements were concerned, but she did enjoy his company and managed to raise a few laughs out of him, which she hoped would put him in a good mood for tomorrow's show.

Nigel thought the entire evening was a tonic and was sure something had happened to Monica that had changed her. He was feeling a lot better, until he tucked himself up on the sofa and set the alarm clock Monica had placed on the coffee table. As he drifted into an alcoholic sleep, he felt the waves of sadness return.

Monica also felt sad as she slid between the covers in the downstairs bedroom. She, too, had enjoyed the evening, but realized the pressure one goes through to keep things on an even keel when one aspires to be a director of a multinational media company. Her last waking thought was of Sir Peter French.

She woke at eight and immediately switched on the radio. There was an extended news because of the

Kuwait situation which John handled with expert care. Nigel took over at five past the hour and fairly jumped out of the radio. His humour was acid, his timing spot on and for his free-choice record he played Chuck Berry's 'Sweet Little Sixteen'. That's my boy, thought Monica. Go out there and get 'em.

Nigel went out there and got 'em until nine o'clock, then went home. Much to his relief, there were no reporters hanging around. Monica had done her job well. He passed Mrs Turner in the garage and inquired about her back. 'I hope I didn't hurt you yesterday, but I was in a bit of a hurry,' he said. She smiled at him and hurried on her way. Amazing, he thought as he rode up in the lift, yesterday's hero is today's despot. He wandered around the flat picking up the bits of broken glass off the living-room floor, cleaning the jacuzzi, making up the bed in the guest room – in fact, anything that would keep his mind occupied. He thought he would be creative and put a new message on the answerphone. The little red light on the machine was flashing away, so Nigel ran back the incoming tape to see if anyone interesting had phoned. The first six callers were all reporters; the seventh was Tony; eight through eleven, more reporters; and number twelve was Sally at the office. 'Don't forget Terry's leaving party is at noon today, she'll be very disappointed if you're not there.'

He showered quickly, changed into a clean, plain white T-shirt, faded Levis and the black leather biker's jacket he'd bought off Johnny Walker a couple of months ago.

He drove the Porsche back to the station and parked it on a meter. He always found that was a good excuse to leave whenever he wanted. With the price of parking violations these days, nobody could afford the price of a clamp. The reception was in full swing when Nigel entered the sales department. His friends said nothing about the weekend papers and his enemies just turned away, but he did notice a few strange looks from a couple of the younger secretarial staff. One in particular, Mandy Stewart from traffic, made it very obvious that she would like to be next in line for the Nigel B. school of naughty bits. He talked to her for a while, but refused her invitation to see her record collection on the grounds that he never went near vinyl after working hours. As he passed through the crowd on his way towards John Thorne he heard Eddy McLeod talking very loudly to some of the junior female sales staff. 'If you ask me,' he was saying, 'that Samantha made it all up. I mean, what's a great-looking woman like that doing with a two-bit disc jockey? If she'd have asked me, I would have taught her a thing or two.'

Whether it was the mention of Samantha, or the thought of her being with Eddy that triggered his mind, he couldn't say, but that was the sentence that broke his cool. He grabbed Eddy by the collar and the seat of his pants, frogmarched him into the hallway, turned him around and punched him on the nose as hard as he could. Blood spurted everywhere: over the floor, over Nigel, but mainly all over Eddy's face. Nigel hit him again in the stomach and, as Eddy doubled over, grabbed his hair and slammed his head against the wall. 'Don't you *ever* mention her name again!' he shouted, then turned on his heel and walked out of the station.

Eddy staggered back into the sales department, blood pouring from his nose and mouth, screaming for somebody to call the police and get him to a hospital. 'Did you see what happened?' he shouted. 'He hit me, for no reason, he hit me!'

No one would admit to seeing anything. A lot of

people at the back of the room started laughing, but, it seemed, no one saw anything at all. John Thorne finally took pity on the fellow and helped him out of the room. 'Come on, Eddy. Let's get you cleaned up.'

Nigel sat in the Porsche trying to calm his nerves. He was not a violent person, but something inside him had snapped. Maybe he was hitting Samantha, maybe he'd just lost control. He smiled to himself as he started the car. 'Couldn't happen to a nicer guy!' he shouted as he roared off down the street.

The phone was ringing as he walked back into his flat. 'If this is a reporter you can fuck off,' he hollered down the receiver.

'Oh, this *is* a reporter,' answered John Thorne. 'But I think you might like what I have to say.'

'I'm sorry, John,' said Nigel, trying to calm himself. 'What's happened? Am I fired?'

'Far from it, old son. You're the toast of the station. You did what everyone has wanted to do since Eddy first came here. Even Monica said that, as far as she was concerned, he fell down the stairs. By the way, she said to tell you she hopes you didn't hurt your hand.'

Nigel suddenly felt like Superman saving a city. 'You're kidding. She really said that?'

'You bet, and there's more. Everyone insists on buying you a drink. Half an hour, at the Grapes.' John hung up before Nigel could protest.

He arrived at the Grapes an hour after the phone call. Nigel knew all about entrances. All the CRFM crowd cheered as he walked through the door. Everyone was there – even Monica sat demurely in the corner sipping a vodka tonic. Nigel also knew all about good manners.

He walked over to Monica and sat down on the only other seat at the very small table. 'Thank you for coming,' he said.

'Thank you for being such a . . . public servant,' she replied. 'I've got a meeting in a few minutes, so I can't stay, but I wanted to make sure you were all right.'

'I'm fine,' he said. He was about to thank her for last night until he thought of all the people who would hear.

She got up to leave and brushed against him as she tried to manoeuvre in the crowded pub. 'If you can't sleep, call,' she whispered, and was gone.

John Thorne pressed a large Scotch in his hand and called for everyone's attention. 'Here's to our fearless fighter,' he said. 'Nigel Barefisted-Clarke.'

Everyone cheered, including the little girl from traffic.

Everyone, that is, except Lizzie. She was busy at the station, making a few phone calls. At lunch, she had slipped out on her own and visited a few phone boxes along the Edgware Road. She had collected as many prostitutes' calling cards as she could and was now busy phoning the numbers and asking the same questions of everyone who answered: 'How much would you charge for two hours between midnight and two o'clock in the morning, and do you visit?' After several failures she finally got a taker. 'I'll pick you up at half past eleven then. Thank you. Goodbye.' She put the phone down and smiled to herself. This was a major game for Lizzie Stephenson.

Nigel's game was proceeding very much to plan. He had done it so many times before, he was an expert. He paid no attention to the target for at least fifteen minutes. Whenever she moved within range, he walked away. Finally he let her get next to him, turned to face her and fired his opening salvo. 'There you are, I've been looking for you. Mandy, isn't it?'

'That's right, Mandy Stewart, I work in traffic.' All her body signs were positive. She took a deep breath that forced her ample breasts out to their expanded best, her left hand rubbed the front of her leg, she took a drink and removed the glass slowly from her mouth. 'I listen to you every morning,' she said.

'A good thing too,' replied Nigel. 'If Monica catches anybody not listening to the station, she has their nipples removed. That's why there's so many flat-chested ladies working for us.'

Mandy squeezed her arms together revealing the most remarkable cleavage. 'I've been a good girl,' she said.

Nigel knew it was time for the main ground assault. He thought of Samantha, and felt even more determined. He pressed the keys to the 911 into her hand. 'The red Porsche in Porchester Place, ten minutes.' He moved away from her without waiting for her reply.

He refused another round of drinks because he was driving and said he had to leave soon to do a voice-over in Soho. He said goodbye to as many people as he could on the way to the door. The last person he came upon was Maggie Lomax who was not fooled by his charade for a second. He gave her a big hug and as he held her, she whispered in his ear, 'You're a bastard, Mandy's too nice for the likes of you.'

'People in glass houses, Maggie,' he whispered back, and slipped out the door.

His evening proceeded along the 'pre-Samantha' routine. Back to the flat, champagne and a joint, some quick-cook food from the freezer, sensual chat over dinner, into the jacuzzi and into bed. She was new, so she was exciting. She was good, so she was enjoyable, but she wasn't Samantha. Damn that woman!

Anthony and Lizzie had dinner in their new flat and made love on the living-room floor. At eleven o'clock Anthony was ready for bed, and Lizzie was about to go out.

'What are you doing?' asked Anthony, as he watched his Lizzie put on her coat.

'Getting us a radio show,' she replied.

'At this time of night?'

'No, I would say Saturday afternoon, if my guess is correct.'

'What *are* you doing?' persisted Anthony.

Lizzie put her arms around him and kissed him full on the mouth. 'I have a plan. It's terribly bad luck to discuss it before it happens, so you'll have to trust me.' She broke away from him and ran out the door, leaving him totally bewildered in the middle of the living room.

She drove to a grubby basement flat in Earls Court and rang the bell. An old lady answered the door. Lizzie was taken aback by her ragged appearance, but she gritted her teeth and followed her plan. 'I'm Lizzie. I've come to collect Nina.'

'Oh yes,' said the old lady. 'Come on in, dearie. She'll be with you in a moment.'

Lizzie followed her down a long dark hallway lit only by a single red light with no shade. The place smelt damp and Lizzie could see mildew adorning the walls. She was led into a small room at the end of the corridor which was also lit by one red light. A double bed took up most of the dingy room with a gas-glow heater next to it. The room smelt of stale body odour and spent sex. Lizzie felt nauseous but held it under control. She turned around and faced the door just as Nina entered the room. She was a pretty girl, in her early twenties. She wore a black leather mini skirt, a white frilly blouse and red high-heel shoes. She stuck out her hand towards Lizzie. 'I'm Nina,' she said. 'Is this outfit all right?'

Lizzie accepted her hand for the briefest of handshakes and pretended to study her clothes. How anyone could fancy that was beyond her. 'Can you wear stockings?' she asked. 'He likes stockings.'

'No problem.' Nina left the room.

When she returned, Lizzie could see an expanse of flesh between the top of the stockings and the bottom of the skirt. This will never do, she thought, she'll never get past security. 'One more thing, could you wear a longer skirt?'

'All my clients love my mini skirt,' said Nina. 'Most of them won't go with me unless I wear it.'

Lizzie felt like telling this silly woman a few facts of life, but didn't have the time. 'Tonight is different, Nina. Tonight you're going to fuck a star.'

'Oh, that'll be nice,' said the girl. 'By the way, I want the money up front.'

Nina changed her skirt, Lizzie paid her a hundred pounds and they drove to the radio station without saying another word. As they arrived, Bernie Bonelli was getting out of a cab in front of the station. Great timing, thought Lizzie as she flashed her headlights. She turned to face Nina. 'Remember,' she said. 'Just like we discussed on the phone, you're a friend of mine from Bradford and when you get inside, you do him for the full two hours.'

Nina was about to answer when Bernie appeared at the car window.

'Hi, Bonelli. Ready to knock 'em dead?'

'Sure thing,' answered Bernie, trying to look past her towards Nina.

'Bernie, this is my friend Nina. She's from Bradford and she'd love to see inside a radio station. We've been at the pub all evening. I'm shattered and I want to get home to Anthony. Do you think you could take her in with you?'

'It would be my pleasure,' said Bonelli, who could now see that Lizzie's passenger was, at least, pretty, with a good set of tits.

Monica was getting ready for bed and musing over the events of the day. She hoped Nigel didn't take her seriously when she teased him in the pub. She knew it was a foolish thing to do, but she couldn't resist. The simple line, delivered at the right time with total surprise, then a quick exit, worked every time. She unbuttoned her dress and let it slide down her body. As she stepped out of it, the phone rang. Oh no, it had to be Nigel, probably drunk, and phoning to take up her offer.

She let the answerphone pick up the call. 'Hello, Monica, this is Lizzie Stephenson. Are you there?'

Monica picked up the phone, very relieved that it wasn't Nigel. 'Yes, Lizzie, I am. What can I do for you?'

'Well, Monica, I was working late and as I passed the studio I saw Bernie Bonelli with a girl I have never seen before.' She tried her best to sound angry and disgusted. 'Personally, I don't care what he gets up to, but in this time of crisis, I don't think it's very smart to have strangers in the building.'

Monica saw a treble play. One, she would rid herself of the obnoxious Bonelli. Two, she would not have to go to a poorly attended leaving party and three, she would finally have something on Lizzie Stephenson she could use at a later date. 'Where are you now, Lizzie?' she asked.

'In a phone box at Marble Arch.'

'Pick me up as soon as you can,' said Monica. 'I'll be waiting outside my flat.'

As Lizzie speeded down Park Lane, she reflected on how a hundred pounds on a hooker could be money *very* well spent.

Monica and Lizzie arrived at the station twenty minutes later. 'You go on home,' said Monica. 'I'll take over from here.'

Monica stormed into reception. 'Did you let a stranger into this building tonight?' she snapped at the night security man.

'No, ma'am,' he replied. 'Just the news people, Bernie Bonelli and his sister.'

'I see,' said Monica, taking the stairs two at a time and bursting into the green room. She could hear 'Riders on the Storm' playing through the monitor speakers but she couldn't see anyone in the studio. She opened the double soundproof doors and found Bernie Bonelli. He was on the floor, lying on top of this woman, pants around his ankles, pumping away between bestockinged legs and trying, unsuccessfully, to keep his rhythm in time with the music. The woman seemed totally uninterested in the whole procedure and looked at Monica as if she half-expected her to join in. Monica thought of the Joe Mace tapes. She was repulsed by the memory of her and Frank playing sex games while listening to them and was thoroughly disgusted by the thought of anything sexual or sensual in relation to the tacky and sordid scene that confronted her on the studio floor.

She stood, legs apart, hands on hips and screamed, 'Bonelli, get out of this station! NOW!'

Bernie jumped off the woman and stood up, half-naked, in front of Monica, then pulled up his pants and zipped his flies.

'I mean it!' shouted Monica. 'You can pick your things up tomorrow. Get out of my sight this instant!'

'Shove your damn radio station!' he yelled, knocked her shoulder as he brushed past her and shuffled out of the studio.

Nina was still on the floor, her blouse undone, her skirt around her waist and her hands between her legs trying to protect what was left of her modesty. 'And who are you, young lady?' Monica asked.

Nina had no reason to hide the truth. 'I'm a prostitute,' she said. 'A girl named Lizzie hired me to screw that guy.'

Monica fitted the whole jigsaw together. She stared at Nina with a look of sad understanding. 'I think your work here is done, don't you?' she said, before averting her eyes from the crumpled mess on the floor.

'Is there some place I can wash up?' asked Nina.

Monica thought that this girl and 'clean' were mutually exclusive, but she felt sympathy for the lady of the night, maybe because she had done enough subtle whoring in her time to feel somehow connected. 'Take your time,' she said. 'The ladies' room is down the hall, third on the left.'

Nina gathered up her things and left the studio in search of the loo. The Doors' record was coming to the end. Monica sat behind the console and punched up the emergency instrumental tape. She walked into the newsroom and found James Grey beavering away in front of the IRN feed machine. She told him the situation and that he would have to finish the overnight show. She then woke John Thorne and told him to arrange some cover in the newsroom, before going off in search of Nina and escorting her off the premises.

In the cab, on the way back to Cadogan Square, Monica rethought her position regarding Lizzie Stephenson. Her game was clumsy, but effective. Lizzie had read the situation well. Monica would offer the overnight to Washington Blake – he was the only candidate – so Lizzie could ask for Blake's Saturday slot to air her show with Anthony, which was already sponsored. Monica admired anyone who could go from receptionist to presenter in under a month, but she also noted her ambition and filed Nina's name in her secrets folder, just in case Lizzie had more adventurous plans.

Lizzie cuddled up to a sleeping Anthony and tried to work out how she would approach Monica to get her show on the air, blissfully unaware that she already had the job.

CHAPTER 15

Maggie Lomax came into the station with John Thorne at half past three on Tuesday morning. She thought it was the least she could do to repay the kindness he and his family had shown her; besides, to be a real newsperson again, albeit for one day, was very appealing. They set about sorting copy from the various agencies and stringing them together into some kind of order for the first bulletin. The main story concerned the Saudis' request to America for troops. Britain had fallen in line behind the States, France was still considering its options and Baghdad were talking hostages.

'Here we go again,' said Maggie, slurping at her third cup of coffee. 'Suez – Mark Two.'

'I fear not,' replied John, studying the feed from United Press International. 'We could be watching the start of World War Three.' John ripped a page from the teleprinter. 'Look at this, Maggie, Iraq owes Kuwait over twenty *billion* pounds in war debts. I think the Royal Family were about to foreclose. Saddam had no choice but to invade before his country went bankrupt.'

'To be honest, I don't think it's about any of those things, John. I think it's about stopping a tin-pot dictator who has already killed more Arabs than anyone in living memory and who, given half a chance, would take over the whole region, hold us all to ransom for the oil and eliminate Israel into the bargain.'

John looked at her over the rim of his coffee cup. 'God, we miss you in news,' he said.

*

Monica's first job of the day was to promote Washington Blake to a daily programme. She loved promoting people because she knew it made them feel beholden to her for their wage packet. Washington made all the right noises when she told him, promising to give his full attention to the show and make it Number One in London. She had just started deciphering the latest rating charts when Lizzie appeared at her office door. It was time for Monica to take control of this situation, and to leave no doubt in Lizzie's mind as to who was the dominant person at this radio station.

'Come in,' said Monica.

'I won't keep you a minute,' said Lizzie, with all the innocence of a roomful of nuns. 'I was just wondering if you had considered a replacement for Washington Blake on Saturdays.'

Monica viewed her over the rim of her glasses. 'At this moment, I'm considering if you have a future with this company,' she said. She could see Lizzie start to disintegrate. 'I had a long chat with, shall we say, your lady friend last night, and I think what you did was underhanded, cheap and totally uncalled-for.'

Lizzie's face turned red. She knew she had been caught out and there wasn't a thing she could do about it. She gathered together what was left of her pride and walked towards the door.

'On the other hand,' said Monica, leaving a slight pause to maximize the effect, 'you have done me a small favour.'

Lizzie spun on her heels and stood very straight in front of her managing director. 'In what way?' she asked.

'By getting rid of Bernie Bonelli,' replied Monica. 'And as long as you will assure me that this sort of thing will never, and I mean *never*, happen again, I am prepared to give you and Anthony a *trial* on the Saturday slot.'

'Oh thank you, Monica, thank you. Can we start this Saturday?'

'If you don't, you won't start at all. Will you be ready by then?'

'We're ready now.'

'Well, off you go then.'

'We'll do a smashing job for you.' Lizzie tried so very hard to keep control.

'I'm sure you will,' said Monica. 'But I mean what I say. One more trick like last night and you will be out on your pretty backside so fast, you won't even touch the pavement. Do I make myself clear?'

Lizzie thought she was the luckiest lady in the universe. 'Perfectly,' she said.

Monica twiddled her toes in the deep-pile carpet and realized that power was the best aphrodisiac in the world. It was such a shame that Frank was . . . That reminds me, she thought, I must phone him, he owes me a meal.

Lady Isobel was having lunch at the Savoy Grill with one of the team of lawyers that kept French Enterprises in with the taxman and out of trouble. She was busy trying to decide which companies should buy into Manchester, when a junior partner in the law firm arrived at the table with a sombre look on his face and a copy of the *FT* in his hand.

'Excuse me, madam,' he said, handing her the newspaper. 'I think you should read the article on page eight.'

Lady Isobel was furious. 'What do you mean bursting in here like this? I'm trying to enjoy a fresh Dover sole at this moment. It is not the time to wave bits of newspaper in my face.'

The young man looked at the senior partner, who was also having a Dover sole. 'Mr Bridgeman, this is important, otherwise I wouldn't have come.'

Mr Bridgeman took the newspaper and began reading. He read the first paragraph and waved his hand at the young man, signalling that he should leave. 'I think you should read this, Lady Isobel,' he said. 'Or maybe I could read it to you.'

'Yes, yes, if you must,' replied the old lady.

The lawyer lowered his voice and half-whispered across the table. 'It has come to this writer's attention that Lady Isobel French, the major shareholder in the multinational property, investment and media company French Enterprises, has been acquiring radio stations in the UK by a method that, although not dishonest, flies very close to the border.'

Lady Isobel snatched the paper from the lawyer's hand and continued reading. The article explained about the below five per cent ploy, naming not only the radio stations, but also the companies involved in buying them. It went on to say that these tactics were only just within the law and that it did not seem proper for a company of French Enterprises' reputation and standing to be dealing in these methods of acquisition. Lady Isobel threw the paper on the floor and continued eating.

'That's a pretty strong article,' said Mr Bridgeman, trying to keep the tone of his comment as light as possible.

'They can say what they like,' replied Lady Isobel. 'The British press have been trying to damn the French family since the Napoleonic wars. One is either guilty or innocent, there is no almost breaking the law. Forget about those talebearers and enjoy your fish. It's delicious, don't you think.'

'This could do your Manchester deal quite a

disservice, coming, as it does, on the eve of our first purchase.'

'Charles, will you please drop the matter? All will be forgotten by tomorrow's editions.'

What a stubborn old lady you are, thought Mr Charles Bridgeman.

Stubborn was the word flying around the newsroom today to describe John Thorne. They all wanted to do their own angle on the Middle East story and John kept 'toeing the party line' and wouldn't let them use anything. He called a meeting following the one o'clock bulletin.

'I know you all want to contribute to the biggest story this year,' he said. 'But I must tell you, once again, this is a local station, specializing in local news. At this moment there are two armed robberies, a fire in Islington and an assault in Chinatown to deal with, and that, ladies and gentlemen, is what you will be reporting on this evening. Are there any questions?'

The news team mumbled a lot and wished that they were head of news and he was going to Chinatown, but they knew the game, and they also knew he didn't blame them for trying.

Maggie sat in his office and read the *Independent*.

John folded his arms on the desk and dumped his head on top of them. 'I'm shattered,' he said.

Maggie stopped reading and looked sympathetically at her friend. 'Nothing like a three o'clock start to slow you down,' she said.

John's phone rang. He reached out an arm and grabbed the receiver. 'John Thorne.'

'All right, my old Culshie? It's Sean Hearty.'

'Sean, hello. Where are you?'

'I'm at Heathrow. Can I see you this afternoon?'

John left a long pause before answering. 'Of course. What time?'

'Are you all right, John?' inquired the Irishman.

Thorne pulled himself together. 'I'm sorry, Sean, I've been at it since three this morning and your call is a complete surprise. Have you got a ride into town?'

'I'll be with you within the hour.'

'See you then. Goodbye, Sean.' John hung up the phone. 'Oh no, I'm never going to survive the day.'

'I thought you got on well with him,' said Maggie.

'I do. It's just I know what will happen. He likes his drink, so we'll get drunk, Patricia will get mad and I'll end up with no supper and no nookie.'

'This Sean Hearty,' said Maggie. 'He sounds like my kind of fellow. Can I help at all?'

John laughed out loud. 'What a great idea. The two Celts in drunken harmony. Sure you can help. If you can entertain him when I fade out, you would do me a great favour.'

'I'll have a go,' said Maggie.

She was in reception talking to Robin Trower when Sean arrived. Robin tucked his newly acquired autographs of Anthony and Cleopatra into his lunch box and went about his duties. Maggie took Sean into John's office and made him a cup of freshly ground coffee. A very tired John Thorne joined them and explained to Sean the reasons for his fatigue.

'Well, there's a lot more to come,' said Sean, taking a sip from his cup.

'What does that mean?' asked John.

'I don't want to sound formal,' said the Belfast reporter. 'Does Maggie have security clearance?'

'Maggie is working for programming now,' replied

John. 'But she is still the best journo we have and she is privy to anything I know.'

'In that case, John and Maggie, here is the bottom line. We have it on good authority that if things escalate in the Gulf Saddam will use his terrorist connections to hit back at the West. We also know that several IRA cells have been training in Iraq and they could be coming straight to the British mainland. Some may already be here.'

'What's that got to do with us?' interjected Maggie.

'It is very hard for them to hit military targets in England. Most camps and bases are locked up tight, so we think their next choice could be the media. The BBC is all but bombproof with their underground studios, the new stations, like KISS and JAZZ, are too new and too small to cause any real waves. That leaves LBC, Capital and you.'

'Do you think it's a real possibility?' asked John.

'I wouldn't have come over from Ireland to see you if I didn't.'

John and Maggie sat in silence as the seriousness of his remarks began to register. John was the first to speak. 'Maggie's been getting some phone calls lately both here and at home. Do you think there's a connection?'

'Doubtful,' said Sean. 'The only phone calls you get are just before the thing goes off. I think your best defence is to shut down your lobby and guard against sounding too macho on the air.'

John phoned Monica on the internal and relayed Sean's story. She agreed to meet them the next morning. She also gave Maggie the night off because of the help she had rendered this morning.

'I don't know what's come over her lately,' said Maggie. 'She's becoming altogether too nice a person.'

'She can be as nice as she likes,' said John. 'As long as she signs my pay cheque. Now, hands up if you want to go to my place for dinner.'

Two hands shot up instantaneously. John phoned home.

Monica was concerned about security now that there was trouble in the Gulf and John's phone call had done nothing to allay her fears, but she would deal with that tomorrow. Her prime objective now was Frank De Wolf. It was time to bite the bullet or, to be more precise, bite Frank De Wolf; and scratch him, and burn him, and hit him on the head with a very large plank. To this end, Monica had purchased a few items of clothing from a small shop in World's End. A black, knee-length, rubber skirt that zipped up the front, a pair of black thigh-length boots that zipped up the back and a black silk singlet with no zips at all. The next problem was getting the timing right. She phoned Freddie to inquire about the state of play regarding the false acquisitions.

'Everything is going wonderfully,' said Freddie, a satisfying chuckle very evident in his voice. 'Pike is trying to buy everything that moves. He must have spent four million already.'

'When do you think you'll pull the plug?' asked Monica.

'Sometime next week,' replied Freddie, now knowing the reason for Monica's call. 'You can dispense with Mr De Wolf at your leisure. Any time after close of play on Friday.'

'Freddie, you're a little gem.'

'I know, and getting smaller every day,' said the chunky aristocrat, as he threw half a chocolate éclair into the wastepaper basket.

Monica phoned Frank at his office and invited him to dinner at her place on Saturday night.

Lizzie was woken on Saturday morning with a multitude of presents. Anthony stood at the foot of the bed, a breakfast tray in one hand and a dozen roses in the other. On the tray, apart from the scrambled eggs, fresh orange juice and coffee, was a small box and a very large card.

'Oh Anthony,' purred Lizzie, taking the tray so he would have both hands free to arrange the roses, 'you are a darling.' She opened the card. On the front was a comic-strip drawing of a football player scoring a goal; inside it said 'Here we go, Here we go, Here we go' in big black type. Lizzie smiled and placed the card beside the roses. She opened the small box. Inside was a plain gold heart attached to a solid gold chain.

She put the breakfast tray on the bedside table next to the roses and held her arms out to Anthony. 'I like my eggs and coffee cold,' she said, pulling him on to the bed and rolling on top of him. 'I have a little surprise for you first.'

They walked into CRFM at eleven o'clock. The promo spots had been running since Wednesday and as they arrived at reception, Robin Trower handed them several cards and fax messages wishing them good luck.

'This is so exciting,' chirped Lizzie, holding on tight to Anthony's arm.

'Let's hope we get the same reaction at the end of the programme,' said Anthony.

They did.

Right from the off, it was apparent the show would be a great success. The phones went mad within five minutes. People wanted the fact sheets, the useful tips' folders and pictures of Anthony and Lizzie. They had so many calls for the guest tradesman, Lizzie had to ask some of them to call back after the show. Mind you, he was good. He was a carpenter friend of Anthony's named Bill Street, who did the first show as a favour on the understanding that, if it took off, he would get the gig on a regular basis. He was funny and informative. He talked about hanging doors, rebuilding old furniture and making stairs safe for children. Lizzie was in charge of the music and she played a lot of Carly and Paul Simon, Stevie Wonder, Tom Jones and Curtis Mayfield. She ended the show with the long version of Marvin Gaye's 'Sexual Healing'.

As soon as the show finished, Helmut Von Krugge phoned David Westbury and confirmed his sponsorship for six months. David phoned Monica and passed on the good news. Monica phoned Anthony and Lizzie and offered her congratulations. The two new stars of radio opened a bottle of champagne and smiled a lot.

Monica was preparing a show of her own. She laid her new outfit neatly on the downstairs bed along with a few new toys she'd bought that morning from the Anne Summers' shop in Soho. She showered, brushed her hair into a pony tail, put on the tightest pair of jeans she could find and the baggiest sweater.

Frank arrived at seven o'clock. She fed him steak and salad, made sure he had no physical contact with her and teased him continuously about the surprise she had waiting for him in the bedroom.

'This is so unlike you,' he said, slurping down the last drop of wine. 'What are you going to do with me tonight?'

'Frank,' she said, standing up and moving towards the bedroom, 'I'm going to take charge of your life.

Take all your clothes off and when I call you, come into the bedroom.'

Frank liked games. He had never seen Monica in such an aggressive mood, but he was confident that he could handle anything she had to offer. He took off his clothes, sat on the sofa and waited.

Five minutes later Monica called from the bedroom, 'Frank, get in here, quick!'

He thought something was wrong and ran into the room expecting to see Monica in some kind of trouble. He didn't expect to see her standing beside the bed dressed in rubber and silk.

Good game, thought De Wolf. 'You look fantastic.'

Monica slithered towards him and wound herself around his body. 'I want to play a new game tonight,' she whispered. 'It's called truth or consequences. I'm going to ask you some questions. If you answer truthfully, I'll do anything you wish. If you tell me a lie, I will have to punish you.'

A wicked grin appeared on Frank's face. 'How will you know if I'm lying?'

'I'll know,' said Monica, sliding her hand down his back and giving his bottom a pinch. 'First of all, what is your name?'

Frank chuckled and decided to lose the first few rounds. 'Andy Pandy,' he replied.

Monica steered him towards the bed and pushed him back first on to the royal blue duvet. She produced a pair of handcuffs from under the pillow and fastened one end to his right wrist. She jerked his arm upwards and fastened the other end to the brass headboard. 'That was a lie,' she teased, kissing the side of his neck and biting gently on his earlobe. 'Now, let's try another one. How old are you?'

De Wolf had not travelled this sexual road before and the newness excited him. 'Fourteen,' he whispered.

'You are such a fibber. I will have to deal with you most severely,' said Monica as she wriggled across his body, produced another pair of cuffs from under the left-side pillow and repeated the procedure on his free arm. 'Third time lucky, Frank. Do you love me?'

'Of course I do, darling. How could I lie about that?'

She smiled and slid down him, the rubber and silk of her outfit mixing in a fusion of pain and pleasure over his hardening penis. Frank closed his eyes and felt the sensations build inside him. Monica dropped off the foot of the bed, retrieved two more pairs of cuffs from under the mattress and in what seemed one flowing movement secured both his legs.

It all happened too fast for Frank to react. Monica moved up between his legs and started massaging him until his penis was at full erection. Frank started to drift into coital ecstasy, the restriction of the handcuffs heightening his sensations. Monica eased herself off the bed and walked slowly to the dressing table, speaking sweet obscenities to him as she went. When she turned back towards him, a Polaroid camera was in her hands.

Frank saw the flash through closed eyes. 'What *are* you doing?' he shouted.

Monica's voice was now soft and menacing. 'Controlling your life, just as I promised,' she said.

'This has gone far enough,' said Frank, rapidly losing his hard-on. 'Get me out of these things!'

'Not on your life,' said Monica. 'You stay there for a while and think about telling the truth. I won't be long.'

Monica walked from the bedroom, camera in hand, and slammed the door. She could hear his vehement protests as she took his house and car keys from the trousers he'd left on the living-room floor, put on her full-length mink coat from the hall closet and rode the lift to the ground floor.

She drove the Bentley to Frank's house and let herself in. She went to his second-floor study, unlocked his desk and started to search. It only took her a minute to find what she was looking for. A small directory with the word 'Clients' on the front. She thumbed through the pages. Freddie was right, all the Aylford companies were there, plus a few private clients, most of them women. She turned his photocopier on to let it warm up and set about addressing envelopes. She made seventeen copies of the Polaroid snapshot, placing one in each envelope. She also took a cassette from her handbag, popped it in a Jiffy bag and addressed it to the Bar Council, along with a handwritten letter she had prepared earlier. She unlocked his stamping machine, rolled off seventeen first-class postage strips and one for fifty pence to go on the Jiffy bag.

She put everything back where she found it, turned off the photocopier, locked all the doors behind her and drove back to Cadogan Square, stopping only once, at the Knightsbridge post office.

When she walked into the flat Frank started shouting at her from the bedroom. She ignored him, removed her coat and replaced the keys in his trousers pocket. She went into the bedroom and looked at him lying spreadeagled on the bed, his wrists and ankles red from trying to shed the cuffs.

He looked at her in total disbelief. 'For God's sake, get me out of this. This is beyond a joke. Where have you been?'

Monica said nothing, just stood at the end of the bed and slowly began to remove her clothing. First the boots that zipped up the back, then the rubber skirt that zipped up the front. She stood in front of him wearing black stockings, lacy black french knickers and the silk top. Frank was even more confused. He twisted and turned inside his bondage. Monica ran her hands over her body, caressing herself through the silk.

Frank began to smile. 'That's better, sweetheart,' he slimed. 'Come and do that over here, so I can watch properly.'

Monica stopped as if a switch had been turned off. She removed her stockings and top with remarkable speed.

'What the fuck is going on?' shouted Frank.

Monica remained silent. She put on her jeans and the baggy sweater, took her hair out of the pony tail and let it fall down over her shoulders. She took two strips of elastoplast from the dresser drawer, walked over to the bed and stuck one piece over Frank's mouth.

She stood over him defiantly. 'You are, without a doubt, the most despicable man I have ever known. You lied to me, you cheated me, you tried to con me from the first day we met, and all in the name of business. Well, my friend, your business is now in ruins. I doubt you will ever work again in this country.' She paused and watched a look of horror come into his eyes. 'I'm leaving now. I'll leave the key so you can get loose. When I return, I want you gone. I never want to see you again.'

Taking a key from her jeans pocket she undid the cuff that held his right hand and quickly stepped backwards to avoid his reach. She stuck the key to the second piece of elastoplast and slapped it on to his testicles.

She heard him scream with pain as he tried to retrieve the key, and smiled to herself as she quietly closed the front door.

Stopping in Sloane Street only long enough for a deep breath of fresh air, she hailed a cab and instructed the driver to take her to the Embankment. She walked beside the river, stopping at the floating pub to order a treble vodka and ponder her situation. She felt satisfied with her destruction of De Wolf and confident that his career was ruined. A very smart young man in a grey suit asked if he could buy her a drink. She smiled sweetly at him. 'Piss off,' she said.

It was half past eleven when Monica returned to Cadogan Square. She made sure the Bentley was gone before she ventured inside. Frank had left a large note pinned to the bedroom door. She threw it away without reading a word. The red light was flashing on her answerphone. It was a message from Nigel. 'Monica, please phone me as soon as you get in, it doesn't matter what time.'

She dialled his number. He sounded very excited and asked if he could come over.

'It's a bit late,' said Monica. 'Can't this wait until tomorrow?'

'I don't think so,' answered Nigel. 'It's very important. I don't want to talk about it on the phone and it involves you.'

'How mysterious, I can't wait,' she said, mocking Nigel's urgency. 'I'll put the kettle on.'

Nigel parked the Porsche outside Monica's flat, picked up the large bunch of flowers from the passenger seat and skipped up the five tiled steps to her front door.

'These are for last Sunday,' he said, handing her the bouquet as he stepped out of the lift.

Monica was pleasantly surprised. 'Why thank you, Nigel,' she said. 'What a lovely thought.'

She placed the flowers in the kitchen sink, poured two cups of coffee and joined Nigel in the living room. 'Now,' she said, 'what's this all about?'

'I've heard from Samantha. You were right, there is more to this than meets the eye.' He handed her a letter. 'Read this, it explains everything.'

Monica took the letter, but did not open it. 'Are you sure you want me to read this?' she asked. 'It's obviously very personal.'

'Go ahead,' he replied. 'You know how I feel about her and I really need some confirmation before I blow up completely.'

Monica studied his face. It was tight with anticipation. She opened the letter and began to read.

'Dearest Nigel,' it began. 'I know you must feel utterly cheated and betrayed by me but please do read on. I must explain what happened and confirm my true feelings. I have lied to you several times, the first being that I lived in Cricklewood. I live in Highgate with my uncle, Wallace Pike.'

Monica stopped dead in her tracks and read the last line again. She looked at Nigel. He grinned at her. 'Go on,' he said.

'I keep a diary. The only explanation I can offer regarding the story is that Uncle Wallace read it and then sold or gave it to the newspaper. I wouldn't dream of making our intimate secrets public knowledge. Your love is very precious to me. My only wish is that you will not hold me responsible for my uncle's ghastly behaviour.

'I made up the story about the holiday, because I go to Geneva with my family at this time every year and I didn't want you to know. The girl you met at the airport is my cousin.

'My family are livid and have threatened Wallace with all kinds of things, but I know that doesn't make you feel any better. I love you so much, Nigel, I am beside myself with worry and regret. I will never speak to my uncle again, but that can't make up for the terrible things he has done to you. I wouldn't knowingly hurt you. I love you. This is my only defence.

'I am enclosing an air ticket to Geneva in the hope that, even if you can't forgive my uncle, you will at least come and see me and meet the rest of my family. They know how I feel about you and will welcome you warmly if you accept my offer. Please come. I love you. Samantha.'

Monica folded the letter and handed it back to Nigel. She thought De Wolf was a low life, but this was the dirtiest trick she had ever borne witness to.

'What do you think?' asked Nigel.

'If you feel you can, you should go to her right away. Tomorrow.' Monica looked at her watch. 'I mean today.'

'What about the show?'

'There are more important things in life than a radio station,' said Monica. 'Not many, I'll grant you, but this is one of them. Take as much time as you need.'

Nigel reached over and put his arms around her neck. 'Thank you.'

Monica hugged him back and silently wished him luck. 'That's quite enough of that,' she said. 'We can't have my reputation shattered by a silly love letter. Would you like another coffee?'

Nigel sat back on the sofa. 'I won't tell anyone,' he said, feeling exhilarated by her confirmation. 'I could do with a large Scotch and a telephone.'

'A telephone?'

'To call Samantha.'

'There's one on the desk,' said Monica, walking towards the kitchen. 'I'll get the drinks.'

First thing Sunday morning Monica phoned Freddie French. She told him the story of Samantha and the wicked Uncle Wallace and how she hoped Freddie would reap his revenge on the son of a kangaroo with the utmost ruthlessness.

'I'd say we have every chance of redressing the balance by a considerable amount,' said Freddie. 'I've just heard that he paid well over the odds for some Capital shares at close of play on Friday. How did you get on with Mr De Wolf?'

'Shall we say, he will now find it difficult to find employment anywhere in the Western world,' said Monica, with more than a touch of satisfaction.

'Peter is thinking of making the deal with Aylford sometime next week,' said Freddie. 'So don't be concerned if pressure is brought to bear on you from inside the station. We don't want to make your board appointment public until we've taken care of Mother.'

'Inside the station?' asked Monica, hoping Freddie was not about to spring another nasty surprise.

'We have a feeling Eddy McLeod has gone to Aylford,' said Freddie.

'Best place for him,' replied a relieved Monica.

'I tend to agree, just watch your back door.'

'I always keep it locked, Freddie. By the way, did you hear Nigel thumped him last week?'

'Yes, Peter told me. That's why we think he's crossed.'

'What is it your mother says?' chuckled Monica. '"It's all like stuffing a chicken to me."'

'Quite so,' laughed Freddie. 'Quite so.'

Chicken was on the menu of SwissAir flight 839 to Geneva, but Nigel couldn't eat a thing. He listened to the rock channel on the in-flight entertainment and lost himself in the music. In half an hour he would be with Samantha. Nothing else mattered.

He cleared customs without being stopped and walked out of the terminal building into the hot Geneva sun. He saw Samantha running across the car-park. She was wearing the same white dress she wore at Trader Vic's, her blonde hair flowing out behind her as she ran. She fell into his arms and held him.

'I love you, Nigel Beresford-Clarke,' she whispered.

He pushed her gently back to arm's length and saw the tears streaming down her face. He took a handkerchief from his pocket and slowly wiped them away. 'I love you too, Samantha Keating.'

They looked at each other, searching, seeking, transferring feeling with their eyes. He knew he would always love her. She knew she had found her man.

They held each other again. 'Come meet my mum and dad, they're longing to see you,' she whispered in his ear.

They took a handle each of Nigel's carry-all and walked across the car-park. Samantha led him to the back of a white Cadillac limousine. As they reached it, the boot popped open.

'Is this yours?' asked Nigel very softly.

'One of them,' answered Samantha, kissing him lightly on the cheek.

Nigel wasn't prepared for this. He knew nothing about her or her family, but this was beyond his wildest expectations. 'One of them? What do you mean, one of them?' he said, throwing in his bag and closing the lid.

Samantha tugged at his arm. 'Come on,' she whispered. She opened the back door of the limousine. Inside were four custom-made seats, two facing front and two facing back, each covered in pleated black leather with its own arm rests. There were various rosewood cabinets built in around the interior, a sunroof and black thick-pile carpets on the floor. Mr and Mrs Keating sat on the front-facing seats. He was a very handsome grey-haired man in his early fifties. He wore an exquisitely cut navy-blue suit, an open-neck white

356

shirt and a pair of Gucci loafers. Mrs Keating was an elegant woman – Nigel guessed her age as anywhere between thirty-five and forty-five – with a smile that matched Samantha's. She wore a white dress with pleats below the waist and a thin navy-blue belt with matching high-heeled shoes.

Mr Keating extended his hand as Nigel sat down on the far back-facing seat. 'Nigel, I'm so glad to meet you. My name is Charles and this is my wife Rebecca.'

Nigel shook hands with them both and sat back in the soft leather seat. As soon as Samantha closed the door the car pulled away with effortless ease.

'Before we go any further,' said Charles, 'my wife and I would like to offer our most humble apologies for Wallace's behaviour. It must have been a most harrowing experience. I only hope we can go some way towards making it up to you over the next few days.'

Nigel looked at them both and could see real embarrassment in their faces. 'Mr Keating, I . . .'

'Please,' interrupted the man. 'Call me Charles.'

'Charles,' continued Nigel, 'as long as I can be with Samantha I couldn't care less what people say about me.'

Samantha reached over and held his hand.

'Very nobly put,' said Rebecca, before turning to her husband and holding his hand in the same way as Samantha held Nigel's. 'They are very much in love, Charles, and that is all that matters to me. I think we should drop this whole subject and rejoice in our daughter's happiness.'

'Splendid idea,' said Charles, turning his attention to Nigel. 'May I offer you a drink?'

'You've said the magic word,' said Nigel with a smile, his confidence flooding back. 'I would love a Scotch.'

'I only have American bourbon, Three Roses. Will that do?'

'I haven't drunk that before.'

'Time to enhance your education,' said Charles, opening the small cabinet beside him. 'Samantha?'

'The same please, Daddy,' she said, squeezing Nigel's hand.

'Rebecca?'

'Vodka tonic, please, darling, but just a small one.'

'No such thing,' said Charles, as he prepared the drinks on the highly polished wooden table that slid from beneath the cabinet. He passed the drinks around to everyone, sat straight in his seat and raised his glass. 'To you, Nigel Beresford-Clarke and to you, my lovely daughter. May you both be healthy, lucky and loved.'

Samantha leaned over and kissed Nigel on the forehead. 'I'll drink to that,' she said.

The limousine pulled into a tree-lined driveway as Nigel finished his drink. 'This is very good,' he said, handing the glass back to Charles.

'You'll never drink Scotch whisky again,' replied Charles, taking the glass and dropping it into its place inside the cabinet. 'Ah good, we're home. Welcome to Casablanca.'

Nigel looked surprised.

'It's my favourite film,' said Rebecca. 'Charles named it for me.'

The Cadillac stopped outside a rambling modern building with high windowless walls and a large central arch. The driver opened the nearside door and they all stepped out into the hot afternoon sunshine. Nigel and Samantha walked arm in arm through the arch followed by Charles and Rebecca. They entered a paved courtyard with an ornate fountain as its centrepiece. A profusion of potted flowers surrounded the fountain and several more pots were placed around the perimeter in a seemingly ad hoc fashion. Through another archway on the opposite side of the courtyard, Nigel could see a large expanse of lawn leading down to the lake.

He wanted to stop and take it all in, but Samantha hurried him along towards a gothic-looking wooden door to the right of the second arch. She looked back at her parents. 'We'll see you at dinner,' she shouted.

'Seven o'clock,' her mother shouted back.

Once inside, the house felt cool and airy. The floors were made of beige marble, cut in large squares and joined with bronze. The walls of the entrance hall were two storeys high and painted white. Two sets of marble stairs hugged the walls and led up to a gallery, along which several wooden doors were spaced equally. On the ground floor were four marble steps leading down to a large living area which was painted light yellow. The floor was made from thick pine planks, highly polished and partly covered by plain Spanish carpets. The furniture was numerous and floral patterned; the far wall was made entirely of glass with views across the lake.

The driver arrived with Nigel's bag, left it in the hallway and quietly closed the door behind him.

Nigel flopped on to the large sofa next to the window wall and looked out over the lake. Samantha walked in from the kitchen carrying an ice bucket and two glasses on a silver tray. In the ice bucket was a bottle of Dom Perignon 1976. She put the tray on the floor beside Nigel. 'Do you want a joint?' she asked.

'With your parents here? Are you serious?'

Samantha laughed and threw back her hair in that perfect arc that he loved so much. 'This is my part of the house. I live here. Mummy and Daddy won't come in unless they call first. It's been like that since they built it for me. We respect each other's privacy in this family.'

'This is . . . yours!'

'All four bedrooms, five bathrooms, two receptions, the playroom and the kitchen. Now, do you want that joint?'

This was all becoming too much for Nigel to absorb. 'I think so,' he said.

'You open the champagne then, I won't be a minute.'

Nigel watched her disappear from the room, then reached down beside him for the bottle.

She returned as Nigel was pouring the second glass. She handed him what seemed to be a tailor-made cigarette. 'This is the way we do it here,' she said. 'We buy fifty at a time, already rolled.'

They drank, smoked and cuddled on the sofa, looking out over the lake and seeing nothing except their reflections in the window.

'I've got to tell you why I did what I did,' said Samantha, stroking the back of his head with her hand.

'You don't have to explain anything,' replied Nigel.

'Yes I do,' she said, turning to face him. 'Ever since I was fourteen men have been swarming around me, trying to find a way to get to me and my family's money. I decided that if I was to have any chance of happiness I had to get away from all this. I came to London last year to study journalism. No one knew me there, so I could live a near normal life. When we met, I didn't want you to find out who I was so I told you lies and fabricated my background. I don't do modelling and I don't live in Cricklewood. I'm just a woman who met and fell in love with a lovely man, then proceeded to lie to him about everything except the fact that I loved him.'

Nigel put his empty glass on the tray. 'I don't know how to answer that,' he said. 'I'm just an average guy with a good radio voice. I like my job, my friends and my car. I've screwed lots of women and when I met you, I wished I hadn't . . . screwed lots of women, that is.'

They both burst out laughing.

'You see,' said Nigel, trying to catch his breath. 'I'm hopeless.'

Samantha moved closer to him on the sofa. 'Nigel,' she said, in a soft but serious voice.

He stopped laughing. 'What?'

'Marry me.'

Nigel couldn't believe what he heard. He would in a second, but this couldn't be happening. 'Are you serious?'

'Very.'

'Wait a minute,' he said, trying to make light of the situation. 'I'm the one who's supposed to ask you.'

Samantha would not remove her stare from his eyes. 'Go ahead then.'

Nigel had reached the moment of truth. She was serious and he did love her, more than anything on earth. He took both her hands in his. 'Samantha Keating, will you marry me?'

'Yes I will, Nigel, I most certainly will.'

CHAPTER 16

Monday morning felt joyously gratifying to Monica Hammond. She had dealt with De Wolf in a most satisfactory manner. She was pleased that Nigel had sorted his life out with Samantha and very pleased indeed with Nigel's replacement, Simon Lewis. He was one of Monica's chance finds. She received hundreds of tapes every month from would-be disc jockeys and aspiring journalists. Ninety-nine per cent of them were, in a word, crap. Simon Lewis was different. He was twenty-six years old, worked at one of the London orbital stations and had a maturity far beyond his years. She liked his voice and, from the picture he enclosed, he seemed very pleasing to the eye. When she met him she was impressed by his smart appearance and easy-going manner. She hired him as a junior fill-in, and covering for Nigel was his first big show. He was no Nigel Beresford-Clarke, but would be given a few more years. Monica sat behind her glass-top desk treating herself to an extra-long toe twiddle before setting about the business of the day.

Her new security measures were working well. Following her meeting with John Thorne and Sean Hearty, she had decided that she couldn't close down the reception area as it was very much part of the station's contact with its audience. A help line, jobfinder and merchandising shop were all located there and she didn't want to stop any of these services. She agreed to have a security desk, manned at all times, installed just inside the main door. Everybody entering the station who didn't have a staff card would be searched and all baggage would be checked. She also agreed to move the telephone switchboard upstairs into the sales office. As for sounding macho on the air, Monica informed Mr Hearty that, war or no war, macho was not part of the station style: anyone found adopting that attitude would be severely dealt with. She signed the report from her Chief of Security and placed the folder in her 'file' tray.

Next, she tackled the latest dip polls. She laughed to herself as she looked at the figures for the breakfast show. Up thirty-eight per cent. Nigel was now clear of Capital by a good eighteen points. She knew they would level off again, especially with him being away, but if she could get a good picture story about his return from Geneva, that would bump them up again. The morning show had returned to its old form, proving that last week was only a hiccup and serving as a reminder to Monica that programmers should never take one set of figures too seriously, be they good or bad. She made some margin notes about breakfast and late night, signed the lead sheet and called her secretary with a request to deliver the file to sales as soon as possible.

Rating figures did not enter the scope of Nigel's thoughts as he woke up on Monday morning in a large king-size bed with Samantha beside him. He thought of being in love, making love, giving love, receiving love; in fact, his mind was set firmly on one track this morning. Samantha wanted to tell her parents about their impending marriage when they knew Nigel a little better. She suggested a dinner at her place on Wednesday, which they would cook together and serve on the patio. Until then it was their secret.

Nigel had packed hastily before his departure from London and took only enough clothes to last a couple of days. He'd brought no suits, ties, dress shoes or evening wear. Tonight the Keatings were entertaining formally and Nigel was expected to be there. Last night at dinner when they'd informed him of this his mind had gone into panic mode, but Samantha eased it with one sentence.

'Over here, Nigel,' she had said, 'when the going gets tough, the tough go shopping.' Everyone at the table laughed, including Nigel. Charles offered him the use of one of the cars and another bourbon.

Nigel propped himself up on one arm and watched Samantha sleeping. He thought of waking her, using the Beresford-Clarke massage method, but decided to let her sleep. He looked around him and took in the simple elegance of the room. He loved the Picasso print above the bed; then he focused clearly on it and realized it was the original, and felt a little foolish. Samantha turned over in her sleep, her arm coming to rest on Nigel's waist. He slid down into the bed, put his arms gently around her and kissed her softly on the lips. She slowly opened her eyes and smiled. Nigel felt so happy he thought he would burst.

'Good morning, future husband,' she whispered. 'I love you.'

'Good morning, future wife,' he whispered back. 'I love you too.'

They had hoped to get an early start at the shopping in order to leave their afternoon free, but as Nigel felt her hand drift lightly up the inside of his leg, he redefined early as any time before noon.

By eleven o'clock they were standing outside the five garage doors that took up most of the east-facing wall of the courtyard. Samantha held a small black box in her right hand. 'I love this bit,' she said. 'Watch.' She pressed the centre of the black box and all five doors started to open. 'It feels like International Rescue,' she giggled.

Nigel started to move like a puppet. 'Gosh . . . Lady P. . . . which Thunderbird shall we use today?'

Samantha mimicked his movements. 'Gosh . . . take . . . your . . . pick, Brains.'

Nigel looked inside the garage. A Rolls-Royce, a Range Rover, a Mercedes-Benz, an E-type Jaguar and the Cadillac limousine stood spotlessly clean in a neat row behind the doors. Nigel had never before seen such a collection of mechanical excellence in one place. 'Do you think your Dad would mind if I drove the E-type?' he asked.

Sam burst out laughing and flung her arms around his neck. She swung her legs up around his waist and kissed him. He held on to her thighs to ease the pressure on his neck. 'Take me to the E-type,' she shouted, pointing towards the car.

As Nigel started the motor and listened to the roar of the V12 engine, Sam sat beside him in the passenger seat, still chuckling away to herself.

'What did I say that was so funny?' asked Nigel.

'This one is mine,' she answered. 'I bought it in London, the day after I met you.'

Nigel joined in her laughter, flicked the car into first gear and thundered out of the garage. 'Where to first, m'lady?'

'Turn left at the road, Parker, and follow the signs saying *Centre Ville.*'

Sir Peter French felt more 'centre stage' than '*centre ville*' as he sat, with his brother Freddie, in Aylford's boardroom and listened to Wallace Pike tell his vice-chairman, Bruce Hamilton, that Sir Peter was a doyen of British media, and how pleased he was that their two companies were at last working together. Sir Peter took it all with a pinch of salt, but thought it best to let him ramble on just in case he let something slip that could be useful to his cause. Freddie hadn't wanted this meeting until Wednesday at the earliest but Pike, apparently, had some urgent business in Geneva and would be out of town for the rest of the week.

'Now,' said Pike, having finished his softening-up speech, 'I think we have several points of mutual interest to discuss. First of all, I believe you are expanding heavily into British radio and I would like to see Aylford right there beside you, blow for blow, every inch of the way. I have been able to purchase a considerable amount of stock recently in several Brit stations and that, teamed up with your, shall we say, firepower and management skills, should ensure that our two companies are instrumental in shaping the future of radio in this country.'

Sir Peter closed his brown leather note-folder and relaxed into his black leather chair. 'I don't know where you obtain your information,' he said. 'But I must tell you that quite the reverse is true.' He watched Pike's face change from cocky arrogance to bewilderment in under a second. 'We have come here today to discuss the possible sale of our UK interests to your company. We are also interested in looking at your satellite holdings in the Far East.'

Pike remembered what Longshore had told him a few weeks ago. He had chosen to ignore it because the information he was getting from De Wolf was much more up to date. He knew the French brothers were buying – De Wolf had said so.

'Of course,' said Freddie, 'we have a very successful operation here, so we are looking for a strong price.'

Pike was now totally confused. 'How much are you looking for?'

'We value the CRFM group, including Cornwall,

Dundee and our interests in ATS, at somewhere in the region of two hundred million,' said Sir Peter.

'I think that's way too high,' said Pike, looking at his vice-chairman for support.

'In that case,' said Sir Peter, 'I feel we have nothing further to discuss.'

'Just a minute,' said Pike, almost in desperation. 'As I said earlier, we have acquired a lot of radio stock recently and the addition of the French interests would put us in a very commanding position. You mentioned an interest in satellite. What do you propose?'

'What value do you place on your Far East operation?' continued Sir Peter.

Wallace Pike considered his answer very carefully. 'A ball park figure, two hundred and fifty million.'

The French brothers didn't look at each other, they didn't need to. 'A straight swap,' said Sir Peter. 'All of ours for all of yours.'

Bruce Hamilton took a large drink of water.

'Done,' said Wallace Pike.

There was a knock on the boardroom door.

'Come in,' shouted Pike, and blessed whoever it was for their timing.

His secretary came into the room and handed him a plain brown envelope and left immediately.

Wallace Pike opened it and pulled out a picture of Frank De Wolf, handcuffed to a bed and sporting a giant erection.

Photographer extraordinaire, Monica Hammond, laughed for a very long time when Freddie phoned her on Wednesday morning to say they had completed the deal with Aylford.

'That's wonderful news,' she said. 'What a marvellous way to start the day.'

They made arrangements to have dinner that evening. Freddie thought a return visit to Le Gavroche was in order and Monica wasn't about to argue, although she did insist that this time it was her treat. Freddie mumbled something about women's lib and tax deductions and agreed to meet her there at nine o'clock. Monica put the phone down and continued getting dressed. She listened to Simon Lewis and knew she'd found a star of the future. She thought of Frank De Wolf and laughed some more. Things were looking extremely good for Monica Elizabeth Hammond.

Maggie arrived at the station at precisely eleven o'clock. She listened to the news on the reception monitor, before handing Robin Trower the last autograph for his sister's collection. 'There you are,' she said. 'With love from Brian "Frosty" Forst. Will that do you?'

'That's great,' said Robin. 'Her birthday is tomorrow – you couldn't have timed it better.'

'I'm known for my timing,' she said, skipping up the stairs two at a time. Wednesday was Bradley day and Maggie was a very happy budgie.

Robin smiled after her and put Mr Forst into his lunch box.

At eleven-fifteen a very serious-looking man arrived at the station. Robin, who seemed to be permanently on front security, asked him the usual questions. No, he didn't have a staff card; no, he didn't mind being searched; no, he didn't have an appointment, but his name was Frank De Wolf, he had come to see Monica Hammond and he wasn't going to leave until he did.

Robin phoned Monica's office. She told him to show Mr De Wolf a seat, and that was all. Monica sat in her office and twiddled, and twiddled, and twiddled. He could sit there all day if he wished; she would go home via the car-park entrance.

At half past eleven Anthony and Lizzie arrived. They were not their usual loving selves; in fact, they were having a good old-fashioned down-and-out scrap. Robin got the gist of the disagreement. Anthony was angry because Lizzie was getting all the roses and he was getting all the thorns. The press, the fan mail, the phone calls were all for her. Anthony felt left out. Robin could understand how he felt – he had worked with Lizzie on reception and knew just how adept she was at those kinds of games.

At eleven thirty-five, a young man carrying a rucksack and an *A–Z of London* came into reception and asked directions to Queensway. He propped his rucksack against the front desk and leaned over the counter as Robin instructed him on how to get to his destination. He thanked Robin very much and left.

Robin watched Anthony and Lizzie fighting away, each blaming the other for everything, and thought he'd better do something about it. He walked over to them and interrupted their scrap with all the panache of a seasoned referee. 'Come on, you two, this is no place for fighting. Monica will have us all on the carpet if she comes down here, and that could be any moment,' he said, pointing in Frank De Wolf's direction.

Anthony saw the sense of this and calmed down. Lizzie stamped her foot, turned, and headed for the door.

'Don't worry, she'll be back,' said Robin, putting his hand on Anthony's shoulder. 'Look, do me a favour, watch the front while I get a coffee.'

Anthony nodded his acceptance and Robin headed for the staff room.

At eleven thirty-nine the bomb in the rucksack exploded.

Anthony didn't see the piece of front desk that

removed his head. Frank De Wolf didn't feel the large piece of plate glass that went into his chest and came out his back, just below his left shoulder blade. Robin Trower saw his coffee cup shatter as he was thrown through the partition wall, he also felt the kitchen knife bury itself in his stomach. The force of the blast knocked Lizzie down the last three steps and into the street. She could feel the warmth of her own blood as it ran down her face and legs, but she couldn't see how badly she'd been hurt. She couldn't see at all.

The blast rocked the whole building. Reception's front walls were blown out causing the ceiling to collapse and part of the floor in the sales department, which was right above, to fall away. The shelves in the library fell like a house of cards, pinning Trevor Jones beneath them. Some people screamed, some froze in shock; others ran to the nearest exit expecting another blast. Mandy Stewart fell to her knees and prayed.

John Thorne, Maggie and Monica knew exactly what had happened. John ran to his desk and pushed the red switch beside his phone. Monica ran from her office towards the newsroom. The hall was full of fine dust. She pulled her dress up, using the hem to cover her mouth. She saw Maggie in the hall. 'Maggie!' she shouted. 'The studio! Check the studio!' Monica ran on to the newsroom. She saw John running out of his office. 'Have you . . .?'

'I've already done it!' John ran past her. 'Come on! It's in reception!'

They ran through the green room which was full of dust and smoke. Monica could just see that the glass partition was still intact, which meant the air in the studio was still pure. She couldn't see either Maggie or Nick Glover, but assumed they were coping. She followed John into reception. The first thing she saw was the headless body of Anthony Parkin. She felt sick.

John called to her. 'Monica, get down here! Robin's still alive!'

Monica ran to him and looked down at this well-mannered young man who had greeted her so often with a warm smile or a piece of naively juvenile advice. She could see that two of his left-hand fingers were missing; the left side of his head looked as if he'd been scalped. There was little blood there, just raw bone. Then she saw the knife handle half-buried in his stomach, blood pouring from the wound.

John took off his shirt and handed it to Monica. 'Hold this on it,' he said, moving Robin's injured hand close to the knife wound. 'Try and stem the bleeding.' She did as he instructed.

Robin looked up at her. 'My lunch box,' he whispered.

She knew she must keep her senses together, this boy's life depended on it. She pressed John's shirt firmly into the wound. 'It's all right,' she said. 'Just stay still.' Robin closed his eyes. His breathing became weaker. 'No!' shouted Monica, 'NO!'

'Is he still alive?' said a voice behind her.

She turned around and saw a man in an orange and white coat. 'I don't know,' she whispered.

'Let me at him,' he said, helping Monica out of the way. He felt for a pulse. 'Jack!' he shouted. 'Over here, bring the crash cart, quick!!'

Monica walked into what was left of the reception area. There seemed to be police and medics everywhere. She tripped over a piece of rubble, fell and, as she looked up, saw the dead face of Frank De Wolf. She opened her mouth to scream, but no sound came out. She sat up and covered her face with her hands, a myriad of memories flashing through her mind. She felt guilt, sadness, shame, remorse, emptiness – then she fainted.

John was pushing his way through the rubble in an attempt to get to the library. After much effort he finally reached the door which was hanging half off its hinges. He kicked it just above the hinge. It swung back on him and hit him on the head. He stepped back and ran straight at it. It gave way under his weight and both he and the door fell into the room. All the shelves had collapsed towards the far side of the room; the fine dust obscured his vision. 'Anyone here?' he shouted. He heard a faint shout from the far side of the room. The shelves had collapsed in a straight line, leaving aisles of visible floor. John ran down the first aisle to the far end of the room. 'Where are you?'

'Right next to you,' came the faint reply.

John looked down and saw the top half of Trevor Jones sticking out from under the fallen shelves, blood dripping from the corner of his mouth. 'Where are you hurt?' he asked.

'My legs mainly, but something's stuck in my gut.'

John looked closer and saw a jagged piece of vinyl had lodged itself just below his ribcage. 'That'll teach you to play Des O'Connor records,' he said.

Trevor laughed. Blood spurted from his mouth.

'I'm sorry, old son, hang on in there.' John turned towards the door. 'MEDIC! IN HERE!'

Within ten seconds two men were standing beside him. 'What have we got?' asked the first.

'Crushed legs, cut wound below the ribcage, right side,' replied John.

'Thank you,' said the second man. 'Give me a hand.' The two men tried to lift the shelving – it would not budge.

'Jacks and bars in this room!' shouted the first man.

Within two minutes they had Trevor free and on a stretcher.

'Were you alone in here?' asked John, as he accompanied the stretcher towards the door.

'Yes, I was,' answered Trevor, grabbing hold of John's hand and trying to smile. 'Thanks for coming in for me.'

Outside the building was utter chaos. There were police cars, ambulances, fire trucks and television cameras – lots of television cameras. Lizzie sat on the pavement being attended by two paramedics. A television news team was crowding in on her. She was covered in blood. 'I can't see,' she kept saying. 'I can't see.'

'Where were you when the bomb went off, Lizzie?' asked the reporter.

'Outside the door,' replied Lizzie. 'Where's my boyfriend? Where's Anthony? Is he alive? I can't see!'

'Who else is in there?'

'I want to see Anthony? Where's Anthony?'

The medic moved in front of the reporter. 'Get the hell out of here!' he shouted. 'This woman is badly hurt! Go away!'

The medics lifted Lizzie into a wheelchair, and one of them held her head. They took her and the chair into an ambulance.

'I can't see!!' screamed Lizzie.

Maggie was keeping things cool in the studio. She went to the rack bay and switched to generator power, made sure the air-conditioning was intact and working, then told Nick to continue for as long as he could while she laced up the emergency tape. Nick made the standard announcement about 'circumstances beyond our control' and switched to the tape.

'Now, let's get the fuck out of here,' he said.

They ran through the debris that used to be reception and out into the street. Maggie found John and hugged him tight. 'Where's Monica?' she asked.

John pointed to a stretcher on the pavement.

'Oh, good God!' shouted Maggie.

'It's all right,' said John, holding on to her. 'She'll be all right. Frank De Wolf is dead – she saw him.'

'Who else?'

'Anthony. Maybe Robin Trower. Trevor's hurt bad.'

Maggie turned her face into his chest and started to cry. He held her tight.

'Bastards,' she sobbed. 'Dirty rotten, stinking, mother-fucking BASTARDS!'

CHAPTER 17

Samantha placed a large bouquet of flowers in a crystal vase on the centre of the pine table that dominated the patio. She stood back and admired her handiwork. Everything was set for this evening's meal. She and Nigel had cooked a large beef roast, prepared the vegetables and the salad, and created a starter of melon, ham, pineapple and port. They had worked all afternoon on this gastronomic delight: peeling, washing, trimming, drinking the best part of two bottles of wine and stopping only twice to, as Nigel put it, make sure they still loved each other.

'They'll be here in half an hour,' shouted Nigel from the kitchen. 'Hadn't you better get ready?'

Sam skipped through the living room and stood framed in the kitchen doorway. She unzipped the front of her yellow summer dress and let it glide down over her body and form a circle around her feet. She wore nothing underneath. 'I'm ready,' she chirped.

Nigel put the salad bowl into the fridge and walked across the room like John Wayne. 'Don't get smart with me, young lady,' he said, doing a very good impression of the late movie star. 'We don't take any prisoners in this guy's army.'

Samantha put both her hands up to her face in an expression of mock horror. 'Why, sir, I will have to tell my mummy and daddy on you.'

'The hell you will,' said Nigel Wayne, picking her up in a fireman's lift and carrying her towards the stairs.

'Put me down, put me down,' teased Samantha.

'Not till I get ya to the jail.'

'Umm, very interesting,' whispered Samantha, digging her fingers playfully into his backside.

They finished dressing just as Charles and Rebecca rang the doorbell. Rebecca commented on how lovely the table looked as she walked beside Samantha out into the warm evening air. Charles and Nigel were getting along famously. Charles saw a lot of himself as a younger man in this brash and confident disc jockey. Charles liked Nigel, really liked him. He made such a change from the limp-wristed sophisticates Samantha used to bring home.

The meal was delicious. Rebecca loved the starter and demanded the recipe. The meat was done to perfection, the vegetables were not overcooked and the salad was crisp and cold. Samantha served the cheese and coffee as Nigel cleared the table.

'Surprise!' said Samantha, as she put a bell-bottom crystal decanter and a brandy goblet in front of her father.

He removed the stopper immediately and poured a small amount of the light brown liquid into the goblet. He cupped it in both hands, turning it in small circles. Lifting it to his nose, he inhaled the bouquet before pouring it into his mouth. He held it there for a few seconds and then swallowed, a wide grin forming on his face. 'Remy Martin, Louis the Thirteenth.'

Samantha hugged her father around the neck. 'Dead right,' she said. 'Carafe number AC1324.'

Nigel looked on in amazement; Rebecca took it as read.

Samantha went inside the house and returned a moment later with three more brandy goblets. She poured a good measure into each glass and passed them around before going to stand behind Nigel and placing her arms around his neck. 'There's something we would like to tell you,' she said. 'And I think Nigel should do the talking.'

Nigel felt the strength flow from her embrace. 'Samantha and I want to get married,' he said.

Charles and Rebecca looked at each other. 'Do you really love her?' asked Charles, turning towards Nigel.

'Yes I do,' he replied.

'In that case, you have our blessing.'

Nigel took Samantha in his arms and kissed her.

Charles and Rebecca walked around the table and joined their embrace, sharing the moment of union with unbridled feeling. Suddenly, Rebecca broke away. 'Where? When? How many people? What about a dress?'

Samantha looked at Nigel. He understood and kissed her lightly on the cheek. Samantha took her mother's arm and they walked into the house.

Nigel and Charles watched the two women walk through the house and into the central courtyard beyond. For the first time, Nigel felt strangely awkward with this kind and cultured gentleman.

Charles sat down on the patio chair, picked up his brandy goblet, warming it in his hands and scenting the bouquet. 'What you felt just then was the sorrow of a father losing a daughter,' he said. 'Not the joy of gaining a son.'

Nigel was unaccustomed to such high mental awareness. He would have to learn.

'Will you continue living and working in London?' asked Charles.

'I have two years left on my contract and Sam wants to finish her course,' replied Nigel.

'I understand,' said Charles. The phone in the living room started ringing. 'That'll be the girls. I'll bet there's an argument over the venue.'

Nigel answered the phone. 'Maggie!' he exclaimed excitedly. 'What a surprise. How did you find me?' His face greyed and collapsed like a sail that had lost the wind as he listened in disbelief to Maggie's story. 'I'll be there on the next flight,' he said and hung up.

'What's the matter?' asked Charles.

'There's been a bomb at the station,' said Nigel. 'My friend Anthony has been killed.'

Charles reached past Nigel, picked up the phone and dialled twenty-two. 'Stanley, please have the plane ready in an hour and a car standing by. Thank you.' He replaced the phone and started walking towards the door. 'I'll get the girls.'

Nigel did not hear him.

Nigel and Samantha landed at Heathrow just before eight o'clock the next morning and went straight to University College Hospital. Robin was still in critical condition after eight hours of surgery and could not be seen. Nigel recognized Robin's mother and sister sitting huddled together on the red bench chairs that fill the reception of UCH. 'Who could do this horrible thing?' sobbed Mrs Trower, her face ashen from a night of pain and worry. 'He was only a boy . . .'

'*Is* only a boy,' interrupted Nigel. 'He's going to make it, Mrs Trower, I know it.'

A nurse called to Nigel from the front desk. 'You can see Mr Jones now, second floor, ward 2B.'

Trevor's wife was sitting by the bed when Nigel and Sam walked into the ward. She looked drained and tired. Trevor looked remarkably perky considering his ordeal. 'You'll have to speak up,' he said, as Nigel greeted him. 'The blast fucked up my ears, I can't hear that well.'

'You never could,' joked Nigel. 'I've heard the music you play.'

Trevor accepted the jibe in his usual 'you don't mean that really' manner, told them as much as he could remember about the events of the previous day and asked them to take his wife home as she needed to rest.

'Where's Lizzie?' asked Samantha.

'They took her to Guy's Hospital,' replied Trevor. 'Something about them having special equipment. I heard she hurt her eyes but no one will confirm it.'

They said their goodbyes, Trevor's wife crying softly as she tried to hug him without touching the damaged parts. They drove her home in the Porsche, Samantha scrunched into the jump seat with her suitcase, before driving on to Maida Vale.

'I'll put the kettle on,' said Samantha as they entered the flat. 'Why don't you fill the jacuzzi? The back of that Porsche is no place for anyone over four feet.'

Nigel took Sam in his arms and kissed her, not passionately or sexually, but slowly, tenderly, holding her tightly and then letting his head rest on her neck.

'I didn't think it was *that* good an idea,' said Samantha.

'It could have been me,' he whispered.

Samantha broke his embrace, held him by the shoulders and looked him straight in the eyes. 'But it wasn't,' she said. 'You were with me and that must tell you something.'

Nigel lowered his eyes from her gaze.

'Why don't you phone Monica?' she continued. 'Find out how she is. I bet she'd like to hear from you. You can call her from the bathroom. I'll bring in the coffee.'

Nigel sighed deeply, looked up at her and smiled. 'I'm so glad I found you.'

Samantha turned him around and patted his backside to send him on his way. 'You only love me because I give good coffee,' she shouted after him.

Monica was pleased to hear from Nigel. It was like a contact from before the event. She remembered Robin Trower, she remembered going into reception, and then she woke up in the ambulance. They had checked her over at the hospital then sent her home with a small bottle of Valium and a word of advice about getting a good night's sleep. A good night's sleep was the last thing she would get. The press had been all over her: at the hospital, following the taxi, at her flat, on the phone, ringing her doorbell; it was another nightmare. Freddie and Peter's phone had been constantly engaged. She deduced they were having the same trouble. She couldn't go to Eaton Square, they would only follow. At half past nine she'd decided to face them. She would wear only a plain black dress, no jewellery and the minimum of make-up. By ten o'clock she'd stood outside her front door and tried not to blink, as the camera flashes lit up her small section of Cadogan Square.

'Ladies and gentlemen,' she had said. 'There is really very little I can tell you about this morning that you don't already know. The police have not been in touch with me as yet, and until they do, I think it would be wrong to speculate on the extent of the damage or the identity of the perpetrators.'

The usual barrage of questions came thundering back. 'Was it the IRA? Has it got anything to do with the Gulf, Maggie Lomax, Jack Flash, the French brothers, Lady Isobel, Nigel B.?'

Monica had let them ask all their questions without saying a word in reply. Finally, during a lull in the proceedings, she delivered her ultimate clichéd statement. 'Whoever is responsible for this murderous outrage has gained nothing whatsoever for their cause, except to add more dead bodies and maimed human beings to their list of atrocities. Business will continue as usual at CRFM. We will not be intimidated. That is all I have to say at this time.' She'd turned and walked into the house, closing the door firmly behind her.

The press had left shortly after.

She'd spoken to Peter on the phone just before midnight. He'd informed her Robin was still in surgery and that it was very touch and go. He'd invited her to Eaton Square, but she'd declined, saying the doctor had prescribed tranquillizers and they were starting to work. Peter had promised to call first thing in the morning.

She hadn't taken the pills, but wandered around the flat, piecing the day together in a methodical manner. It was her only defence. She finally fell asleep on the sofa watching the late news on ITV.

The press coverage this morning had been remarkable. The tabloids linked the bombing with Saddam, the serious papers hinted the same, but stated the other possibilities. Every one of them carried a picture of Lizzie Stephenson, her face and clothing covered in blood, silently shouting for her dead Anthony.

They all spelt her name correctly.

Monica told Nigel everything she could remember. Samantha listened in and held on tightly to Nigel's arms. They knew this was the release that Monica needed and Nigel said nothing until he was sure she had finished.

'Would you like to come over to us?' he asked.

'Thank you, no,' replied Monica. 'I want to go to the hospital to see Robin and Lizzie, and then I must go to the station. Business as usual. Mustn't let them shut us down.'

Nigel and Sam looked at each other and Nigel began

to understand high mental awareness. 'We're going there too,' he said. 'Stay where you are, I'll pick you up in ten minutes.' He replaced the receiver before she could object.

'Well done,' said Samantha, kissing him on the cheek. 'That lady needs to be with someone. I'll bet she hasn't eaten all day. You pick her up and I'll get some food together.'

Peter and Freddie picked at their food in a private room supplied by their club. They had just returned from Guy's Hospital, where they had told Lizzie that Anthony was dead. She seemed to sense he was before they told her. She cried long silent sobs. Sir Peter had held on tightly to her hands.

The doctor had good news for Lizzie. The tests showed that there was no permanent damage to her eyes and she would see perfectly again within a very short time. She cried again, but this time, they were totally different tears.

'I wonder what all this will do to our share price?' asked Peter, turning a stubborn piece of lettuce slowly around his fork.

'I should think it'll go sky high,' answered Freddie. 'All this press could double our rating and push turnover up by fifty per cent. I think we should re-evaluate our deal with Aylford.'

A black-suited man appeared at the door. 'Phone call for you, Sir Peter. A gentleman called Pike.'

The brothers smiled at each other. 'Speak of the devil,' said Freddie, gesturing at the man to come in. 'We'll take it here.'

The man plugged the phone into the wall socket and placed the receiver on the table. Peter waited for him to leave before picking it up. 'Wallace,' he said. 'How nice to hear from you.'

Wallace Pike offered his sympathies for Anthony and inquired about Lizzie and Robin. Sir Peter thought how inept Pike was at formal conversation but decided against any comment. Finally, Wallace Pike revealed the true intention of the phone call. 'Peter, old sport, I trust this is not going to affect our deal in any way. We are due to sign the heads of agreement tomorrow and I wouldn't want the game plan changed at this late stage.'

'We might have a small problem in that department, I must admit,' said Sir Peter. 'Our share price could easily double as a result of this unfortunate incident.'

'We have a bloody deal!' shouted Pike.

'We have an agreement to make a deal,' corrected Sir Peter. 'That is not quite the same thing.' He could feel Pike's apprehension through the phone and decided to try his luck. 'It would, however, be a shame to spoil a transaction which is so beneficial to both of us. If we put our minds to it, Wallace, I'm sure we can find an amicable solution.'

Pike knew exactly what the Englishman was suggesting and he didn't like it one bit. Unfortunately there was not a lot he could do if he wanted to consolidate Aylford's holdings in British radio. He had already told his Australian parent company that the deal was set; to call it off now would mean they would use his balls for badger bait and he would be lucky to get a job selling plastic pouches to kangaroos. 'How much do you bloody want?' he asked.

Sir Peter winked at his brother who sat in the chair opposite, arms folded in front of him, grinning like a Cheshire cat. 'I think five per cent should do it, Wallace . . .' he left a slight pause, '. . . in cash, on completion.'

'That's daylight robbery,' said Pike hoping he could find at least some room to negotiate.

'No, Wallace. That's business,' stated Sir Peter, leaving him no room whatsoever.

'You'll have it tomorrow,' said the defeated chairman before slamming down the phone.

Sir Peter replaced his phone gently on to its cradle and smiled at his brother. 'Another twelve and a half million for the kitty,' he smiled. 'And this time in sterling.'

'Nothing better to replenish the appetite,' answered Freddie reaching for the bowl of new potatoes.

When Nigel and Monica arrived back at Maida Vale they found a table full of food. Samantha had done a quick shop at the corner store, then got very busy raiding the freezer, defrosting in the microwave and heating in the oven. Arranged neatly on the living-room table were chicken on a stick Thai-style, lamb in a curry sauce, breaded deep-fried mushrooms and sliced ham with pineapple, all encircling a large bowl of fresh salad. Beside the array of food was an ice bucket containing a bottle of champagne and three crystal glasses.

'What's this?' asked Monica. 'I thought we were going to the hospital.'

'When was the last time you ate?' asked Samantha.

Monica tried to remember, but couldn't.

'I thought so,' said Samantha, sounding much more like a headmistress than a schoolgirl. 'You must eat or you'll be ill. We will all go to the hospital when we've eaten. Besides,' she said, reaching over and holding Nigel's hand, 'we have something to tell you and you'll need a drink.'

Monica's eyes lit up. For that brief moment she forgot about the last twenty-four hours and all the horror they had brought. She looked at the two of them tenderly holding hands and confirmed her guess. 'You're getting married!'

'Yes, we are,' said Nigel. 'And outside Sam's family, you're the first to know.'

Monica felt elated. She hugged them both, asked them when and where and immediately started filling a plate with chicken and salad.

'We don't know yet,' said Nigel. 'We were getting to that when Maggie phoned.' He opened the champagne and poured three glasses. Monica proposed a toast to the happy couple and they drank, ate, and laughed for the first time that day.

Mrs Trower sat with Maggie in the small waiting room beside intensive care. She talked about Robin as a child, his first job as a paper boy, his first girlfriend, how good he was to her and his sister, and how could anyone do this thing to such a good boy. Maggie listened and tried to comfort her the best way she could. 'It'll be all right, Mrs Trower,' she said. 'Robin's a strong boy, he'll pull through.' As she spoke, she felt overwhelming guilt at the thought that this whole heinous affair was her fault, that the bomb was planted by the Flash Jack yobbo who had threatened her on the phone.

A white-coated doctor walked into the room. His face was serious and foreboding. Maggie felt her stomach knot a thousand times; she clenched both fists and lifted them to cover her mouth. Mrs Trower clasped her hands in prayer.

'Mrs Trower,' said the doctor, 'as long as there are no unforeseen complications, Robin will live but – I'm afraid we've had to amputate his hand.'

The two women fell on each other crying tears of bitter joy. The doctor walked from the room, leaving them alone to share their moment of thankful sadness.

Maggie felt a strong hand on her shoulder. She looked up through bleary eyes and saw Bradley standing over her, clutching a large bouquet of red roses in his free hand.

'You look like you need a nice cup of tea,' he said.

Lady Isobel French was not at all happy. It was Monday, 20 August and her seventieth birthday. She sat alone in the dining room at Eaton Square with only her two boiled eggs and a stealthily hovering Simmons for company. There was no sign of her sons, not even a birthday card waiting for her at the breakfast table. She sat back, resigned to this sorry state of affairs.

The door of the dining room suddenly flew open. Lady Isobel was so startled, she flipped her toasted soldier across the table. In the doorway stood two enormous displays of red roses, each over five feet high and fanning out to fill the entire entranceway. They slid into the room on small hidden wheels. As they neared the table Peter and Freddie stepped out from behind them.

'Happy birthday, Mother!' shouted her sons in unison.

The old lady's face suddenly seemed thirty years younger, but old habits die hard: her response was edged with criticism. 'Good God, you could have frightened me to death,' she said, before finishing her answer in a manner befitting the gift. 'They are, without a doubt, the most beautiful roses I have ever seen. Thank you both, very much.'

The ever-hopeful Freddie was determined to give his mother the benefit of the doubt, at least on her birthday. He took the tone of her answer to be a genuine sign of affection and embraced her lightly around her shoulders. 'You're very welcome,' he said. 'Peter has something else we think you'll like.'

'You smell very fresh this morning,' said Lady Isobel, moving away from his touch as if he were a slug. 'That's two days this month you haven't been drunk – that must be close to a personal best, Freddie.'

Peter put a red and blue folder on the table in front of his mother before Freddie could react. He winked at his brother over Isobel's head, while directing his remarks at the old lady. 'As this is a very special birthday, we thought it appropriate to give you a very special present,' he said.

Lady Isobel opened the folder and surveyed the contents. Inside were various tags, labels and information leaflets half-hidden beneath a letter stating that a first-class passage was booked for her and three of her friends on the QE2 departing Southampton at noon on 10 September. The first port of call would be Rio and the cruise would return on 17 January 1991. She looked at the letter in stunned silence. 'I can't do this,' she said to Peter. 'The deal with Manchester will be near completion in September. I can't go gallivanting around the world when my place is here running a business. What *are* you thinking of?'

'Manchester is not going to happen,' said Peter in a soft but commanding voice. 'We have sold all our interests in UK media to Aylford. We have obtained franchises from twenty-two countries to broadcast satellite television and Freddie and I will soon be going to the Far East to consolidate our position regarding technology.'

'You can't do that!' shouted Lady Isobel, slamming both hands on the table. 'You can't move that kind of money without my say so! I won't allow it!'

Freddie slammed his hand down beside his mother's. 'For once in your life listen to what's being said!' he shouted. 'You have no say anymore! This is our money!'

'Freddie! Please!' interjected Peter. 'There is no need to shout.'

Lady Isobel sat back on the Louis XIV dining chair

and came to the realization that she had been outflanked by her own sons. She pondered the glossy tickets in front of her. 'Is this true, Peter?'

'Yes, Mother, it's true. The media operation is now funded by new money. We had hoped for your blessing, but if you choose to fight, we will leave French Enterprises and trade through our own companies.'

'Well, this is some birthday,' said Lady Isobel, letting both her arms drop on to the table. 'Lovely roses, a world cruise and the sack.' She looked at her elder son, an expression of sadness and defeat on her face. 'Will you keep me informed?' she asked.

'Every step of the way,' replied Peter.

'In that case, I'd better call Gwen and talk Rio. I suppose they already know about the trip?'

'They're awaiting your call.'

Lady Isobel picked up the folder, stood up and walked from the room without saying another word or, in any way, recognizing the existence of her sons.

Monday morning at CRFM sounded almost normal. Nigel B. was back on the air and flying. The police report of the bombing led the eight o'clock news. John Thorne delivered the bulletin with his customary impartial professionalism. The police could not determine who was responsible: it had all the hallmarks of an IRA attack, yet there were doubts surrounding the type of explosives used and type of bomb produced. A police spokesman said that as nobody had claimed responsibility and they couldn't say for sure where the device was made, they were keeping an open mind until the forensic report was completed.

Nigel responded by playing 'Gertcha' by Chas and Dave on his free-choice spot.

*

Monica was having a late breakfast at the Connaught with Sir Peter French. He seemed very lively this morning, complimenting her on her Chanel suit, telling jokes about Dennis Thatcher and ordering an extremely large breakfast. She thought it unusual he had not dined at home, especially as it was his mother's birthday. It was not until they were on to their second cup of coffee that Sir Peter imparted the reason for his high spirits. 'Mother has left the board of French Enterprises,' he said.

Monica's reaction was cautious. 'Just like that?' she asked.

'Just like that,' answered Sir Peter. 'She'll be leaving on a world cruise next month with three of her friends and won't be back until next year.'

Monica rewrote a cliché. If a week is a long time in politics, she thought, then a minute in media can be an eternity. That one sentence had transformed her life.

'If I may,' continued Sir Peter, 'I would like to conclude our arrangement so we can press on with the job in hand.'

'You may,' said Monica, in a manner befitting royalty.

'We would like to formally invite you to join the boards of French Enterprises International, Colby Electronics and World Television Productions, at a fee of two hundred thousand pounds per annum plus usual benefits. We will require the stock you hold in CRFM to complete our deal with Pike, so we propose exchanging it for stock in all three companies of which you are a director, at a rate of two for one.'

Monica looked slightly puzzled as she tried to do some quick mental arithmetic.

'That will come to a value of two point four million sterling,' continued Sir Peter. 'Congratulations. You are a millionairess.'

'In that case, I think I should pay for breakfast,' she cooed, trying with all her might not to go stark raving loony and dance on the table top.

'Wouldn't hear of it, old chap,' answered Sir Peter. 'Comes under usual benefits.'

'What about CRFM?' asked Monica. 'When can I leave CRFM?'

'Now, if you like. Resign. Use any wording you wish.'

Monica did a MEGA toe twiddle under the polished oak table.

On Tuesday morning the news of the Aylford 'take-over' of CRFM became public. Harry Connaught phoned Monica on her private line – no answer. He called her home and got the answerphone. On his other line a secretary from the Home Office was holding on with a message from Whitehall.

Nigel and Samantha were visiting Lizzie in Guy's Hospital when they heard the news on Lizzie's portable radio.

'I must get back to the station,' said Nigel. 'Monica will be devastated.'

'I'll come with you,' said Samantha, giving the wounded ex-receptionist a small hand-squeeze. 'We'll call later, Lizzie, and tell you all the news.'

After they'd left, Lizzie felt sad and lonely in her dark world. She knew it was temporary, but right now, that seemed irrelevant. Her bedside phone rang. It was Thames Television.

'I don't think I can stand another interview,' she said.

'We don't want to interview you,' came the reply. 'We want to talk to you about working for us once you've fully recovered.'

Lizzie made arrangements to meet a Mr Rogers at

noon tomorrow. She hung up the phone, sat back in bed and put on her hospital headphones. She felt much better now.

Nigel and Samantha walked unannounced into Monica's office and found Eddy McLeod sitting behind her desk with his feet on the glass top talking on the telephone.

'What the fuck are you doing here?' shouted Nigel.

Eddy hung up the phone and sneered at the astonished couple. 'I'm the new managing director of this station and you, my macho young man, had better start toeing the line, or you'll be out on your ear.'

'You astound me, McLeod,' hissed Nigel. 'If you think, for one second, that I would even contemplate working for you in any capacity, you're a bigger asshole than I thought. Take your breakfast show *and* your radio station and stick it where the sun don't shine.' He turned to face Samantha. 'Come on, sweetheart, it smells of horse shit in here.'

'Come back here!' screamed Eddy. 'I have a contract on you for another two years and you're going to honour it!!'

Nigel walked over to him and tipped the cup of steaming hot coffee into his lap. 'Consider the contract broken,' he said, 'on the grounds of gross insubordination.'

As Nigel and Samantha stormed out of the office, slamming the door behind them, Eddy contemplated just how hollow his victory could be. No more Nigel meant no more number-one breakfast show, which is the key to success in any radio station. No more Brian Callaghan meant no more hard aggressive sales force, which had to translate to lower revenue. He tried, without success, to wipe the coffee stain from his trousers and thought briefly about joining the Church.

★

'I'm proud of you,' said Samantha as they left the station for the last time and walked towards the Porsche. 'You handled that ever so well.'

'I don't know,' answered Nigel. 'I don't have a job anymore. Where can I work?'

'Anywhere you want. Right now I think we should visit Monica. She might be taking this very hard.'

They arrived at Cadogan Square to find a jubilant Monica, dancing around the flat in her bath robe and pouring continuous glasses of champagne. She told them about World Television, Lady Isobel, and how Pike had to pay well over the odds for his foothold in British radio. Samantha told Monica about Nigel's resignation speech and how he nearly beat up Eddy for a second time. Monica applauded loudly and offered more champagne.

'How long will it take to get WTV on the air?' asked Nigel.

'About three years,' replied Monica.

'Will you offer Nigel a job?' asked Samantha.

Monica looked at them both and smiled. 'I most certainly will.'

'Good,' said Samantha, holding on tightly to Nigel's arm. 'That will give us enough time for a decent honeymoon.'

It was ten o'clock at night when Nigel and Samantha finally left Cadogan Square. They also left the Porsche and cabbed it home, due to the overconsumption of champagne.

'What did you mean by enough time for a decent honeymoon?' asked Nigel, as he settled back into the cab seat and stretched his legs.

'If you mention money, I'm going to hit you,' said Samantha.

Nigel smiled. 'I only . . .'

'Don't,' interrupted Samantha. 'Let's go back to Casablanca tomorrow. There's nothing more we can do here and, in case you've forgotten, we have a wedding to plan.'

Nigel fell against Samantha as the cab took a sharp turn into Sloane Street. 'Wedding,' he said. 'What wedding?'

Samantha hit him where even the softest of touches can hurt.

Monica had also overconsumed on the champagne, and at eight o'clock the next morning felt the full impact of her error. She stood in the shower for fifteen minutes trying to rid herself of the headache. Today she was flying to New York on Concorde and she didn't want to miss a second. She and Freddie were stopping off for a few days in New York on their way to Seoul.

By ten o'clock she was ready. The last remnants of her hangover disappeared when the driver rang her front doorbell. He placed her bags with great care into the boot of a new, long-wheel-base Turbo Bentley. Monica settled in to the elegant luxury of the back seat and surveyed the technological marvels that confronted her. Two telephones, a fax machine, a word processor that doubled as a television and a drinks cabinet were all built into the rear compartment and finished in polished rosewood. She had never seen such a beautiful automobile.

The driver handed Monica a white envelope with her name handwritten on the front. She opened it, expecting another itinerary or change of plans' information. She was surprised to find a letter from Sir Peter.

Dear Monica,
As a director of French Enterprises, it is only right

that you should have the most up to date transport available. We both hope you enjoy the Bentley for many years to come. Kindest regards,

Peter and Freddie.

Monica folded the letter with great care and placed it in her handbag.

It had all been worthwhile. Mothering Maggie with her paranoia of pop music's low life, nursemaiding Nigel with his juvenile heart and pampering Lizzie with her unsubtle ambition. She had bent to their wills without relinquishing an ounce of her power; she had traded CRFM for a seat on one of the most powerful media companies in the world; and she had gained personal financial security. She concentrated her mind on the next target. Sir Peter could be a problem, she thought, but she was sure Freddie would soon be eating from her hand.

'To the airport?' asked the driver.

'To the airport,' replied Monica.